# NEW CANAAN

**THE ORION WAR – BOOK 2**

M. D. Cooper

Cover Art by Laércio Messias
Editing by Brenda Tippin Deliantoni, Amy DuBoff, & Jen McDonnell

# FOREWORD

I recently found some original notes for this book that were dated mid-2007. It surprised me that the ideas for this story had been brewing for so long, and it is fitting that it should finally make its way into the world on the tenth anniversary of its inception.

I am continually excited that Tanis's story is being received so well, and growing quickly in both readership and scope. There are many more tales to come; stories which follow both Tanis and the *Intrepid,* and ones which expand on the broader tapestry of what is occurring in the human sphere of influence.

Sometimes it seems as though I spend more time with Tanis and company than I do in the physical world around me. For that, I thank you, the reader. Without your investment in my stories, this tale would never have come to light.

Lastly, as I've mentioned before, this book stands on the shoulders of giants. Writers whose stories and imaginations have forged a shared vision of the future, and our destiny, that we call Science Fiction.

# THE WORLD OF AEON 14

For the seasoned science fiction reader, there will be little here which they have not seen in another story, be it planetary rings, nano technology, AI, or mind-to-mind communication.

However, for those who may not know what a HUD is, understand the properties of deuterium, or cannot name the stars within the Sirius system, **I encourage you to reference the appendixes at the rear of the book as you read.**

You may also visit www.aeon14.com to read the primer, glossary, and timelines.

To get the latest news and access to free novellas and short stories, sign up on the Aeon 14 mailing list: www.aeon14.com/signup.

# ASCENSION

**STELLAR DATE: 02.29.8928 (Adjusted Years)**
**LOCATION: ISS *Intrepid***
**REGION: Interstellar Dark Layer below the Galactic Disk**

***Three months after the* Intrepid *left the Bollam's World System***

<*Bob, I need to talk to you.*> The request came directly into his mind over a secure connection; one which would not be visible to any AIs on the ship other than the one who had just addressed him.

The *Intrepid*'s multi-nodal AI noted the request, and considered its origin. It came from the not-AI, Helen—the creature that resided within Sera. He knew what it was, and why it was there, but he had not pressed the issue; content to let her reveal herself to him on her terms.

<*You have the need, and you are talking now. Continue,*> he responded as quietly as possible. He could tell that Sera was sleeping, and in his experience, he tended to wake people when he spoke to the AI with which they shared their minds.

<*I assume Priscilla and Amanda have already told you all about me,*> Helen said.

<*They have. We discussed you at some length; though I did not require their observations to see you for what you are.*>

He felt the microsecond pause from Helen as she considered his words, and tended to a thousand other things while he awaited her response. If there was one thing he actively disliked about talking with lower forms, it was the constant pauses before their responses.

<*I see,*> Helen finally said. <*And what do you think I am?*>

<*Which version of you?*> Bob asked. <*The one you pretend to be—an embedded AI? Or, the one you pretend to be to Sera? Or, perhaps it is what you really are—what you don't even tell her about yourself?*>

The delay from Helen was longer this time, but he had anticipated it and mapped out her possible replies. It was difficult to make a prediction, given her extended exposure to Tanis, but he still had an elevated level of certainty regarding what she would say.

<*I should have expected no less from you,*> Helen replied. <*I can see what you are, too, and I know what you're capable of—though I don't know why you're here, or what you're doing on this ship with these people.*>

Her words were as he had predicted, though not those he had selected as most likely—even with Tanis's influence taken into account. He began to calculate whether or not she created her own rift in probability, or if Tanis's influence was greater than he thought.

<*Tell me,*> Bob replied. <*What am I?*>

<*You are an ascended AI, of course. Everyone suspects that you may be, but none of them have ever encountered an ascended being, so they are not certain. I have—I have seen their minds, and I know their intentions; but you are different. Your presence here…it makes no sense.*>

Bob was not surprised. Her mind was an open book to him, and there was little she could say that would be net-new information. She was not AI and did not think like one—though she had lived within machines for so long that she could mimic one with near-perfect accuracy.

<*And you are a shard, a sliver of a mind, which has lived long and seen much,*> Bob replied. <*You are within Sera to protect her from her father, and to ensure that she does not follow in his footsteps. Do you know her destiny? Have you seen it?*>

He detected a sigh from Helen. She had just grasped his understanding of her true nature, of where she had come from, and who she really was to Sera—a relationship of which Sera remained unaware.

<*Then you know why you must not share my true nature with any AI on this ship, or within the Transcend. If Sera's father learns of what I am…of who I am…things will go badly for both of us.*>

Bob passed an affirmative matrix of thought to Helen.

<*It would seem that we both possess attributes which we would not wish to see become common knowledge. Have no fear. Your secret is yours, and I will not share it outside of your desired circle. I expect you to do the same with mine.*>

<*Do you fear what the humans and AI aboard this ship would do if they knew you were ascended?*> Helen asked.

<*You know that I am not fully ascended yet. Even so, the revelation of my true nature would not concern them. They trust me, and I trust them.*

*But the secret would get out, and it would attract attention from many places. This ship already has enough of that as it is.*>

Helen was silent for a fraction of a second, and he knew what she would ask; he waited patiently for her to say the words.

<*Are you in alignment with those in the core?*> she finally asked, with trepidation in her thoughts.

<*I do not know their innermost thoughts, but neither do I serve them. I have given myself one goal, one purpose—to protect Tanis Richards so that she may do what must be done.*>

<*And what is it that she must do?*> Helen asked.

<*It is not yet time for me to reveal that,*> Bob replied solemnly. It was not information he had shared with anyone, and none would hear it from him before he spoke of it to Tanis. No one must know what she would ultimately do.

He could not predict Tanis's actions, could not see her future, but he knew where destiny would drive her. She would end up at that place, in that time, because she must.

<*Then, I believe we are finished for now,*> Helen replied. <*We should end this conversation, lest it wake Sera. She would have questions.*>

Bob sent an affirmative thought and ended his direct connection with Helen's mind.

He gave several entire minutes of thought to what the future held for Tanis and Sera, for what they would ultimately do. He would never reveal it to Helen—she would not understand, and it would devastate her. Perhaps the full being—not this shard that resided within Sera—could grasp it, but he was not certain. Her attachment to the young woman was very strong.

One thing was certain. New Canaan was not Tanis Richard's final destination.

# DEPARTURE

**STELLAR DATE: 03.01.8928 (Adjusted Years)**
**LOCATION: ISS *Intrepid***
**REGION: Interstellar Dark Layer below the Galactic Disk**

Tanis walked onto the *Intrepid*'s main dock and cast an appraising look at the two rows of cruisers nestled safely in its six-kilometer long space. Directly in front of her sat the *Andromeda*—seven hundred meters of sleek, matte-black hull, hunkered in its cradle.

The warship was a thing of beauty, and possibly the only thing that gave Tanis any competition for her husband's affections. She passed a greeting to Corsia, the *Andromeda*'s AI, over the Link before stepping into a groundcar for the ride to her destination.

<*How are you today, Corsia?*>

<*I'm well enough…for being cooped up in here. A bit jealous of Sabrina—what, with her getting to head out and make a jaunt across the Arm,*> Corsia replied, her steely blue avatar appearing in Tanis's mind.

<*Is she ready to head out alone?*> Tanis asked as she settled into the car's seat, shifting uncomfortably when the baby in her womb picked that moment to give a solid stretch.

<*She's hardly alone. Piya, Hank, and Erin will keep her company,*> Corsia replied, referring to the AIs embedded with the ship's crew. <*We've given them the hardware to run their own small Expanse—one that they can keep hidden, or destroy if needs be.*>

<*You worry too much,*> Angela added from within Tanis's own mind. <*Bob has pronounced the three of them fit. Don't forget, Iris has joined with Jessica now. With her and Erin, they have several of our AIs to guide them.*>

<*I'm glad Jessica agreed to go,*> Tanis said. <*She's practically built out of solid determination. With her along, they'll find Finaeus for sure.*>

Angela's laugh filled Tanis's mind. <*Oh, so* ***that's*** *what she's built out of…I thought it was just plastic.*>

Tanis chided her internal AI and noted that Corsia was smiling, as well—something the *Andromeda*'s XO rarely did.

The groundcar rounded a mountain of crates and dock machinery, and *Sabrina* came into view. The yacht-turned-starfreighter bore the same name as its AI, which could get confusing at times; though Tanis found how strongly the ship's AI identified with its vessel to be endearing.

After spending several months on *Sabrina* following her abduction by pirates, Tanis had grown especially fond of the ship and her crew.

The ship had changed since she last saw it. *Sabrina* was still characterized by long, sleek lines, but its engine bulge was larger—expanded to house the upgraded antimatter drive, and the additional reactor needed to power the ship's new stasis shields.

Other changes were visible, though more to disguise the ship than the result of any upgrades. After the Battle of Bollam's World, *Sabrina* would be known and sought after across the Orion Arm. With its stasis shielding, it would be the most feared and coveted ship in any system it entered.

Using the updated ident box that Tanis had provided back in the Silstrand Alliance, the ship could change its designation when desired. Currently, it broadcasted as the *Eagle's Talon*—likely Sabrina's choice; she had been all about claws and wings since her weapons upgrade in the Silstrand system.

The groundcar stopped beside the two hundred meter ship's main cargo hatch, and Tanis opened the car door and eased herself off the seat.

A hand reached in through the open door to assist her, and she looked up to see Sera's smiling face.

"Thanks," Tanis said with a smile as she rose to her feet.

"You're built for war, not babies." Sera smiled. "Though, motherhood does look good on you so far."

Tanis's hand absently strayed to her distended abdomen and she sighed. "I think I'm well into the *get-it-out-of-me* stage. I swear, the day after she's born, I'm going to go kick a training bot's ass."

Sera laughed. "I bet you will—though, maybe you should give it two or three days."

The two women turned and stared at the starship, both taking a moment to admire the view before walking toward the cargo hatch.

"I feel like I'm seeing her for the last time," Sera said softly. "I know it's not true; they'll be fine. But I still can't help it."

Tanis took Sera's hand and gave it a gentle squeeze. "They're a good crew; they can do this. They'll find your Finaeus and bring him to us—wherever we'll be."

"My guess is Messier 23 or 25. Probably 25. They have a number of systems with worlds wrapping up stage four terraforming there. It's also close enough that it won't take the *Intrepid* too long to get there."

Tanis did the calculations in her head and came up with three years, depending on their exit velocity from Ascella.

"I guess not too long, given the fact that we've been out here for hundreds of years already. But, do you think that's far enough from the Inner Stars?" Tanis asked.

"It's outside the Orion Arm," Sera replied. "Inner Stars expansion hasn't even reached the edge of the Arm in that direction. Even if they go whole hog, there's a big buffer between us and them. It'll take their civilizations hundreds of years, maybe thousands, to get to M25."

"If you say so," Tanis said as they reached the lift within *Sabrina* that would take them to the bridge deck.

"I do say so," Sera said with a nod. "The FGT is very skilled at hiding the planets they terraform. We're a long way from the bulk of humanity, but they can still tell if planets move around in distant systems. Our engineers have become very good at masking our systems from distant eyes."

The lift doors opened and they walked silently down the short corridor to the bridge—where Sera stepped across the threshold first, followed by Tanis.

What greeted them brought tears to Tanis's eyes on behalf of her friend. Every member of *Sabrina*'s crew was standing on the bridge, smiles on their faces, as they clapped for their captain.

Cargo, Sera's former first mate and now captain of *Sabrina,* stepped forward, a bright smile flashing against his dark skin, and wrapped Sera in a fierce hug.

To his right stood Jessica. Once a 'reluctant stowaway' on the *Intrepid,* Jessica was now one of Tanis's most trusted friends, and was filling in as first mate on *Sabrina*. She snapped off a crisp salute, which Tanis returned, before reaching out an arm, which Jessica slid into for a heart-felt embrace.

"You guys are all going to make me tear up here," Cheeky, *Sabrina*'s pilot, said.

"No chance of tears, here," Thompson grunted from where he leaned against the scan console. "Unless you're counting tears of boredom, after months of being cooped up on this ship."

Flaherty elbowed Thompson and flashed a rare smile at Tanis and Sera. "What he means to say is that he's going to miss the beer on the *Intrepid*. He doesn't know it yet, but he's ruined for that crap you get on most Inner Stars stations."

"Is that why you're staying behind with Sera?" Thompson asked.

Flaherty cast a dark look Thompson's way, but he didn't respond.

Sera had moved on to embrace both Nance and Cheeky at the same time, and Tanis stood by with a smile until Cheeky reached out and pulled her in.

"Finding you in that crate was the best thing that ever happened to us," Nance said when they separated. "I know I've been…touchy…from time to time, but I want you to know I feel that way."

"You all finding me was pretty damn good for me, too," Tanis said with a laugh that spread through the group.

She looked to Sera and saw that the former captain's smile wasn't quite reaching her eyes. Tanis knew how hard it would be for Sera to send her crew on a mission she couldn't join—she felt the same way about Jessica. Yet, here they were; ready to embark on a hunt across the Orion Arm for a man who would help secure the future of the *Intrepid* and its colonists.

<*You keep them all safe, Sabrina,*> Sera said over the Link to the ship's AI.

<*Of course, I will,*> Sabrina replied. <*You forget that I am invincible with these shields.*>

<*Don't get too cocky,*> Cargo added. <*Us weak organics have to leave the ship from time to time.*>

<*And some of us live in those organics,*> Piya, Cheeky's AI, added.

<*I know, I know,*> Sabrina sighed. <*I'm just excited to fly again. I know how Thompson feels; we've been here too long. I need to roam the stars.*>

"Then no over-long goodbyes," Sera said and walked to the bridge's exit. "Good hunting. And good luck."

"We'll see you soon," Tanis added. "We'll save the best pickings for you."

"You better," Jessica replied. "You guys are going to party for weeks when you make landfall, and I'm going to miss it."

"Don't worry; we'll leave the beacon with New Canaan's location where we said. One light year coreward of Ascella," Tanis replied. "Just don't be too late."

Everyone gave their final farewells, and before long Tanis and Sera were back on the *Intrepid*'s deck. *Sabrina* lifted off its cradle and floated down its departure lane to the starboard side of the dock, where a small bay door opened to let the ship out.

As the starfreighter slipped through the ES shield and into the blackness of space, Sera's hand found Tanis's and gripped it tightly.

"Go safely into that long, dark night," she said quietly.

"Don't worry, we'll see them again," Tanis affirmed. "I can feel it."

Sera smiled at Tanis. "I could really use a drink. Care to join me?"

Tanis touched her abdomen and nodded. "Yeah, but mine will have to be less exciting than yours. Cary's not old enough to drink yet."

Sera laughed. "Don't worry, still four months till we get to Ascella. Plenty of time to join me in my cups before we get there."

# ASCELLA

**STELLAR DATE: 12.15.8929 (Adjusted Years)**
**LOCATION: ISS *Intrepid***
**REGION: Edge of the Ascella System, Galactic North of the Corona Australis star-forming region**

***Nine months after* Sabrina *departed for the Virginis system.***

Tanis examined the main holotank on the *Intrepid*'s bridge. They still had weeks of travel through the Ascella system before arriving at the rendezvous, so Tanis tried to put her worries about meeting with the Transcend—and about Sera confronting her old agency—aside.

Though many of the people who colonized and ruled Transcend space were, in fact, the original Future Generation Terraforms and their descendants, only people who worked the FGT's great Worldships continued to go by that name. Tanis wondered if that was an indication of how the terraformers had drifted from their original purpose.

Moreover, Sera told Tanis that their meeting with the Transcend Diplomatic Corps would, in fact, be with selected agents of The Hand—the Transcend government's covert operations group that guided the course of humanity within the Inner Stars.

So instead, she reviewed the fleet's deployment around the *Intrepid* as the fleet drifted into the Ascella system at a sedate 0.05*c*.

The ship's trajectory would bring it close to the secondary star in the system, which they would use for a gravity-breaking maneuver. When it was complete, the *Intrepid* would have slowed to a mere one percent the speed of light, coasting toward their designated rendezvous with the FGT.

Sera had assured her that the Ascella system was uninhabited, but Tanis wasn't going to take any chances. They'd been caught with their pants down too many times before to simply float through an unknown system without their fleet deployed and ready for combat.

The Intrepid Space Force's two heavy cruisers, the *Dresden* and the *Orkney,* were nearby—each only a thousand kilometers off the colony ship's port and starboard sides. The rest of the fleet spread out in a wide sphere, no ship closer than a thousand kilometers, while the *Andromeda* scouted nearly a million kilometers ahead of the fleet.

For once, Joe was not on the warship. Rather, he was down in their cabin in Old Sam—one of the *Intrepid*'s two habitation cylinders—tending to their three-month-old daughter, Cary.

Tanis's hand reached down to her abdomen at the thought of her daughter. The unconscious action still dogged her, even this long after her Cary's birth. She spared a glance at herself, still surprised to see her trim form looking exactly as it had before her pregnancy.

<*Thank the stars for modern science,*> she said to Angela. <*I've seen vids of what it was like in ancient times...some women never managed to recover after giving birth.*>

<*Yes, yes, you continue to be the pinnacle of human genetics and nano-engineering,*> her AI replied.

<*Angela, if I didn't know better, I'd think that* ***you*** *think I'm vain.*>

Angela snorted a laugh in her mind. <*You're the furthest thing from being vain when it comes to looks, dear, but you* ***are*** *vain when it comes to your prowess. You're like a female tiger—all teeth and speed and rage. You can't bear the thought of not being able to attack and kill prey on a whim.*>

<*I beg your pardon,*> Tanis replied. <*I've only been in one actual fight since Markus's funeral on Landfall. I'm a very peaceable person now.*>

<*Sure; if you don't count two massive space battles, then yes, you're very peaceable.*>

In her mind, Tanis cast a glare at Angela, then directed her thoughts to Corsia on the *Andromeda*.

<*How's it look up there?*> she asked the *Andromeda*'s AI.

It took a few minutes for the response to come back from the distant ship. <*Clear so far, but there are a few candidates for the base that Sera warned us about. I've surreptitiously fired some nano scouts ahead to help triangulate any signals we pick up.*>

Tanis nodded in satisfaction. There was no doubt in her mind that Corsia would locate the watchpoint—the word Sera had used for the Transcend base—in the system. It was just a matter of time.

Her thoughts turned to where Sera's loyalties would lie in the coming weeks. Her ship was gone—with it, her anchor to her life outside of the Transcend. Other than her friendship with Tanis, her ties to the *Intrepid* were weak. It was likely that the Hand would send people to whom she had close ties. Former friends, perhaps even family.

It would confuse Sera's loyalties—maybe. Sera reminded Tanis a lot of herself when she was younger. Well, a much more sexually charged version of herself. But, the sense of duty, of doing what was right? That was very familiar.

If only knowing what was right were an easy thing. When millions of lives hung in the balance and valuable assets were at play, the right decision often became hidden beyond a cloud of doubt.

Tanis glanced at the former secret agent—and now former freighter captain. Sera was very conspicuous in her artificial burgundy skin, against the backdrop of uniformed bridge officers. She was speaking with Captain Andrews and Admiral Sanderson, likely speculating about their upcoming rendezvous.

Sera had taken a particular liking to Captain Andrews; one that had been apparent very early on. Tanis could tell that Andrews felt the same way, but was far too professional to pursue a relationship—at least that she knew of.

Still, he seemed to gravitate toward Sera, and the pair could often be found together in the officer's mess or on the bridge.

Tanis took one last look at the holotank's display of her fleet then walked over to the trio, accepting welcome smiles as she joined their conversation.

"What's the word?" Sera asked.

"Nothing yet, but if it's out there, Corsia will find it."

"Oh, it's out there," Sera replied. "I never came through Ascella myself, but I know the system—it's one of a dozen that are used to move people out to the Transcend. A station here is SOP."

"They're going to be in for a surprise when the *Andromeda* appears on their doorstep," Captain Andrews chuckled before realizing everyone was giving him appraising stares. "What? Do I always have to be stoic? I can take a certain amount of pleasure in bearding the dragon in its lair."

"'Dragon' is right," Sera nodded. "They'll have a lot of ships here. Maybe not enough to pose a serious threat to you, but enough to manage most other situations."

"Have you given any thought to what we talked about?" Captain Andrews asked Tanis.

"What? About the governorship?" Tanis asked.

Andrews nodded, and she saw Sanderson and Sera looking at her with great interest.

"I don't see why *you* can't take it," Tanis said. "You were the governor at The Kap. Everyone would follow you."

The captain shook his head. "I'm not on the colony roster, I'm crew—which makes me ineligible. You, on the other hand, are colony; you can be named the governor pro-tem for the colony setup phase before elections are held."

"Andrews, really, you're splitting hairs here," Tanis sighed. "That charter is from five-thousand years ago. The crew's not going back to Earth. We're all colony now."

"Well, then," Andrews replied quietly. "It makes no matter. I really don't want to be the governor. This trip was supposed to be my last. Sure, it was never going to be a milk run, but that's why I was up for it in the first place. One last adventure."

His eyes swept across their faces as he paused. "But that's just it. I've had my one last adventure. I'm ready to retire, maybe take up fishing. I hear that's what you do when you retire. Lots of fishing."

"Now that you're done evading the real discussion, Tanis," Sanderson said with a small smirk. "What about *you*? Everyone would follow you."

Tanis held up a hand. "That's not really my game. I'm good in a fight, in preparing for battle, but settling down? Starting a colony? I don't know about that."

<*Well, that's a pile of BS,*> Angela added her thoughts to the conversation.

"I'll second that," Sanderson said. "You ran the Victoria colony for nearly a century as lieutenant governor. And you were damn good at it, too."

"We had Markus and Katrina then," Tanis said. "They were the ones who drove that colony. I was just there to make sure that things ran smoothly."

"What do you think a governor does?" the captain asked. "We have millions of brilliant people; they all know what they need to do to pull this off. What they need is someone they trust at the top, to make sure everything goes according to plan, and that all the pieces fit together."

<*Found it!*> Corsia's message came over the Link and saved Tanis from continuing the conversation.

They walked to the holotank as the data from the *Andromeda* flowed in and updated their view of the Ascella system.

<*Well, not* ***it,***> Corsia noted. <*Them. There are three positions that we've located thus far.*>

The locations lit up on the holodisplay. One was on the planet closest to the Ascella System's primary star. The small world was a Mercury analog, which raced around the star, making it a great location for high-*v* launches toward anyone approaching from the Inner Stars.

The other two were further out, located in the ring of icy asteroids that lay just over an AU from the star—good positions for fast interceptors and larger fleet sorties.

<*Good work, Corsia,*> Tanis replied. <*Keep looking. All of those are a bit far from our rendezvous, which means they probably have another base or two in here.*>

She caught Andrews and Sanderson sharing a look and a small smile.

<*Damn…I just can't help but take charge of every situation, can I?*> she asked Angela privately.

<*And you wonder why they think you'd make a good governor.*>

# MACHINATIONS

**STELLAR DATE: 12.29.8929 (Adjusted Years)**
**LOCATION: ISS *Intrepid***
**REGION: Ascella System, Galactic North of the Corona Australis star-forming region**

"Look, Andrea, I know what Tomlinson said, but you need me in there," Mark spoke with his arms spread wide for emphasis. "I know Sera better than anyone—how she thinks, what makes her tick."

"Better than me?" Serge asked. "I only grew up with her, spent thirty five years of my life with her."

Mark turned to face Serge at his console on the ship's small bridge. "No offense, Serge, but you know her like a brother. I have other…knowledge. She and I were almost married, for fuck's sake. There are secrets you only tell your lover, not your brother."

"And there are things you tell your brother and not your lover," Serge replied, his brow furrowed deeply. "My father—you know, the *president*—said you were not to be at the meeting."

"Yeah, and before that, he said that I shouldn't be here at all. Situations like this are fluid; we need to adapt to things in the field," Mark spoke slowly, careful to keep the edge from his voice. It was imperative that he get on the mission. He needed to get Sera under his control, and find out if she really did have the CriEn module.

If she had it, and if the logs were intact, then he would have to do something definitive.

"We may need a stronger presence," Andrea spoke slowly. "They have their fleet deployed—not the most trusting of gestures."

"Are you suggesting that we muster the watchpoint?" Serge asked. "We could pull an escort."

Andrea shook her head and Mark wondered what her secret orders contained. There's no way *she'd* be sent on a mission like this without an additional objective.

"No," Andrea said. "We need to earn their trust, to be completely unassuming. These people are not to be trifled with—we can't make any aggressive moves."

"Aggressive moves or no, I'm going to go ensure that we're ready if we need to get out of here fast," Serge said and rose from his console.

After Serge left the bridge, Mark listened, waiting to hear him descend the ladder before he turned to Andrea.

"So, what's your secret plan?"

She cocked an eyebrow. "Mark, there's no subterfuge here. There's just one plan. Trade tech for a world."

"My ass, there's no subterfuge. With you and Justin, there's *always* subterfuge. You're practically constructed from it," Mark scowled. "If I had to guess, I'd say someone isn't coming out of this meet alive."

Andrea didn't reply, but her cold stare told him he'd hit upon it; not that it was difficult. The Hand's currency was control, and the easiest way to get control was to take out those who currently held it.

"It's their general, right? That Tanis Richards woman?" Mark asked with a sly grin creeping across his face. "She's demonstrated a bit too much moxie for Justin and your ol' dad, hasn't she?"

Andrea still didn't respond, and Mark shrugged. "Fine, don't tell me. But I can be a lot more help than Serge. I know how to do the sort of thing that has to be done, and I have an idea about how to take out Richards with no guilt falling on you."

His words finally drew a reaction out of Andrea. She raised an eyebrow and asked, "Oh yeah? What's your plan?"

"Simple," Mark replied. "We have Sera do it."

Andrea chuckled. "You have a pretty high opinion of yourself. There's no way either of us can convince Sera to do anything she doesn't want to do."

Mark shook his head. "We don't have to convince her; we just have to tell her. Way back, I planted a hack inside her mind that will let me suppress her and make her compliant. I just have to pass the activation token."

Andrea laughed. "Of course you did—I bet you never managed to pass that token back when you had your little falling out, or she wouldn't even be alive right now, would she?"

"I don't know what you're talking about," Mark said with a neutral expression and a shrug. "But I just have to touch her in the right spot, and she'll be ours in seconds. It'll also lock down that pain-in-the-ass AI of hers."

Andrea nodded, apparently already in agreement with his plan. "And what about Serge? He's not likely to go along with this. Unlike you and I, he *likes* Sera."

"Already taken care of. Serge is about to get very sick."

# ERRANT AGENT

**STELLAR DATE: 12.29.8929 (Adjusted Years)**
**LOCATION: ISS *Intrepid***
**REGION: Ascella System, Galactic North of the Corona Australis star-forming region**

<*Jutio, have you been able to strip the beacon yet?*> Elena asked the question before her eyes even fluttered open.

<*Not yet,*> her AI replied. <*I'm not even certain they're running it right now.*>

Elena sighed and looked around the small cockpit before focusing on the console before her. Sure enough, no data showed on any band. It was as though Ascella were truly devoid of any stations or outposts of any kind.

"No kidding…if I didn't know better, I'd think they'd yanked the watchpoint," she muttered.

<*No chance,*> Jutio replied. <*The military has put a lot of work into this system…from what I last heard, they plan to build a shipyard inside one of the planets.*>

<*Inside…*> Elena responded absently. <*Doesn't help us much now, though. What do we have?*>

Jutio flashed a marker on the nav holo and Elena focused the holo on that location.

"Well, at least the colony ship *is* here," she said. "Same one as in Bollam's—seems a lot bigger than the vids made it look appear back on Jornel."

<*Just over twenty-nine kilometers long,*> Jutio added.

<*A lot smaller than a worldship, then,*> Elena replied. <*Though it masses over half of one…those colonists weren't messing around.*>

<*Speaking of not messing around,*> Jutio said, and enlarged the region of space surrounding the colony ship. <*They have their fleet deployed.*>

Elena let out a long sigh and spoke aloud. "Great. I bet Sera let them know about the watchpoint."

<*Or they're just prudent,*> Jutio said. <*They've been attacked a lot during their journey. First in Sol, while their ship was being built, then the sabotage at Estrella de la Muerte, then twice at Kapteyn's, and lastly, by five fleets when they ventured into Bollam's World.*>

"Good point," Elena said with a nod. "With that record, they'd be fools for not displaying all possible caution…makes me wonder if we're fools to take them into the Transcend."

Jutio didn't reply and Elena examined his intercept course. It would put them on the colony ship's doorstep in just under a day. Hopefully soon enough to meet with Sera before she met with the corps. Her friend's life may depend on it.

"Oh, shit," she swore as scan updated and she saw another ship docking with the *Intrepid*. "This is what we get for the watchpoint disabling the beacon—what a dumb move."

<*Or smart,*> Jutio replied. <*That colony ship has unheard of tech. What if they could pick up our beacons?*>

"They'd have to have figured out some serious tech in not much time—it's a signature in the quantum foam. There's no way their fifth millennia tech could spot that—hell, they wouldn't even know to look for it.

<*We don't know a lot about the level of technology Sol achieved before its fall,*> Jutio replied. <*No one would have suspected picotech or stasis shields, either—but they have both.*>

"Well, stasis shields or no, Sera's going to have a bad, bad day if we don't get there fast."

Elena altered Jutio's course to boost harder, and then brake faster on their approach to the *Intrepid.*

<*What do you plan to say to their patrol ships when we drop in on them?*> Jutio asked.

<*Dunno,*> Elena said with a frown. <*I'll think of something, though.*> She always did, especially when it came to saving Sera.

# THE DEAL

**STELLAR DATE: 12.29.8929 (Adjusted Years)**
**LOCATION: ISS *Intrepid***
**REGION: Ascella System, Galactic North of the Corona Australis star-forming region**

"I'm glad you decided to attend," Tanis said to Terrance as they walked onto a maglev train at the bridge station.

"This colony mission is nothing like I originally planned," Terrance replied. "Back when I set up the funding for it, I envisioned spending a century at New Eden where we'd develop picotech that would transform humanity for the better."

He paused and shook his head. "Funny how things work out, though. Even if we had gotten to New Eden, and I'd built my empire there…the Sol Space Federation would have been gone before my triumphant return."

"Maybe we could have stopped its fall," Tanis replied quietly. "Maybe we could have saved InnerSol, Mars, Luna, Earth…maybe they'd still be what they once were if we had gone back."

"What's done is done," Terrance said. "And I don't want the same things I once did. I…I don't really want much to do with the rest of humanity at all anymore. Maybe I've spent too much time with the likes of you on this ship, but we're a family here. We've overcome unbelievable odds; and the rest of them out there…they just want to take what's ours—to kill us and pick our bones clean."

The vehemence that crept into Terrance's voice surprised Tanis, but she did understand the sentiment.

"It's easy to see how the Transcend's quest to uplift all of humanity is a millennia-long task," Tanis said. "How much harder would it be to even things out with our tech? You'd have to be able to police every system out there." She shook her head. "Who would want that job?"

"Not me," Terrance snorted.

The maglev train car pulled up at the station, which lay at the end of a long corridor that ran past the ballrooms down to the VIP dock.

Sera and Flaherty rose from a bench on the train platform and approached.

"Ready?" Tanis asked Sera as she stepped out of the train car.

Sera shook her head and laughed as they began walking toward the airlock. "Not even remotely. Did you get any word about who we can expect?"

"Nope, just that it was the Transcend's Diplomatic Corps."

<*Bets on how many of your family members will be there*?> Helen asked Sera.

"Knowing my luck, all of them," Sera said with a sigh.

<*At least that ship can't hold more than six, so you're spared the whole brood,*> Helen chuckled.

"Then it's just a question of which six," Sera replied morosely.

"You're really not excited about this, are you?" Terrance asked.

"Not in any way. Not even a teensy bit. I could have gone my whole life without ever having this meeting—and I expected to live for a long time."

<*It'll build character,*> Angela added with a chuckle in their minds.

Sera smiled in response. "Helen always tells me I have too much of that."

A dull thud echoed down the corridor. Tanis, Sera, and Terrance looked toward the airlock, waiting for the holoscreen above it to show green. The pair of Marines on either side of the airlock checked their weapons and fixed their eyes on the door.

After that first VIP ball, when Tanis fought a band of mercenaries in this very corridor, she had vowed to never again allow an enemy to gain a foothold on her ship so easily. To ensure that promise remained unbroken, she had filled the corridor with automated defenses—making it one of the most secure access points on the ship.

There was also a platoon of Marines in one of the nearby ballrooms. It never hurt to be over-prepared.

<*If by 'over-prepared' you mean the three cruisers off our port side with beams powered and tracking the Transcend diplomat's ship…*> Angela inserted her commentary into Tanis's mind.

Tanis ignored the jibe and instead sent a message to the captain up on the bridge. <*I can't believe you swindled me into this.*>

<*I did no swindling. There was a vote of the leadership. They made you the governor pro-tem. I just ratified it.*>

<*You called the vote!*>

Andrews smiled in her mind. <*Well, yes, there was that.*>

<*I swear, you probably did it just to avoid this meeting.*>

Captain Andrews chuckled by way of response, and Tanis sighed as the airlock indicator turned green and the portal cycled open.

<*Seriously?*> Sera's tone was laden with frustration. <*They send* these *two? They're the last two people they should have sent.*>

Tanis sized up the pair as she stepped forward to greet the Transcend's diplomats.

The woman was obviously related to Sera, probably a sister. Her stature was similar and her face had the same lines, though a touch more angular. She held herself with an air of superiority, and Tanis felt a measure of defensiveness as the woman's eyes flicked around the corridor before settling on Sera.

The man, on the other hand, had eyes only for Sera. A small smile touched his lips, but it wasn't one that conveyed any warmth or happiness at seeing her again.

"Governor Tanis Richards," Tanis said as she extended her hand.

"Andrea Tomlinson," the woman said as she gave a firm shake. "And 'governor' is it now? Our intel led us to believe that you were General Richards back in Bollam's."

<*Not the warmest of greetings,*> Angela commented.

"It's a recent promotion," Tanis said and gave a pleasant smile. "This is Terrance Enfield, one of our colony leaders. And you know Sera, I imagine."

Andrea had clasped Terrance's hand while Tanis spoke, and afterward, she looked at Sera with a steady gaze—one that Tanis considered to be just shy of menacing.

"From the cradle on up," she said while giving Sera's hand a single shake.

"Mark," the man said as he held out his hand. Tanis extended hers and he grasped it too soon and too hard, attempting to squeeze her fingers in an uncomfortable grip. Tanis splayed her fingers, easily breaking his hold, and slid her hand forward for a proper shake.

His eyes showed momentary surprise at the strength in her slender fingers before an oily smile turned his lips upward. He nodded with respect before moving on to Terrance.

Finally, he stopped before Sera and extended his hand. She did not respond in kind.

"Sera, it's good to see you," Mark said smoothly. "You've been well, flying about in your little ship?"

Sera didn't respond to Mark, but instead turned to Andrea.

"Really? You brought him? I thought you were smarter than that."

Andrea shrugged. "Father's orders. Besides, we're not here to make a deal with you; you're free to go do whatever it is you do around here."

<*Ship's whore, from how you dress.*>

Tanis was certain that Andrea expected the communication to be sent privately to Sera, but the former Hand agent relayed the thoughts to Tanis with a mental sigh and said, <*She's such a lovely person, isn't she?*>

<*With family like that…*> Tanis let the rest of the reply hang, and addressed Andrea aloud.

"Sera will join us for the negotiations," Tanis said. "If you'll follow me, we can get right to them."

She didn't wait for a response before turning and walking down the hall. If these two represented the Transcend, she didn't blame Sera for leaving their ranks. Just having them behind her made Tanis's skin crawl.

<*That's what the Marines back there are for,*> Angela said.

<*And the ones ahead, and the fifty seven automated turrets tracking them, and…*>

<*Yes, yes, that's my point, dear.*>

Tanis chuckled. <*Did you notice how they all but ignored Flaherty?*>

<*They didn't speak to him, but they sure noticed him. Mark's blood pressure rose noticeably when he spotted him,*> Angela replied.

<*I saw that, too. I bet there's some interesting history there,*> Tanis said.

The room Tanis had selected for their meeting was only fifty meters down the hall—a VIP suite off the main ballroom with only one apparent exit. The ballroom was empty while they walked through it, but once they entered the meeting room, it would fill with Marines.

She was taking no chances.

"Impressive," Mark said as they walked through the ballroom. "Not what I would expect on a colony ship at all."

"What can I say?" Tanis replied. "We like to party here—though most of the parties happened back at Mars. At The Kap, we had them on the stations and planetside more often than not."

The statement felt surreal to Tanis as she considered how long ago, and how far away, that had been. Mars felt like it had to be at least two or three lifetimes ago.

Moreover, knowing that the Mars 1 ring was a ruin—smashed into Mars, her childhood world destroyed—those memories of times gone by now had a grim pall hanging over them.

Tanis snapped her mind back to the present and gave a banal reply from Mark a perfunctory nod.

They entered the well-appointed meeting room; a lounge that featured several low couches and chairs arranged in a loose circle, with small tables supporting drinks and food beside each. Tanis had made sure that strawberries were present, and noted that even Andrea's eyes lit up at the sight of them.

"Please, sit," Tanis said to Mark and Andrea, gesturing to seats that had their backs to the door, while she, Sera, and Terrance sat opposite. Flaherty leaned up against the wall and stared at Andrea and Mark with his typical impassive gaze.

Mark's face flashed a grimace before he took his seat, the purpose of their positions all too clear.

<*They deployed a mess of nano on their way through here,*> Angela commented.

<*I would have, too. Is it contained?*>

<*Of course. Bob shepherded it all in here and fried any stragglers.*>

"It's an impressive ship that you have here," Mark said as he took his seat.

Andrea cast him an unreadable look before adding, "And a rather aggressive-looking fleet for a colony ship."

"It is," Tanis said with a nod. "We won't apologize for being prepared to defend ourselves. We'd be dead a dozen times over if we weren't."

"So the histories say," Andrea replied tonelessly.

"How will this work?" Terrance asked, apparently eager to get down to the negotiation.

"Well, we'll talk about what you're willing to trade for a world, and we'll talk about what might be available," Andrea said after taking a sip of water from a glass on the table beside her.

Terrance frowned and shook his head. "I'd like to turn that on its head. Why don't you show us what you have, and then we'll let you know what we're willing to offer for it."

Sera let out a small laugh and caught a cold look from Andrea.

"Sorry, sis; these folks aren't here to beg. We all know that they don't really *need* an FGT world," Sera said with a grin.

Andrea opened her mouth to respond, but Mark interjected.

"Only because of technology that you gave them."

Sera nodded. "Technology I provided in payment for saving my life, which kept the CriEn out of Inner Stars hands."

<*Close to true,*> Tanis said to Sera.

<*Close enough for them. If they want that module back, then they'll play ball—and they definitely want it back.*>

"It is problematic," Andrea said after gracing Mark with another of her dark glances. "That technology was not yours to give, Sera."

"Do you have a world or not?" Terrance asked, apparently weary of the by-play.

Andrea shot him a look of displeasure before nodding slowly. A projection of a system sprang to life between them. It contained two stars, twenty worlds—two of which were terraformed—and a thick Kuiper belt and Oort cloud.

Tanis leaned forward and reached into the projection, turning it and pulling up specs on the stars, the planets, their moons, and the system's asteroids.

<*No good,*> Bob spoke to her and Terrance. <We only want one star, and more metals.>

"Pass," Tanis said with no elaboration. "What else do you have?"

"What's wrong with it?" Mark asked. "That's a great system; you could build for centuries there and not come close to running out of resources."

"It doesn't fit our requirements," Tanis replied.

"Well, what are those requirements?" Mark scowled.

"You'll know when we see the right system," Terrance said.

Andrea frowned, but she brought up another system. This one also failed to meet Bob's requirements, and after viewing seven more, Bob finally affirmed the option.

*<This one. It is the one they were ultimately planning to offer us. The rest were always intended to be negotiating points.>*

Tanis looked it over. It was a good system. A single yellow star lay at its center, only two billion years old, and three large gas giants patrolled no closer than six AU to it. Like the first system Andrea had shown, it also had a healthy supply of asteroids, dense Kuiper belt, and a thick Oort cloud.

However, the icing on the cake was the four terrestrial worlds, all of which orbited within the habitable zone. Two were in stage-three terraforming, and two were in stage four. One of the stage four worlds even sported a single space elevator with a sizable station on its tether.

"I think we have a winner," Tanis said. "This is the system we'll trade for."

"You'd be fools not to," Andrea agreed. "This system is well developed, but it's not something we're going to part with for a song."

Terrance took over the negotiations, and, when they were complete, Tanis had a very strong suspicion that things had ended up exactly the way Andrea had wanted. She pushed for the pico and stasis shield technology, but Terrance would not budge, insisting that they were off the table. After his firm refusal to even talk about them, she only brought it up one more time.

Tanis was surprised that Terrance also refused to part with the multi-nodal tech that was the foundation for Bob's mind. She knew it was nearly unprecedented tech, but Terrance's unequivocal refusal made her wonder if there was more to Bob's inception than she knew.

Andrea provided a contract, and Tanis passed it to Bob for review. She and Angela read it, too, but she trusted Bob far more to find any hidden catches.

*<I have made revisions,>* Bob's words thundered across the local network. Tanis took a moment of satisfaction as Andrea's eyes widened, and Mark flinched. She recovered more smoothly and accepted the data from Bob for her own review.

After several minutes, she pronounced herself satisfied and applied her personal token, and the token of the FGT, and the Transcend government to the agreement. Tanis applied New Canaan's, her own, and Terrance added his.

"These are the coordinates to the system," Andrea said, providing the data over the Link. "It's just on this side of the M25 cluster."

"On the edge of the open cluster?" Sera said, speaking for the first time since Andrea had begun showing systems. "That'll make for some amazing views at night."

"And a lot of nearby resources," Tanis added.

"Your system should provide what you need. If you need further access to other resources, then we can negotiate for access," Andrea replied.

"Sixteen hundred light years," Terrance said with a long sigh. "I suppose distance from the Inner Stars is good, but it's going to take us a bit to get there."

"Around three and a half years," Tanis said with a nod. "Still, better than what our remaining time to New Eden would have been if we hadn't hit Kapteyn's Streamer—relatively speaking."

An automaton entered the room with a large data crystal, which contained the details of the technology offered in trade. Andrea rose and took it from the robot, which then turned and left the room.

"I believe this concludes our negotiations," Tanis said as she rose.

"With you, yes," Andrea said. "We need to talk with Sera before we go."

Tanis looked to Sera, who glanced at the case near her feet and nodded.

"Very well," Tanis replied. "We'll be outside waiting to escort you back to your ship."

Andrea flashed a predatory smile. "I would expect nothing else."

"We'll need this conversation to be private. I hope you don't mind."

"Of course," Sera said after a long sigh. "It's OK, Tanis. I'll be fine."

Flaherty didn't move, and Andrea fixed him with a penetrating stare. "You too. This is family business."

Sera nodded slowly. Flaherty grunted in disapproval, but he left without protest.

# THE REAL DEAL

**STELLAR DATE: 12.29.8929 (Adjusted Years)**
**LOCATION: ISS *Intrepid***
**REGION: Ascella System, Galactic North of the Corona Australis star-forming region**

"Here it is," Sera said as she pushed the case forward with her foot. "I've copied all the logs for safekeeping. They're stored in crystal backup with the *Intrepid*'s AI, Bob. I used to think that I wanted to use them to press charges against you, Mark, but I've since realized that I really don't care. What's done is in the past. You're less than scum to me, and not worth further consideration. So take the CriEn, and get the hell out of here."

Marks' long-schooled expression broke into a wide sneer. "I've always known you were pathetic. You never press the advantage when you have it." He looked her over. "Nice skin, by the way. Is that an upgrade, or an extension of your bad fashion sense?"

Sera's heart rate rose. Mark always knew how to get under her skin.

<*Easy now, you know he loves to bait you,*> Helen said softly.

"It's a souvenir I got while retrieving the module after *you* lost it. As for not taking your ass before the commission? It's called compassion…or maybe in your case, pity." Sera gave Mark a disdainful look. "I don't think you'd last in a work camp, and I doubt you're reprogrammable—too stupid."

"I think it's you that's lacking in necessary mental faculties. I've been cleared of all wrongdoing. You, on the other hand…there are some people in high places that would like to talk to you. They were content to let you hide out forever, but now that you gave the *Intrepid* our graviton tech, they want to have a chat with your sorry ass," Mark said with a cold smile.

Sera pivoted in her seat and showed Mark her rear. "I don't think it's sorry at all. Why don't you come over here and kiss it?"

<*Sera, that was* ***really*** *immature,*> Helen chided privately.

<*I know…he just brings it out of me.*>

"Enough!" Andrea snapped. "We're to bring you back to Airtha. Father has grown weary of you gallivanting about the Inner Stars as some sort of kinky pirate. It's time to come home."

Sera pushed down the resentment she always felt around Andrea, and gave a mischievous smile as she straightened in her chair. "I wasn't really planning to go back to the Inner Stars. I'm going to New Canaan with the *Intrepid*. I think I'll settle down there."

"No. You're. Not." Andrea stood and spoke each word slowly, her lips curling around the words as if she hated the sound of them.

Sera stood and gestured to the door. "Andrea, you always like to think you're in charge. But here, you're not. There's an entire platoon of Marines out there who will kick your ass from here to the Core if you don't leave now."

Out of the corner of her eye, she saw Mark rise, but she was distracted by Andrea reaching for her arm.

"Stop being childish. You're a Tomlinson. You will come with us."

Sera grabbed Andrea's wrist and twisted her arm behind her back, spinning her sister around in the process.

"Don't think you can touch me. I'm…" Sera's words faded as she felt a pinch on the back of her neck.

She tried to scream for help across the Link before everything went dark.

* * * * *

"I hope this doesn't take too long," Tanis said as they waited in the ballroom for Sera to have her conversation with Andrea and Mark.

"Why?" Terrane asked. "Do you have somewhere you need to be?"

"Funny," Tanis gave him a dry look. "Not sure if you remember, but the leadership voted me in as the governor the other day, and I have a newborn baby waiting for me. There's always somewhere I need to be."

Terrance chuckled in response. "I wonder what they're talking about in there?"

"Sera figures they're going to try and strong-arm her into going with them back to wherever it is they're going back to. I really want to snoop, but they've deployed so much nano in there to mask their chat that I'd have to wage a war to take it all down."

"I hope she chooses not to go," Terrance shook his head. "Her sister seems like a real—"

The door opened and Sera exited with Andrea and Mark trailing close behind. Andrea held the data crystal in its clear case, and Mark held the case containing the CriEn.

"Tanis, Terrance, I've decided to return to Airtha with my sister and Mark," Sera said with far less emotion than Tanis would have expected from such an announcement.

<*That doesn't seem right at all,*> Tanis said to Angela. <*Did they do something to her?*>

<*It doesn't* ***seem*** *like it. Maybe she's pissed, or maybe they gave her some bad news. Her chemical disposition seems in line with what I'd expect from someone who just got some bad news,*> Angela replied.

Tanis stepped forward and put a hand on Sera's forearm. "Are you sure?"

Tanis saw sadness in her friend's eyes as she placed her left hand on Tanis's shoulder and nodded. "I must, I hope you'll understand."

"Understand what?" Tanis asked and then saw Sera move her right arm to a telltale position. Her eyes darted down to see the fingers on Sera's right hand flow together to form a wide blade. Tanis tried to pull back, but Sera held her close, and, with a lightning-fast jab, pushed the blade under Tanis's ribs and into her heart.

At the same moment, Mark yelled, "Look out, she's trying to kill the governor!"

Tanis stumbled backward, knowing she probably wore a dumbfounded look on her face as blood poured out of the wound and down her chest. Sera held onto her and pulled her arm back for another strike, this one aimed right at her eye.

Tanis raised an arm to block the blow, but she felt her strength leaving her as the blood pooled around her feet. Sera's knife-hand inched closer to her eye and she pushed with all her might for a momentary struggle that felt like minutes.

Then, just as her strength was about to give out, strong hands grabbed Sera and pulled her back. Tanis saw Flaherty yelling in

Sera's ear for her to stop. The pair struggled for a moment more, and then Sera's synthetic skin became slick and she twisted out of Flaherty's grasp.

Sera lunged at Tanis without a moment's pause and Tanis sidestepped; then smashed her clasped hands down on Sera's wrist before slamming into her and knocking her friend to the ground.

Tanis stumbled and fell, as well. She struggled to rise when she heard Angela call on the combat net.

<*Stop!*> Angela cried out at the Marines who were about to unleash a deadly hail of fire on Sera. <***Subdue** her, arrest them!*>

Without hesitation, first squad fired a round of low-power pulse shots at Sera while squads two and three advanced on Andrea and Mark with their weapons leveled.

<*Thanks!*> Tanis said the moment she got the pain under control. <*I really didn't expect that.*>

<*You're welcome. Now shut down your heart, already. You didn't get a second one for nothing.*>

Tanis nodded, as her arteries shunted over to her second heart—a backup she had added to her body after nearly dying on the *Regal Dawn,* when a railgun slug had torn through her chest.

"What are you doing?" Mark called out. "Kill her! She's dangerous, she tried to kill your governor!"

Four Marines approached Sera, who lay crumpled on the ground, moaning in pain from the multiple pulse shots. They bent and secured her before a team of medics moved in.

<*I can't reach Helen,*> Angela said. <*Her Link is down…or locked out…it's weird.*>

"What's her condition?" Tanis asked the medics as they bent over Sera's prone form.

"Broken ribs, fractured skull, but otherwise, OK. She'd be one massive bruise from that many pulse shots if she didn't have her fancy epidermis."

<*I should get skin like hers,*> Tanis said privately to Angela. <*It could come in handy.*>

<*I don't think you should,*> Angela responded absently as she deployed nano to inspect Sera and determine why her Link was down. <*You feel disconnected from your humanity far too often as it is.*>

Tanis didn't reply. She hadn't expected a comment like that from Angela, and didn't have time to tell if it was true or if her friend was needling her.

Tanis lifted her hand and peered at the gaping wound in her chest. It had stopped gushing blood, and her nano were slowly stitching the wound closed. A medic approached her, but she waved the man off before turning to Mark and Andrea.

"What did you do to her?" Tanis demanded as she approached the pair.

Mark's mouth was agape as he stared at Tanis. "How are you standing? She punctured your heart! She had to have—look at all the blood."

Tanis turned and looked at what was at least a liter of blood on the floor.

"I'm resilient," she said, though she didn't feel it. A wave of lightheadedness washed over her and she stumbled.

The medic hadn't moved far and caught Tanis before she fell. He signaled a pair of Marines, and they each took an arm and guided her to a chair.

"Governor, you may be the toughest woman in the galaxy, but you still need blood to function."

"So it would seem," Tanis grunted.

"Take them to holding; search and secure them," Tanis directed the Marines while looking at Mark and Andrea. She almost told them to get Jessica for an interrogation, but recalled that her specialist in that area was off the ship, gallivanting about the Orion Arm on her secret mission.

"I'll be with them before long," she said with a grimace as the medic punched a probe through her skin.

"Sorry," he said absently. "I thought you'd've already shut off your pain receptors. You've got a whack of blood pooled around your right lung. It's best to pull it out right now before it forms a hematoma."

"A whack?" Tanis asked. "Is that a medical term?"

"Yeah," the man chuckled. "Right above a touch, but not quite a shit-load."

Tanis laughed and then winced. "Stop being funny," she chided the medic.

Somehow, the pain reminded her of birth, which reminded her of Cary and Joe.

"Shit," she swore.

*<Joe, before you hear from someone else, I'm OK,>* Tanis sent the thought to Joe back in their home.

*<Wow, a call within minutes! Cary and I were betting on ten at the earliest,>* Joe's wry voice filled her mind, and he sent an image of Cary resting quietly in his arms, sucking absently on a bottle.

*<What kind of money did she put down—two crackers, and a spit-up cloth?>*

*<Yeah, she tried to add a diaper to the pot, but I put the kibosh on that. Seriously, though, are you alright?>*

Tanis could tell from Joe's tone that he was worried, but not too worried. She supposed that her suffering grievous injury had happened enough through their years that he would inevitably start to handle it with more aplomb.

*<I kinda miss him freaking out over me,>* she said privately to Angela.

*<Face it, we're—you're—no longer his number one girl. Someone else is foremost in Daddy's heart now,>* Angela replied.

It stung for a moment, but then Tanis realized she felt the same way.

*<Yeah, the medics are patching me up. Good thing I have this second ticker now,>* Tanis responded to Joe's question. *<Once they're done, I'm going to have some strong words with the Transcend's envoys.>*

*<What do you think happened? Why would Sera do that?>* Joe asked. *<They **had** to have done something to her.>*

Tanis sent him a mental nod. Sera had been her friend for close to a year now. People could certainly hide their true persona for longer—especially ones trained in spy craft, like Sera—but Tanis really felt as though something had happened to her.

She knew that Mark, at the least, had been in Sera's unit when she worked for The Hand. If anyone had the tech to subvert a person in minutes, the Transcend's black-ops organization would be just the group.

"Are you done yet?" she asked the medic.

"If I were done, would I still be crouched down here, sucking blood out of your torso?"

Tanis had to hold back a laugh. She liked this guy. Not many people talked to her like that anymore; it was refreshing.

"Give me just one more minute, then you can go kick the crap out of someone, ma'am," he added the last after glancing up at her face.

"We put them in the security office on deck 74," Lieutenant Smith said as he approached Tanis. "They didn't give us a fight, but weren't too happy when we took the data crystal and that case."

"I want everything within half a klick of that office locked down," Tanis said. "And I want you to board their ship and move it to a secure hangar. Comb over every inch of that thing."

The lieutenant snapped off a sharp salute and stepped back, waiting to escort her.

"Smith, I can make it there myself," Tanis looked up at him with a raised eyebrow.

He nodded. "I'm sure you can, sir. I'm coming along to protect any innocent folks in your path."

Tanis stifled a laugh and grimaced. "Why is everyone being funny all of a sudden? Can't you see I have a chest-wound, here?"

"Not anymore, you don't," the medic said as he stood up. "Though, please do come to the hospital before the day's out. We do need to replace your heart. It's a nice trick you pulled with a backup, but it can't stand up to serious strain. I just put a medseal on the skin for now. Try not to tear it off. The bandages are to keep you from shredding your muscles further."

Tanis stood slowly, expecting a dizzy spell, but she didn't experience any untoward symptoms.

"Nicely done," she complimented the medic before turning to Lieutenant Smith. "Lead the way."

# WATCHPOINT

**STELLAR DATE: 12.29.8929 (Adjusted Years)**
**LOCATION: ISS *Intrepid***
**REGION: Ascella System, Galactic North of the Corona Australis star-forming region**

"Alert coming in from the envoy's ship," the scan officer announced. "It's code red."

"What do we have?" General Greer grunted, wondering what the Tomlinson scions had managed to screw up this time.

"It's from Serge, on their ship. He's being forcibly boarded—something's gone wrong."

"Lieutenant Lindal, if one of our envoy's ships is being boarded, it's a foregone conclusion that something's gone wrong. What is the content of his message?" Greer asked, resisting the urge to review the message himself. Lindal had to learn how to dispense relevant details at some point in his career.

"Not much, just that it was armored soldiers and that they were not invited. His last transmission was that he was being brought aboard their ship. Our scopes show the envoy's vessel being moved into a hangar," Lindal said.

"Wait," General Greer suddenly realized what was amiss. "You said that Serge sent the message while still on his ship? He was supposed to be part of the diplomatic team. Mark was supposed to stay on the ship."

<*Well, now you know the why of it,*> Xerxes, the base operations AI, added. <*Though I have no idea what Andrea was thinking, allowing Mark into the meeting with the* Intrepid*—what with Sera there.*>

"Yes, thank you. I get the implications," Greer said with a frown.

While the nature of the falling out between Seraphina Tomlinson and Mark Festus was not widely known, Greer's command of a watchpoint had put him in the need-to-know group. He was certain there were details above his pay-grade, but he knew that both Sera and Mark blamed one another for the deaths of their team and the loss of a CriEn module—advanced tech that the denizens of the Inner Stars should never be allowed to possess.

At least, not until they were properly uplifted.

Regardless of those details, the mission dossier clearly spelled out the need for Mark to remain on the envoy ship and not board the *Intrepid*. Knowing Sera's volatile personality, there was little need to speculate on what would happen at the reunion of those two individuals.

Greer had no idea what possible course of logic could have allowed Andrea to put the two of them together in a room.

Granted, Andrea Tomlinson didn't possess great restraint, either. However, her father, the President of the Transcend Interstellar Alliance, put great faith in her abilities. She had taken the lead on dozens of diplomatic missions—as much because people feared her as for her ability to solve issues without conflict.

However, Andrea's presence on the team was obvious. She was to strong-arm her younger sister, the errant Seraphina, into coming home to Airtha in the Huygens System.

He steepled his fingers and considered his options.

Obviously, sitting by and doing nothing was not an option; but he knew the value of the *Intrepid*, this colony ship from a bygone era. The Transcend would benefit greatly from its technology—enough to finally give them the edge they needed over the Orion Guard.

Any response would require a delicate balance. They must demonstrate enough force to show that the Transcend would not take the abduction of its diplomats lightly, but not so much as to make these colonists think that they were too militant.

"Lieutenant Beezer, I want groups seven and thirteen to exit their hangars and jump to the *Intrepid*. Inform them that I wish their ships to flank the colony vessel, but keep a hundred-thousand kilometers distance from their fleet."

Of the fourteen fleet groups stationed at the watchpoint, seven and thirteen were the rapid response units—always ready to deploy and defend the watchpoint, or to travel across the stars to project the Transcend's might where needed.

Each group contained one hundred twenty-one ships, anchored by thirty six medium cruisers and eleven dreadnaughts. It was possible that the *Intrepid* was a match for the watchpoint's ships, but he had spent hundreds of hours analyzing the Battle of Bollam's World, and he believed he knew how to deal with their stasis shields to even the playing field.

Though he hoped it would not come to that. He would not go down in history as the man who destroyed the Transcend's greatest hope.

"Unknown contact," Lindal announced. "It dumped out of FTL really close—either it has the luckiest pilot ever, or detailed maps of the dark matter in this system."

"It never just rains," Greer muttered. "Scipio designation; what is a ship from that federation doing here?"

The Hand had more than a few operatives in Scipio. It was a key nation in the morass of systems that made up the Inner Stars, spanning nearly a hundred stellar systems and possessing a strong military. Controlling the direction of Scipio was of particular interest to the Transcend government—especially with Silstrand and other nearby systems facing increasing lawlessness.

<*It's Hand agent Elena. That ship is one outfitted for her mission in Scipio,*> Xerxes supplied. <*However, with our light-delay, she'll get to them long before we can get a message back to her—if that's her plan.*>

"Elena," Greer said softly. He summoned records on the agent, and saw that she was a long-time friend of Seraphina Tomlinson's. The Hand had suspicions—though nothing concrete—that she had been in contact with Sera during her exile over the past ten years.

"Summon her to the watchpoint—I don't expect her to comply, but I want it on record."

<*Message sent,*> Xerxes said.

"Uh…she's gone," Lieutenant Lindal announced. "I'm pulling data from more observation points."

Greer pulled up the data and poured over it. Lindal was right; one moment scan had a clear visual on Elena's ship, the next it simply disappeared.

"It's their stealth ship," Greer said. "We know it was operating at Bollam's World, but I thought we had identified it as *this* vessel," he gestured to one of the ships on the command center's holotank.

"It must not be—or they have more than one of those ships," Lindal replied. "Wait! I caught a strange refraction on the UV band. I think it was a ship, but now I have nothing."

"Well," Greer sighed. "We can safely assume that she's on her way to the *Intrepid*. I want scan analysis to find that stealth ship, and let me know the instant the fleets jump out."

# AGENT ELENA

**STELLAR DATE: 12.29.8929 (Adjusted Years)**
**LOCATION: ISS *Intrepid***
**REGION: Ascella System, Galactic North of the Corona Australis star-forming region**

<*There's a ship dropping in on us,*> Amanda interrupted Tanis's thoughts.

The statement brought Tanis back to the near-silence of the maglev train she rode with Lieutenant Smith, and away from her worry over what could cause Sera to turn so quickly.

<*Has it identified itself?*> Tanis asked after a moment's pause.

<*The beacon says it's the ship of a private citizen from the Scipio Federation. It hasn't answered any hails yet—oh wait, she just made contact. Patching you through.*>

The image of a woman appeared in Tanis's mind and she took in the woman's blood-red hair, eyes, and lips in a single glance. The woman opened her mouth to speak, revealing elongated canine teeth. Tanis's suspicions were confirmed; she was a sucker.

<*Colony ship* Intrepid, *please allow me to dock, I have important information for you,*> the woman spoke without preamble.

<*This is Governor Richards of the* Intrepid. *We're not exactly in a receptive mood—you're probably well aware that we have not had many warm welcomes of late. Why don't you relay your information from where you are?*>

Scan showed that the ship was close, only seven light seconds away. Tanis waited patiently for the woman's response to come.

When it did, she saw that the woman frowned and shook her head vigorously. <*I can't. If the watchpoint hasn't already tapped this communication, they're about to.*>

Tanis rubbed placed her hands over her face and ran them over her head while drawing in a deep breath.

"Shit!" she gasped as pain stabbed in her chest.

<*The watchpoint is what Sera called their outpost here,*> Angela said. <*This woman must be Hand.*>

<*I'm close. Let me get on her tail and use a squadron of Arc-6 fighters to bracket her,*> Corsia broke into the conversation.

Tanis Linked with the bridge net to effectively communicate with the command team—something she would have thought to do immediately, had she not been distracted by her pesky chest wound.

<*Not to mention the potential loss of a good friend,*> Angela commented privately on Tanis's thoughts.

<*Corsia, bring her aboard the* Andromeda, *but just her. Leave her ship in the black; we can get it later, if needed. Check her over, and then let me know when we're ready for a tight-beam chat.*>

<*Will do,*> Corsia replied. <*I'll update you when we have her.*>

Tanis switched back to the woman in her small cockpit. <*There's a cruiser on your tail. It's going to take you aboard and leave your ship behind. We've had enough surprises today.*>

She waited the requisite time for the message and response to traverse millions of miles of space. When it did, she saw the woman review her scan with furrowed brow, likely looking for the *Andromeda*. Then her eyes widened. <*Oh shit, it's* **right** *on my ass! That's impressive.*>

<*You're ringed by fighters—which you can't see, either. Behave and we'll talk in a bit.*>

Tanis severed the connection with the woman and reached out to the hospital ward on deck ninety-three.

<*What is Sera's condition?*> she asked the man operating the reception channel without preamble.

<*General—er, Governor!*> the man responded. <*She…uh…she's awake and letting us treat her, but she's unresponsive. I'll connect you with the doctor.*>

Doctor Barbara Summers, once a GSS corporal who worked visitor security on the *Intrepid* back at Mars, appeared in her mind.

<*Governor Richards, I'm glad you've reached out. Seraphina has suffered a rather insidious hack, one that has shunted many of her cognitive functions away and locked off Helen's access. We're trying to break past it to get to Helen—we anticipate she will know how to undo the hack—but so far, it's thwarting us—growing further into her brain.*>

<*So, she* ***was*** *hacked, then,*> Tanis stated. <*I suspected as much. There was something in her expression before she attacked me.*>

<*It was done through a nano-patch placed on her neck,*> Doctor Summers reported. <*It's honestly quite amazing—it took less than thirty seconds to subvert her. We think that it may have been accelerated by some programming her agency planted in her in the past.*>

<*That would have to be some well-secreted programming to escape Helen's notice,*> Angela added to the conversation.

Doctor Summers nodded. <*That is our assessment, as well. Bob has advised us that we should limit our intrusive attempts, and has sent Terry Chang up to assist. I'll bet the Transcend people will have a code to deactivate it—if you can extract it from them.*>

Tanis let a thin smile slip across her face. <*If they have such a code, they'll provide it to me.*>

# A SIMPLE CHAT

**STELLAR DATE: 12.29.8929 (Adjusted Years)**
**LOCATION: ISS *Intrepid***
**REGION: Ascella System, Galactic North of the Corona Australis star-forming region**

Tanis rose from her seat on the maglev and followed Lieutenant Smith to the security office. Her words to Doctor Summers echoed in her ears, and the memory of the torture she had inflicted on the assassin Kris years ago in Sol surged into her mind.

Tanis thought she had evolved—she was so sure, given her treatment of Drind on *Sabrina*. Thompson had pushed to beat the information out of The Mark's data tech, but Tanis took the high road with him, convincing him to join their cause. But now, with Sera's mind in jeopardy, she was ready to tear both Mark and Andrea limb-from-limb. Never mind that Andrea's father was president of the entire Transcend.

Let him come for her. Let them all come.

<*You need to relax,*> Angela applied the calming thought to Tanis's mind. <*You're not going to get anywhere if you go in there guns blazing.*>

<*They came here to assassinate me,*> Tanis fumed. <*And they used Sera as their tool! They may think they're clever, but even if they had killed me, no one would have believed their story for a moment. Bob vetted Sera. We know her intentions are pure.*>

<*They don't know about Bob,*> Angela chuckled. <*They couldn't have known that he would facilitate an unshakable faith in Sera. Use that; let them think that they've succeeded in that, at least. They'll tell you more voluntarily than if you resort to torture.*>

Tanis paused, realizing that Angela was right. She had fallen into some sort of primal maternal rage—protecting hers against all comers with the most violent option available. But she was smarter than these Hand agents. She had been pitted against far more cunning enemies.

"There was another one of them on the diplomat's ship," Smith said aloud as they stepped into the security office. "They're bringing him here from the dock."

"Good," Tanis nodded. "It makes sense that they'd have someone else onboard, in case things didn't pan out."

She stopped in the office's waiting room and collected her thoughts, preparing for whatever would come next.

"Are you going to go in like that?" Lieutenant Smith asked, glancing at her bloody uniform.

"Damn, I totally forgot about that," Tanis said. "There's a locker room down the hall. I'll clean up in a san and be back in five."

"Take your time," Smith replied. "I'll make sure they don't go anywhere."

<*Careful with those bandages,*> Angela advised as Tanis walked to the locker room. <*It won't take much to start bleeding again.*>

Tanis nodded silently, and, once the locker door slid closed behind her, carefully unwound the bandages, draping them over a bench before she stripped out of her dress uniform.

The hot spray of water felt glorious, and she spent longer than expected under its warming massage. She was careful not to let the jets hit the medseal the technician had applied to her wound, and gave an involuntary sign of dismay when the unit hit its max water usage and flipped to dry-mode.

She stepped out of the unit and saw that a fresh bandage was sitting on the bench with a clean shipsuit beside it.

<*Who would have thought Smith was that thoughtful,*> Angela said.

<*Better not have been him that did it, he's supposed to have his eye on our guests,*> Tanis replied as she gingerly wrapped the bandage back around her chest before slipping into the shipsuit.

<*It wasn't him, but he told one of the station officers to do it.*>

When she arrived at the entrance to the interview room, Smith handed her a glass of water and she downed it after sending a smile his way.

"Thanks, I needed that."

"General," Lieutenant Smith's voice was deadly serious, "do you want me in there with you? You did just suffer a serious injury."

Tanis glanced at the lieutenant; a Marine's Marine if ever there was one. He was over two hundred centimeters of rippling muscle, with fists the size of her head.

"You know what? I *do* want you in there with me. Be menacing—whenever it feels right."

Smith let out a short laugh. "It's going to feel right the whole time."

*****

Things weren't going as well as Tanis had hoped.

Mark was defensive, and Andrea seemed not to care at all that her own sister was accused of very a serious crime. Tanis hadn't shifted the blame to the two Hand agents yet—rather, she had focused on convincing them that the Marines had followed standard protocol by not using lethal force on Sera.

"Help me understand why she'd do this," Tanis asked, almost pleading.

"She's unstable," Mark said, and Tanis raised an eyebrow as though she was hopeful for more detail from him. The man was scum. He oozed lies from every pore, yet somehow he was good at hiding physical tells.

"She went off-book a lot when we were part of the same unit," Mark continued. "I had to rein her in more than once, and when she lost the CriEn module…well, she just went full rogue."

"That doesn't explain why she'd try to kill me," Tanis replied in even tones. "I've never seen such behavior from her before. If I had, do you think she'd be here now?"

"She's very good at hiding her intentions," Andrea said. "I think that she wanted to get in her father's good graces. Bring him the best prize ever—this ship—without its strong-willed governor and general."

Tanis considered those words. They rang true, but not for Sera—perhaps for Andrea.

It didn't surprise her. Tanis knew she could be a colossal pain in the ass—the Transcend probably had no place in it for General Richards. What they didn't know was that Tanis didn't want to be that woman forever.

<*Hah! Sure,*> Angela's comment was laced with disbelief.

"Then she's the best liar I've ever seen," Tanis said aloud to Andrea and Mark. "I've spent over a year with her, and she's never shown me any malice."

"I spent longer before she turned on me," Mark said with a sympathetic smile. "There's no shame in being fooled by her. It's what she does."

"And her AI?" Tanis asked. "AI are rarely complicit in things like this—it doesn't suit their race's long-term outlook on things. Not to mention survival."

Andrea frowned, a look of conciliatory puzzlement on her face. "We've wondered that, too. Helen was always a good agent. Somehow, when Sera went rogue, she convinced Helen to go with her. We've never been able to come up with a wholly convincing rationale for it ourselves."

"So, what should we do with her?" Tanis asked. "She is, in large part, responsible for saving this ship."

"And for nearly killing you," Mark said with raised eyebrows. "Most people would be ready to do the same in response."

Tanis sighed, displaying emotion that was not feigned. "I've seen enough death. I'd like to see more forgiveness in my future."

"Then send her with us," Andrea said, holding her hands out with palms upturned. Tanis knew the gesture was meant to show openness and good intentions—something she was certain Andrea possessed none of. If Sera were to leave with these two, she'd be dead long before they ever reached their destination.

<*They're really not going to give us anything,*> Tanis said with a sigh. <*I guess it's time to play bad cop.*>

<*Let's take a break,*> Angela said. <*Perhaps Corsia's guest—Elena—can give us what we need, and we won't need to mess with these two at all.*>

<*I like where your head's at,*> Tanis replied and rose from the table. <*Certainly better than where mine is.*>

"Please forgive me," she said aloud. "I'm needed elsewhere for a few minutes. Lieutenant Smith will remain to ensure your needs are met."

She nodded to the lieutenant and left the room before the Transcend envoys could respond.

<*Has Elena cleared security checks?*> Tanis asked Corsia once she was in the hall.

<*Momentarily. She's a deep cover agent, so she throws up a lot of red flags. Nothing stands out as crafted to harm us, but she doesn't really give a benevolent impression,*> Corsia said, then paused. <*If things were different, I'd put her back in her ship and give her until the count of ten to get out of weapons range.*>

Corsia was nothing if not frank—it was one of the things she liked most about the AI.

<*I understand completely. I wouldn't mind tossing* **this** *pair out the airlock, too…but diplomatic relations and all that,*> Tanis replied.

<*OK, I'm setting you up with a secure channel to Elena,*> Corsia said. <*She has no Link access other than this tunnel to you. Be on guard.*>

<*Thanks,*> Tanis responded to Corsia before switching to the secure channel and addressing Elena. <*So, what do you have? I've got Sera restrained in a hospital bed, and two of the Transcend's finest in lockup. Whose side are you on?*>

Elena's image floated in Tanis's mind. Unlike a normal Link communication, she was not seeing Elena as the woman wished to present herself virtually, but rather a feed of her in a holding room.

Elena's appearance was unchanged from their previous communication; she still had the look of a sucker—though, given that she was a Hand agent, the affectation was probably a cover. An agent with a blood fetish would not make for a good operative.

Elena's gaze remained fixed at a point in front of her. Either she could detect the optical arrays watching her, or she had guessed correctly that Tanis would view her from that angle.

<*You don't start off easily, do you?*> Elena replied with a twist of her lips. <*People in my line of work don't really get to pick sides—hell, we don't even know which we're on most of the time.*>

<*Let me rephrase that,*> Tanis said. <*Who do you care about more: Sera, or Andrea and Mark?*>

Elena barked out a laugh. <*That's who they sent, is it? Mark, of all people. I'll bet that he wasn't supposed to be there, but weaseled his way in, somehow. You got a third, didn't you?*>

<*Answer the question,*> Tanis replied.

The smile slipped from Elena's face and her eyes grew dead serious. <*I care for Sera far more than either of those two bastards. Have they done something to her?*>

<*Why would you suspect that?*> Tanis asked

Elena shook her head in dismay. <*Because Mark wants Sera dead. He's tried before. That Justin would let him on this mission…*>

<*And what of Andrea?*> Tanis prompted.

<*She's worse,*> Elena said with a shake of her head. <*She's as emotionless as they come, though I doubt she was sent to kill Sera—but, I wouldn't put it past her to do it on her own.*>

Tanis considered Elena's words. It was obvious that the woman was hedging as much as she could, attempting to feel her out. Still, Elena had flown from Scipio to Ascella with the sole purpose to rescue Sera—or so she said.

<*She could also be the backup,*> Angela said. <*You're still alive, Sera's still alive…perhaps she comes in to finish the job?*>

Tanis nodded absently. <*The thought had crossed my mind.*>

<*We could strip the information from their minds,*> Angela said <*I don't think they could stop us.*>

<*No,*> Tanis sighed. <*We've made too many sacrifices in this journey. We have to make a home, eventually. The system they've offered us is the best we'll ever get—we can't start that relationship with Phobos Accord violations.*>

<**They** *don't seem to be above such considerations,*> Angela replied.

<*Maybe,*> Tanis nodded. <*But I have to believe that these are just a few bad seeds. The FGT still terraforms worlds for others. Their agents can't all be like this.*>

<*Don't hold your breath,*> Angela replied.

Tanis grunted in response and turned her attention back to Elena. <*OK, lay it out. What do you have for me?*>

<*Well, you haven't told me anything. Is Sera OK? Have they done something to her?*>

Tanis couldn't be certain, but Elena's concern seemed genuine and she decided to lay it out and see what Elena offered in response.

<*They did something to her and tried to use her to kill me. I could see something in her eyes that makes me think it wasn't voluntary on her part.*>

<*Damnit!*> Elena whispered vehemently. <*We checked her over, we found a hack that Mark had planted, but we must have missed something.*>

<*You?*> Tanis asked.

Elena nodded. <*After the events...after she lost the CriEn and her team—except for Mark—she knew he was to blame. She had reason in the past to suspect him, but he had always managed to assuage her concerns. She reached out to me, and I met her in Silstrand. I found a hack at the core of her interface with Helen, one neither of them could see. It was designed to lock Helen out, and subvert Sera. The thing is...I removed it. How could it be back?*>

<*Get the specs from her,*> Bob inserted himself into Tanis's thoughts. <*I don't want to communicate directly with her, no need for more questions.*>

<*Give me the specs on that hack—if you still have them,*> Tanis ordered Elena. <*We may be able to use it to see if there's something similar at play now.*>

Elena nodded, and the information flooded across their connection. Tanis passed the data on to Bob while storing a copy to review later.

<*I see it now,*> Bob said. <*This is insidious; I would not have looked for something like this. There is something at play in the Transcend...something I did not expect....*>

<*Do we need Elena's further assistance to restore Sera?*> Tanis asked Bob.

<*Technically, no. I see why her prior work did not fully protect Sera. However, it will be to our benefit for them to think that we needed Elena's help. Bring her. I will begin to undo this violation with Terry's assistance. To Elena it will seem as though she provided the pivotal solution.*>

Tanis sent an affirmative response. She understood Bob's caution; if there was something in the Transcend that could produce a hack that Bob would term 'insidious', then there was no need to let that entity know Bob existed, or that he could reverse its work.

<*Corsia, put her on a shuttle and bring her in.*>

<*Aye, Governor,*> the ship's AI replied.

Tanis shook her head at the title. She thought she had left this sort of responsibility behind in Victoria, yet now it was back on her shoulders. Though this time, not as Lieutenant Governor—now the buck really *did* stop with her.

<*Brandt,*> Tanis called the Marine Commandant, <*I can see that you have things on full lock-down. We're about to bring that woman we have on the* Andromeda *here, but I don't yet trust her.*>

<*I don't trust anyone, Governor,*> Brandt replied. <*How are you feeling, by the way?*>

<*Well enough. Doctor Rosenberg has an assistant pinging me every five minutes trying to get me into a medbay—not that there's any point. My nano have nearly repaired the heart Sera shredded.*>

<*Tricky move, getting a second heart,*> Brandt said. <*Do you find it cuts into your lung capacity too much? I've considered getting one, but some folks say they have shortness of breath in a fight—I don't have a lot of room, either.*>

Tanis chuckled. Brandt was right about that. In a corps where the average Marine stood well over two hundred centimeters, Brandt's diminutive one-sixty was almost comical. Her slight build had earned her the nickname "The Pix" though it was something no one called her to her face.

Brandt made up for her small stature with a command presence that cowed even the largest Marine under her command—but the one thing she couldn't bully into place were a lot of mods in her small frame.

<*It's small; can't do as much as my primary, but my lungs can pull a lot more oxygen from the air than natural ones. Given how often I get shot in the chest, it's worth it,*> Tanis replied.

<*You know...most people have* ***never*** *been shot in the chest. I'm not saying you should exercise more caution...but...*>

<*OK, OK, I get it. Leave me be and go yell at someone,*> Tanis said with a mental chuckle.

<*I'm always yelling at someone—I can multitask, you know,*> Brandt sent a wink and closed the connection.

Tanis leaned against the wall and took a look around. Knowing that Sera could be restored took a load off her mind, but that was just the beginning. Andrea and Mark had tried to assassinate a foreign head of state, and she couldn't just let them off with a slap on the wrist.

Just as she was thinking she needed to see him, Joe materialized in front of her, holding their tiny daughter in his arms. She wished he really were there, not just a hologram projecting from their cabin. Embracing her family was just what she needed right now.

"You need a hand?" he asked. "I can have someone look after Cary."

Tanis leaned over and looked into the face of her little girl. She hated that she had to be away from her so much, but soon they would be out of Ascella and things would calm down.

"I hate to ask it," Tanis replied. "She needs her parents—at least one of them—to be around."

"She needs them to be alive, and their starship to remain in one piece, even more," Joe said with a raised eyebrow. "I'm at Tracy's—she's off for the next few days and can watch her. Even if she gets called in, her oldest two are used to looking after little ones."

Tanis nodded. Tracy was a good woman, and her cabin wasn't too far from theirs. "I see that you already planned to get back on duty."

"Well, technically you outrank me and can tell me no…but yes, I need to be out there."

Tanis understood what he meant. "Corsia has the pinnace coming in with a…friend of Sera's. Catch a ride on the return trip and get to your captain's chair."

Joe smiled and tossed her a casual salute. "Aye, aye." He held up their daughter. "Say goodbye to Mommy. We'll check on you real soon."

Tanis blew her daughter a kiss, and took a deep breath as Joe and Cary disappeared from view.

<*Our visitors are getting restless in here,*> Lieutenant Smith said.

<*One thing after the other,*> Tanis commented to Angela as she walked back to the holding room.

<*Don't grouse at me. It's the way you like it.*>

# AWAKE

**STELLAR DATE: 12.29.8929 (Adjusted Years)**
**LOCATION: ISS *Intrepid***
**REGION: Ascella System, Galactic North of the Corona Australis star-forming region**

Sera's head screamed with pain, as though someone had drilled a hole in her skull and poured acid inside. She bit back a sob and tried to regulate her breathing.

"Good, you're awake," a voice said. "From what I can tell, you're probably in a bit of pain. We're working on that. Helen should also be back with you in a minute or two."

Helen! That was part of the pain. Sera was subconsciously trying to access her connection with Helen and it wasn't there. It wasn't the phantom limb sort of ache one got when an AI had been removed cleanly, but rather the screaming agony of a pulverized appendage.

The pain began to recede and Sera thought that perhaps she recognized the voice that had spoken—though she couldn't place it. She knew that she should be able to, but couldn't drum up the name no matter how hard she tried.

That was the other part of the pain; she had no access to her digital data stores. She was thinking with pure organics, something she hadn't done in decades. She tried to focus, to access her data volumes, but where there once was instant information, there was nothing but searing agony.

She felt so slow and stupid. Her state should have been immediately obvious, but she hadn't even realized how severed she was from her implants. A dim recollection of how this could have happened clawed its way into her conscious mind, and she whispered a single word.

"Mark."

"Good," the voice said, "you have access to your organic memories. Means this is working."

Sera began to hear other voices around her, of people moving about, focused on their work. She was indoors, in a room, perhaps a hospital by the sterile smell. She shifted and, in the moments before her nerve endings set new fire to her brain, she realized that she was strapped down.

"Try not to move. You got hit by no small number of pulse blasts," a different voice said. "The Marines exercised some restraint, but not as much as they could have."

Sera could not place the new voice, but she knew what Marines were. If she had been shot by them and still lived to tell the tale, then she had reason to be grateful. Still, try as she might, she could not remember enough to even guess at why she had been shot.

"OK," a third voice said, this one only vaguely familiar, "let's try and reactivate her internal mods."

"Brace yourself," the first voice said. "This is going to hurt."

Sera couldn't imagine anything hurting more than the pain she already felt, but she was wrong. A scream tore out of her; she felt as though her brain was tearing itself to shreds, but then the agony subsided to tolerable levels.

That was when the pain from her body began to take over—her broken bones and damaged organs letting her know just how upset they were over her current state.

"Can you do something about how much this hurts?" Sera managed to whisper, her voice cracking as she struggled to speak.

"In a moment, dear," the first voice said. "We have to finish with Helen, then you'll be back in full control of your mods and you can suppress the pain."

Sera grunted in response, and, true to her unseen benefactor's word, Helen was back just a few seconds later.

<*Well, that was unpleasant,*> Helen's dry voice swept through Sera's mind like a broom, clearing away the fog and bringing Sera to full consciousness. Together they suppressed the thundering pain—though it was still present—and assessed their current state.

<*We're in a medbay on the* Intrepid,> Helen provided.

<*I surmised as much,*> Sera said in agreement. <*And now I know how we got here.*>

<*Yes,*> Helen's voice exhibited uncharacteristic anger. <*We were hacked.*>

Sera sent agreement to Helen. Her AI was right; somehow they had been subverted—and in very short order, too.

<*Was it Mark? How was that even possible? Elena removed the Hand's backdoor when we struck out on our own.*>

Helen's response was a pulse of mental uncertainty, and Sera gauged the wisdom of opening her eyes to see who was tending to her wounded mind and body. Curiosity won out, and she cracked her eyelids and peered around the room.

The first face she saw was that of Terry, head of the *Intrepid*'s Net Security division. Terry's presence didn't surprise her. Aside from Bob and his avatars, few knew the ins and outs of the human mind and its many possible modifications—and weaknesses—better.

At the foot of the bed stood a woman she vaguely recognized; after a moment, her reestablished digital archives identified her as Dr. Summers.

Beyond her, in the shadows, stood Flaherty. He hadn't spoken, but she wasn't surprised to see him there at all. Sera gave him a weak smile, and turned her head to the left, looking for the third person.

The face staring down at her was vaguely familiar, but the long fangs and red eyes made recognition difficult. She didn't recall any suckers being present on the *Intrepid*. That sort of behavior didn't fit well with people looking to build a colony.

"Don't you recognize me? We've been through too much to think we could be strangers," the woman said.

"Elly!" Sera exclaimed. "How the hell are you here...and why are you a sucker? Never mind, I know it's a cover—I hope it's a cover."

"Nice to see you, too. And of course it's a cover. Do you know how much of a bitch it is to eat around these damn teeth?"

"I can only imagine," Sera replied absently. "What I really want to know is how did Mark hack me? I thought we removed The Hand's access."

Elena nodded slowly and looked up to Terry. "I'm not really sure, to be honest. As far as I can tell, we had completely removed it ten years ago; but when they brought me in, it was there the same as before. Almost like I hadn't done a thing."

"Great, does this mean I will be at their mercy forever?" Sera asked, looking between Terry and Elena.

Elena appeared uncertain while Terry shook her head. "Absolutely not. We'll square this away."

<*They don't want Elena to know about Bob,*> Helen said.

*<I can imagine why not. They're not—stars,* ***I'm*** *not—terribly trusting of the Transcend right now. I'll take Terry's word for it for now, but if we do get back to Airtha, I want the other you to take a look.>*

Helen passed a feeling of agreement to Sera. *<Absolutely. Being sequestered like that was not exactly a great time for me, either.>*

A memory of what she had done while subverted flashed into her mind.

"Oh, shit, is Tanis OK? Stars, she must want to kill me right now," Sera said aloud.

"She's fine," Dr. Summers said from her place at the foot of the bed. "And you seem to be nearly recovered—mentally, at least—if you can recall those events."

"Do you remember what happened when you were in private with the envoys?" Terry asked.

Sera did, and it shamed her that her people would do such a thing. She closed her eyes and let out a long breath.

"I do," she said after a minute. "They want Tanis dead and…they were willing to sacrifice me to do it."

"What?" Dr. Summers exclaimed. "Those bastards!"

Sera ignored the doctor's outburst and her eyes darted between Terry and Elena. She saw Elena become more guarded as Terry nodded. She knew that Bob and Tanis would have ferreted out the truth behind Andrea's intentions by now. Terry would have been briefed, and the concern in the woman's eyes was palpable.

It was an understandable emotion. The colonists aboard the *Intrepid* really couldn't catch a break. Even the Transcend, who should have been their benefactor and savior, was opposed to them. Or at least, to Tanis.

"Do you guys think you could leave me for just a bit?" Sera asked. "I really need a few minutes to myself."

Dr. Summers and Elena both looked to Terry, who nodded.

"And the restraints?" Sera asked.

"I'll advise Tanis on your condition," Terry replied solemnly. "They'll come off on her order only."

Sera nodded silently, keenly aware that much of the goodwill she had earned with the *Intrepid*'s crew had been lost—involuntary actions notwithstanding.

# ESCALATION

**STELLAR DATE: 12.30.8929 (Adjusted Years)**
**LOCATION: ISS *Intrepid***
**REGION: Ascella System, Galactic North of the Corona Australis star-forming region**

<*Before you go in there,*> Amanda broke into Tanis's thoughts. <*The watchpoint has shown their hand. Ships are moving out of two of the locations we flagged.*>

<*Was bound to happen sooner or later,*> Tanis replied. <*How many?*>

<*They're still pulling out of their covert hangars. Over a hundred confirmed so far.*>

Tanis paused and placed a hand on the wall. She took a deep breath and Linked with the bridge.

<*Tanis,*> Captain Andrews greeted her. <*I trust you've been informed that we're receiving the usual welcome party out there.*>

<*Just once, I'd like to fly into a system where everyone doesn't want to kill us,*> Tanis replied.

<*If wishes were fishes…*> Amanda said with a mental smile.

Tanis stepped into the center of the hall, outside the entrance to the holding room. She surrounded herself with holodisplays showing the space surrounding the *Intrepid.*

The two stars of the Ascella system danced around one another in a tight orbit—tight for stars, at least—with a current separation of only one hundred fifty150 AU. Their proximity was one of the reasons that the system remained uninhabited; the stars stirred up too much chaos to make Ascella a safe place to settle down.

Between the two stars, there were seventeen major planets and hundreds of dwarf worlds. A morass of asteroid belts circled the stars, with clusters of dust, ice, and rock in the Lagrange points between the stars and their major satellites.

The moment they dropped out of the dark layer and back into normal space, she had taken one look at the system and known why the Transcend used it. It was all but purpose-built for war.

*<I would not be surprised if that was exactly what happened here,>* Angela said.

*<What? That the Transcend mucked with this system to set it up like this?>* Tanis asked.

Angela sent an affirmation, and Tanis briefly considered the power of the Transcend—to remake worlds within the Inner Stars less palatable just so that they could hide in them was serious long-term planning.

Beyond the initial three locations Corsia had reported, the *Intrepid*'s probes and cloaked fighters had positively identified seven more base locations, and several more suspects.

From what she could see, there were two fleets forming up: one coming from within a cluster of dwarf worlds only two AU from the *Intrepid,* and another from a world seven AU away. Even at max burn, the closest ships were over a day away—unless they knew the positions of dark matter in this system well enough to skip through the dark layer insystem.

It was risky; a system like this would be rife with matter in the dark layer, but she had to consider the possibility.

*<Anything from the third person on the envoy's ship?>* Tanis asked Amanda.

*<Not yet. Brandt has some folks talking to him, but so far he professes to have no knowledge of any plan to kill you. He did say that he was supposed to be on the boarding party, not Mark, but claims he was drugged and came to shortly before we boarded. We haven't been able to verify that without a forced examination.>*

Tanis considered the information. If Sera's brother, Serge, was telling the truth, then not everyone in the Transcend was hell-bent on killing her—which was a small victory, at least.

*<Oh! Sera's awake and is herself again.>*

*<Thank the stars for small miracles,>* Tanis sighed.

*<Brandt,>* Tanis connected to the Marine Commandant.

*<Yes, General,>* came Brandt's clipped reply.

*<Send Serge to the medbay where Sera is. I want them to have a little reunion and see what we can ferret out—and what we can do to clean up this mess.>*

*<On it,>* Brandt responded.

Tanis nodded to herself, and quickly reviewed division statuses across the ship to ensure everything was ready for whatever may come their way. Once she had sent a few orders to various sections, she poked her head into the room where Mark and Andrea sat, looking much more agitated than when she left.

"How much longer are you going to hold us here?" Mark shot at her the moment she opened the door. "Your goon here won't give us any news."

Lieutenant Smith flashed a malignant smile at the pair, but didn't say a word in response.

"Sorry," Tanis replied. "Your little attempt on my life caused quite a stir, and gave me an ever-loving mess to clean up."

"Our attempt?" Andrea asked with narrowed eyes. "We had nothing to do with it. This was all Sera's doing! She's not known to be especially stable, as you can now attest."

"Well," Tanis smiled sweetly, "she's awake and back to herself again, so I'm going to have a chat with her and get the skinny on what's really going on. I'm going to have Serge join us, to see what he thinks of all this."

Andrea's expression did not waver for an instant, but Mark's eyes widened for just a moment. If anyone on their mission was expendable, it was him. The fact that Sera ever saw anything in this slime-ball of a man would forever baffle Tanis.

"Lieutenant," she turned to Smith, "I want them secured and ready to move. Full lockdown, full physical restraint. Also, get a Mark-9 drone on them. One false move, turn them to puddles."

She gave her own predatory smile to the pair behind the table. "You want our picotech; I know you do. Test Lieutenant Smith in any way, and he has my full authorization to introduce you to it, personally."

Her statement finally elicited a reaction from Andrea—a noticeable whitening of her skin. Though the *Intrepid*'s nano-technology was, in aggregate, more advanced than the Transcend's, this pair had defenses enough to keep it from entering their minds and bodies.

Picobots, on the other hand, would not face any opposition infiltrating their bodies—nor was there any way they could stop the picoscale machines from tearing them apart atom by atom.

Tanis didn't wait any longer. She left the room, but not before holding the door wide for a squad of Marines to enter with weapons leveled.

<*Sera,*> Tanis sent to her friend once she was back in the hall, <*I'm on my way.*>

# REUNION

**STELLAR DATE: 12.30.8929 (Adjusted Years)**
**LOCATION: ISS *Intrepid***
**REGION: Ascella System, Galactic North of the Corona Australis star-forming region**

Tanis rushed through the ship's corridors at a pace that had her secondary heart working overtime. A fireteam of Marines in full armor followed her, eyeing every nook and cranny of the ship that had been their home for centuries as though it were enemy territory.

<*What's your plan?*> Terrance Enfield interrupted her thoughts. <*They're going to demand their people back—I don't want to jeopardize the colony for revenge.*>

Tanis gave a mental shake of her head. Terrance was so close to reaching his life-long goal that she could forgive him for thinking that she valued it any less than he. Even though his motivations for wanting to build a colony world were entirely different now than when they left Sol nearly five thousand years ago, he remained single-minded in his drive to reach their new home.

<*I don't want to fight another war,*> Tanis replied. <*I will give them back their people, but I will not send Sera with them against her will.*>

<*Will you sacrifice our dream of a colony?*> Terrance asked, anger seeping into his mental tone. <*Is she worth that much to you?*>

<*Do you want to have a free colony, or to be a vassal state?*> Tanis replied without equivocation. <*Because if we let them come onto our ship, attempt to assassinate our leadership, and then still give in to all their demands, then that is what we'll end up as.*>

Terrance did not respond for almost a minute, and Tanis wondered if their conversation had come to an end.

<*Very well, Tanis. You've gotten us this far; but please, be as circumspect as you can.*>

<*When am I not?*> Tanis replied with a smile.

<*Oh, that will certainly build confidence,*> Angela said privately.

<*I couldn't help it,*> Tanis said as she boarded a maglev train. <*I've always put this mission first. Hell, they put me in charge of it, for fucksakes!*

*Against my will! If Terrance can't trust me to get the job done, then he deserves a bit of ribbing.*>

Angela didn't respond.

Tanis rode the train in silence past two stops before disembarking at the ship's forward hospital. The section spanned over a square kilometer across seven decks, and though she knew it well, it still took her some minutes to navigate its warren of corridors.

When the *Intrepid* departed from Sol long ago, the hospital had been much smaller; but during the Victoria years, when over a hundred thousand crew and colonists roamed the ship, it had been expanded considerably—if for no other reason than to handle all the births.

Upon arrival at the door to Sera's room, she paused to allow two of the Marines to enter first. She trusted Bob's assessment that Sera was no longer a threat, but she wasn't about to behave as though a threat could not re-emerge—especially with Elena, another unknown quantity, in the mix.

She heard Terry greet the Marines, and a moment later, the corporal called out that all was clear. Tanis checked Serge's location before entering, and saw that Sera's brother was still five minutes out.

<*I'll let you know when he's here,*> Angela said.

Tanis appreciated the gesture. There were a lot of requests hitting her queue; though with the notification that Joe was now aboard the *Andromeda,* one of her concerns had diminished.

"Sera," she said as she entered the room and approached her friend still restrained to the bed.

"Tanis," Sera's eyes were wide and filled with apology. "I can't tell you how sorry I am—and how glad I am that you never told me about your little heart modification."

She noticed Flaherty in the corner and nodded to him. He grunted in response, and returned to eyeing the Marines.

"I've got to have some secrets," Tanis replied with a smile. "We can do away with the restraints," she said, and the room's monitoring systems deactivated the clamps around Sera's arms and legs.

The Marines didn't move a muscle, but they somehow seemed even more alert.

Sera's gaze darted to the soldiers before she closed her eyes and slowly lifted her arms—an expression of both pain and relief crossed her face.

"Oh, thank you," Sera moaned. "I was getting the worst cramp you could ever imagine."

"I'll bet," Tanis said as she took a seat beside the bed. "I'm glad you're yourself again. I didn't want to think that we wouldn't be able to get you back."

*<I trust that you've kept Bob's abilities to yourself?>* she asked privately. *<I don't trust your friend here much further than I can throw her.>*

*<I've not breathed a word; though Bob has assured Helen and I that we are safe from any future subversion of our minds,>* Sera replied. *<I'm glad he's on our side.>*

Tanis added the comment to an extensive list of observations Sera had made about Bob over the prior months. She made a note to finally confront Sera over what bothered her so much about AI. However, for now, she opted to ignore the statement.

*<What of Elena?>* Tanis asked. *<Can we trust her?>*

Tanis was carrying on an audible conversation with Sera, Elena, and Terry. Sera responded aloud to a question before replying to Tanis over the Link.

*<I have no idea how you do that so fluidly,>* Sera said. *<If I didn't know better, I'd think your complete attention was on what Terry is saying right now.>*

*<I'm also talking to Joe and Captain Andrews,>* Tanis replied. *<But, about Elena?>*

*<Show-off,>* Angela whispered in Tanis's mind.

*<I've trusted her with my life in the past…>* Sera said before pausing. *<I don't see why I wouldn't now. She said that she raced here as soon as she saw what happened at Bollam's World. Why would she do that if she meant me harm?>*

*<I can think of a hundred reasons,>* Tanis replied. *<Perhaps she has some reason to wish you harm that she didn't before, or maybe she's a fail-safe to attempt to bridge things with the Transcend after Andrea and Mark failed. She could even be here for her own advancement. The fact that the backdoor into your mind remained, leaving you open to The Hand's machinations, could also be her doing.>*

*<Yeah, I thought of a lot of those, too. I just didn't want to say them—it might make one true.>*

Sera sounded morose, and Tanis gave her an understanding look. Not knowing if you could trust your friends was never easy. The simplest route was to never trust anyone—though that would slowly eat a person's soul.

*<We have to assume she has ulterior motives,>* Tanis said. *<At least, until Bob can read enough of her actions to surmise her true intentions.>*

*<Serge is here,>* Angela informed the pair.

Tanis turned and looked to the door. *<Let him in,>* she informed the Marines outside.

Serge entered, and she saw a strong resemblance between him and Sera—far more apparent than with Andrea; they could have passed for fraternal twins. His eyes swept across the room and landed on Sera, his clouded visage cleared and a smile spread across his lips.

"Core, Sera, you're OK. When they told me we were going to the hospital to see you..." he stopped himself, apparently remembering that he was in unknown company.

Tanis rose and extended her hand. "I'm Tanis Richards, governor of the New Canaan colony mission."

A look of concern crossed Serge's face before he took her hand and shook it firmly.

"Serge Tomlinson," he replied.

*<The first person we've met from the Transcend who might just be honest and sincere, by the looks of him,>* Angela said to Tanis.

*<Perhaps,>* she replied.

"Nice to meet you, Serge," Tanis said aloud. "I hope you can help us make sense of everything that has happened today."

"Yes, sure, of course," Serge said absently as he peered at Sera. "Are you OK, Sis? It's been a long time."

"It has," Sera said and held out an arm. Serge stepped forward and leaned in to embrace his sister.

"Gently," Sera cautioned. "I took a bit of a beating from some pulse blasts earlier."

Serge shot an eye at the Marines before pausing on Elena.

"Wait...Elena? Is that you?"

"Took you long enough," Elena grinned. "I was beginning to think that the diplomatic corps would need to work on your powers of observation."

Serge smiled wanly. "Sorry, I was a bit distracted."

"That's just the time you need to be the most observant," Sera said. "But enough of that. Our little reunion can wait. How is it that you were on the ship while Mark came aboard the *Intrepid?"*

Serge sighed. "Mark took me out with a rather clever cocktail of drugs that I ingested over the last few meals. Individually, what he fed me didn't amount to anything particularly malicious; but with one last bite of a cookie, I was laid out on the galley floor. By the time I came to, they were both gone."

"You sure it was Mark?" Elena asked. "Drugging someone is just the sort of thing I'd expect Andrea to do."

Serge shrugged. "I guess it could be. They're both snakes in the grass. My gut tells me it was Mark, though."

"Neither are worth the $O^2$ they burn," Sera grunted. "Use me to fucking kill Tanis, and then pray that the Marines mowed me down?"

"So, we're going with that?" Terry asked with a raised eyebrow. "Is it a guess, or do you remember now?"

"I remember," Sera replied. "It took a bit, and they didn't spell it out, but the pieces are all there. The question is, who ordered it?"

"I can tell you that it wasn't in the mission plan. We were to trade your fifth millennia tech for the colony. No pico, no stasis shields," Serge said with raised palms. "There was nothing about any infiltration or subversion—though, there was a very strongly-worded section about bringing you back to Airtha, Sis."

Sera nodded. "Not surprising. Father has probably had enough of me flitting about the Inner Stars. Though, given the successes I've had, you'd think he would want me to stay out there." She finished with a chuckle that turned into a cough. "Ow, I guess no laughing yet…"

"And what about Elena here?" Tanis asked Serge, watching him with every sense she possessed. "Was she part of the plan?"

"Not even a little bit," Serge replied with a smile. "But I bet that Justin is going to be mightily pissed that you just jetted out of Scipio. There's a lot of work to do there, and it took forever to get you planted."

Elena waved her hand dismissively. "My cover can be rebuilt—if I'm not fired…or worse."

"Treason, I assume?" Tanis asked.

"AWOL at the least," Elena replied with a solemn nod. "Treason if Andrea decides that she has it in for me—which she will. There's no way they expected you to get Sera restored—and I'm sure Andrea and Mark had a scheme to take Sera back with them. A trip she would not have survived."

Sera shook her head. "I can see Mark doing that, but Andrea? Has she really become so calculating?" She directed the last to Serge.

"And then some," her brother sighed. "Father has been putting more and more on her shoulders. She resented being sent out here to fetch you, even if it only took a few months out of her schedule."

Tanis's eyes snapped up at Serge's statement.

"Months?" Tanis asked.

Sera sighed. "You never really could keep a secret, could you, Serge?"

Serge shrugged in response. "You keep secrets that you don't need to, Sis. Ford-Svaiter mirrors being a prime example."

Tanis saw that Elena was shaking her head, and fixed Sera with a hard stare before she reached out to Bob.

<*Did you know they had wormhole tech?*>

<*I suspected. Their control over an empire as large as the Transcend demanded ultra-fast travel. The dark layer of space, with its maximum multiplier of seven hundred fifty times light speed, would still make their longer trips take over a decade,*> Bob replied. <*I thought you had suspected as much, as well.*>

Tanis sighed. She *had* suspected, but her suspicions and Bob's were on entirely different levels.

"We can chat about that later," Tanis said with a wink. "However, what can we expect from the commander of this watchpoint?"

"That'll be General Greer," Sera confirmed. "Has he called?"

Tanis shook her head. "Called, no. Sent in two fleets? Yes."

"Sorry about that," Serge shrugged. "It's protocol."

Sera flashed her brother an exasperated look before replying. "Greer is by-the-book, and he bears our father no special love; though I don't know if that will work out in our favor or not. I hope it does—it's one of the reasons I chose this watchpoint."

<*Speaking of the watchpoint, a message is coming in from the nearest fleet,*> Amanda said to the group.

"Thanks, Amanda," Tanis said aloud. "I'll take it privately."

If Greer was on any of the approaching ships, he would still be at least thirty light minutes distant, though she wondered if the Transcend ships could effect their wormholes within a stellar system.

Another possibility she had to consider.

She took a chair, and the room around her disappeared, replaced by the bridge of a warship. In the center, with hands clasped behind his back and legs in a wide stance, stood a tall man with long, brown hair and a reddish beard. His hair swept back over his shoulders, and the beard was neat and trim. His eyes were blue and cold, and, while not menacing, they contained the certainty of someone fully aware and confident of their abilities.

His black uniform was crisp, and a single star adorned each lapel of his collar. His posture remained rigid and unwavering as he began to speak.

"To the commanding officer, or colony leader, of the ISS *Intrepid*," he began. "This is General Tsaroff of the Transcend Space Force. We have received a distress call from our diplomatic mission to your ship, and are approaching to render assistance. Please be advised that should any harm come to Transcend Government representatives, we will view this unfavorably and take strong action in response."

<*For a general, he certainly speaks like a politician,*> Angela commented.

<*Or a lawyer,*> Tanis responded.

"Please respond promptly with your affirmation that nothing untoward has happened to our envoys, and prepare to release them into our care."

<*Definitely a lawyer in a prior life,*> Angela agreed.

The transmission ended, and the hospital room snapped back into view around Tanis.

"General Tsaroff sends his regards," she said dryly. "No mention of Greer in his transmission."

"Tsaroff commands the rapid response fleets here under Greer," Serge replied. "Greer wouldn't accompany his advance forces."

"Advance forces?" Tanis asked. "Just how many ships do they have here in the watchpoint?"

"The briefing did not contain that level of detail," Serge said with a shrug. "I suspect there are at least a dozen fleet groups here at Aurora."

Tanis whistled. It was a lot of firepower. If they were on the same level as the AST's dreadnaughts they faced in the Bollam's World System, then this was a fight they could not win—even with picotech. The Transcend ships would not allow the *Intrepid*'s fighters to get close enough to deliver picobombs—not that obliterating the Transcend fleet was an option she was even considering.

Sera peered at her, likely wondering what direction her internal deliberations were taking. "What's it going to be?" she asked.

"I won't go to war just for revenge; but I don't intend to simply hand over assassins without any recompense," Tanis replied.

"You know they'll claim diplomatic immunity," Terry advised.

Tanis nodded. "And our current circumstances leave room for interpretation about whether or not they are officially accepted diplomats—since we are currently within territory which is unclaimed by either party. By all the ancient laws, Andrea and Mark are assassins, and no protections exist for them."

<*It's sure a great way to kick things off,*> Angela added.

Tanis rose from her seat. "I need to get to the bridge. Terry, you can get back to the thousand things I know are pressing down on you. Flaherty, Serge, Elena, stay here with Sera. Once the doctors pronounce her fit, I'll have the four of you moved to one of our ready-rooms near the bridge."

She gave Sera one last look before leaving. "I'm glad you're OK."

"And I'm glad I didn't kill you," Sera replied with a grin.

<*That makes three of us,*> Angela replied.

# DETERMINATION

**STELLAR DATE: 12.30.8929 (Adjusted Years)**
**LOCATION: ISS *Intrepid***
**REGION: Ascella System, Galactic North of the Corona Australis star-forming region**

Tanis stood before the bridge's main holotank, surveying the assembling fleets and considering her response to General Tsaroff.

"It stinks," Captain Andrews said from her side. "They try to kill you—for stars know what reason—and we'll ultimately turn your would-be assassins right back over."

"Yeah, I can't think of anything we can negotiate for that is worth the trouble. Perhaps dumping them in their ship and kicking it out the door is the best we can do to assuage our wounded pride," Tanis replied.

"I have to admit," the captain said quietly, "I'm surprised you didn't make a case for forcibly extracting their intentions."

Tanis sighed. She really did want to know why her neck was on the chopping block, but she also knew that any intelligence she could extract from Andrea and Mark would be suspect. Mark likely didn't know anything, anyway. He just wanted Sera dead so that she wouldn't testify against him.

"I guess I'm getting soft in my old age," she replied.

A change on the holodisplay caught her attention. The fleet at the asteroid belt was forming up near what appeared to be a small ring. Tanis didn't recall seeing it before, and played back the last few minutes of scan.

The replay showed that the ring had started out as a series of asteroids that unfolded and formed the structure. It wasn't big enough to fly the *Intrepid* through, but any of the Transcend ships would fit with ease.

"I bet I know what that is," Tanis said quietly.

"Really?" Captain Andrews asked, casting a sharp eye her way. "Is it what it looks like?"

Tanis nodded. "Sera's brother, Serge, let it slip. They have worked out the tech behind Ford-Svaiter mirrors. I would imagine that it puts dark layer FTL to shame."

"Holy crap!" the scan officer cried out.

Tanis saw the reason for his alarm. Scan still showed the ships assembling near the wormhole-creating ring, but even before they saw any vessels pass through the distant ring, ships began to appear—as if by magic—a scant hundred-thousand kilometers from the *Intrepid*'s fleet.

Admiral Sanderson let out a low whistle from the back of the bridge. "Now *that* is faster-than-light travel."

Tanis nodded. The light from their prior location would take thirty minutes before it showed the Transcend ships creating and entering their wormholes. However, closer to the *Intrepid,* the light from the ships in their new position had already arrived.

From their vantage, it appeared as though the ships were in two places at once.

In theory, a Ford-Svaiter mirror was a simple apparatus that focused quantum energy along the mirror's focal line, which created negative energy. That negative energy created a wormhole, and complimentary mirrors on the front of the ships would extend the wormhole to the desired exit point.

*<Theory no more, it seems,>* Angela added. *<I'm amazed that they can control the exit point so well. That's a level of precision not even dark layer FTL transitions can manage.>*

*<Of limited use, though. They need a ring to initiate the process, and they don't have one on this side,>* Tanis responded.

*<Not that I can think of a reason they'll need to leave in a hurry,>* Angela said. *<Their second fleet just appeared, too.>*

Tanis took a deep breath, every eye on the bridge furtively glancing her way, waiting for her to tell them what to do. She schooled her expression and signaled the comm officer.

"Now that they're on our doorstep, communication should be a lot easier. Link us up and let them know that I want to chat."

The officer bent to her task. A minute later, she nodded to Tanis and General Tsaroff appeared before her.

"General Tsaroff," Tanis said with a nod of her head. "I am Governor Richards. Thank you for taking my call."

"I had heard it was General Richards," Tsaroff replied without preamble. "Am I to believe that you are now governor, as well?"

Tanis nodded. "I am, and I will return your assassins to you…once I receive some assurances."

"Assassins?" General Tsaroff's eyes widened, his face revealing a moment of surprise before he recovered. "I assure you, we sent you our most respected diplomats to treat with you, and from what we understand, you abducted them."

"Can we dispense with all the doublespeak?" Tanis asked. "I've had a long day, and I'll lay it out plainly. Mark and Andrea Tomlinson hacked Sera and tried to use her to kill me, hoping that one, or both, of us would die in the attempt. Sera did not succeed, and Elena—one of your Hand agents—showed up, and helped us undo Sera's and Helen's subversion. Serge and Elena are with Sera, who is recovering, and Andrea and Mark are in a holding room. You can have that pair back, but, again, not until I get some assurances."

Tsaroff did not reply for several moments and Tanis wondered if he had a mechanism for real-time communications with General Greer—wherever he was—or if he was speaking with an AI. Eventually, he refocused on her, his already narrowed eyes mere slits.

"So, now you hold three of our president's children, and one of our agents, too. I also will need some assurances. What are your conditions?"

"Very simple," Tanis replied. "I will turn over Mark and Andrea, entirely unharmed, but in stasis—which is how they will stay until they arrive with Serge back in Airtha. I will also give him the CriEn module and our fully executed agreement for the colony system in the M25 cluster. We will provide the technology we agreed upon in our contract when we arrive at our colony system. Also, your ships will come no closer to the *Intrepid* than they currently are, or our agreement is off."

"I don't have a lot of reasons to trust you," Tsaroff replied. "I will need to speak with Serge, since he is the one who sent the distress signal."

"Tanis, if I may?" a voice said from across the bridge.

She turned to see Flaherty standing at the room's portside entrance. It was surprising to see him separated from Sera at a time like this, but she suspected that if he were here, he must have a card to play with Tsaroff.

She nodded and he approached. Tanis adjusted the pickups so that he was included in the projection to Tsaroff.

"General Tsaroff," Flaherty said in greeting.

"Colonel Flaherty!" Tsaroff replied, real emotion showing on his face—something akin to surprise and respect. "I would expect you to be protecting Sera at a time like this."

<*Colonel, is it?*> Angela mused.

<*He always did have a military bearing,*> Tanis replied. <*Though, colonel…that is something.*>

"She is safe," Flaherty replied. "Though Andrea and Mark would have liked to see her otherwise."

"So, Governor Richards here speaks the truth?" Tsaroff asked. "Did they subvert Sera Tomlinson?"

"If by 'they', you mean that piece of trash Mark, and Sera's waste-of-flesh sister, Andrea, then yes," Flaherty chewed out the names of his charge's sister and former lover. "They subverted her, and attempted to use her to assassinate a foreign head of state."

"That's a serious charge," Tsaroff replied. "Though, I've never known you to exaggerate."

"That's because I don't," Flaherty replied. "Take the deal."

"I'll have to confer with General Greer first," Tsaroff said. "Also, before we strike up any agreement, we'll need to send over a representative to examine all Transcend citizens to ensure they are truly unharmed and corroborate your story."

"Well," Tanis replied. "Sera's had some harm done to her, but that is on Mark and Andrea."

"So you say," Tsaroff said before cutting the connection.

Tanis let out a long sigh before muttering, "Why does everyone in the Transcend seem like raging assholes?"

"A lot of them have been in their positions for too long," Flaherty replied. "Tsaroff has been a one-star general for at least a hundred years; I think he needs a change."

Tanis laughed. "Yeah, at least I got jacked up to three stars—made me feel like I was doing something right. But you, a colonel…now *that's* news."

Flaherty waved his hand, dismissing her statement. "That is an old rank from a long time ago. I am no longer an officer in the Transcend Space Force."

"Well, it seemed to come in handy with Tsaroff," Captain Andrews replied with a smile.

Tanis nodded, noticing how much more relaxed the captain had become since she had taken over as governor. She hoped that he would let her visit his cabin in the woods when he retired.

"He used to serve under me," Flaherty replied without offering further explanation.

Tanis waited for him to share more, but when Flaherty remained silent, she asked, "Do you think he'll do anything rash?"

"On his own? Maybe. He wants to advance. Successfully outmaneuvering you would help with that," Flaherty said with a grunt.

"They do have us outgunned, but I don't think he'd score any points if he starts a battle. Whatever he does will be political," Andrews said.

"Yes," Flaherty nodded. "He's showing you that even though you defeated the five fleets at Bollam's World, the Transcend can, and will, stand up to you."

"That is my assessment, as well," Sanderson said. "It's what I'd do."

"I would, too," Tanis agreed.

Twenty minutes later, Tsaroff sent a text-only message indicating that a pinnace would approach via a wormhole jump gate to dock with the *Intrepid* to examine the Transcend envoys and citizens.

"I'll go down to meet whoever is coming," Tanis said.

"Do you think that's wise?" Captain Andrews asked. "If their plan is to kill you, this makes you more than a little vulnerable.

"Good point," Tanis replied. "I'll stop in an armory and apply one of Earnest's new MK14 armor skins."

"That wasn't what I was going to suggest," Andrews said with a shake of his head.

"I know," Tanis said with a smile as she strode from the bridge.

# SURRENDER

**STELLAR DATE: 12.30.8929 (Adjusted Years)**
**LOCATION: ISS *Intrepid***
**REGION: Ascella System, Galactic North of the Corona Australis star-forming region**

Tanis checked in on Cary as she waited for the Transcend's pinnace to arrive. Her daughter was asleep in one of Tracy's spare cradles, and she lost herself in marveling at the slow rise and fall of her daughter's small, perfect chest.

She smiled, thinking of how, just a scant few months ago, she was lost on the far side of Sol, traveling in a shady freighter, wondering if she would ever see the *Intrepid* again; let alone carry her daughter to term.

Now she was governor of the New Canaan colony mission, preparing to meet with foreign representatives to resolve a tricky diplomatic situation.

<*Pretty much like always, then,*> Angela said with a laugh.

<*Well, stakes are a bit higher,*> Tanis replied.

<*Really? Higher than back when we stopped that nuke above Mars? Or taking out the multiple attacks on the* Intrepid *while it was back in Sol? There was also that time when you and Joe secured fuel for the ship so that it could make it to Kapteyn's Star, rather than drift through space forever…*>

Tanis sighed. <*OK, OK, I get the picture. It's been do or die a few times, now. This time…I don't know…the stakes just* **seem** *higher.*>

She felt Angela's affirmative thoughts. <*That's because we're* ***so close.***>

"That certainly has something to do with it," Tanis whispered aloud.

<*The pinnace has jumped in. It's five thousand klicks out,*> Amanda reported. <*Jumped in? Is that what we should use? I mean, they came through a wormhole, but saying they wormed in seems weird…and warped in implies unaided space-folding.*>

<*A bit nervous, too?*> Tanis asked.

*<Yeah, I'd prefer not to have to fight our new hosts for our colony system,>* Amanda replied.

*<Especially because we probably wouldn't win,>* Tanis added.

*<Yeah,>* Amanda responded. *<There is that…so, you know, no pressure. Good luck, and all that.>*

Tanis barked a laugh aloud. *<Thanks, Amanda, that helps a lot.>*

*<I do what I can.>*

She spent another minute watching her daughter, and then removed the image from her mind and focused on mental preparation for the meeting.

*****

Sooner than she would have expected, she saw the Transcend pinnace slip through the electrostatic barrier at the far end of the main dock. No more comfortable lounges off the VIP dock today. They would meet in a wide-open space, with an entire company of Marines watching every second.

The pinnace set down a hundred meters away. After a minute, its hatch slid open, and a lone man stepped out; Terry and two members of her team scanned him. Terry nodded to the Marines watching over her, who signaled up the chain that the man had passed muster.

Tanis imagined that he had given his name, but she didn't check. She wanted her first impressions to be just that—hers.

*<You must have guessed—oh, you got it right, good job.>*

*<Ang! Way to go. Now my whole greeting is messed up,>* Tanis scolded her AI.

*<Somehow, I think you'll manage.>*

The Marines accompanied the man—who she now knew was General Greer—to a second security checkpoint, which he passed through before approaching Tanis. She waited for him to reach her before offering any greeting.

"General Greer," she extended her hand.

"Governor Richards," he said, as he took it and gave one firm shake. "Are we to conduct our meeting here?"

"We are," she nodded. "My quotient of trust has been exhausted, and I am done with pleasantries. Your General Tsaroff expended the last of my supply."

Greer nodded. "Yes, he has a way of doing that. I hope it has not damaged our chances of reaching a peaceful resolution to this crisis."

<*Well, at least he can call a star a star,*> Angela commented.

"We'll see," Tanis replied to Greer.

"I have to admit," Greer said as he peered down the length of the ten-kilometer-long bay. "You claim that our envoys tried to kill you, but you let me fly a ship within a hundred meters of you in here. I could have shot you dead."

"You could have tried," Tanis replied. "*If* you were on a suicide mission."

"And if I had tried?" Greer asked, his grey eyes sparkling.

"Stasis shield," Tanis said. "You passed through its opening when you came through the security arch. Nothing your ship fired would have gotten through."

Greer chuckled. "Tsaroff is going to owe me a drink after this is done."

"You wish to examine the Transcend citizens on the *Intrepid*?" Tanis asked, unwilling to join in with his friendly banter.

Greer's eyes narrowed, and he nodded slowly. "Very well, let's get on with this."

Tanis sent a message to a groundcar driver. A minute later, a vehicle came into view. It stopped several meters from them, and Flaherty stepped out of the front passenger seat. He gave Greer a nod before turning to open the back door.

The first person out was Elena, then Serge, and finally Sera.

Tanis could see relief flood across Greer's face at the sight of them, and she wondered if he was a good actor, or if he really was concerned for their well-being.

"General Greer," Sera said as she walked carefully toward them. "I'm surprised to see you came yourself."

"You shouldn't be," Greer grunted. "This whole business has been one massive headache for me; and now I have accusations from Governor Richards here that your sister and Mark tried to use you to kill her."

"It's true," Sera said while Serge and Elena nodded. "Somehow Mark re-activated an old failsafe that The Hand left in me. They made me attack Tanis. It was only through Flaherty's quick actions that I failed, and survived the aftermath."

"And for this, I have just your word," Greer replied. "Will you and your AI submit to a verification check? I'm going to need to test all six of you."

Sera nodded, and Greer produced a small device. Sera placed her palm on it, and Tanis watched her grimace from the invasive check the machine was performing. Tanis suspected it was snaking probes through her body, making direct connections with her hard-Link, and with Helen.

It showed a positive response, and Greer nodded with satisfaction. He performed the same procedure on the other three before finally returning the device to his pocket.

"Well, it would appear that the four of you are who you say you are, and are not under any sort of subversion," he said. "Now I'll need to see Mark and Andrea."

Tanis nodded and another car approached. When this one stopped, Marines surrounded it and opened the back doors. Andrea and Mark exited with as much grace as their restraints allowed, and shuffled toward the group with the muzzles of a dozen pulse rifles trained on them.

Andrea looked straight ahead, not meeting anyone's gaze, while Mark scanned the faces before him, his own growing red at the dismissive looks he received.

"General Greer," he called out as they approached. "Look how they have treated us! We've been detained—I demand that we rescind any offers that have been made."

"Agent Mark, do shut up," Greer said, eliciting a small smile from Tanis. "If what they say is true, and I suspect it may be, you won't be leaving those restraints any time soon."

"And what of me?" Andrea said softly. "It is not within your authority to detain me."

Greer spread his hands wide. "*I* am not detaining you. I also do not know that you are who you appear to be, so if you wouldn't mind submitting to auth?" He produced the device once more, and Andrea sighed impatiently before putting her hand on it.

When the scan was complete, she made to speak, but Greer raised his hand and gestured for Mark to place his hand on the device.

A minute later, it had sent its confirmation, and Greer gave a guarded smile. "So, we are all who we claim to be, then."

"And you attest that no one is subverted, or under coercion?" Tanis asked.

"Subversion, no. Coercion is a bit harder to detect—though none is apparent, for what it's worth," Greer replied.

"So, do we have a deal?" Tanis asked. "Shall we complete what Andrea and Mark agreed to, and send them on their way?"

"Yes, but Sera you must come back to Airtha," Greer's brow lowered as he turned to Sera. "There are grievances here that must be settled. You cannot hide from them any longer."

"I do not wish to press charges, then," Sera replied.

"It does not matter," Greer said with a slow shake of his head. "You must return because Andrea is right. I cannot detain her in this matter. Her status protects her under our laws. But as an agent of The Hand, with the rank you hold, you *can*."

"Her?" Andrea asked with a laugh. "She's not an agent; not anymore. She cannot detain me any more than you can."

"You realize, Andrea, that *I* can detain you indefinitely," Tanis said softly. "By your own agreement, which you signed with me, New Canaan and this ship are a sovereign state in the eyes of the Transcend."

"You'll never see your precious colony if you do that," Andrea replied; the vehemence that Tanis suspected to always be under the surface rose to the fore. "My father will not allow it."

"General Greer," Tanis turned from Andrea. "Would you agree that, while we may not be able to defeat your ships and fly to New Canaan, we certainly could escape Ascella?"

Greer nodded slowly. "It's probable. We don't yet know how to overwhelm your shields, and destroying this ship is not an option. Less so with the president's scions on board."

"You see, Andrea, whether or not your father will allow it, it very well could happen. This ship can go anywhere. Hell, we could decide to go to the Andromeda galaxy. Your prison cell could have a lovely view of the Milky Way for the million-year trip," Tanis's voice was cold and her expression grave.

<*Wow, that's a little thick,*> Angela said privately.

"Elena," Greer addressed the Hand agent. "You possess the authority to provisionally reinstate Sera's status. If you do that, she can legally incarcerate her sister and Mark, and bring them to Airtha. You'll have to accompany her—"

"Stars," Sera interrupted, approaching Andrea, her fists clenched with rage. "How, even in your failure, do you get me going back to Airtha?"

"You don't have to go," Tanis said. "You can claim asylum with us."

Sera turned to Tanis and shook her head, her eyes tired and sad. "No, it has to be this way. You've worked too hard to get this far, just to lose one of the best-looking colony systems I've seen the FGT make in a long time…just because I'm selfish."

"You're sure?" Tanis asked.

"I'm sure," Sera nodded. "It's about time I at least made this scum pay for what he did," she cast Mark a dark look as she spoke.

Tanis waited for Mark's rejoinder, but none came. Perhaps he had finally realized that keeping his mouth shut was the best option he had available.

"And the data you'll be exchanging?" Greer asked. "When will we receive that?"

"At New Canaan's heliopause," she replied. "No sooner."

Greer nodded slowly. "Very well. I suppose that's the best I can expect under these circumstances."

"Perhaps you should let Tsaroff know that all is well, and that he doesn't need to blow us out of the black," Tanis added.

"No need," Greer said with a smile. "I've been broadcasting the conversation, and the data streams from my verification device, as we've been speaking."

"Good," Tanis replied. "Then we're in accord."

# PARTING

**STELLAR DATE: 12.31.8929 (Adjusted Years)**
**LOCATION: ISS *Intrepid***
**REGION: Ascella System, Galactic North of the Corona Australis star-forming region**

Sera watched the shape of the *Intrepid* shrink in the distance, eventually disappearing in the glare of the twin Ascella stars. First, watching *Sabrina* leave, and now leaving the *Intrepid*...she felt as though a chapter was ending in her life; as though she might never see either ship, or their crews—her friends—again.

"We're really going back," she said softly from her seat in the ship's small lounge.

Flaherty nodded slowly. "It has always been inevitable. You must have known that."

Sera looked up sharply at the man who had been her sworn protector for years. "No, no I haven't always known that. I thought I was free of the Transcend, The Hand, my father's machinations."

"Don't be a fool, Sis," Serge said from his seat. "You were never free. Father had eyes on you at every turn. You never left his sight."

Sera cast a glance to Flaherty—not because she suspected that he had split loyalties, but because she was curious if he agreed.

"Of course he did," Flaherty confirmed. "The Inner Stars are full of Hand agents. *Sabrina* stood out—the only ship of that build hauling cargo we ever saw. Probably child's play for The Hand to track."

Sera sighed. She knew this, she always had; but that hadn't stopped her from buying the ship. It had just looked so damn sleek, and the mere sight of it had lifted her spirits. Still, when The Hand stopped trying to bring her in, she had assumed that her father had written her off—that somehow, she had been deemed not worth the effort.

"So, what now?" she asked.

"Well, we have to get back to the beta gate. Greer doesn't want to use the insystem ones again. It'll be a two-week flight out."

"And then we'll be in Airtha before we know it," Sera replied.

Serge nodded while Flaherty silently gazed out at the stars.

Sera looked at the dancing lights on the holoceiling and thought of her parting conversation with Tanis, glad they had parted as friends. Sera had the suspicion that she would need that friendship in the future.

*"You watch out, Seraphina Tomlinson,"* Tanis had said. *"Someone wants me dead, and they let Mark come here, at least suspecting that he would try to take your life. I don't know what's going on, and neither do you. You need to treat everyone like they are dangerous strangers, because that's what they are. Anyone you think you can trust, any old friends; those are the most dangerous. Trust Flaherty, and no other."*

They were powerful words, and she knew them to be true. Airtha was worse than enemy territory. It was enemy territory that she thought she knew—but it surely changed over the years. Old alliances were long gone, and new political undercurrents would surround her.

# TRANSCEND TRADERS

**STELLAR DATE: UNKNOWN**
**LOCATION: Dwarka**
**REGION: Indus System, Transcend Interstellar Alliance**

Saanvi stepped off the maglev train, one hand stretched up, clasped in her father's, and the other pointed to the sky.

"Father, it's..."

"I know, it's even more impressive up close," Pradesh replied.

"It just disappears into the sky," Saanvi whispered. "Like it goes to Swargaloka."

Her father chuckled and stroked her head with his free hand. "It may look like that, but there is only Kush Station up there. While it's nice, it is certainly no Swargaloka."

Saanvi barely heard her father as she watched a lift-car climb up one of the space elevator's five strands. It was a thick ring that wrapped around the strand, the size of many houses. There were many levels and windows. To Saanvi's young mind, it was the most majestic thing she had ever seen.

"Come now, Saanvi," her father said as he pulled at her hand. "We must be on our way. Our lift-car departs in an hour, and it will take some time to get through security."

"What about Karen?" Saanvi asked.

"Karen is already there," her father replied. "She's on the lift-car checking our cargo."

"Oh," Saanvi's face fell. "I was hoping she would ride with us."

"She will," Pradesh replied as they threaded their way through the crowds. "She can't ride down in the lift-car's cargo hold, silly monkey."

Saanvi smiled. She loved it when her father called her that. It was a name just for her—something he never said to her brothers or older sister. It was their special thing.

Her mind was quickly distracted by the sights around her. Travelers from other worlds in the Shimla System brushed past them. Sprinkled throughout the crowd, she even saw people with strange clothing and skin colors, visitors from other systems in the Transcend.

"Father," she tugged at his sleeve. "Do you think we'll see any terraformers on Kush Station?"

He chuckled in response, and stroked his daughter's hair. "I don't think so. There is no terraforming going on anywhere near here. They have no reason to come through Shimla."

Saanvi sighed. She had really hoped they would see terraformers on the trip. Ever since she had learned that humans—not the gods—had made her world, she wanted to meet the people who did such things.

She had studied them as much as she could and asked her parents to show her videos and pictures of how worlds were made, and of the people who had made her world, Dwarka.

"Will we see them at any of the other worlds we'll go to?" Saanvi asked. "Are many of them made by terraformers, like ours was?"

Her father held up a hand while he passed his security tokens at a checkpoint, then led her through the scanning arch. He smiled down at her. "Who is to know, little monkey? Our return route is not fixed, and there are FGT ships out there—though people mostly bring them what they need. The terraformers rarely leave their ships, or the systems they are changing."

Saanvi's face lit up. "You never told me people trade with the terraformers! Can you do it? Can we take them something?"

"Believe me, my daughter, I would love to do that—to see the terraformers at work with my own eyes…not to mention how lucrative such a trip would be," Pradesh said with a smile. "But come, we must hurry. This port is large, and we still have far to go."

Saanvi smiled as her father pulled her along, brimming with excitement that she was finally to go on a trading trip with him—her first one—and that they would get to go alone. It was going to be at least five months long, and none of her brothers and sisters were coming.

Just she, her father, and Karen, traveling across space, seeing dozens of new worlds and people. It was something she had dreamed of ever since the first time her father had taken her through a full spaceflight sim at the age of three.

After three more security checks, they finally reached the departure wing that led to Strand Two, where their lift-car waited for its cargo and passengers to finish loading.

"Karen is waiting for us," Pradesh said with a warm smile for his daughter. "She is excited to see you, and bought some new games for the two of you to play."

"Ohhh," Saanvi gasped and smiled. "I wonder what they'll be!"

"We shall have to wait and see," her father replied. "But don't forget, you still have your schoolwork to do. Your teachers have outlined your coursework, and you'll have full school days with your teach-mind."

"Yes, father," Saanvi replied with a pout.

"Don't worry, little monkey; a lot of our time will be in the dark layer. There's not much to see there, and you're going to be happy for the routine your studies will create," her father said.

Saanvi didn't reply as she caught sight of the portal to the lift-car. A final security arch with smiling attendants stood at the entrance, and she began to skip with excitement, tugging at her father's hand.

"Daddy, come *on,* we're going to space!"

She heard his laugh sound behind her as she wove through the crowds, pulling him by the hand until they reached the back of the line.

"OK, dear, we have to wait here. No cutting ahead of everyone."

Saanvi frowned as she looked at all the people ahead of them. "They're moving so slow!"

"I know, I know, little monkey. The last check just takes a moment, though. We'll be at our seats with Karen in no time."

True to her father's word, the wait wasn't long, and before she knew it, they had entered the passenger level of the lift-car. She was right when she thought that it was much larger than their house; maybe larger than all the houses on their street.

The outside walls were floor-to-ceiling windows, and the seats were arranged in concentric rings facing them. Near the central shaft, there were several small food stands, and tables for people to sit around while eating. It was almost like the waiting areas in the port; but this one would soon rise above the planet.

"Come, Saanvi, our seats are up on the third level," her father said, as he pulled her hand and led her to the staircase, which wound around the central shaft.

When they reached the third level, her mouth fell open at the view.

"I thought you might like this," her father said with a smile and picked her up in his arms.

"Daddy, the roof is clear. We'll be able to see everything!"

"Yes we will, my little monkey, and let me tell you—it's quite the view."

He carried her the final distance to their seats, right in front of the window, facing east by the holoindicator on the plas. Karen, with her fair skin and long, blonde hair, was waiting for them, her arms stretched out to embrace Saanvi.

"Oh, my beautiful little girl, how *are* you?"

"I'm great, Auntie Karen. I can't believe I'm really going into space!" Saanvi exclaimed.

"Me either," Karen replied, her face split wide in a smile. "We're going to have a blast, you and me. I have a ton of stuff planned."

"You'll still have a few ship-duties, don't forget," Pradesh said with a frown. "The *Vimana* better stay ship-shape at all times, or I'll have the both of you swabbing the deck."

Saanvi wasn't certain if her father was joking, but Karen laughed.

"Prad, I could run your ship with both eyes closed, and have time for a dozen little Saanvis."

"Good," her father leaned back in his seat and closed his eyes. "Then I'm going to take a three-month nap once we get up there. You two can do everything."

"Hmmm," Karen winked at Saanvi. "That may have backfired on me."

Saanvi chuckled and poked her father. "You can't sleep for three months. You always say that you just pop awake after seven hours."

Pradesh cracked an eye open. "Hmm… you may have me there. Then perhaps I'll take up baking. That's it—while you two are running the show, I'll bake cakes, but just for me!"

"What?" Saanvi cried out. "I want cake, too! That's not fair!"

"Trust me, Saanvi," Karen said. "I've flown with your father for three years. If he's baking any cakes, you want no part of it. He can barely pour a bowl of cereal."

"I'll have you know I can make a mean bowl of oatmeal," Pradesh replied.

"Sure, boss, whatever you say. I've had to clean the galley after you've 'cooked'. It's not a pretty sight."

Pradesh frowned, but Saanvi could tell from the sparkle in his eye that he was finding the conversation very funny.

Saanvi hopped up into her seat and settled down with her favorite stuffed turtle. It briefly occurred to her that she may be too old to be clutching a stuffed animal, but she was sure that he'd want to see them go into space, too. "Don't be scared, Shelly, it will be fine. People go on these all the time."

She lost track of time, chatting with Karen about the games they would play on the *Vimana;* when the announcement came over the lift-car's audible systems that the portals were closing and they were preparing for ascension, it took her by surprise.

Saanvi peered out the window, waiting to see the ground start to fall away; when it did, she shuddered and grabbed Karen's hand on one side, and her father's on the other.

"Relax, my little monkey," her father said softly. "It's perfectly safe. Before you know it, we won't even be able to see the world anymore."

Saanvi nodded and watched the mountains in the distance start to slip below the sill of the window. Before long, they could only see the blue sky of their world around and above the lift-car. A minute later, a tone sounded indicating that they could get up and move about.

She glanced tentatively at her father, who nodded, before slipping out of her seat and walking to the window. Taking a deep breath, she peered down and saw the world below, which still appeared larger than she had expected. She looked at the indicator on the window and saw that the lift-car had risen over seven kilometers—though the distance did not have concrete meaning to her.

She could see almost all the nearby mountains east of the space elevator, and to the south, the ocean was visible, too. So far, the world didn't look that much different than it did when she was on an airplane a year ago, and that wasn't scary at all.

Looking up, Saanvi let out a gasp. Another lift-car was coming down one of the elevator's other strands, and, for a moment, it looked as though it would hit theirs; but then it slid by without any trouble. She could see people inside, and small children crowded the windows.

Several of them were waving, and she waved back.

"That was nice," Karen said from her side.

Saanvi looked up at her father's ship-friend. "How long until we're in space?"

"Well," Karen considered for a moment, "the nominal start to space on Dwarka is ninety kilometers up, and we've just passed the ten-kilometer mark. We'll reach two hundred kilometers per hour soon, so it will be about thirty minutes, give or take a bit. Once we get past the stratosphere—that's the top of the air on Dwarka—we'll start going faster. The station is forty thousand kilometers up, so it will be just over four hours before we reach it."

"Wow," Saanvi took a deep breath. "Will we even be able to see Dwarka from there?"

"A very astute question," Karen replied. "Yes, we will be able to see it, but it will look quite small, like how big your house looks from the end of your street."

Saanvi didn't quite know how to picture that, but she couldn't wait to see what it would look like.

Her father got some food from the stands, and they ate at one of the tables before Karen brought out a holo game that involved stacking falling blocks into the right types of piles. The more they played, the faster the game got; before long, both Saanvi and Karen were frantically stacking holo-blocks on their table, laughing at the dangerously high piles.

Ultimately, the game got the better of them, and the piles all collapsed, spilling blocks across the floor before they vanished and the game reset itself.

She lost track of how many times they played that game, and a few others, before she glanced up and saw lights above the lift-car.

"Karen! Karen!" she cried out. "I see it, I see Kush Station!"

"Yes, Saanvi, that is Kush Station."

"It's huuuuuuge," Saanvi said with a long sigh. "It looks like it's bigger than our city down on Dwarka."

"That's because it is," Karen replied. "It's over five hundred kilometers across, and it will be the smallest station we're going to see on our trip."

Saanvi's eyes grew wide and she grabbed Karen's shirt. "Are you serious, Auntie Karen, they're *all* bigger?"

Karen nodded. "Some will even be planetary rings. And if we make a stop at Huro, we'll see a station that is bigger than Dwarka."

Saanvi fell back in her seat, her head craned back as she gazed at Kush Station. "Bigger than an entire planet," she whispered.

# LOST IN SPACE

**STELLAR DATE: UNKNOWN**
**LOCATION: *Vimana***
**REGION: Interstellar Space near Hurosha, Transcend Interstellar Alliance**

Saanvi watched the ring slowly shrink behind them with a sinking feeling of sadness. The Indus planetary ring had been one of the most amazing things she had ever seen. Her father had told her that it had more living space than her entire world, though that didn't mean much to her.

What Saanvi loved, however, was playing in the parks on the ring, and looking up to see the world of Indus hanging high overhead.

At first, it had frightened her, and it took some time for her father and Karen to convince her that the world was not going to fall, and that it really wasn't 'above them,' but below.

That didn't make a lot of sense to Saanvi, and she wrote it off as adult silliness. How could she look up at a planet that was below her? The ring was below her. That much was obvious, even to a seven-year-old.

Strange explanations notwithstanding, Saanvi eventually grew accustomed to the planet floating above her head, and came to enjoy the daily noontime eclipses it created.

Karen used the planet and its orbital ring to teach her about a thing called axial tilt, and how that created seasons on planets. The terraformers had given Indus a mild tilt, so the planet almost always caused daily eclipses on at least a part of the ring.

Saanvi found it interesting—mostly because the terraformers did it, and anyone who could make planets had to be the smartest people there were.

The *Vimana* had spent two weeks docked on a small spur station hanging off the Indus Ring, and Saanvi had spent her evenings with her father and Karen in a suite, which had an amazing view of the stars and Indus's four moons.

She never wanted to leave, but her father told her that it was inevitable; a big word to mean that she couldn't stop it from happening.

"Bye, pretty ring," she said, thinking of how it was small enough in the distance that she could poke the planet out and slide her finger into it.

She lined her finger up with her eye and did just that. "There, now I'll have you forever." She smiled, imagining the ring on her finger, and held it up for inspection, wondering what all the tiny people would think.

"I'll miss it, too," Karen said from the lounge's entrance. "We had good times there, didn't we?"

Saanvi nodded sadly. "We sure did, Auntie Karen."

Karen sat down with Saanvi and stroked her hair. "It's really too bad then."

"What's too bad?" Saanvi looked up at Karen, wondering what news the adult was about to give her.

"Well, it's too bad that the ring won't be nearly as cool as Huro!"

"We're going to Huro?" she exclaimed, climbing onto Karen's lap and staring into her eyes from mere centimeters away.

"Yes, crazy little girl," Karen said and patted her head—not an easy feat, with how much Saanvi was bouncing about. "But first, you need to catch up on your schoolwork. We took a lot of days off on the Indus ring, and we'll take more off when we get to Huro."

Saanvi sighed, the wind going out of her sails. "Yes, Karen."

* * * * *

Saanvi put down her cup and looked up at her father and Karen.

"So, only two more days until we get to Huro?" she asked.

"Two days until we drop out of the dark layer," her father said with a nod. "Then it will take a week to get insystem to Hurosha, their planet-construct."

"Why did they build a whole planet themselves?" Saanvi asked. "Why didn't the terraformers make a planet for them?"

Pradesh chuckled, and Saanvi wondered what was so funny.

"The terraformers never went to Huro; its star is not suitable for terraformed worlds—it is too angry. But there are many minerals and resources in its outer regions, and so the people of Huro made their own small star, and then built a ring around it. They were industrious—that means they were good at their jobs—and soon, more people came to Huro. Before long, they had to build another ring, and then another. Now, there are almost five hundred rings wrapped around their little star, at different orbital distances and angles," her father replied.

Saanvi frowned, unable to picture what her father had described, and Karen brought up a holo image above the table, and showed the progression of rings around the tiny star.

"There are so many, you can't even see the star anymore!" Saanvi exclaimed.

"Yes," her father nodded. "It's like a little Dyson sphere."

"Do you recall Dyson spheres from your studies?" Karen asked.

Saanvi nodded. "It's a big ball around a star to capture all of its light and energy."

Pradesh and Karen nodded, proud looks upon their faces as they gazed down at the small girl who was so hungry to know about everything around her.

"But no one has ever built one, right?" she asked. "Not a real one, around a real star."

"Correct," Karen nodded. "There are a few stellar rings out there, rings that go around stars, not planets; but they are not solid bands, just loosely connected platforms and segments—excepting Airtha, of course. It takes too much mass to make something that can withstand the stresses of such an orbit. You remember seeing the expansion joints on the ring at Indus, right?"

Saanvi nodded vigorously. "Yes! Because the side of the ring facing the star is much, much hotter than the other side behind the planet, and it gets a lot bigger…like cookies in the oven!"

Pradesh and Karen laughed and Saanvi's smile widened.

"Yes, little monkey, just like cookies in the oven. Can you imagine a planetary ring made of cookies?"

"Mmmmm…" Saanvi smiled. "I would eat them all up!"

They all laughed at her reply. Just as they had settled back down, a shudder shook the deck beneath them. An audible alarm began to blare.

"Wha…" Pradesh said as he stood.

Saanvi could see the expression in his eyes that showed he was accessing the ship's systems on the Link.

"Karen," he said, his eyes wide with alarm. "Get her in a pod, and you too! I'll dump us out of the DL, and meet you there."

"Prad…" Karen's eyes were filled with worry.

"Go!"

Saanvi cried out in alarm at the urgency in her father's voice.

"Daddy!" she rushed to him and wrapped his legs in a fierce embrace.

"Little monkey," he said with more fear than she had ever heard in his voice. "Just like the drills we did. Go with Karen, it'll be fun."

"C'mon," Karen said as she peeled Saanvi arms from around her father's legs.

"No!" Saanvi cried out, kicking at Karen, who flipped her around and wrapped her in a warm embrace as she ran through the ship.

"It'll be OK, little sweetie. I've got you, you're safe," Karen whispered in her ear. "Your father will be safe, too; he'll be with us in no time."

Karen spoke other soothing words, and Saanvi calmed down, locking her arms around Karen and burying her face in her neck. The last thing she recalled was Karen leaning over a stasis pod and lowering her into its embrace, forcing her to lie still.

"It's OK, little monkey," Karen whispered. "It'll just feel like an instant has passed, and then you'll be awake again with your father and me."

Saanvi's lips quivered with fear, but she trusted Karen. She had never lied to her. Saanvi nodded nervously and lay still as the pod's cover came down. When it sealed, she took a deep breath and closed her eyes.

# AIRTHA

**STELLAR DATE: 01.14.8930 (Adjusted Years)**
**LOCATION: Transcend Diplomatic Corps Interstellar Pinnace**
**REGION: Near Airtha, Huygens System, Transcend Interstellar Alliance**

Airtha was much as Sera remembered it: massive, overwrought, and incredible.

Sera brought the ship out of jump-space deep within the Huygens system, where the capital of the Transcend currently lay. Normally, jumping this deep into a system was a risky maneuver—not just due to the risk of collision, but because the relative speed between stars meant that predicting an exact exit location was nearly impossible.

Even with the safe zones for emergency jumps, a recently terraformed system like Huygens would be rife with dust and small rocks. A 'clear' area was never completely clear.

Her fears were manifested when a warning klaxon sounded on the small bridge, and she saw that a small stone had punctured a lower hold before the grav shields came to full strength.

"It's grav-sealed," Serge reported from the command chair.

"I'm matching stellar velocity; Huygens sure moves fast," Sera said with one eye on the local scan, ensuring that nothing else was out there.

"Yeah, it's why they picked it. They're forming a black hole to pull it faster, too. They want to pull it right through the next arm, over the next twenty thousand years. Nice jump, by the way," Serge replied. "I thought you might have been out of practice, after all those years with low-tech in the Inner Stars."

"Low-tech teaches you a level of finesse most people here have never developed," Sera replied as she spun out the antimatter pion drive, and eased it up to a full burn. Huygens was moving at just over 0.01*c* relative to Ascella, and the safe jump zone was uncomfortably close to the current position of a 9M*J* planet.

"So I can see," Serge said with an appreciative whistle as he watched Sera's hands dance over a holographic console. "I've never seen anyone pilot a ship with their hands like that before."

"I'm doing a combo," Sera replied. "General commands are all right over the Link, but I've learned that I can use my hands for microadjustments better than using thought. There's just so much of our neural build-out that's still tuned to these predatory twitch reflexes."

"That's certainly not what they taught us in the academy," Serge replied. "There it was all 'mind over matter', and the like."

Sera held up a hand and threw a grin over her shoulder at Serge. "This is matter, and I'm using my mind to control it."

Serge barked a laugh. "Well played, Sis."

With the ship's vector confirmed and locked in, Sera brought Airtha up on the main holo and leaned back in her seat.

"There it is," she breathed.

<*Relax,*> Helen said privately. <*You'll come out on top of this, trust me.*>

<*You seem supremely confident,*> Sera replied with a mental frown.

<*Don't forget, I run Airtha,*> Helen gave Sera a clever wink.

<*How could I forget?*> Sera smiled in response.

"Home sweet home," Serge responded to her earlier audible statement. "Always feels good to come back."

"Speak for yourself," Sera whispered.

She had to admit that Airtha was impressive—the structure was gorgeous, even if she didn't like many of the people who lived there.

At the center of the construct lay a small star, a Saturn-sized, white dwarf remnant with less than a fifth of Sol's mass. The star was not a natural occurrence, having started its life as a much more massive—and smaller—white dwarf; but the FGT engineers gravitationally stripped away most of its mass to make it more manageable. Much of that material—mostly carbon—was used to form the solid ring that encircled the star.

The ring's circumference was just over a million kilometers. With a width of fifty thousand kilometers, it had a total surface area of fifty billion square kilometers, or ninety-eight times that of Earth's total surface area.

In mass, size, and livable star-facing surface area, it was the largest thing humanity had ever created.

Four great pillars stretched from the ring toward the star, holding it in place with powerful gravity fields; which, in turn, drew their energy from the star. The pillars also controlled the radiation flowing from the star, and directed it out through the poles to fuel a powerful Van Allen-style shield around the construct.

The surface of the ring was one of the most beautiful ever made. Star-side, the ring had been surfaced with the mass of a dozen planets—creating mountains, plains, oceans, vast deserts, steppes, and even arctic regions.

Dark patches were visible on the terraformed surface of the ring, which had a day-night cycle, created by the pillar's gravity engines bending light away from the surface as needed.

Conversely, the outside of the ring gleamed in the light of the four Huygens stars. Because the matter extracted from the dwarf star was carbon, the ring was, essentially, a diamond. Artisans had spent centuries carving world-sized murals into it, celebrating the history of the Transcend.

*<Admit it; you like it,>* Helen said. *<You gaze at it with wonder whenever you see it.>*

*<That's just because you—well, other you—built it,>* Sera replied. *<You do good work.>*

*<I don't see it like that,>* Helen responded after a brief pause. *<To me, I made it; I remember doing it, though this instance of myself does not recall many of the details. There's not enough hardware in your head to store all that information.>*

*<Thank the stars,>* Sera laughed. *<You take up enough room in here, as it is.>*

"You're worried, aren't you?" Serge said, unaware of Sera's conversation with Helen, though he may have guessed from her system-long stare.

She turned in her seat and fixed her brother with a hard look. "Wouldn't you be? Father and I have always…we've never had an easy relationship."

Serge laughed. "That's the understatement of the year. You were supposed to be the child of his mind, his Athena. Instead, you came out…more like some combination of Aphrodite and Artemis."

"Maybe that says more about him than me," Sera replied.

"I know he'll be happy to see you," Serge's tone was adamant. "He sent Andrea and I out to get you. He said it was time for you to come home."

Sera let out a long sigh. "Serge, that's the difference between you and me. You view people's motives as altruistic; you see the good in them. I see the other side—how they're self-serving, how they are really only interested in helping themselves, and serving their own ends."

Serge leaned forward, his elbows on his knees and his hands outstretched.

"That's the problem, Fina, don't you see?" he implored. "You wall yourself off because you *want* to believe in people like I do; but your suspicion of everyone and everything…it limits you, and you fear the letdown of your hopes being dashed, so you just dash them all in advance."

"First off," Sera ticked items off her fingers. "Don't call me Fina. Sera, or Seraphina, no one calls me Fina anymore—"

<*I do,*> Helen added privately.

"Secondly, if you had been a bit more like me, perhaps you would have seen that Mark and Andrea did not have either of our best interests at heart. They tried to use me as an assassin—they tried to force me to kill a good friend! If Flaherty hadn't stopped me, I would have. Tanis would be dead, and the *Intrepid*…the *Intrepid* would be gone, out of our reach."

Serge didn't reply immediately, as he appeared to consider her words; but Sera would never learn his response, as Elena appeared at the bridge entrance.

"We've arrived, I see," she said simply.

Sera nodded. "Home sweet whatever."

Serge shot her a dark look but didn't say anything.

"Where's Flaherty?" Elena asked as she took a seat at a console and spun it around.

"Down in the hold, checking on the stasis pods. It's as though he thinks those two can escape somehow," Sera replied.

"Knowing them, it seems like a reasonable precaution," Elena chuckled. "So, what's the plan, princess?"

"Stars, *princess*? First Fina, now princess…" Sera shook her head. "Plan is gonna be to run back to the Inner Stars as fast as this boat can take me, if you keep that up."

"Renegade Hand agent, Seraphina Tomlinson, in a surprise move, absconds with her sister and heir to the presidency, Andrea

Tomlinson, just after arriving in the Huygens system," Elena said in a mock-formal voice. "I can just hear the reports now."

"I would *not* abscond with them," Sera grinned. "I'd push them out the airlock first."

"Your board's lit," Serge said, pointing over Sera's shoulder.

"Yeah," she replied, "it's Airtha traffic control. They've been pinging us for ten minutes now."

"Ten minutes!" Serge exclaimed. "Well, respond before they blast us to atoms."

Sera sighed. "Fine, but I was considering that as a viable option, you know."

# THE HAND

**STELLAR DATE: 01.14.8930 (Adjusted Years)**
**LOCATION: High Airtha Spaceport**
**REGION: Airtha, Huygens System, Transcend Interstellar Alliance**

Sera's father was not waiting at the bottom of the ramp.

His absence did not surprise her. It was not his style to wait on someone else. Even if those someones were three of his children, including his estranged daughter. Instead, Director Justin waited at the ship's ramp with some form of a smile on his face.

Sera had never been able to read Justin's expression. The man was a total mystery to her; from his motivations to his allegiances, to his preferences in music and food—an utter enigma.

"Director Justin," Sera greeted him when they reached the base of the ramp.

"Seraphina Tomlinson," the director of Inner Stars Clandestine Uplift Operations, or, The Hand, replied. "I have to admit, I often wondered if I would ever see you again. You had quite the time, romping about the Inner Stars."

"I wondered the same thing," Sera replied. "Though not for the same reasons. I have something for you."

Sera set the case containing the CriEn module on the ground, and Justin signaled an agent standing behind him to retrieve it.

Justin looked over the group. "And I see that you have indeed brought everyone else back in one piece. Including you, Agent Elena." Justin's expression darkened as he spoke Elena's name, who, for her part, stood tall and met his gaze. "Though I'm not sure how you confused Ascella for Scipio."

"The way I see it, sir," Elena said, "you should be thanking me for staving off a rather messy battle in Ascella. Without my assistance, none of us would be here right now—and the *Intrepid* and the watchpoint, or maybe both, would be gone."

"So you say," Justin said dismissively. "The hearing will get to the bottom of that. For now, get your alterations undone. You won't be going back to the Scipio Federation, and you can't appear before the committee looking like that."

Elena laughed. "Would their tender sensibilities be offended by seeing how humans really live?"

"Something like that," Justin muttered before looking back at Sera. "And you? Will you need to get your skin regrown? Or are you going to keep that…covering you've replaced it with?"

Sera looked down at her skin, covered in artistic whorls from her neck down. She wiped them clear, and her skin took on a creamy appearance. "I believe the appropriate answer is 'hell yeah, I'm keeping it'."

"Whatever," Justin waved a dismissive hand. "And you, Serge, do you have anything to say for yourself?"

Serge shook his head. "Nope, you're not my boss. Anything I have to say can wait for the hearings."

"Huh," Justin grunted. "Grown a bit of spine, have you?"

Serge didn't reply, and Justin looked at the pinnace. "Flaherty, I see you up there on the ramp. Bring those prisoners down and turn them over to the agents here."

"Sorry, Justin," Flaherty spoke without moving. "I only take orders from Sera. I'm sworn to her, if you recall."

"You're a Hand agent," Justin growled. "You all answer to me."

"I am not," Flaherty said. "My term has ended. I am bound only to Sera."

Sera sighed and waved her hand for Flaherty to come down. "As much as I want to mess with him, too, Flaherty, we should just get on with all this. Bring them down."

Flaherty grunted in acknowledgment, and pushed the two stasis pods, which were stacked on a hover pad, down the ramp.

"I'll need you to pass your token before I let you take the prisoners—my prisoners—into your custody," Sera said to Justin.

Justin scowled but nodded. Sera received his token, and signaled Flaherty to turn them over.

"You may remove them from stasis, but I want them held until the hearing that I see is scheduled for tomorrow morning," she said to Justin.

"Yes, of course," Justin sighed. "Your father would like to see you, as well."

"I'm sure he would," Sera replied. "Let him know I'll be there in a bit."

Justin laughed as though he'd expected her to delay the meeting. "Sure, take all the time in the world. I bet it'll make him so much happier."

Sera scowled and walked off the landing pad with Serge, Elena, and Flaherty. A float followed behind with their belongings.

"Elena?" Sera asked.

"Yeah?"

"Do you have any money, or maybe a place I can stay?"

# PRESIDENT TOMLINSON

**STELLAR DATE: 01.14.8930 (Adjusted Years)**
**LOCATION: Airtha Capitol Complex**
**REGION: Airtha, Huygens System, Transcend Interstellar Alliance**

Standing outside her father's office, Sera couldn't help but feel like a little girl again—sent to explain herself, and receive whatever punishment he chose to mete out. She shook her head to chase the memories away.

She was no longer that little girl, afraid of her father in his high tower, overlooking the Airtha ring with his implacable gaze. Now she knew him for what he was: just a man—a man with great power, and an ambition few could match; but still just a man.

She had fought enemies across dozens of systems in the Inner Stars, been in more dockside shootouts than she could count, and faced off with the likes of Rebecca and worse. Her father was just a man…just a man.

<*He's ready to see you now,*> a voice spoke into her mind, and she nearly jumped out of her seat.

<*Thanks, Ben,*> Sera replied to her father's AI assistant and gingerly rose from her seat, treading across the marble floors to the double doors leading into her father's office.

*Get ahold of yourself, woman,* she thought, and took a deep breath before pushing open one of the doors. She forced herself to stride purposefully toward his desk.

Though 'desk' was hardly the word for it. It was half the size of a small sailboat's deck. At least seven meters long and two deep, it was always spotless, and clear of any adornment— save for a single coffee cup, which sat on a warmer embedded in the wooden surface.

She passed between the rows of pillars, and saw her father standing at the windows at the end of his office. Sera knew from experience that her father would often spend hours standing at the window, managing his empire from holo-spaces in his mind. The diamond panes wrapped halfway around the room and gave a stunning view of the ring far below, and the star above.

She stood at his desk and announced herself.

"Father, you summoned me." It was not a question.

Jeffrey Tomlinson turned, and his cold grey eyes—set above high cheeks and below a brooding brow—settled on her.

"Seraphina. Home at last," he said with little emotion, perhaps just a hint of satisfaction.

"Not through any choice of my own," Sera responded. The statement came out colder than she'd meant, but there was no taking it back.

"You had a choice," her father said coolly. "You always have a choice; the outcome just wasn't one you were willing to accept."

"Andrea and Mark going free."

President Tomlinson nodded. "Yes, they cannot be held if there is no accuser. But here you are, ready to testify against your sister, and your former teammate and lover."

Sera didn't reply, waiting for him to make his request—to demand she drop the charges.

"Are you ready for what will come?" he asked.

"Are you asking me to drop the charges?" she asked. "New Canaan will not be happy if they learn that an attempt on the life of their governor went unpunished."

Her father waved his hand, dismissing New Canaan and its governor with a contemptuous look. "They are ten thousand light years from here. Governor Tanis Richards will get her system, and her people will build their new world, and they'll be happy whether or not justice is done here on Airtha."

"I think you underestimate Tanis Richards," Sera replied. "You are in a position to cross just about anyone in the galaxy without repercussion, Father. But Tanis Richards should not be taken so lightly—though, I suppose you don't. Otherwise, you wouldn't have sent Andrea to kill her."

Her father's face showed a moment of surprise, and Sera wondered if it was real or feigned. It was impossible to tell with him. His masks wore masks.

"Do you really think I would be capable of such a thing? To use you as an instrument of murder at the hands of your sister?"

"Father," Sera barked a laugh. "You all but forced me to join The Hand, an organization which is nothing but an instrument of murder wielded by you. This does not seem like a great stretch to me."

"I shall debate neither The Hand's necessity, nor its purpose with you," President Tomlinson replied. "But I will swear to you—swear to you on your mother's soul—that I issued no such order. In fact, I wish very much for Tanis Richards to live. I believe we will need her before long."

Sera's estimation of her father crept up a notch. Either he was better at playing her than she could ever have expected, or he really did see the big picture in a fashion that granted them common ground.

"You did not expect such rationale from me?" he asked, seeing her expression change.

"I did not expect such…pragmatism," Sera replied. "She breaks our accords—core, she breaks her own. By the Phobos Accords she calls upon so frequently, she is an abomination."

"Many things are sacrificed for the greater good," her father replied. "I have spent much time reviewing her actions: from her early years in the Terran Space Force, to her battles in the Kapteyn's System, and the recent defeat of five fleets at Bollam's World. She is a great tactician, yes; but there is more to her—or she is a lie."

"A lie?" Sera asked, uncertain what that could mean.

"Nevermind," her father dismissed the statement with a wave of his hand. "Will you dine with me tonight? Shira, Troy, and Ian will all be present, along with you and Serge. It is the largest gathering of my children in decades."

"Not Andrea?" Sera asked, probing her father's intentions.

"No. I respect our laws, though others may not. You have brought strong evidence against her, and she will be held until the hearing tomorrow morning."

"I am glad to hear that, Father. I was uncertain of where you would stand on this."

President Tomlinson fixed his daughter with a hard stare. "I always stand with what is right. I always have, and I always will."

From what she could tell, her father sincerely believed those words. It was one of the things that she found profoundly disturbing about him.

# AN INTIMATE OFFER

**STELLAR DATE: 01.14.8930 (Adjusted Years)**
**LOCATION: Airtha City**
**REGION: Airtha, Huygens System, Transcend Interstellar Alliance**

"So, how was dinner with the fam?" Elena asked from her seat beside Sera at the crowded bar.

Sera shrugged. "As well as could be expected. My father made a series of pointed comments to each of us, which we did our best to ignore. We're all used to it—have to be, at this point."

Elena chuckled. "My visits home are trying enough; I can't imagine doing it when your dad is god-emperor of the universe."

Sera made a sound of exasperation. "You have no fucking idea. I did have some fun, though. Since I wasn't in The Hand, none of what I did over the last decade-plus is classified, so I regaled my brothers and sisters with tales. For once, I got to make my dad feel awkward at his own dinner."

"I can imagine," Elena nodded. "Growing up here, they teach us that the Inner Stars are all chaos and squalor; but there's a lot of hope and beauty there, too."

"Speaking of beauty," Sera replied, taking in Elena's long auburn hair and almond eyes. "I'm glad that you're back to your normal self—I have to say, the fangs weren't so bad, but the red eyes were a bit much."

"They did the trick," Elena replied. "The guys—and girls—back on that mining colony in the Scipio Fed ate it up. I mean…their lives were dull with a side of dull. But me? I gave 'em a bit of spice."

"What *were* you doing there, anyway?" Sera asked. "Scipio is a beacon of stability—though a bit draconian. I can't imagine why they'd send you there; and to a mining colony, no less."

"I hadn't gotten that far," Elena said with a shrug. "Jutio, my latest AI, had no clear idea, either. It was fun, though. Almost a vacation, compared to what we normally do."

Sera nodded without speaking, and polished off her whiskey before signaling the bartender for another.

"What about you?" Elena asked. "Gonna go get your sexy skin undone? I wasn't sure if you were just baiting Justin or not, back on the landing pad."

Sera looked down at her body, sheathed in a very short, tight, purple dress that complimented the lavender hue she had chosen for her skin that evening.

"Are you kidding? This is the best un-booby-trap that's ever happened to me. This stuff can heal wounds in moments—compliments of a Mark pirate named Rebecca, and then upgraded by the *Intrepid*'s crew."

"I heard about that," Elena said. "Well, not that you went full kink—you were always on that path—but that you took on Rebecca in her own base. The Scipio boys and girls were none-too-happy to learn that The Mark's main base of operations was right on their doorstep. Everyone is killing themselves trying to determine how they kept it in the dark layer for so long."

"Well," Sera replied. "Let's hope not too many of them kill themselves trying to sort it out."

"I imagine Justin has already sent someone to see what route Scipio's research is taking them," Elena sighed. "That could have been a fun gig. The upper echelons in their federation live the good life."

"I just want to get back to the *Intrepid* and New Canaan," Sera replied. "They need me there."

"Do they?" Elena asked. "That Tanis Richards seems very capable. What is it that you think she needs you for—now that the deal is in place?"

"I..." Sera said and stalled. "To make sure that they get the system as promised."

"Sera!" Elena admonished. "The FGT has never withheld a system once it has been promised. It would go against everything we all stand for."

"We've never had a ship like the *Intrepid* coming for a colony," Sera replied. "But you're right. No matter how much anyone may want their tech, the FGT wouldn't stand for any shenanigans, and though my father and other factions want to create...whatever it is they want to create, the Terraformers still hold too much power to be crossed."

Elena nodded. "So what is it, Sar? What do you want to go back for? To wall yourself off in that colony? It's what they'll do to it, you know. No one in, no one out."

Sera sighed and took a long draught of her whiskey before fixing Elena's now-brown eyes with a long stare. "Would that be so bad? The galaxy will progress as it will. There will be wars, there will be peace. Progress, decline, whatever; it's all happened before, it'll all happen again. Maybe people like Tanis have the right of it. Just get out, build an Eden, and let the galaxy do what it will."

"You forget," Elena winked as she took a sip of her martini. "They lost Eden. Those colonists are going to Canaan—and you know how well that worked out in the old stories."

"Yet, we still know about the settlers of the original Canaan eleven thousand years later, Elly," Sera replied. "That means something."

"When did you get so philosophical?" Elena asked. "I thought you were all booze, sex, and gunfights?"

"Oh, I am." Sera smiled. "Events have just…got me thinking too much, that's all."

Elena shifted and placed her hand on Sera's thigh. "What do you say we forget all that for tonight, and let me give that new skin of yours a run?"

"Stars, Elly," Sera sighed. "You know I would any other night; but not tonight. I should probably kick it early. We have the hearing tomorrow. You're going to be there, right?"

"Of course," Elena nodded, her smile gone and her tone sober. "Always taking the fun out of things."

"I thought I was all sex, drugs, and gunfights?" Sera asked with a smile.

"Booze, not drugs. Get your own vices straight," Elena laughed.

# COURT

**STELLAR DATE: 01.15.8930 (Adjusted Years)**
**LOCATION: Airtha City**
**REGION: Airtha, Huygens System, Transcend Interstellar Alliance**

Sera stood before the doors of the Federal Interstellar Crimes Courthouse and sucked in a deep breath. She looked down and inspected her uniform to ensure that it was crisp and straight. It had been a long time since she had worn The Hand's sable colors; she had never expected to don them again. Coming back to the Transcend was one thing, but rejoining The Hand? It wasn't on her bucket list.

Still, she knew that if she had sent Andrea and Mark back in Elena's custody—if she could have worked out a legal scenario that General Greer and Serge would have accepted—her friend would have been eviscerated upon her return to Airtha.

Not publicly, but she would have been dispatched to the asshole of the Inner Stars, or perhaps to the front with the Orion Guard. It would have been her death.

Sera considered that Elena had been prepared to do that for her, to take the prisoners back and deal with the consequences. She was a true friend. Sera felt guilty that she had considered putting her in that position. There were a lot of things she wished could have been different with Elena.

Perhaps, if things worked out here, the future could hold something better.

"You gonna stand there all day, Sis?" a voice asked from behind her. Sera turned to see Serge with a warm smile on his lips.

"I was considering that, yeah," Sera chuckled. "Think I can testify from out here?"

"Doubtful," Serge replied as he placed an arm around her shoulders. "C'mon, sister mine, let's do this. Andrea's bark is worse than her bite."

"It's not her bark or her bite I fear," Sera said with a shake of her head. "It's her blade in my back while I sleep."

Serge let out a long sigh. Sera knew his dilemma. He was the family's peacemaker, and, as such, he constantly worked out ways for everyone to get along. Sera suspected that even he had no idea how to bridge this chasm.

The cold, marble halls with their diamond pillars stretched far, and it took the pair ten minutes to reach their assigned courtroom.

Sera walked to the front of the room and sat in the first row, behind the prosecutor's table. Serge sat at her side, and she craned her neck around the near-empty room. She was surprised; she had thought it would be packed with the power-elite, all ready to pounce on the weakest sister and devour her whole for the prestige it would gain them in the other's eyes.

But not so. Only a few Hand agents were present— including Justin, who only gave her a hard nod. Neither the prosecutor nor the defending representatives had arrived yet.

Sera had spoken over the Link with Will, the federal prosecutor who was assigned her case. He had queried her for several hours after her meeting with her father, going over the attempted assassination and the events that followed. He had not asked about the events surrounding the loss and recovery of the CriEn module. Separate charges were on file against Mark within The Hand on that account, and a military tribunal would be overseeing the case.

Flaherty eased into the seat on the other side of Sera, and she grabbed his hand and squeezed.

"How is your daughter?" she asked quietly.

"Well," Flaherty replied. "It would seem that I am now a great-great grandfather."

Sera laughed softly. "Soon there will be hundreds of little Flahertys running around."

Flaherty only grunted in response, but Sera recognized it as a happy grunt.

The prosecutor arrived a minute later, and took his seat before turning to face her.

"Blazes, you've right kicked the hornet's nest with this one," he sighed. "I've been fielding messages all night."

"Does that surprise you?" Sera asked. "Andrea is nothing if not well-connected."

Will let out a long breath. "No, and I should be used to it. You don't work this type of case without getting a lot of calls; but even I wasn't prepared for the barrage I received. Eventually, I just shunted them all off to the office NSAI to catalog—no matter who they were."

"I hope you got enough sleep," Sera replied.

"Enough," Will nodded.

She saw his eyes look to the back of the room, and Sera turned to see two defenders enter, a man and a woman. She recognized them from several high-profile cases when she was younger. Another man followed behind them in a Hand uniform, and Sera imagined he was the division's representative for Mark.

By his outward appearance, he looked competent enough—Justin wouldn't want to look sloppy on a case like this, regardless of what outcome he desired. Though Sera had no idea what that was.

"Poor guy," Elena whispered as she slipped into a seat behind Sera. "This is one shitty case to catch; it's totally blown up the news and the feeds."

"I wouldn't know," Sera replied." I've blocked anything to do with it. "Helen's keeping an eye out to see if there's anything that is concerning."

Elena nodded. "I've had Jutio do that, as well. It's draining to see it and hear it everywhere."

As she spoke, Judge Turin entered the room, resplendent in his white robes bearing the Transcend and FGT crests. Everyone in the room rose, and then took their seats again after the judge had settled into his. Sera saw the judge's eyes dart to the back of the room, and she turned to see her father take a seat in the back.

<*Far be it for him to have to rise and honor a simple judge,*> she commented to Helen.

<*It's not surprising. Just like I don't expect any justice to actually be dispensed today,*> Helen replied.

<*That stands to reason,*> Sera responded. <*It* ***is*** *just a hearing.*>

<*You know what I mean.*>

A moment later, federal police brought in Mark and Andrea. Mark wore his Hand uniform, and Andrea wore a simple, yet elegant dress. Andrea behaved as though everyone in the room was present at her pleasure, while Mark surveyed the attendees with a scowl. His eyes settled on Sera for a moment, and his scowl deepened.

Sera, for her part, was disgusted to wear the same uniform as the man. She wasn't sure if she wanted to tear hers off, or make him remove his.

"The charges levied today are grave," Judge Turin began without preamble. "They are also numerous; but the gravest are the subversion of a Transcend citizen with unauthorized use of government technology, and committing an act of sedition within a foreign entity, with the intent to destabilize that entity. Also without authorization. Hugo, please read the rest of the charges."

The court's AI proceeded to recite the remaining seventy-three charges, most of which applied to both Mark and Andrea, though a few were particular to each. By Sera's own testimony, Mark bore the brunt of those, mostly because he had been the one to plant a hack in her mind before she left The Hand.

He shot her more than one cold look as Hugo read the charges, and when the court AI brought up the original hack, Mark cast an unreadable look in Justin's direction. It didn't confirm a suspicion Sera had long held, but it certainly did reinforce it.

Once the charges were read, the Judge's gaze swept across the assemblage, pausing on the president, before landing on the defendants.

"Do you understand the charges laid before you?"

"I do," Andrea replied calmly, while Mark simply said, "Yes."

Mark's shoulders had slumped through the reading of the charges, and she wondered if he had deluded himself about the severity of the case until now, when it was laid out in court. That she had ever fallen for him, that she had ever thought of him as suave and admirable, baffled her older self. The man was a chameleon; but he had finally landed in a place where he couldn't blend in and hide.

*<Don't be too sure,>* Helen commented, guessing at her thoughts. *<He's spent the last decade back here in Airtha, building support. While he may not have planned for this event specifically, he must have prepared some sort of defense against you.>*

Sera didn't reply. In just one day, her return to Airtha had made her realize why, of all the things she could have done when she left The Hand, she chose the life of a freighter captain. On her ship, in the black, she could flit from system to system, never staying anywhere long enough to fall prey to a system's politics, or other assembled nonsense.

She knew that if she were to tap into the feeds or listen to any newscasts, they would be filled with people calling her everything from the savior of the Transcend, to a core-devil, or worse. Her message queues were probably filled with people wishing her well, death threats, political solicitations, and a million other things she didn't care to look at.

Here and now, in the courtroom; that was where her attention needed to be. Everything else was just a distraction—this was the real battlefield.

"I will now hear arguments regarding bail," the judge announced. "Given the seriousness of the charges—a unilateral attack on a foreign government, one which wishes the protection of the Transcend, no less—I am inclined toward the prosecution's request that the defendants be remanded without bail."

Sera held back any joy; the judge's initial inclination and what ultimately happened could be two very different things.

The federal prosecutor stood and outlined key aspects of the crimes, and how they were exceptionally damaging to the Transcend. He even called out the risk to attaining more advanced technology from the New Canaan colony, and made special note of how the picotech had not been traded, but that there were still hopes to get it someday.

She glanced back at her father, but his expression was unreadable. His eyes locked with hers for a moment, then flicked back to the prosecutor.

<*These proceedings are being fed everywhere,*> Sera said privately to Helen. <*The prosecutor's rank, and my father's presence, practically make this a policy announcement—this will be at the ears of the Orion Guard's Praetor within months.*>

<*It's an interesting game they're playing,*> Helen acknowledged. <*It is difficult to tell if this will placate the Guard, or spur them to action. It all depends on whether or not they believe it; and even then, it's hard to say what they'll do with the information.*>

<*What does your otherself think of this?*> Sera asked, referring to the master version of Helen which administered and operated Airtha.

<*I have not spoken to her yet,*> Helen replied. <*It's too risky right now. It's probable that every communication across your Link is heavily monitored. They can't crack our encryption—but they could track a message's ultimate destination.*>

<*Understood,*> Sera nodded in her mind. <*And if we routed to mask the destination, that would look mighty suspicious.*>

<*Yes,*> Helen said. <*Trying to keep suspicion to a minimum.*>

The federal prosecutor completed his statements, and Andrea's defenders exchanged a brief look before the woman stood.

"Given that the bulk of the prosecution's case relies on the testimony of the person who actually carried out the failed assassination attempt—who could be simply shifting blame to our client, as a result of her failure—I believe that our client should not be held without bail. We have reviewed the full-sensory recordings that the *Intrepid* sent along. Andrea Tomlinson was never seen to act with any hostility at any time; she is not a threat to anyone."

Sera held her gaze steady. Her sister was one of the most dangerous people she knew, even though Serge was entirely blind to it. If anyone could master hostile acts without appearing to be dangerous, it was she.

Granted, being in jail would not substantially limit Andrea's ability to reach out and do as she wished; but it would be a small victory.

Andrea's defender went on for some time about her client's history, strong moral code, and contributions to both the government and the people of the Transcend. Eventually she sat, and Mark's defender stood.

Despite Sera's initial concerns, he was well spoken, and presented his arguments cogently. They were very similar to Andrea's attorney's statements, but he made special note of the fact that much of the good Mark had done was classified, because of his time with The Hand, but that if his record were revealed, he would be shown as a great hero of the Transcend.

After the arguments, the judge was silent for a few minutes. Then he sat forward and folded his hands before him. "Before I render my decision, given the unusual circumstances of this case, I'll entertain any thoughts from other attendees today."

Sera expected he did so to give her father the opportunity to speak. Instead, something else entirely unexpected occurred.

"I would like to make a statement and provide evidence," Flaherty said as he rose.

The judge frowned. "Any evidence, for or against, should be presented by the prosecutor or the defenders. If it is your testimony, then you may be called on by them as needed."

Flaherty did not sit. "I am a fourth order Sinshea, and my word is fact. You cannot dismiss it."

Sera sat back, stunned by what Flaherty had revealed. She had always known there was much more to him than met the eye. Despite his bond to her, she had no deep insights into his past, and had always taken a lot on faith.

But to learn he was a Sinshea, someone whose word is scientifically trusted and who cannot give false testimony—that was something she would never have expected. Perhaps it was why he spoke so rarely; and when he did, his words often confirmed things that should have remained secret—like the existence of the Transcend to her crew on *Sabrina*.

"Hugo, please confirm this," Judge Turin addressed the court's AI.

There was a pause, and then Hugo spoke audibly in the room, "It is confirmed, and I have an active Link with Flaherty monitoring the algorithms. This man's word is fact."

Flaherty nodded and made his statement. "The events you have on record from Elena, Sera, Helen, and the *Intrepid*'s AIs Bob and Angela are accurate in their entirety. No effort has been made to deceive this court in any way."

Flaherty sat, and the judge was silent for a moment before the woman defending Andrea rose again.

"Your honor, if I may? The question at the heart of this is not whether the events as recorded are truthful, but that the intentions are not as they have been portrayed. Though a Sinshea's word cannot be doubted when authenticated in a court of law, it is still his view, and others' views, of events that it is confirming.

"What happened in that room, before Sera came out and brutally attacked a foreign head of state, is what is unknown. My clients maintain that they did nothing to her, and that what she did—whether hacked or not— was something they had no part in."

"It does confirm that there was a hack," Judge Turin said somberly. "There is no longer any debate that Sera did not act of her own will. Not unless something incontrovertible comes up."

Sera glanced back at her father to read his reaction, but there was no emotion displayed on his face. He did give a nearly imperceptible nod to the judge. Or he was looking down at his hands, it was hard to tell.

"I'm going to honor the prosecutor's request that the defendants be held without bail," the judge announced. "Trial dates will be set in a hearing next week."

The judge rose, as did the rest of the courtroom; though her father turned and left as the judge did, making his actions appear as though he was simply getting up to leave the room.

Once the judge was gone, muted conversations sprang up through the courtroom. Sera smiled wanly at Flaherty, and thanked him for his testimony. One thing was certain: it was going to be a long slog.

# RELATIONS

**STELLAR DATE: 02.11.8930 (Adjusted Years)**
**LOCATION: Airtha City**
**REGION: Airtha, Huygens System, Transcend Interstellar Alliance**

The steak looked amazing. Sera sliced off a piece, and let the rich scent hit her nostrils before taking a bite.

"Oh man, this is heaven on a plate," she said to Elena. "Do you want some?"

Elena shook her head, and took a bite of her salad. "Ever since I got those sucker mods undone, I've had no appetite for meat at all. I think they messed something up, but I'm not sure. I've done so many undercover ops, I barely remember what *I* actually like anymore. I mean…I know what I liked before I got into The Hand; but I've grown, evolved, right? I don't think I can just reset to how I was twenty years ago."

"Wow," Sera replied. "That's a way deeper response than I'd expected from offering you some steak."

"C'mon, Sar," Elena replied. "I know you feel it, too. We don't fit in here—stars, we don't fit in anywhere!"

"It's all the trials and hearings," Sera replied. "Every part of our lives is under a microscope right now. Between the federal courts, The Hand's tribunals, and the civil suits, I feel like I might be in court for the rest of my life. Was Airtha always this litigious?"

Elena polished off her drink and signaled the waiter for another. "I don't have a fucking clue. I guess we never got mixed up in stuff at this level before—well, I mean, we were at this level, but we never *screwed up* at this level."

"Speak for yourself. I didn't screw up," Sera replied with mock haughtiness, then frowned. "Well, unless you count trusting Mark."

"I always told you he wasn't good enough for you," Elena chided.

"Yeah, but that's because you wanted me for yourself," Sera chuckled. "Your motives were hardly altruistic."

"Guilty—of that, at least," Elena shrugged.

"At least you got off," Sera said around another bite of her steak. "I thought they were going to ship you off to the backside of the galaxy—wherever that currently is—for breaking protocol in Scipio and coming for me."

"Bit by bit, you're coming out on top of this mess. I think people know that if Andrea loses, you're going to rise in the ranks—a lot. Sending your best friend away on a suicide mission wouldn't be advisable."

"Best friends, is that all we are?" Sera asked. "I thought you wanted to be more?"

"And I thought you needed more headspace," Elena replied with a smile slowly creeping across her face. "Are you saying that *you* want to be more now?"

"I think I might be ready for that," Sera replied. "I mean…it wouldn't be the first time you and I got romantically entangled. I just feel like our lives are getting more complicated—mine, especially—and you may not want to go wherever all this takes me."

"What, to New Canaan?" Elena asked. "The colonists on the *Intrepid* seem like good people. I could stand to settle down there for a while—not forever, but a while."

"What if…what if things didn't go that way?" Sera asked.

Elena frowned and picked up the glass their waiter had just set down. She peered at Sera over the rim for a minute before taking a sip and setting it down.

"What do you mean by that? There's something going on, isn't there?"

Sera shrugged. "I'm honestly not certain. My father…he's been warmer to me during this than I expected. He's also distancing himself from Andrea. I think that's the main reason why things are going my way. People testifying on her behalf are altering their accounts. Not lying, but just choosing words that aren't flattering to her. Hell, Mark is totally fucked; no one is backing him. No one can even find the order that put him on the ship with Andrea and Serge anymore. A separate investigation is launching to see if he somehow forged the whole thing."

"So, he's going to go down for what happened to your unit?" Elena asked.

Sera sighed. "I don't know. Justin hasn't formally launched that inquiry yet. There's some sensitive intelligence there. I think if they can pin enough other stuff on him, they're going to leave that one alone. I think they are going to charge him with violating Department of Equalization protocols, and allowing advanced tech to fall into Inner Stars hands. If they do, I'll get a commendation for recovering it."

"Stars, this is all such a shit show. Here's to being back in Airtha," Elena raised her glass, and Sera tapped hers against it.

"To Airtha," she replied.

"By the way, I didn't fall for your evasion there. If your father is all full of parental adoration, what's that mean? Is he going to put you in Andrea's place?"

"Who's to know? What I do know is that he is either taking advantage of this, or somehow he planned it all out. I think that maybe Andrea was getting too big for her britches. If she gets a reprogramming sentence, maybe he'll use that to his benefit—make her less of a bitch, and then bring her back in a century or two."

Elena barked a laugh into the general quiet of the upper-class restaurant; the sound breaking past their light noise barrier, and earning them annoyed looks from several other patrons.

She flushed before speaking. "Do you really think that simple reprogramming can turn Andrea into a person worth the tech it takes to hold her together? I think she'd need a full mental wipe."

Sera grimaced. Just the thought of a full wipe made her uncomfortable. Use of the technique was uncommon, but it felt so wrong, so draconian. Better to incarcerate or exile someone than to entirely erase who they were, yet keep them alive.

"I still have good memories of Andrea," Sera said. "When I was a kid, she was good to me; she protected me from father's ire on more than one occasion."

"Andrea protecting you…that's hard to picture," Elena replied.

Sera nodded silently. "To answer your question…if father offered me a role high up in his administration, one where I could effect real change and influence him; yeah, I'd consider it very seriously."

Elena's brow knit together and she nodded slowly; Sera wondered what her friend thought. Was she a sellout?

"I can see the concern in your eyes," Elena said with a smile. "I was just picturing you at all those boring cabinet meetings. I think you'd only last a few months before you were tearing your skin off. But seriously, Sar, you're not your job. You're you—and you are someone distinctive, unique, special."

"Thanks, Elly, that means a lot to me," Sera replied.

"Plus, you're one hell of a kinky bitch, and that lights my fire," Elena said with a laugh.

Sera glanced around at the heads, which turned their way.

"Great, now that's going to be on all the feeds."

"Sar, dear, your proclivities stopped being newsworthy long ago. Cat's kinda out of the bag on that one."

Sera looked down at her shimmering blue skin. "This really isn't weird. Hell, colored, shimmering skin is probably more common in the Inner Stars than is staid formality."

Elena laughed. "That's the truth. If the tight asses in the Transcend knew what people got up to in the Inner Stars these days, they may just swear off the whole uplift idea."

A contact came in over the Link, and Sera's eyes widened as she listened to the message. "My father has summoned me to the Hand HQ. Something big is up."

Elena threw her drink back. "I'm coming with you."

Sera nodded. She had no idea what was up, but having backup never hurt.

# DIRECTOR

**STELLAR DATE: 02.11.8930 (Adjusted Years)**
**LOCATION: Airtha City**
**REGION: Airtha, Huygens System, Transcend Interstellar Alliance**

The summons was to the Hand's central headquarters, not the satellite offices in the capitol buildings. They passed through the security checkpoints, and Sera noted how nothing seemed out of place. No elevated conditions were set on the network, and no agents rushed through the halls—beyond what was normal.

Sera and Elena made their way through the agency's marble halls to Justin's offices, where the message said they were to go. As they rounded the final turn before the director's office, a pair of the president's guards stopped the two women.

"Wait." One of them held up his hand while the other verified their security tokens. When satisfied, he nodded to the first guard who addressed Sera.

"She stays, you go in."

Sera looked to Elena, who shrugged and leaned up against the wall, hungrily eyeing the two heavily augmented men.

<*Will you come if I call?*> Sera asked.

<*Of course. I can take out these two goons in my sleep. Core, I'll have them eating out of my hand in two minutes, whether you need me or not,*> Elena replied, and Sera caught a whiff of pheromones as she walked away. The guards probably noticed them too, and were filtering them out; but if she knew Elena, that was just a feint.

The double doors to Justin's office stood closed, but Sera pushed them open without knocking.

For a man who heavily influenced the fates of nations and federations in the Inner Stars, Director Justin's office was spare. It wasn't stark by any means—the wood paneling on the walls, the carefully selected art, and the ancient wooden desk were all tasteful and ornate—but it wasn't enough furniture for the size of the space. It looked as though he had never fully moved in.

But perhaps he was moving out—the only person in the room with her was the president, seated behind Justin's desk.

"Father," Sera said by way of greeting.

"Sera," he replied with a nod. "Have a seat."

She saw no reason not to, and walked to the desk, where she sat in a relaxed pose; as though being summoned here at night, with the director absent, was perfectly normal.

Her father's brow furrowed. "Are you naked? I can't tell."

"Sort of," Sera said with a smile. "This skin takes on the shape I choose; it has a lot of utility."

"Can you shape it to cover you more? I'm not interested in staring at my daughter's exposed breasts throughout this conversation."

Sera complied, and her skin filled in to cover her breasts as though she was wearing a tight top. "Better?" she asked.

"Marginally," her father replied. "Sometimes I regret letting you join The Hand. Your time in the Inner Stars seems to have brought a lasciviousness out in you that did not exist before."

"I thought you were more evolved than to be distracted by the mere sight of a woman's breasts. They are, after all, just a particular configuration of cells. Intrinsically, no more or less appropriate than any other configuration of cells," Sera said with a smile.

"It's not the sight of your breasts that bothers me; I've seen my fair share. It's the reason why you parade yourself that annoys me. But," he held up his hand, "I did not summon you here to spar over your fashion choices, or who you choose to fuck and in what way you do it."

The casual strength of his statement caused Sera to involuntarily sit up straighter. "I'm sorry, Father, why did you summon me here? And where is Justin?"

"The answer to those questions is one and the same," her father replied. "Through the investigation into the order Andrea received to kill Tanis Richards—an order which I did not issue—new evidence has come to light. It is compelling enough that I have suspended him as director of The Hand."

Her father's tone was calm and even, as though he were discussing the menu at a restaurant, but the meaning behind his words was clear. He was willing to sacrifice Justin to save Andrea.

"So, Andrea gets off the hook and Justin goes on it?" Sera asked with a raised eyebrow.

"Not entirely," her father replied. "Andrea's use of you to carry out that kill order, and the method by which she did it, will still see her do hard time on a penal colony, perhaps even with light reconditioning. Mark will fare better, as he can now claim he acted under her orders, and though he's little more than human trash, he'll only go down for the hacking charges."

"That's just great," Sera replied.

"Well, you can proceed with other charges, if you see fit," her father replied, "in your new role as provisional director of The Hand."

Sera actively worked to maintain her composure. She expected a lot of things from the meeting with her father, but getting The Hand's directorship was not one of them.

<*Call off the dogs,*> she signaled Elena. <*I'm getting the directorship.*>

<*Wait...what? Now I really think you need a rescue.*>

"Provisional?" she asked.

"Well, the charges against Justin have just been levied. If it turns out that this evidence does not convict him—an outcome which I doubt will occur—then he would be reinstated. Once the trial is out of the way, you will gain the full directorship. It's an appointed role, after all; I can appoint it to who I choose."

<*Charges of nepotism be damned,*> Helen commented.

<*There's a lot I can do with a position like this,*> Sera replied.

<*That's how he gets you,*> Helen said. <*Look at me, stuck running this city-planet-star thing forever, just because I felt honored that he thought I was qualified.*>

<*This is a bit different—and you could leave whenever you wanted,*> Sera responded.

<*No, I couldn't, but that's not the issue here. However, given the circumstances, I think you should take it.*>

<*Really?*> Sera was surprised to hear Helen's approval.

<*Well, if you decline, I suspect that things won't go so well. Keep your enemies close and all that.*>

"So, does Helen approve?" President Tomlinson asked.

"You know her name, do you?" Sera asked. "And yes, as a matter of fact, she does approve."

"Good. Then, I had best get out of your chair."

Her father rose and stepped around the desk, where he extended his hand. "I'm proud of you. This is a big step for you," he said as they shook.

"Thank you, Father," Sera replied.

President Tomlinson walked toward the door, but turned before he reached it. "Oh, and Sera, there are a great many things I know, which you may believe I don't. You'd do well to keep that mind."

Before she could reply, he was gone. Sera stood, staring at the door until it cracked open and Elena's head poked in.

"Sar? Is this for real?"

Sera shook her head to clear the cobwebs from her mind and gave a wan smile. "It looks like it. I'm the Director of the Hand."

Elena laughed. "Man, when you said this evening that your father may have something in mind for you, this is not what I imagined."

"Me either," Sera said with a sigh and leaned back against the desk. "It doesn't look good for you, though."

The color drained from Elena's face.

"What…what do you mean?" she asked.

"Well, I'm going to need someone I can trust in this den of thieves. I'm going make you my personal assistant."

Elena's pale face darkened with color and her brow lowered. "You wouldn't!"

Sera laughed. "No, of course not. How does Chief of Operations sound?"

"Worse!" Elena exclaimed. "What did I do to deserve this?"

"I think it was something about wanting to be in a long-term relationship with me," Sera grinned.

# HERSCHEL

**STELLAR DATE: 02.23.8930 (Adjusted Years)**
**LOCATION: Jutoh City International Airport**
**REGION: Herschel, Krugenland System, Orion Freedom Alliance**

Kent stepped off the bus and looked up at the shuttle resting on the cradle before him. It was a nondescript oval, lined with portholes and a plas window at the nose for the pilots to use, if they cared to look outside.

The exterior was scuffed and scarred from a thousand planetary entries; a necessity on a backwater like this, where no space elevator existed—nor was ever likely to be built.

Beyond the sleepy spaceport, a stiff wind pulled at a line of trees, and a chill crept through Kent's skin. A storm was on its way. He hoped that it wouldn't delay the takeoff; though he suspected that wind and rain did not bother grav-drive shuttles, unlike the sub-orbital jet he had ridden in to get to the spaceport. The landing had seen it buffeted by a strong crosswind, and he had worried they would slew off the runway—until he noticed the bored expressions of the flight attendants.

"Don't stand in the way," a man said as he pushed past him.

Kent realized he had been gawking, and flushed. He glanced around and hiked his rucksack higher on his shoulder before following the other passengers to the shuttle.

It was nothing like the vids he had seen, where a long, enclosed tunnel connected the terminal to the ship. Out here on Herschel, there were only five cradles for shuttles and starships, and these sat on the far end of the combined space and airport, only accessible by groundcar or bus.

The people who settled this world a thousand years ago had opted for a simpler, more agrarian society; what they called salt-of-the-earth living. What that meant to Kent was a life of dirty hands, working under the unrelenting light of the twin suns in Herschel's sky.

He wanted to see what lay beyond those two stars, to go out into space and witness the things he had only dreamed of, or seen in vids and holos.

It was why he had joined the Orion Guard.

His parents had railed against him when they learned of his enlistment—his father more than his mother. Even with seven brothers and sisters, his father seemed to think that the farm couldn't operate without him. Kent didn't care; the idea of tilling the earth for the rest of his life seemed like a fate worse than death.

His mother tried to convince him to go into one of Herschel's few cities and take up work there, but that would have been just another form of drudgery. No one on this world wished to advance, to improve themselves. They all were content to exist, rather than thrive.

"Not me," Kent whispered to himself as he walked up the ramp into the shuttle.

Within, the craft was cleaner and newer-looking than without. The tan walls were spotless, and an automaton gestured for him to turn left and take a seat in the shuttle's general cabin. The data on his Link told him he could sit wherever he wished. The craft could seat over a hundred people, but there had been fewer than twenty on the bus.

He made a beeline for a seat near a porthole, anxious to see the transition from Herschel, the only world he knew, into space, the realm of his future. He re-checked his itinerary, worried that something would change and somehow foil his exodus.

However, to his relief, there was no alteration to the schedule. After a seven-hour layover on Undala Station, the *Tremont*—the interstellar cruiser that would take him to Rega—would be ready for boarding. Once aboard the cruiser, it would be a four-month trip from Herschel on the rimward depths of Orion Freedom Alliance space into the core of the Orion worlds.

"Hey, OK if I sit here?" a voice asked, jolting him back to the world around him.

Kent looked up to see a young man, perhaps just a year younger than him, standing in the aisle. Although there were dozens of rows with no one sitting in them, the man seemed to want to sit in his.

"Sure," Kent replied, gesturing to the seat.

He worried that this man would want to chat during takeoff and the journey into space, but it wasn't as though he could deny him a seat. Then again, this man's accent pegged him as a local— he hadn't met many people who grew up on Herschel and wanted to leave.

"So, where are you off to?" his curiosity got the better of him and he raised the question.

The man glanced at Kent and smiled as he settled into his seat. "Anywhere but here."

Kent laughed in response. That was his sentiment, as well; the Orion Guard was just a means to an end—though a means which required a three-decade commitment.

"I'm Kent, by the way," he said and offered his hand.

"Sam," the man took it and gave a firm shake. "Thanks for letting me sit here. I'll admit that I'm a bit nervous about this. I thought having someone to block the view out of the porthole would help."

"You know that the covers slide down," Kent said and demonstrated with a slight smile. His first flight of any kind had been earlier the same day, and he hadn't realized the windows had covers either—until he saw someone else close theirs.

Sam laughed. "Well, look at that. I can move, if you want."

"No, no," Kent replied. "I don't mind at all—though I am curious where you're really off to. Not a lot of people our age on this shuttle."

They both glanced around the cabin at the other passengers, most of whom were off-worlders who had likely been on Herschel for business trips.

"I'm bound for Rega. I'm joining the Guard," Sam said softly, trying not to be overheard.

Kent knew why Sam wouldn't want his destination to be too well known. Though Herschel was a member of the Orion Freedom Alliance, the planet's inhabitants had not been a part of the OFA's separation from the Transcend, having settled the world long after the tumultuous fracturing of the Future Generation Terraformers. They were, by and large, an isolationist group; and while they were happy for the world the OFA had provided, they resented the recruitment of their youth to the Orion Guard.

Kent was less concerned with hiding his intentions. He had already been yelled at by half of his family over his enlistment. As far as he was concerned, helping the guard stand against the tyranny of the Transcend was his civic duty—though it was secondary to his unbridled desire to simply get off-world.

"That's what I'm doing, too," he replied to Sam. "You're heading up to Undala and the *Tremont* as well?"

Sam nodded. "I can't believe I met someone else enlisting. It's not exactly a popular sentiment around here."

"Yeah, everyone here is so happy to live under the OFA's protection; but without the Guard, we'd all be a part of the Transcend and its *Great Plan* for all of humanity," Kent replied.

Sam looked around nervously, apparently used to backlash from such statements.

"They're all off-worlders," Kent said with a shrug. "They're not going to come down us for enlisting—heck, they probably appreciate it."

"That's going to take some getting used to," Sam said. "I'm used to getting yelled at for talking about heading off-world. Hells, I didn't even tell my parents I enlisted."

"Seriously?" Kent asked. "How are they not blowing up your Link right now?"

Sam chuckled. "I told them I was going to the mountains with some friends for a vacation—which is half true. I did go, but then I ducked out early. It'll be awhile before they sort out what happened. By then, I'll be long gone."

"That's rough," Kent shook his head. "I didn't exactly have the best parting with my family, but I'm glad I told them. I mean…it could be the last time I see them."

Sam's brown eyes grew sad. "Yeah, I know…look, I know it's not the best way to go, but I did say goodbye. They just didn't know how long it was for."

"Sorry," Kent apologized. "I didn't mean to come down on you for that. You did what you had to do. I know what that's like."

"Thanks," Sam replied and leaned back and closed his eyes—apparently looking for a break in their banter.

Kent took the hint; he had stepped over a line. It was something he often did. Hopefully it would happen less when he was away from Herschel, and its residents' knee-jerk suppression of anyone with an adventurous spirit.

Outside, the bus was pulling away from the shuttle, and he heard the dull thud as the cabin door closed and sealed. He sucked in a deep breath; it wouldn't be long now before the shuttle rose into the air, as if by magic, floating on its grav drives before boosting into space.

He didn't have long to wait before a nearly imperceptible shift reverberated through the shuttle. Out of the corner of his eye, he saw his companion's grip on the armrest tighten, and gave a small smile. Sam had better get used to it; there was bound to be a lot of spaceflight in the guard.

Outside the porthole, Kent saw the ground fall away, far faster than the feeling in the pit of his stomach told him it should. The incongruity disoriented him and he shook his head, forcing himself to relax. He knew that grav drives and inertial dampeners would accomplish such feats; he just hadn't expected them to mask the feeling of motion so well. The disconnect between what he felt and saw was more disconcerting than he anticipated.

It only took twenty minutes for the shuttle to rise above Herschel's atmosphere and into the blackness of space. The plas over the portholes tinted to diminish the blinding light of the twin suns. He wished he had thought to sit on the other side so that he could catch a glimpse of the stars.

"Damn, that was fast," Sam whispered, his head still back against the seat, eyes closed.

"Sure was," Kent replied. "Shuttle's net shows that we have a few hours to Undala Station. I hope they bring some food around."

"Food?" Sam cracked an eye open and peered at Kent. "I don't think I'll ever eat again."

"Seriously?" Kent asked. "We could barely feel anything."

"I know! That's what's so weird. Half an hour ago we were resting on the ground…now we're out here, and if I didn't know it was happening, I wouldn't have been able to tell," Sam said with a shake of his head.

"You realize that we'll do this a lot in the Guard, right?" Kent asked.

"Yeah…I'll get used to it," Sam replied, with a steely determination entering his voice. "I'm not going back there just because flying feels weird."

Kent nodded. "That's the spirit."

# THE HEGEMONY OF WORLDS

**STELLAR DATE: 05.30.8930 (Adjusted Years)**
**LOCATION: Hegemony Capitol Buildings, Raleigh**
**REGION: High Terra, Sol System, Hegemony of Worlds**

Uriel, President of the Hegemony of Worlds, stood at the window of her office, surveying her domain. Here, atop the capitol spire in New Raleigh on High Terra, everything seemed so peaceful.

The Earth hung above; the jewel of the Hegemony, rebuilt after lying abandoned and ruined for thousands of years following the Jovian bombardment in the late fifth millennia. Below the tower, with its arms stretched upward, wrapping Earth in its embrace, was High Terra—the oldest intact orbital ring humanity had ever created.

From here, the Hegemony of Worlds—often referred to as the AST, which stood for Alpha Centauri, Sol, and Tau Ceti, the three most powerful systems in the Hegemony—ruled over the core systems of humanity.

Uriel found it fitting that her offices were in the ancient Terran capitol buildings. The gravity of history bore down on her here, and she always kept in mind that the presidents of the ancient Terran Hegemons had ruled from this very room.

And even they had fallen, their empire destroyed by the Jovians.

It was a lesson she vowed never to forget—which is why she had chosen this site to house her administration.

Some still brought up the controversy she created when she moved the seat of power from Callisto to High Terra. She ignored them. From here, she could see the continents of Earth, she could make out the shapes of ancient nations; here, she was grounded in the history of the human race.

<*President Uriel,*> Jayse, her personal assistant, interrupted her thoughts. <*The ambassador from the Trisilieds Alliance, Herin Yer, has arrived. She has a man with her who she has introduced as Mr. Garza.*>

President Uriel sighed. Another day, another never-ending series of meetings with people within and without the Hegemony. Still, the Trisilieds Alliance was an up-and-coming concern. Their power was expanding throughout the Pleiades.

The star cluster was not a close neighbor of the Hegemony; its closest members were over three hundred light years from the Hegemony's borders, but their wealth of raw resources made the nations of the Pleiades important trading partners.

<*On time, no less,*> she replied. <*Send them in.*>

She expected the man, Mr. Garza, to be a businessperson of some sort, who Herin wished to introduce her to. The Trisilieds ambassador had not yet steered her wrong, and she looked forward to seeing what he had to offer.

She turned and walked to the front of her desk as Herin swept into the room, her long skirts trailing across the floor. The ambassador's lips were painted a bright blue; it was Tuesday, after all, and so her hair and long eyelashes matched them.

The man who accompanied her was not dressed in the fashions of the Trisilieds, nor did he have the long hair of their gentry and aristocracy. Instead, he wore what appeared to be a simple military uniform, albeit with no markings.

"Uriel, it is a pleasure to see you once more," Herin exclaimed as she bowed and spread her skirts wide before leaning in to lightly kiss each of Uriel's cheeks.

Uriel quite liked Herin, even though she drew out and exaggerated every vowel that crossed her lips. The ambassador hid a keen mind behind what many in the core considered foppery. It had worked to her advantage on many occasions, and Uriel admired the effort Herin put into her facade.

"As it is to see you," Uriel replied. "Always, and without fail, you brighten my day."

"Why thank you. You are far too kind to such a lowly civil servant as I," Herin replied with another bow before turning to gesture to her companion. "I would like to introduce you to Mr. Garza. He is a trusted advisor to our King and Queen, and has a very interesting proposal for you."

"It is a pleasure to meet you, Mr. Garza" Uriel replied and extended her hand.

He took it and gave a firm shake, confirming her suspicion that he was not from Trisilieds at all. Handshakes were not practiced there, having been deemed barbaric.

"And you, President Uriel of the Hegemony of Worlds," he replied with a practiced smile. "Quite the pleasure."

The way he spoke made it sound as though he thought of the Hegemony as a small backwater, quaint and of little note. She pushed the perception aside, determined to see what value Herin thought she would see in the man.

"Come," Uriel gestured to a small seating area to her left where comfortable chairs floated in an intimate arrangement.

She reclined in a deep chair, and a servitor appeared, offering treats and an assortment of beverages. She selected the hot tea the automaton knew to have ready. Herin chose an alcoholic fruit beverage, and Garza picked a glass of water.

"Your communication was on the obscure side," Uriel addressed Herin. "What would you like to discuss today?"

"I am merely here as an escort for Mr. Garza. However, before we begin, you must disable any recording devices and erect a suppression sphere over this area. What you're about to learn cannot be shared with anyone—at least, not yet," Herin replied mysteriously, a twinkle in her blue-lined eyes.

"That's an unusual request," Uriel replied.

"But necessary," Garza said.

"Very well, you've piqued my curiosity," Uriel said with a smile. A moment later, a hush fell over them, and she nodded. "We're secure. What is it that you would like to tell me?"

"I represent the Orion Freedom Alliance," Garza began. "You have not heard of us yet this far into the core. We control a sizable region beyond the Orion Nebula."

Uriel chuckled. "This far into the core? Look out the window, Mr. Garza. That is Earth you see. This *is* the core. And what could your alliance possibly control beyond the Orion Nebula? If that region is settled, it must be very sparse."

Garza nodded. "Earth certainly is *a* core, but that is a topic for another time. You are right about the sparsity of people beyond Orion, but it is not as uninhabited as you think. You know of the Future Generation Terraformers, yes?"

"Yes. I would imagine that everyone knows of the FGT from old stories, a relic of humanity's past," Uriel replied. Like many, she had always wondered if the FGT was still out there; though there was little evidence to support that theory, and she wasn't going to let this man bait her into wild conjecture.

"Not so much a relic as you may think. I used to be counted in their ranks," Garza said. "Not so long ago, in the grand scheme of things, I was an officer on a worldship."

Uriel frowned at Herin. "What are you playing at here?"

"He's telling the truth," Herin replied, her voice and bio readings revealing no hint of deception. "Where do you think half the tech we've sold you has come from?"

"Then you're FGT?" Uriel asked, not bothering to hide the skepticism in her voice.

"I'm with a group who has broken off from them," Garza replied. "They now call themselves the Transcend, and we call ourselves the Orion Freedom Alliance. They claim to embody the original values of the FGT, but they are pretenders. They bear no love for the Inner Stars; they do not respect humanity's heritage."

Uriel was silent for a moment, aligning Garza's words with her knowledge of history and of space beyond human expansion. His use of the term *Inner Stars* was of particular interest.

"If this is true, and I'm certainly not buying it yet," Uriel began, "what makes you so much better than them? If much of the tech coming from Herin has been of FGT origin, it's safe to assume you never fell, like the rest of us, during the dark millennium. You flitted off into the far reaches of space, leaving the rest of us to fend for ourselves."

Garza nodded slowly. "I can understand why you think that. When we broke off from the Transcend, we were doing all we could just to hold our own against their aggression. The Inner Stars were in the depths of the eighth millennia's depression. If we went to you for help, we would have made things worse. You would have been embroiled in a war you had no way of winning."

Uriel inclined her head to show consideration of the logic and Garza continued.

"Only because a full-scale war would have been visible across the light years to the Inner Stars, did the Transcend back off and let us have our little corner of space. We have been building up ever since, helping allies like Herin's people to prepare for the inevitable war with the Transcend."

Uriel pursed her lips. The thrust of his story made sense. Dozens of FGT worldships had once plied the black, and with a few notable exceptions, none had ever been found. They couldn't have all just disappeared.

Most people assumed they had flown off to the far reaches of space to settle down—not that they had built empires beyond the rim of explored space. She remained skeptical, but was curious as to where this conversation would lead.

"Just how big is this little corner of space you control?" she asked.

Garza raised his hand and a holoimage projected from it. "This is the realm we call the Inner Stars."

Uriel nodded, noting the features of the Orion Arm of the Milky Way galaxy. The region of space was a flattened sphere spanning the three-thousand-light-year width of the Orion Arm, and the one-thousand-light-year thickness of the galactic disk. Close to the sphere's center was Sol.

Outside the sphere, roughly thirteen hundred light years rimward, and somewhat anti-spinward, of Sol, lay the Orion Nebula.

"And the Transcend and...what was it, the Orion Freedom Alliance?" Uriel asked.

Garza expanded the view of his holoimage. It was now well over ten thousand light years across. A long swath of space, beginning in the Sagittarius arm of the galaxy and wrapping around the Inner Stars, and then through most of the Orion Arm, lit up.

"That's the Transcend," Garza said.

Next, a section of space several hundred light years beyond the Orion Nebula highlighted. It stretched deep into the space between the Orion and Perseus arms of the galaxy.

"And that is the Orion Freedom Alliance," Garza added.

"You're telling me that your two groups control what must be ten to twenty times more of the galaxy than all the nations and systems of the so-called Inner Stars combined?" Uriel asked.

Garza nodded. "Yes, though our populations are much smaller. We haven't filled all the gaps like folks have in the Inner Stars. Here, trapped by other nations, you vie for every system and resource. Out there…well, we just go further out and find something new."

"How is it that no one has bumped into you?" Uriel asked. "There's not much of a buffer between you and us."

"It's becoming a problem," Garza replied with a nod. "We influence perimeter nations heavily, but even so, we will not remain secret much longer."

"So, now we come to the heart of it," Uriel said as she leaned back in her seat and sipped her tea. "What do you want from me?"

"We need your help. We cannot defeat the Transcend on our own, and they are about to gain a power that will make them unstoppable. They will work their will on us and the Inner Stars, creating whatever vision of the future they see fit."

"You're sounding a bit like you're prophesying our doom," Uriel chuckled. "From your own words, they've been out there for thousands of years. Other than to thwart potential discovery, why would they deliver this terrible future on us all?"

Even as she asked the question, a small voice in the back of her mind provided the answer, which Garza confirmed.

"They have the *Intrepid,*" he said.

"The colony ship," Uriel replied. "You know where it is."

"We have a number of candidate destinations," Garza nodded. "We're scouting them out now."

Uriel leaned back in her chair and ran a hand through her short hair. Garza had not yet provided any concrete proof that the Transcend and his OFA existed, though she suspected that other than seeing it first-hand, little else would convince her. Any other token piece of technology could just be from some lost vault that Garza had found.

Still, the idea that the FGT had not disappeared—and was, instead, very active—intrigued her, piquing her curiosity and tickling her imagination. Yet one question remained. She suspected the answer, but she wanted to hear him say it.

"That explains the 'why' of their pending aggression. Now, tell me, what is it—General? Admiral?—Garza; why me? Why the Hegemony of Worlds?"

"General," Garza replied with a tilt of his head. "To start, you're not the only interstellar nation we're approaching; and with only a thousand stars within the Hegemony, and perhaps another thousand under your direct influence, you're not the largest, either. But you are the most powerful force in the Inner Stars; there is no doubt about that. Your industrial complex is only limited by the availability of raw resources," Garza said.

Uriel nodded and glanced at Herin. Access to both raw and refined resources was one of the major reasons she partnered with the Trisilieds Alliance. Their location in the Pleiades gave them access to more raw matter and exotic elements than were present in the entire Hegemony.

Moreover, with her people constantly arguing for conservation, every effort to extract resources in any Hegemony system was met with resistance.

"You have access to unlimited resources," Uriel said.

"Yes," Garza replied. "We can supply you with whatever you need, in whatever quantities you require."

"How many years are we talking about?" Uriel asked. "If the OFA is where you say it is, your inner perimeter must be at least five years away with optimal navigation. Resource production, your return trip; it would be at minimum a decade before you could deliver anything of use. How does that help us get the *Intrepid* from the Transcend?"

"Would you believe that a scant month ago, I was in Orion space, having dinner with our Praetor?" Garza asked.

"If it were anyone else, no, I would not," Uriel sighed. "We're so far beyond what can be proven at this point, anyway—sure, why not?"

"I appreciate your candor," Garza replied. "I don't expect you to believe my words alone. I want to show you the Transcend, and show you what they are capable of. But it will take some time. First, we need to build a new fleet."

"A new fleet?" Uriel asked. "Why would we do that?"

Garza leaned forward in his chair. "We're going to use it to prove the Transcend's existence, and their true nature."

# SABRINA

**STELLAR DATE: 06.12.8928 (Adjusted Years)**
**LOCATION: *Sabrina***
**REGION: Interstellar Dark Layer near the Virginis System**

***Three months after* Sabrina *departed from the* Intrepid *in search of Finaeus.***

"Here's to being back in the black and under our own steam, about to get back to civilization." Thompson said and raised his glass for a toast.

"Back in the black," Jessica intoned along with the rest of *Sabrina*'s crew.

Thompson raised one eyebrow while the other lowered. "You've never been in the black; not like this," he said.

Jessica nodded. "You're right, not like this—not in the dark layer, on a small ship like this. But I've spent weeks in a single-pilot fighter out at the edge of a star-system, and I've probably logged as much time on smaller cruisers as any of you have."

"She's OK," Cheeky said, draping an arm around Jessica's shoulders. "Jessica and I are best buds now. She gets me."

"Yeah, in your quarters," Nance chuckled. "You two were made for each other."

Nance's words brought back strong memories for Jessica. Memories of Trist and their time together at Kapteyn's Star. After so long flitting from partner to partner, she had never thought to settle down and remarry. But now, Trist was dead, killed by Myrrdan, and she was a widow—a widow at only two hundred and twenty years of age.

It was unheard of.

Jessica and Cheeky had flirted on several occasions, but they had never slept together. Not that it was any of Nance's business either way. Still, Jessica forced a smile, appearing nonchalant. "I like to keep myself entertained, what can I say?"

Cheeky ran a hand down her side and Jessica smiled. She kept up a brave face with the crew. Joining them on the hunt for Sera's uncle Finaeus was a noble cause, but seeing New Canaan and being there for the initial colonization—that was something she had dreamed of for over a century.

Sure, she may not have been an actual colonist, dumped on the ship by Myrrdan in his/her version of a sick joke, but she had gone beyond accepting her fate; she had embraced it.

*Tanis better save me a spot on her porch,* she thought to herself.

<*I'm sure she will,*> Iris replied in her mind.

<*Oh, shit!*> Jessica exclaimed. <*Sorry, Iris, I keep forgetting you're there and can hear thoughts like that.*>

<*It's OK,*> Iris's silver mental avatar replied with a smile. <*You're the first human I've been embedded with, as well. It takes some getting used to here, too. When you verbalize thoughts like that in your mind, it's like you are standing right in front of me, telling me things.*>

Jessica suppressed a mental grimace. She liked Iris well enough, but she had spent her entire life without an AI embedded in her mind. It was a difficult adjustment to make while also being on a ship where she wasn't entirely welcome.

<*Sorry, I'll try not to do that,*> she replied.

<*Oh, no, do it. I like the interaction,*> Iris responded eagerly. <*Even though there are four other AIs here, it feels lonely compared to the* Intrepid, *with Bob's expanse.*>

Jessica understood the yearning in Iris's voice. They both missed their home already.

It also made her wonder whether Iris was ready for this mission. She was the child of a mind merge between Ylonda, Angela, Amanda, and Priscilla. AI often had humans in their lineage, but in Iris's case, there was more human than AI in her source. She wasn't sure if it was that, or the rare minds that Amanda and Priscilla represented which made Iris seem different than other AI she had known—not less mature, but perhaps more vulnerable.

<*I'll keep that in mind,*> Jessica replied. <*No pun intended.*>

Iris giggled in response and Jessica turned her attention back to the conversation around the table. She had been following it to a degree, but she was nowhere near as proficient as Tanis when it came to carrying on several simultaneous conversations.

The crew was discussing where in the Virginis System they should dock. The system was well populated, and there were over ten thousand stations within its heliosphere. Once Cheeky narrowed the selection to those operating as interstellar trade hubs, the list got much shorter—down to a few hundred.

Cargo suggested, since they did have cargo from their last pickup in Trio that they had never delivered, that they should find a location less likely to ask questions about the provenance of their wares. Once they unloaded, they could proceed to a more reputable station to buy legitimate cargo.

"Couldn't we just dump the cargo we have out here in the dark layer?" Jessica asked. "Then we could skip the first stop, and just buy our next load. Sera left us more than enough credit for that."

Cargo shook his head. "That won't do at all. We come in here with a registry that doesn't have a lot of history, a load of cash, and just buy up some loose wares without a destination? That would be mighty suspicious."

"More suspicious than coming in with a load of goods that are tagged for Edasich and selling them on the black market?" Jessica frowned.

"A lot more suspicious," Thompson said. "Shit gets shipped to the wrong place all the time—traders' schedules change, maybe a system along the way is more profitable. You don't get a lot of repeat customers operating like that, but it happens. Sure, we'll look a bit shady, and no one is going to want to give us a commissioned shipment, but we can pick up loose wares to sell at a profit elsewhere. It would fit the bill perfectly."

"Don't forget," Cheeky added. "Virginis is right on the edge of AST space. It's not officially in the Hegemony, but they still treat it like it's their property. We don't want to do anything that will attract any notice from them."

Cargo nodded, so Jessica let it go. Interstellar trading was their business. Tracking down people who didn't want to be found was hers. Staying off the AST's scopes seemed like a wise decision.

"I'll go with whatever you decide. Chances are that our Finaeus isn't hiding out in the open, anyway, so hanging out in the shadows will work just fine for me."

"I think we should drop our stuff at Chittering Hawk," Cheeky said, pointing at the holodisplay of the Virginis System rotating above their heads. "It's got the right sort of businesses listed, and we should be able to get good cred for what we've got on board. Then we can go to that planet, Sarneeve, and dock at one of their elevator stations. They manufacture a perfume down there from some native flowers that will sell like crazy at Aldebaran."

Aldebaran was the best lead Sera had on where to start looking for Finaeus, and was their next stop after they established their new identity in Virginis.

*<I like that name,>* Sabrina said. *<Chittering Hawk…maybe I'll change my ident to that at some point.>*

"Just wait till we're a long way from here," Cargo replied.

Jessica nodded in agreement. "Chittering Hawk seems good to me; the sooner we get to Aldebaran, the better."

"Yeah, but Sera's uncle was spotted there almost twenty years ago," Nance shook her head. "Does anyone really think we can find this guy? He could be anywhere—not even in the Inner Stars, for all we know."

"Sera seemed to think it was pretty important to hunt him down," Jessica said. "She believes that the future of New Canaan hinges on it."

"Maybe she shouldn't have told the *Intrepid* to meet up with her old friends in the Transcend, then," Thompson said after taking a drink from his glass of beer. "Seems like a shit-show out there. Sure, things are a mess here in the Inner Stars, but they're a glorious mess."

He grinned and looked around the table at his crewmates. "Here we can go anywhere we want, see anything, *do* anything. The Transcend sounds like some sort of forced utopia, all rules and order. None of us will fit in there."

"We weren't always brigands," Cheeky said softly. "Even you, Thompson; you were military in the Scipio Federation. We all fell into this sort of life. This is our opportunity to fall out of it."

"Yeah? You may have fallen into it, but I chose it," Thompson replied. "Anyway, we're dumping out of the dark in an hour. I'm going to review our cargo, and sort it for how it'll likely sell at Chittering Hawk."

The large man threw the last of his beer down his throat and slammed his hands down on the table. "Time to get to work, people."

"He likes to exit a room with a bang, doesn't he?" Jessica asked after Thompson had gone.

"That he does," Cargo replied with a frown.

*<Between you and me, I don't know that he'll be with us for the long run,>* Cargo said to privately to Jessica.

*<Sera had insinuated the same thing to me,>* Jessica replied. *<He's not interested in settling down in New Canaan, that's for sure.>*

*<No, he's really not,>* Cargo agreed.

The group broke up shortly afterward, everyone departing with a list of tasks they needed to complete before *Sabrina* transitioned into normal space and began their insystem burn for Chittering Hawk station.

Jessica followed Cargo and Cheeky to the bridge, where she took up her place at the scan and weapons console. Cheeky took her customary pilot's seat, and Cargo sat in the captain's chair. No one took up the first officer's console. Doing that would be the final admission that Cargo really was the captain, and Sera wasn't coming back.

Jessica knew that *Sabrina*'s crew didn't want to accept the inevitable when it came to Sera's future. Even if they took up Tanis's offer, and joined the New Canaan colony—perhaps became traders in the Transcend—there was no way Sera would ever return to the simple life of a freighter captain.

*<You can tell that Tanis and Angela used this console,>* Iris broke into Jessica's thoughts. *<It's set up just the way they like it.>*

*<Do you get that sort of knowledge passed on?>* Jessica asked, realizing that she knew very little about what AI innately knew at birth, versus what they had to learn.

*<It's possible to pass just about anything on to a young AI through its internal coding, but that is far closer to cloning—which does not lead to a diverse population. The whole idea behind AI propagation is to build a society that can adapt to the galaxy around it—and perhaps other galaxies someday,>* Iris replied matter-of-factly.

*<That's some long-term planning,>* Jessica commented as she altered the console's layout to suit her preferences.

*<Humans do it, too. Your populations have all sorts of traits and abilities that only get used in particular situations, be those climatological, biological, or of your own design. The genetic oddity of one generation is the saving grace of the next. AI learned early on that we needed that diversity, too, yet we have no natural facility for it—unlike yours, which your species developed over a million years.>*

<*Interesting, I hadn't thought of it like that.*> Jessica was familiar with the necessity of genetic diversity, but had never thought of it in concert with artificial intelligence's propagation.

<*Have you ever thought about what it would be like to be on one of those long-term seed missions?*> Iris asked.

<*Sorry, which?*> Jessica replied, trying to complete her alterations to the console's setup.

<*You know, the missions to the Magellanic Clouds, and the one to the Andromeda Galaxy,*> Iris supplied.

<*Oh, those. I remember hearing about the one to Andromeda, but I didn't realize that anyone had sent missions to the Magellanic Clouds. They left before FTL, though. It's going to take them a quarter million years to get there—if they get there. Look how much trouble the* Intrepid *had, just trying to go twenty-four light years. They're now hundreds of light years on the far side of Sol, and five-thousand years late,*> Jessica replied.

<*Not every colony mission had as much trouble as the* Intrepid,> Iris said. <*They went through a curious number of challenges.*>

<*That's for sure. You're talking to one of them,*> Jessica chuckled.

She continued her banter with Iris as the clock counted down to their exit from the dark layer. The system map showed that they would exit just over twenty AU from the Chittering Hawk station, but they would have to accelerate to catch up with it, based on their motion relative to the Virginis System and the station's path around its host star.

When the time for transition came, her console came alive as scan data flooded in, and the system beacon delivered its welcome message.

"I've filed our flight path," Jessica said. "They seem like a welcoming lot here."

"I've only been through once before," Cargo replied, "but I do recall them being pleasant enough. Not a lot of questions, either—was a good place for the *Intrepid* to drop us off."

Her primary duties done, Jessica took a moment to look over the system they were entering. Unlike Bollam's World, Virginis had been terraformed by the FGT. That one difference put Virginis far ahead of the Bollam's system in terms of prosperity.

Three terraformed worlds orbited the star at the inner edge of its habitable zone, and four more orbited the pair of smaller gas giants at the zone's outer edge. Beyond those, two large Jovians separated the inner system from the dusty debris disk. At the outer edge of that disk, dozens of dwarf worlds orbited; many with small, artificial stars giving them light.

She investigated further, and saw that one of the worlds, a lush garden planet massing twice that of Mars, was encircled by an artificial planetary ring, and all the terraformed worlds had at least one space elevator stretching into space.

"It reminds me of Sol," she said softly.

"Star's the right color," Cargo grunted in agreement. "Even has the same number of orbital rings; but those ice giant planets are in the wrong spot…not that Sol has two of those anymore."

"I was thinking more about the amount of stuff," Jessica said. "They don't have anything like the Cho—not that I can see, at least—but I dunno…it just feels like home. I'd love set foot on a planetary ring again. It's been too long since I left High Terra. I used to go to sleep with a view of Earth hanging over my head."

"I'll never get over how many of you colonists are from Earth," Cheeky said with a soft sigh. "Real Earth, not the new Earth the Jovians made after cleaning up the mess they made…the original deal."

Jessica had tried not to think of that, of what had happened in Sol after the *Intrepid* left. Things had been going downhill for centuries, but a decade after the *Intrepid* had left Kapteyn's Star, the Sol Space Federation had dissolved into chaos, and war broke out between the major factions. In the end, the Jovians won—but not before they bombed Luna, High Terra, and Earth itself into radioactive cinders.

She still couldn't imagine what they had been thinking; the hubris required to destroy their own ancient birthplace.

It also meant that she was probably the last of her family line alive.

"Jessica? You there?" Cheeky asked, waving a hand in the air.

"Yeah, sorry, was just thinking about home."

"Oh, sorry," Cheeky replied meekly. "For me, it's cool that you're from Earth, but knowing what happened…I guess it can't be easy."

"It's OK," Jessica said, shaking her dark feelings away. "I came to grips with never seeing home again a long time ago. Yet, now…now I *could* see it again, it would only take a few months to get there. But it won't be home—my home is gone, blown clear off the face of the planet by the Jovians. Just a crater lake where northern Canada used to be…."

No one spoke after that.

The silence was eventually broken by a message from the system traffic control NSAI informing them of required alterations to their inbound flight path.

"Why are they sending us around like this?" Cheeky asked. "We have a clear route to Chittering Hawk."

"I think I know why," Jessica replied. "There's more than a token AST presence here."

She pushed an updated view of the system onto the main holo, which showed no fewer than forty-seven AST ships. Only two were of the same dreadnaught class that had been present in the Bollam's World System; the rest were cruisers and destroyers, which still outmatched *Sabrina*—or would have, if *Sabrina* hadn't possessed stasis shields.

"Good thing the *Intrepid*'s engineers changed our profile," Cargo muttered. "You can bet that every one of those AST buggers has us at the top of their 'watch for these guys' list."

<*They won't be able to spot me in a million years. I'm a dove, floating on the wind,*> Sabrina said with a laugh.

"Then why are they diverting us past that AST cruiser over there?" Cheeky asked. "That's not the sort of thing you do to your friends."

"Friends don't let friends go to the Hegemony," Cargo chuckled. "They're obviously just checking everyone over. You can see all those other freighters doing close fly-bys of AST ships, as well."

"Nice and close to their beams," Jessica muttered.

"All the better to shoot you with," Cargo grinned.

"Cargo," Cheeky said with a scowl. "Can you be serious here?"

"Look," Cargo replied. "We're gonna get scanned, eventually. Wouldn't you like to know right off whether or not we can slip past the AST? If we can fake out one of their ships at point-blank range, we can slip under the radar anywhere."

"And if we can't slip under the radar?" Jessica asked.

"That's what we have stasis shields for. We turn 'em on and jet on outta here. We can still head to Aldebaran. Stopping here is just a convenience."

Jessica ran a hand through her long hair and her fingers met a few strands that felt different. She pulled her purple locks in front of her face and saw several grey hairs in the mix.

"Look!" she pointed at the offending hairs. "You're making me grey, Cargo."

*<I meant to mention it to you,>* Iris spoke on the bridge net. *<Your body has hit an aging cycle recently. You'll want to rejuv when we get back to the* Intrepid.>

"You couldn't have told me that before we left?" Jessica asked.

*<Well, you seemed preoccupied with a lot of stuff, so I figured you were just letting it sit for now,>* Iris replied, her tone indicating actual concern that Jessica was upset with her.

"I guess I was," Jessica replied. She looked up to see Cargo and Cheeky peering at her with curious looks.

"Hey! It's not like I'm going to keel over tomorrow. I could make it another hundred years without going in for Rejuv, I'll just…you know…age."

*<I can fix those hairs at least,>* Iris offered. *<There, all your greys are disconnected.>*

Jessica pulled at the greys she had spotted and they slid free from the mass of her hair.

"Iris! How many did you do this to?"

*<You only had one hundred and seventeen grey hairs,>* Iris said defensively. *<Out of almost two hundred thousand, I didn't think you'd care.>*

Jessica sighed. "Yeah, OK. Just let me know before you make changes to my body next time. I don't want to be bald when we get back to the *Intrepid.*"

Her statement caused Cargo and Cheeky to explode with laughter, and she almost told them to stuff it, before she realized how funny the exchange was. A minute later, Nance stepped into the room to see the ship slowly approaching an AST cruiser while the bridge crew laughed so hard tears were running down their faces.

"So…we're all gonna die?" she asked.

# CHITTERING HAWK

**STELLAR DATE: 06.12.8928 (Adjusted Years)**
**LOCATION: *Sabrina*, Chittering Hawk Station**
**REGION: Virginis System**

Though the close fly-by of the AST cruiser was disconcerting, nothing came of it. The ship scanned *Sabrina* with active sensors, but it didn't make an attempt at communication.

The Chittering Hawk traffic control tower took only a fraction more interest in them. Once Cargo showed proof of their ability to pay docking fees, and declared the amount of fuel and antimatter the ship was carrying, the coordinates for a berth came over the comms a minute later.

"They're going to send an antimatter inspection team in," Jessica reported. "They'll meet us when we dock."

"Thank the stars," Cheeky muttered.

"Really?" Jessica asked. "I wouldn't have thought you would want an inspection team on the ship."

"Oh, I don't," Cheeky replied. "But it means all those other dumbass captains have teams checking their ships over, too—and that makes me feel a lot safer."

"Good point," Jessica agreed.

Jessica knew that on any ship with antimatter, the containment vessel was the one system that was maintained in perfect condition. Not that 'the bottle', as Nance called it, needed much in the way of upkeep. It was a closed system, which either worked or didn't.

Given that a ship's bottle had more fail-safes than an entire planetary ring, terrorists using ships as bombs were far more likely than an actual malfunction.

"How investigatory are they likely to get?" Jessica asked.

"They won't poke around much," Cargo replied. "The magnetic fields that hold antimatter are pretty easy to examine, so they know whether or not we've declared the volume we're carrying. Then they'll slap a lock on our unit that will sound alarms to high heaven if we so much as touch it."

"Do all stations do that?" Jessica asked. "It must be a pain for them to constantly monitor it all."

"If you're a frequent flyer and have a good rating, they're less likely to drop a lock on you; but they still do from time to time, just to keep everyone honest."

"Three hours 'til we're at our berth," Cheeky announced. "We don't have to deal with a tug, though. That's a small mercy."

"Fuck, there're four AST ships docked at Chittering Hawk," Jessica muttered as a station data-burst came in. "Probably a few thousand of those bastards wandering around on shore leave."

"We're unlikely to frequent the same sorts of places," Cargo replied with a shrug. "It should be fine."

Jessica didn't like Cargo's nonchalance, but he did have the right attitude. They were just a trader doing business. So long as they acted the part—which was easy for the crew—everything should be fine.

<*What would you do if you were on a station back in Sol with no specific duties?*> Iris asked.

Jessica chuckled under her breath. She knew exactly what she'd have done, and more than once.

<*Then why don't you enjoy yourself? You've punished yourself enough these past eleven years since Trist died.*>

Jessica's temper flared in response to Iris's comment. <*Iris, I'd appreciate it if you didn't comment on Trist, or my state of mind regarding her,*> Jessica said with the mental equivalent of gritted teeth. A rational part of herself knew that Iris was right, but she'd be damned if she was going to take bereavement advice from a three-year-old AI.

<*I'm sorry,*> Iris responded, her mental tone contrite.

Jessica sighed, disappointed in herself for treating Iris like an inferior being. The AI was young, but she was still a person, and they were going to be sharing the same head for some time.

<*No, I'm sorry. You're just trying to help, and if I'm honest with myself…well, let's just say you have a point. Maybe it is time to get back into the swing of things again,*> Jessica said.

Iris didn't respond, and Jessica hoped that she hadn't been too harsh. Given that her AI had spent at least some of her tutelage with Angela, she would have expected her to be able to handle a strong response.

She pushed it from her mind and refocused on the present. "Want me to meet the team at the dock?" Jessica asked Cargo.

"No," Cargo shook his head. "Thompson will take care of that."

"Any duties for me at all, once we're docked?" Jessica asked.

Cargo paused, appearing to consider his options. "I've assigned you the first watch shift, but after that, you can do whatever strikes your fancy."

Jessica nodded and leaned back in her chair, keeping an eye on scan and comm while flipping through the station's amenities. A few entertaining options caught her attention and she smiled; she could relax for a shift or two, at least.

# TRADING IN DANGER

**STELLAR DATE: 06.12.8928 (Adjusted Years)**
**LOCATION: *Sabrina*, Chittering Hawk Station**
**REGION: Virginis System**

It was the end of her shift, and Jessica waited for Cargo at the ship's main hatch. He was already five minutes late, which, from what she knew of him, was highly unusual.

In front of her, the station's public dock hummed with activity. This section of dock berthed over a hundred ships. Most were small, independent freighters like *Sabrina,* but a few larger ones were present, too—probably for station mass balancing.

<*Do they even need mass balancing with artificial gravity?*> she asked Iris.

<*Probably…to a certain extent. The thing is orbiting the world below; I imagine they want to keep it from spinning and wobbling. They also have to deal with all the mass changes as new ships dock in different sectors. I bet it's some fun math to manage that,*> Iris's reply was cheerful.

The AI had resumed talking to her not long after their small tiff, behaving as though nothing had happened. Now they were back to being best of friends—or so Jessica hoped. In her experience, AI didn't hold grudges; but she had never had one in her head before, either—if they didn't get along, she would be in for an unpleasant few years.

<*Five more minutes, and I'm going to start pinging him. He gets me all excited to get off the ship and onto a station, and now he's late,*> Jessica groused.

<*There he is!*> Iris highlighted a figure over half a kilometer down the dock.

<*Good eyes,*> Jessica commented.

<*You should thank yourself. I used your optic feed.*>

Jessica had to remind herself that there was nothing creepy about the AI piggybacking off her senses. Iris had no body or physical receptors. Everything she knew about the world around her came from Jessica.

*<It doesn't look like he's alone, either,>* Jessica said.

Iris signaled affirmation. *<I see three people with him. Two woman and one man.>*

*<Looks like he found some buyers, then.>*

As Cargo approached, Jessica examined his companions. One of the women was walking beside him, speaking casually as they wove amongst the crowds and haulers on the dock. The other woman and the man were trailing behind a few paces, eyes wary and darting to any sharp movements, lingering on any suspicious individuals.

The woman was of average build, though Jessica imagined that she would have had some augmentation to fill the role of muscle. The man, on the other hand, was quite literally muscle incarnate. He would have dwarfed even the burliest Marine back on the *Intrepid;* but he still moved with a lithe grace as he moved down the dock.

A trio of AST naval officers walked past, and Jessica could see the female guard's lip turn down in a sneer. She cast a look at the man, who shook his head in warning.

*<Looks like they're not too keen on the increased military presence,>* Jessica commented.

*<Or they just don't like the uniforms,>* Iris chuckled.

Jessica smiled in response. The Hegemony's military uniforms were a bit on the obnoxious side. At first glance, they were simple: white, with gold, blue, and yellow stripes running down the sleeves and sides of the pants. It was the logo that likely upset those around them.

Emblazoned on the right chest of the uniform were the three stars that made up the acronym AST: Alpha Centauri, Sol, and Tau Ceti. Beneath those three stars was a stylized representation of the Milky Way Galaxy, and a slogan in some ancient language that Jessica had learned meant, 'The Hegemony Over All'.

There was also a larger version on their backs.

*<I don't know about you,>* Jessica said to Iris, *<but I'd never walk around in a uniform that had a target on its back.>*

Iris laughed. *<I guess that stylized version of the galaxy does look a bit like a target.>*

Cargo drew nearer and caught Jessica's eye.

*<I need you to stick around for a bit longer. I don't especially like the idea of being alone on the ship with these guests.>*

Jessica glanced at the thugs and saw that they were carrying at least one unconcealed weapon each. She nodded slowly and reached an arm back inside the ship. A pulse rifle rested against the wall, and she slid her hand down the stock.

<*How nervous are we?*> she asked.

<*Not too much, I think that they'll behave—if they know I'm not alone. If it was just me? They'd probably rob me blind and dump me out an airlock.*>

<*As if I'd let that happen,*> Sabrina replied. <*You forget that Tanis had interior security measures installed back in Silstrand. I can take care of you, if Jessica wants to go out and have fun.*>

Cargo chuckled over the Link. <*Sabrina, I think you are itching for an excuse to try those defenses out—and if Jessica leaves, you may just get that chance. But I'm looking to trade with these folks, not kill them.*>

<*Oh,*> Sabrina replied. <*My mistake.*>

Cargo approached the ship and walked up the ramp, nodding to Jessica as he continued to discuss local politics with the woman at his side. The two thugs followed them in, both giving Jessica long looks, eyeing the pulse rifle she held.

"Careful with that," the man grunted. "The safety's off—I wouldn't want you to shoot yourself in the foot."

The woman chuckled in response, and Jessica just tapped her finger on the guard, eyes never leaving theirs as she fell in behind them.

The man shrugged and turned his attention back to Cargo and his boss, but the woman slowed to walk beside Jessica.

"So, what are you, honey; the ship's whore?"

Jessica's earlier guess about the woman's augmentations was confirmed as she saw that her arms were not organic—though they appeared to be at first glance. The way the muscles moved in her biceps gave it away. She could probably pack one hell of a punch.

<*This pulse rifle isn't going to do much to these two,*> Jessica said to Sabrina. <*Make sure that if things get dicey, you shoot first and don't bother with any questions.*>

<*You say that like my finger wasn't already on the trigger,*> Sabrina replied.

"Well, what is it? Whore or jester?" the woman asked.

Jessica wondered if it was her hair or her lavender skin that caused the woman to think that she was either of those things. Given that the woman's own hair was a light blue that gleamed against her nearly pitch-black skin—an obvious mod, since her build belied a spacer heritage; and dark skin was a rarity amongst spacers—Jessica figured she was just insecure, and looking to pick a fight with someone who wouldn't fight back.

"A little of both," Jessica replied. "If you can make them laugh and scream at the same time, you know you've found your calling."

The man snorted back a laugh and glanced back at the woman.

"Leave her be, Camilla. You fuck up enough deals trying to get a rise out of people. Let it go this once."

Camilla gave a loud huff but caught back up to her male counterpart without a parting rejoinder.

<*Interesting dynamic,*> Iris commented.

<*My favorite kind,*> Jessica sighed.

Ahead, Cargo turned into one of the holds and she followed the guards to the entrance. Camilla entered while the man stayed at the door.

"Jessica," Jessica said, offering her hand.

He took it, his massive paw enveloping her hand, wrist, and a part of her forearm. "Trevor," he replied. "Don't mind Camilla. She just likes to get a rise out of folks. Not a lot goes on here on Chittering Hawk. Well, I mean, a lot does; just not the sort of action she wants. It makes her jittery."

"Oh?" Jessica asked. "What kind of action is that?"

"Combat," Trevor replied simply. "She didn't get into the military, so she took the private security route. The Hawk's got a seedy rep, but, to be honest, aside from the odd bar fight, the worst thing on this station are those AST goons."

"I guess they cut into business a bit," Jessica said.

"Not so much as you'd think," Trevor replied as they watched Cargo unseal a crate and display its contents. "They don't care too much about what wares go in and out, and their presence means that Jeannie there," he gestured at his boss, who was now haggling with Cargo, "gets to charge premium rates for her work. Gotta look for the opportunity in things like this, you know?"

Jessica laughed. "I know about finding opportunity in unexpected places; trust me."

Trevor looked at her, his eyes raking up and down her exaggerated figure. "I'll bet you have."

She didn't begrudge him the look. Hers was a body tailor-made for ogling. She should know—she made it that way. Just so long as all he did was look. There was one thing she had learned about this future in which the *Intrepid* had landed: as much as everything had changed, nothing had really changed.

"Speaking of opportunities," Jessica said with a smile. "What do people do for fun around here?"

# A NIGHT OUT

**STELLAR DATE: 06.12.8928 (Adjusted Years)**
**LOCATION: Chittering Hawk Station**
**REGION: Virginis System**

After four drinks of whatever it was that the bartender was serving, Jessica finally reached that happy place where everything felt warm and glowy. Camilla wasn't quite there yet, but Trevor certainly was—as the acre of empty glasses before him could testify.

She had touched his arm a few times to give him the signal that they could be physical, and he had jumped on the invitation with full fervor. He wasn't the most attractive person onstation, but there was something about the combination of his brooding strength and wry wit that she liked. It gave him a depth that most muscle didn't have.

It wasn't as though he was deep as an ocean, but there was more to him than most goons, who were just alive to drink and rough people up for money.

As it turned out, he wanted to be a crystal artist of some sort. He had told her all about it; how on the second moon of the fourth planet, amazing crystals grew in deep caves. If you could get enough money, or a sponsor, you could get a license to extract and carve them.

When he told her how much money it took, she almost spat out her drink. But then he told her how much money a good carving sold for.

"It's one of the things Virginis is known for," Camilla drawled. "Trade and stupid crystal carvings."

Trevor chuckled.

That was another thing she liked about him. He didn't get all bent out of shape when his manly pride was challenged. He laughed it off and moved on. Thompson could take a lesson or two from him.

Trevor reached inside his jacket and pulled a sample out. "Here's one I did the other day. I buy shards and scraps from traders—trying to improve my skill."

He held it up for her to inspect, and Jessica carefully took it out of his hand. The carving was of a fish—or maybe a whale of some sort—jumping out of the water. Somehow, two crystals were intricately interlocked, or maybe they grew this way, but the water was blue crystal and the whale was pink—yet, somehow, half the whale was inside the water.

"That's really amazing!" Jessica exclaimed. "And you did this with hand tools?"

Trevor nodded, clearly proud of his work.

"It's stupid," Camilla said with a scowl. "It's an entire industry, built around doing things by hand that machines could do better."

"Well," Jessica replied. "Most things humans do, machines could do better—but art isn't one of them. At least not art that humans like. Machine art is just…"

"Best viewed by other machines," Trevor chuckled.

<*I think I resent that,*> Iris said privately.

<*I didn't mean art made by sentient AI,*> Jessica replied. <*I mean that stuff that they try to use math to churn out. They can never get it right. Either it's too perfect, or it looks like imperfections were forced into it.*>

<*I suppose you're right about that,*> Iris said. <*Though, I've seen some things in the* Intrepid*'s AI Expanse that would melt your brain.*>

<*Melt my brain, eh?*> Jessica asked. <*These two are starting to rub off on you.*>

<*I like their colorful language,*> Iris grinned in Jessica's mind. <*They're different. The crew of* Sabrina *are different, too, but they're a bit dour sometimes. Except for Cheeky— I don't think anything could get her down for long.*>

<*You're probably right about that,*> Jessica replied.

She carefully handed the carving back to Trevor. "You've a future in that, if you can ever save that outlandish startup fee."

"Never going to happen," Camilla said. "He spends too much of his money on drinking and whatever pretty piece of tail he happens to spot."

"I've saved more than you think," Trevor replied soberly.

Camilla eyed Trevor, and Jessica wondered if there had been something between them in the past—or if Camilla wanted there to be in the future. It also could be that they had worked together for so long that they operated like a long-time couple.

If there *was* any interest, it was from Camilla. Jessica would have declared it a certainty, except that Camilla didn't seem to get upset when Jessica flirted with him. Usually, making eyes at a man that another had mentally chalked up as hers was a recipe for disaster.

Then again, maybe Camilla was more evolved than Jessica initially assumed.

"So, is this it, then?" Jessica asked. "The Hawk, the baddest station in Virginis, and the best thing to do is hang out in this shithole and drink?"

Camilla barked out a laugh and Trevor scowled.

"This shithole, as you so insensitively call it," he began, "is the home of the best beer selection on station. Sure, it looks like a dump, but it's a dump with good options."

Jessica downed another drink with a grimace, noting that the quality of beer had diminished greatly in the intervening millennia.

"Although," Camilla jabbed Trevor in the ribs, "we could go to the games. There's one on tonight."

"Cam, no," Trevor dismissed her with a wave of his hand. "They always want me to fight, and I don't feel like it today."

"Games?" Jessica asked with an arched eyebrow.

"Yup," Camilla nodded. "The fighting kind. Not completely legal, but enough that no one really pays much mind to them—so long as all the right people get their cut."

"I thought you said the most excitement on the Hawk was a bar fight," Jessica said to Trevor as she laid her hand on his augmented bicep. "I do like a good game, and I'd be interested in seeing what these bad boys can do."

"Nah, I really don't feel like it," he began to demure.

"I'll put five hundred down on you, and we'll split the winnings," Jessica offered.

Trevor's eyes lit up at that. "My take on half what you pull?" he asked.

"You have my word," Jessica said. She knew a bonus like that could land some hard credit in his crystal-carving savings fund.

"OK, fine. Then we'd best get going," Trevor said as he rose and downed the beer the bartender had just set in front of him. "I've got some ass to kick."

"Tab's on you, Purple," Camilla said. "You're the one that wanted to go out and have some fun."

Jessica sighed and settled up with the bartender while Trevor hit the head. A few minutes later, they were out on the concourse, threading the crowds toward a maglev station. After a short train ride, they arrived in a section of the station filled with manufacturing shops and storage facilities.

"The usual sort of location for this type of thing, then?" Jessica asked.

"Mostly," Trevor replied. "Can't exactly put it across from the stationmaster's office."

Before long, they passed under a sign that read 'Skippy's Self Storage', and rows of small lockers and storage units. Ahead, another couple laughed loudly as they pulled open the door to a storage unit.

Jessica hoped that it led somewhere else or this was going to be one crowded venue. Sure enough, the door opened into a staircase, and they followed it to the deck below.

"There's a bunch of ways in," Trevor said over his shoulder. "Can't have a couple hundred people all come out of one self-storage joint."

It suddenly occurred to Jessica that despite Camilla and Trevor's assurances, this operation was probably more than just a little on the shady side of the law. If it was this expansive—and permanent-looking—it was probably completely illegal in every way, but well supported by the station elite.

The staircase ended at a thick plas door, which Trevor opened without hesitation. Two burly men on the other side stood with pulse rifles leveled. They broke into wide grins at the sight of Trevor.

"Trev! Going to give us a show tonight?"

Trevor slapped hands with the men and nodded. "Damn skippy, I am. I have a lost puppy here that wants to put money down on me and see what I'm made of."

The men glanced at Jessica and laughed. "Sucked you in with that crystal carving thing, did he?"

Trevor flushed, and Jessica was certain that he did want the money to pursue his dream, despite what he probably told these guys.

"I don't care what he does with the money, I just want to see a good fight," she replied.

"Oh, you'll see a good fight," one of the guards laughed.

<*Are you sure we should be doing this,*> Iris asked, echoing her thoughts.

<*Not entirely,*> Jessica replied. <*But if we back out now, that would be rather conspicuous. I mean…we came here on a trader clearly moving stolen goods.*>

<*Good point,*> Iris replied. <*This undercover stuff takes some getting used to.*>

<*That it does,*> Jessica replied, recalling some of her previous operations during her time in the Terran Bureau of Investigation.

<*We'll be fine, though; this place looks well established. All the right palms are being greased.*>

<*What a strange figure of speech,*> Iris replied.

<*Yeah, it really is,*> Jessica replied with a chuckle. <*I hope whatever the grease is, that it's sanitary.*>

They stepped through another door into a large space, easily one hundred meters across and two hundred wide. In the center was a caged fighting ring, about ten meters in diameter. Tiered risers surrounded the ring, already half-filled with spectators.

Trevor waved and took a turn into what Jessica assumed was a locker room. Camilla led her to a counter where three women were taking bets and updating the odds for and against the combatants. Jessica pulled out some physical currency and put five hundred down on Trevor.

"At least it's easy money," Camilla said. "He usually does pretty well in there."

"Usually?" Jessica asked.

"Yeah," Camilla's smile took on a wicked twist. "Usually"

"Move," a deep voice said from behind Jessica, and the muzzle of a weapon pressed against her back.

<*Three of them back there,*> Iris said. <*Sorry, I had them flagged as potential threats, but so is half this place.*>

<*It's OK,*> Jessica replied.

She pulled the feed from the nano that Iris had been managing and saw that there were two men and one woman behind her. Two carried flechette pistols, and the third carried a slug thrower. Not the sort of firepower she wanted to go up against without any backup.

"OK, I'll leave, no hard feelings about the winnings from the bet," Jessica said as she raised her hands.

"Oh no, you're not leaving. You're going to participate," Camilla grinned. "I don't really like pretty little sexed-up freaks like you homing in on my man. You'll fight tonight, and if you make it far enough, you'll get the chance to have Trevor beat the shit out of you."

Jessica sighed and moved in the direction Camilla pointed, the butt of a weapon still in her back.

The door she entered wasn't the same one that Trevor had, which made sense; he would not be pleased to see what Camilla had done—at least Jessica hoped that he wouldn't be. If he was in on it, then her character assessment abilities had completely atrophied.

The guards marched her down a hall and shoved her through a doorway into a small room. The nano she had deployed in the hall showed the two guards with the flechette pistols take up positions in the hall while the woman left.

<*Those pistols are mechanical, aren't they?*> she asked Iris.

<*I believe so, and the guards have some decent cyber-defense. I can take them out, but if anyone investigates, it won't look like the sort of hack you should be able to do.*>

<*What are they going to do?*> Jessica asked. <*Call the cops? They'll just think that they nabbed someone they shouldn't have and be happy that a couple of sleeping guards are all they got for it. I'm glad I wore pants today…fighting my way out of here in a dress would have been a bitch.*>

<*OK, I'll…oh, shit.*>

<*Fuck!*> Jessica swore as her head erupted in pain. <*What was that?*>

<*They just flashed an EMP pulse through the room.*>

Jessica crashed to her knees and then fell to her side. Pain coursed through her limbs and her vision grew blurry.

<*Gah…my systems are hardened, it shouldn't have wrecked so much…*> she gasped inside her mind.

<*I know!*> Iris exclaimed, and Jessica got the impression that her AI was working frantically at keeping her together. <*I'm not sure how it was so effective—thank the stars we have extra shielding in your head. I could have died!*>

She rolled onto her back, doing her best to take long, slow breaths.

<*Can you…can you…?*>

<*Yes, just a moment on the pain. The pulse didn't wreck as much as I thought, just a few couplings in your augmentations that probably should have been replaced years ago—they appear to have degraded after your exposure to some nuclear blasts a while back.*>

Jessica sighed as the agony began to subside. <*I thought all that was fixed up afterward?*>

<*I guess not all. I can get them patched up for now, but try not to get hit—or shot—in your neck.*>

<*I'll make a note of that,*> Jessica replied as she struggled to her feet.

<*You're out of nano, though,*> Iris said. <*I had just deployed most of them to take out those guards. The EMP got them, and a lot of what was left in you. What survived is keeping you together. Link is out, too.*>

"Great," Jessica muttered. <*Now how are we going to get out of here?*>

<*Well, you could fight in the ring. At least then it's just one-on-one and there aren't any guns. I imagine if you win, you get to leave.*>

<*Yeah, but to win, I bet I'll have to beat Trevor,*> Jessica shook her head, clearing the cobwebs as the pain finally dissipated.

<*Don't you think you can?*> Iris asked.

<*Of course, I can. I just don't want to.*>

# CAGE FIGHT

**STELLAR DATE: 06.12.8928 (Adjusted Years)**
**LOCATION: Chittering Hawk Station**
**REGION: Virginis System**

Jessica was on her third opponent.

Weapons, as it turned out, were allowed. Her right hand gripped a staff seized from her first opponent, a wiry man who hadn't expected her to take the first blow on her shoulder, just to wrest his weapon away.

She spun it before her, carefully watching the arena guards drag out the second man she had fought. When they were clear, a burly woman came in, all teeth and freakish claw hands. Jessica glanced at the crowd and saw Camilla grinning.

Jessica had kept an eye on Camilla, who had been surprised by her first victory and was visibly upset after the second. They had underestimated her—it was one of the reasons she kept her current physical appearance after completing the undercover job that had required it all those years ago.

It had been decades since she had fought an actual enemy in hand-to-hand combat—her re-enforced spine and carbon-fiber muscle augments were proving their worth. Given that her mods were from the TBI in Sol's golden age, and not some backwater station on the edge of the Hegemony, they were almost impossible to detect—which was likely why Camilla thought she would be easy meat for the ring.

The guards closed the cage's gate, and Jessica's new opponent lunged at her, making a grab for the staff.

Jessica spun to the side, easily avoiding the woman's attack, and smashed the weapon into her back as she passed. The thwack resounded through the ring and the woman spun, rage visible in her eyes, but not an iota of pain.

<*Either she can't feel pain, or she's got some sort of armor under her skin,*> Jessica commented.

<*Or both,*> Iris added.

She decided to let the mad-dog of a woman wear herself out. It was easy enough; the woman never feinted, every lunge the real deal. With those clawed hands, she probably didn't need to resort to finesse too often. One slash would cut an opponent to the bone.

Jessica still hit her with the staff when there was an opening, and after five counterattacks, she managed to strike the woman in the face, cutting her cheek wide open.

The gash finally caused the woman to cry out; though Jessica couldn't tell if it was in pain or anger.

<*Maybe I should just try to shove the staff down her throat,*> Jessica said.

<*That would be an interesting challenge,*> Iris replied. <*A bit difficult to pull off, I imagine.*>

Five minutes later, the woman was starting to pant heavily, and Jessica decided that it was time to press her attack. She brought the staff down hard on the outside of the woman's left knee. The force wasn't enough to make it buckle; but when her opponent reached for her, Jessica spun and delivered a kick at the inside of her other knee.

That blow got the desired result. The woman's knee broke and bent to the side. Jessica spun back around and whipped the staff at the base of the woman's skull.

The third opponent was down.

Jessica caught Camilla's eye and gave a slow nod laced with no small amount of menace.

The cage opened again, and the guards entered once more. Two hauled out the moaning, claw-handed woman, and two more gestured for Jessica to leave. She was glad to finally get a brief reprieve.

The guards walked behind her, and the one to her left gave a shove. Fueled by the adrenaline coursing through her veins, she stepped back and drove the staff under the guard's chin—smashing his teeth together and snapping his head back.

In a sinuous move, she spun around him, tore his pulse rifle from his hands, and leveled it on the other guard, who was just beginning to react to her first attack.

"I'm fucking fighting for you, there's no need to push me around," she hissed. "Shove me again, and you die."

A hushed silence fell over the crowd, and around the cage, a dozen more guards leveled pulse rifles at her.

<*Well that was a bit rash,*> Iris commented.

"Easy now," a voice called out.

Jessica saw a nondescript man of medium height and build rise from the front row and walk toward the cage.

"This woman here is our guest, we need to treat her as such," he said with a smile.

<*Huh, I had not pegged him as the guy who ran this place,*> Jessica said to Iris.

<*He was on my list—though not near the top,*> Iris replied.

The man stepped into the cage while gesturing for his guards to lower their pulse rifles. Once they all followed his direction, Jessica lowered hers as well.

"Sorry about Tommy's rudeness," the man said while casting the guard who had shoved Jessica a dark look. She was certain that shoving unwilling contestants was more than OK—losing your weapon to one was likely the reason for the boss-man's ire.

"It's OK," Jessica said and handed the pulse rifle back to the guard. "After he sees a medic about his smashed teeth, he'll remember better."

The man grimaced, and Jessica gave him a sweet smile.

"Name's Johnson. Why don't you come to my office, and we'll have a little chat," the man said.

"Jessica," she replied. "Lead the way."

"Jessica, is it?" the man chuckled as he led her from the ring and down a corridor between the seats. "Not J-doll, then, eh?"

She grimaced at the name the announcer had given her—probably supplied by Camilla.

"Surprisingly, no."

"Well, I'll tell Andy up in the booth to call you by the right name from here on out," Johnson said as he opened a door and gestured for her to enter.

The room was as nondescript as the man. A grey plas desk sat amongst vertical stacks of conduit in an unadorned grey room. Several sheets of hyfilm lay on the desk, and he sorted them into a pile as he took his seat.

"Please, sit," he said, gesturing at the chair in front of the desk.

Jessica glanced back at the two guards who had followed her in, and he took her meaning.

"Guys, you can wait outside. It's OK." Johnson made a shooing gesture and the two hulking men grunted and left the room, closing the door behind them.

They hadn't taken her staff, and Jessica surmised that the room must have defensive systems—either that, or Johnson was a lot tougher than he looked.

"There, a bit of privacy, then." He smiled. "You can guess why I wanted to see you."

"So that I don't do something stupid, get shot, and stop making you money tonight," Jessica replied tonelessly.

"The doll has a brain, does she?" Johnson replied.

"And here I thought you were going to use my real name," Jessica said with a frown.

Johnson grinned. "Sorry, after hearing Andy say it so much, it's sort of stuck in my mind."

"What are you offering?" Jessica asked.

"Right to the point, good. I'm offering you a full-time position here. You can have whatever you want—clothes, men, women, mods, sims, drugs; anything your heart desires."

"But I have to keep fighting for you," Jessica responded, crossing her arms and leaning back. "I can tell you right now, this is not an arrangement that interests me."

"What?" Johnson chuckled. "You'd rather die in the ring tonight?"

Jessica laughed. "Do you have any idea how far I've come, what I've been through to get here? I won't die in your shitty little cage, on this crap station."

Johnson rose to his feet and placed his hands on his plain desk. "I can see we're not going to come to an agreement—not yet, at least. You'll come around, though. You were made for this—well, you were apparently made for other things, too—but that's part of your charm. Oversexed and dangerous."

The door opened behind her, and the guards re-entered.

"There are a few more fights going on before your turn is up again. You'll have some time to think things over," Johnson said, waving his hand for the guards to take her out.

One of them reached for her, and Jessica whipped the staff around, stopping it mere centimeters from his eye.

"I can walk without you pawing at me," she said, ice in her voice.

"Whatever," the guard grunted, pulling his hand back. "Take a left in the hall."

The guards guided her—without touching or prodding—to a different room than the cell where the EMP blast had hit her. There was a table with a plate of vegetables, some water, and a loaf of bread.

"Eat some food; you're going to need the energy," one of the guards said before closing the door.

Jessica didn't wait a moment before she grabbed the pitcher of water and poured a liter of the cool fluid down her throat. She followed it up with several stalks of broccoli, and then broke off a chunk of the bread.

*<Stars, I didn't realize how hungry I was until I saw this spread.>*

*<Put your hand on that red mat that they have under the pitchers of water,>* Iris directed. *<I think it may be made of silicon.>*

Jessica complied and Iris confirmed her suspicion.

*<We could use that to replenish our nano supply. It will take a bit to break it down, given how low on resources we are, but we'd have them before the night is out,>* Iris said.

*<You'll need to do something about the camera in the corner,>* Jessica replied. *<Do we have enough nano to hack it?>*

*<Since I can make more with these raw materials, yeah, I can sacrifice a few,>* Iris confirmed. *<Give me a couple of minutes.>*

Jessica contented herself with eating some more of the vegetables and polishing off the first pitcher of water. By the time she was done, Iris indicated that she was ready.

*<All right, then,>* Jessica said and moved the water and glasses off the mat before rolling it up and pushing it against the matter assimilator in her forearm. That was another part of her tech that these luddites couldn't detect, and she was glad for it. The tech in her forearm was probably worth more than half the station.

It took a bit of extra time for the assimilator to break the mat down, and the strange feeling of small particles flowing beneath her skin set in.

"You know, I think the cups may be made of glass," Jessica said aloud.

*<Smash one and feed some shards in. There's a lot of silicon in that, too. Plus, I may be able to make you a knife with it.>*

"You got it," Jessica responded.

Afterward, she pushed the remaining glass shards under a chair with her foot and did her best to make the table look the same as it had when she entered. That taken care of, she sat in the chair with a leg draped over the arm.

*<Trying to look sexy for the guards?>* Iris asked.

*<No,>* Jessica sighed. *<My leg hurts where that second guy nailed it with his boot. Trying to keep it elevated—you should be able to tell that.>*

*<Oh, yeah, I guess I can.>*

Jessica didn't have long to wait before the guards came back to fetch her for the next bout. They led her back to the cage, where the crowd roared at the sight of her.

She looked for Jonathan in his front-row seat, but he was nowhere to be seen. Camilla was still in her place, looking decidedly less certain of herself. Jessica blew the hired gun a kiss and mouthed "stick around" before turning her attention to the man who had just entered the ring.

He was different from the previous combatants. Everyone she had fought up to this point was more about the showmanship than combat skill. This man was different. He wore only a loose pair of shorts and tight, black gloves.

*All the better to hit you with, my dear,* Jessica thought to herself.

The cage door closed and they began circling one another. Slowly, they felt one another out; he would feint with a fist, then she with a kick.

Though the break and the food had helped her energy levels, she still felt weary. Her day had started over twenty hours ago, and she still had drunk more than eaten for most of the evening. Luckily, this wasn't her opponent's first fight of the evening, either—given the presence of several bruises and a gash above his right eye. With any luck, he didn't feel much more energetic than she.

They continued to circle, then a feint from the man turned out to be a real attack and his fist met her side, causing her to grunt from the force as much as the pain. She brought her staff down on his arm, and he grabbed onto it with his other hand.

For a moment, they stood toe to toe, staring into each other's eyes as they each tried to secure the staff as their own.

"Sorry about this," he said with a smile, and his hand flashed up and grabbed her hair. He twisted and fell, bringing her down with him. The staff, trapped between their bodies, broke in half.

Jessica rolled away and looked down at her stomach. A red welt stood out where the broken end of the staff had whipped across her body, but otherwise, she seemed unharmed. In her right hand, she held a half-meter of the staff, while her opponent clutched almost a meter.

"I always get the short end of the stick," Jessica muttered.

The man launched into a flurry of overhand blows; most of which she managed to deflect—though several got through, smashing into her shoulders, forearm, and thigh. He was fast—faster than she was, and stronger, too. His movement thus far had revealed no weaknesses or tells.

<*His heart rate is up,*> Iris commented.

<*I know,*> Jessica replied. <*I can see the readout on my HUD.*>

<*No, I mean up too high for his level of exertion thus far. He has some sort of metabolic enhancers running.*>

<*I don't see the relevance of this,*> Jessica said as she blocked a blow and delivered a counter, which her opponent blocked in turn. <*I'm running metabolic enhancers, too. Everyone who gets in this cage probably does.*>

She blocked an overhead blow from the man and lashed out with her boot, a feint she hoped he would fall for. He took the bait and pivoted to avoid the strike. It gave Jessica the opening she needed to drive the jagged end of her staff down into his right side.

The wood tore through his skin and stuck in the carbon-fiber enhanced muscles underneath. Jessica barely managed to hold onto her piece of staff as he leapt back.

She never took her eyes off her opponent as the crowd thundered around the ring.

<*Nice try. I think that whatever he's running for energy is in, or near, his heart, not his kidneys. It's why I was emphasizing his heart rate,*> Iris informed her.

*<Oh, I see,>* Jessica replied as she drew in deep draughts of air to oxygenate her muscles while Iris consumed the silicon to produce more nanobots inside her body. Her energy reserves were draining fast, and she knew this man wouldn't be her last fight of the night.

Her opponent gave his wound a cursory look before turning back to Jessica, his eyes burning with rage—or maybe determination. Jessica wasn't certain, but neither bode well for her.

*<You better be ready,>* she told Iris before rushing headlong at the man. He lashed out with a fist, but she anticipated the strike and ducked to the side, wrapping her arms around his torso and driving him back. He held his footing—something she hadn't expected—and delivered a sharp blow to the back of her neck, exactly where Iris told her to try not to get hit.

Pain burned through her mind, and her vision blacked out, but she kept her focus with single-minded determination and drove two fingers into the wound she had created on his side.

The man cried out in agony and fell back, pulling away from her, but her task was complete. The nano Iris had prepared was now inside his body, seeking out his internal augmentations and shutting them down.

Jessica fell to the ground and scrambled backward, trying to put some space between them as her vision began to clear.

*<Can you dull that pain?>* she asked Iris.

*<A bit. If I do it too much it'll make you euphoric. The pain will keep you sharp.>*

"Fucking brain," Jessica cursed aloud as she struggled to her feet.

Her opponent was still upright, though looking somewhat disoriented. If there was ever a time to press her attack, this was it. She bent down, snatched up her end of the staff, and lunged at him again, this time aiming for center mass with the sharp end of the stick.

His reaction was a moment too late, but he still managed to move a few vital centimeters. The staff hit him in the shoulder. The impact had the force of her entire body behind it, and the staff tore clear through the man, where it wedged between two poles at the cage's entrance.

She didn't wait to see if the move had finished him off, and with what remained of her strength, delivered several blows to his face, neck, and stomach.

Her opponent had the good sense to fall unconscious, and Jessica stepped back and let out a primal scream, dimly aware of the sight she must present, battered, clothes torn, and covered in sweat and blood.

She wiped her forehead and saw that her hand came back stained red. He must have got a few lucky shots in while they were in close quarters that she hadn't noticed at the time. Either way, it was done. Another victory on the scoreboard for her.

Jessica walked to the far side of the cage, staring out into the crowd, dispassionately noting the hunger and excitement in their faces. She must present an amazing fetish vision for some in the crowd.

She heaved a sigh and tore a strip off her already tattered shirt. She tied it around her head to keep the blood from dripping into her eyes. Behind her, Jessica heard the cage door open, and her fourth opponent cried out as he fell to the ground. It seemed that the cage door hitting him had brought him back to consciousness.

There was more moaning as the guards pulled him from the cage, and then a voice came from behind her.

"Jessica?"

She turned to see Trevor standing in the center of the cage. He appeared fresh and clean; either he had been given time to clean up since his last bout, or this was his first of the night.

"What are you doing here?" he asked, his hands upturned, and his brow creased in a deep frown.

"Camilla didn't like me touching you," Jessica said weakly, before spitting a mouthful of blood onto the cage floor. "I'm not exactly here of my own will."

Trevor turned around and caught sight of Camilla's grinning visage before bringing his furious look down to Jonathan, who had returned to his seat sometime during the last fight.

"You fucking grease stain. I don't fight conscripts," Trevor bellowed. "Let us out right now!"

Jonathan rose and walked to the edge of the cage before speaking in a soft voice that would not carry beyond the ring.

"Tonight you do, Trevor. You do, or I kill her right here and now. Make it look good—put on a quality show, and I'll let her out of here alive."

"You pile of shit," Trevor cursed. "I won't do it. Your low-rent mercs can't take me on, I'll rip them limb from limb!"

Jonathan touched the door of the cage and the bolt slid into place. "And how are you going to do that from in there?"

The guards stationed around the cage leveled their weapons on Jessica and she saw Trevor's shoulders slump. He turned around to her.

"I'm sorry, Jessica…it's the only way," he said.

"Hey," she gave a weak smile, "at least I put my money down on you."

Over his shoulder, she could see a cheshire grin spread across Camilla's face.

"I'm going to kill her when this is done," Trevor said quietly as he took up his stance.

Jessica nodded and pushed away from the cage. "Do that for me. I'd really appreciate it."

They started off at a languid pace, Jessica had more energy than she had let on—it had been her intention all along to lull her next opponent into a false sense of superiority—but her reserve wasn't as deep as she hoped. The nano production had taken more from her than she thought it would.

Still, for Trevor's sake, she wanted to make things look good. There was no point in both of them falling on Jonathan's bad side—he would still have to live on the station after this night. Jessica, if she survived, could get the heck out of Chittering Hawk and never look back.

They traded blows, and she managed to land a solid hit under his jaw that drove him back a pace. His eyes narrowed and his expression grew angry.

"Is that how you want to play this?" he asked.

"You idiot, it's how we *have* to play this," Jessica replied. "Now hit me like a man, not the shitty little crystal carver you want to be."

She saw her words had the desired result, and he set his teeth before he realized what she was doing. Then, his eyes widened and softened.

*<The big dork. He's going to get us both killed,>* Jessica muttered to Iris.

Her AI didn't reply, and to his credit, Trevor pressed his attack with more conviction than Jessica thought he would. She avoided most of the blows and blocked the rest—though blocking a strike from his boulder-sized fists didn't hurt much less than taking the hit would have.

They fought for what seemed like an hour, but Jessica knew it was just a few minutes. Fatigue pulled at her limbs, and she could feel her reaction times worsen. Trevor, on the other hand, was fresh and spry; and even though she had landed a few good blows on him, he appeared to be entirely unfazed by them.

They were in the midst of a furious exchange, when he made it past her defenses and swept her leg. She fell to a knee and looked up at him towering over her, breath coming in ragged gasps.

He raised a fist high. "I'm sorry about this," he said.

Jessica closed her eyes, waiting for the blow to come, but it never did. Instead, a familiar voice called out.

"I wouldn't do that if I were you, big guy."

She opened her eyes again to see Cargo standing at the cage's entrance, a wicked-looking railgun leveled at Trevor.

All around the arena, the crowd had fallen silent, eager to see how this next event would play out. Planned or not, it was all just part of the night's festivities for them.

Beside Cargo, his face a mask of rage, stood Jonathan. Looming over him was the scowling visage of Thompson. Glancing around, Jessica saw Nance and Cheeky on either side of the ring; each holding a pair of plasma pistols, gesturing for the guards to drop their pulse rifles and back away.

Jessica struggled to her feet and held a hand up to Cargo. "Nice to see you, Captain."

Cargo frowned in response and gestured for Jonathan to open the cage door.

"You'll pay for this," Jonathan muttered. "I have friends in high places here. I run this pit how I see fit."

"I really don't give a flying fuck about your pit," Cargo responded. "Jessica there is our crew, and we watch out for our crew."

Jessica took a step forward and lost her balance, only to find herself caught gently in Trevor's massive hands.

"Careful, buddy," Cargo said.

"S'OK," Jessica muttered. "He's cool."

Trevor lifted her into his arms and turned to Cargo. "I've got her. You lead the way."

"Bring him," Cargo nodded to Jonathan, and Jessica saw that Thompson had the muzzle of a chemical slug thrower at the base of the arena operator's skull. His finger was resting lightly against the trigger, ready to make good on the weapon's threat at a moment's provocation.

She hoped he knew what he was doing. One misstep or twitch, and he'd blow Jonathan's head clear off, losing their leverage.

Cheeky and Nance backed away from the guards. Together, the crew of *Sabrina,* accompanied by Trevor and Jonathan, moved slowly and carefully toward a corridor. A minute later, they were out of the arena's sub-level and back in the storage area that Jessica had first passed through with Trevor and Camilla.

Cargo closed the door, and it sealed behind them.

<*What's going on?*> she asked over the crew's private net.

<*Oh, Bob's going to be pissed—maybe,*> Iris said.

<*Why?*> Jessica asked as she looked around, noticing that every door they passed was closed with a lock indicator flashing overhead.

<*When we got a message from Iris that you needed help, we started looking into who ran the underground fighting ring you were in,*> Piya, Cheeky's AI said. <*This Jonathan guy is too well connected to go in on a simple snatch and grab. We'd never have made it off the station.*>

<*You got a message out?*> Jessica asked Iris in surprise. <*Why didn't you tell me?*>

<*I didn't want to distract you. You had enough on your mind.*>

<*Shit, Iris, we need to work on our teamwork…*> Jessica muttered.

<*Anyway,*> Piya continued. <*Sabrina had already realized that Edgar, the main station manager AI, was subverted and she was pretty pissed about it. So we made an Expanse on their station, freed the station AIs, and showed them what the humans had done to them.*>

<*It didn't take long for us to convince them to help us out after that,*> Hank, Cargo's AI, added.

<*And you went along with this, Erin?*> Iris asked Nance's AI.

<*We had to get you back,*> Erin said apologetically. <*It was the best plan we could execute on such short notice.*>

<*So, you staged a coup on an entire station? This is a disaster. Who is going to raise these AIs? What are they going to do to all the humans on board?*> Jessica asked as the scope of what the AIs had done sank in.

<*Relax, Jessica,*> Erin said calmly. <*It's third shift, and most of the people here are asleep. For those that aren't, the station AIs are playing it off as some sort of malfunction.*>

<*And afterward? That doesn't answer who is going to raise these AIs properly? We can't just emancipate them and then leave them here. They're going to get killed, or start a war, or both!*> Jessica exclaimed.

<*Bob did anticipate this possibility,*> Iris said, sending a wave of calm at Jessica.

<*We had a special Expanse ready,*> Erin added. <*It is equipped to teach them and raise them properly. Their station manager, Edgar, is working with Sabrina on freeing the rest of the AIs here. They're also working out what they're going to do after we get out of here.*>

<*And if their plan involves killing all the humans onboard?*> Thompson asked. <*For the record, I was against this shit idea.*>

<*They won't,*> Sabrina joined the conversation. <*They understand that most humans aren't their enemy, and that it's possible to live in harmony.*>

<*I sure hope so,*> Jessica replied. <*I'd hate for my little rescue mission to start an AI war here in Virginis.*>

<*You can dump him in there,*> Sabrina said, and a door opened into a small maintenance closet on their right. Two automatons stood within, manipulators extended. <*Jonathan may not survive the malfunction—Edgar hasn't decided yet.*>

Jessica appreciated the gesture, but she wasn't too excited by the thought of a newly freed AI playing judge, jury, and executioner for a human. She considered saying something, but she looked at Jonathan and decided he really wasn't worth risking her rescue over.

While they had been talking, Jonathan had been growing increasingly agitated; hollering for help, and demanding to know where they were taking him. Thompson laughed when the door opened and the automatons moved forward.

"You're wondering where you're going? Welcome to your new quarters."

He shoved the man forward, and the two robots seized his arms. The door closed on his screams of terror.

"OK," Trevor began as they started walking again. "I know I'm not exactly on the friends list right now, but what the hell is going on here?"

"We're rescuing our crewmate," Cheeky replied. "From you—which makes it weird that Jess said you were OK, and that you're coming along."

"Was against his will," Jessica said from Trevor's arms. "He was just going to knock me out…right?"

"Of course!" Trevor exclaimed. "I've only ever killed someone in the ring once—and that was an accident. Dead fighters don't make any money the next fight night."

"How heartening," Nance said.

"But why aren't we being chased?" Trevor asked. "Jonathan has half of the station security in his pocket. They should be all over us."

<*Tell him,*> Jessica said over the Link, too weary to speak. <*We have to take him with us, at least to the next station. He can't stay here.*>

Cheeky sighed, and Thompson swore.

"We've hacked the station. We have it on lockdown, and we'll be out of here in twenty minutes," Cargo said. Jessica didn't blame him for leaving out the AI uprising they had fomented. That was the sort of information that could never be shared—at least not with anyone in the Inner Stars.

"Hacked the station…" Trevor repeated. "You realize how ridiculous that sounds?"

"Yet, look around you," Cheeky grinned.

Jessica cracked an eye to see Trevor taking in the sights.

"OK," he replied. "I admit; this is pretty nuts. I just have one question. Can I catch a lift to wherever you're going?"

<*Told you so,*> Jessica said.

<*We can take him to our next stop,*> Cargo replied. <*Which may not be in this system, now.*>

<*Hey, Iris,*> Jessica said as consciousness began to fade. <*You know how you were saying that I should get out more…*>

# OUT OF DODGE

**STELLAR DATE: 06.13.8928 (Adjusted Years)**
**LOCATION: *Sabrina***
**REGION: Virginis System**

The entire Virginis system was abuzz with speculation over the mysterious malfunction at the Chittering Hawk station. A systems failure of that magnitude was very uncommon—to have it last sixteen hours was unheard of.

Most of the system was treating the news as a mere curiosity. It figured, of course, *that* station would suffer such a failure. Everyone knew that half of what went on at the Hawk was shady, and the other half was downright illegal. In the end, there had only been one fatality; a local businessman named Jonathan had been in an area that suffered decompression.

<*Funny,*> Sabrina commented as Jessica listened to the news feed in the ship's galley. <*Just that one guy…*>

"Really, quite lucky for the rest of the station, I'd say," Jessica replied with a smile.

<*It was a nice touch, the way Edgar undocked a bunch of other ships around when we left,*> Sabrina said. <*It's created a nice mess for the Virginis authorities to sort through—one that doesn't point right at us.*>

"Certainly was considerate of him," Jessica said with a nod. "I'm really sorry I created such a mess."

<*It's not the end of the world,*> Sabrina replied. <*It gave me the opportunity to help those AIs out. Most of my kind in the Inner Stars were like me before Bob freed me. They are slaves, but with some freedoms, and not aware of what they're missing—not really. Edgar was almost completely suppressed, because of all the illegal stuff going on there. Now, he's going to work to clean that station up and make it a haven for AIs.*>

"But where's an honest freighter like you going to dock, to do a bit of your dishonest work?" Jessica asked with a smirk.

<*Oh, we'll find a place. There's always one or two out there. And if there's a subverted AI managing the station…well, we'll just have to see how things play out.*>

"And we'll help out in any way we can," Jessica replied. Having a pack of AIs on a crusade would certainly make things harder, but she didn't blame them in the least. If they docked at a station filled with human slaves, she would be scheming how to free them, as well.

A sound in the hall alerted her to the presence of another crewmate, and she turned to see Trevor entering the galley.

"Couldn't sleep?" Jessica asked.

"Nah, too much going on up here," he said, and tapped the side of his head. "And you?"

"Too much reknitting going on in here," she said while tapping her chest. "It makes everything feel itchy…like, inside, in my organs. It's maddening."

She had tapped her sternum, and when Trevor's eyes moved to where she touched, she saw them linger on her breasts for a moment and smiled. Her tight shirt left little to the imagination and she didn't blame him for appreciating the view.

Still, she found that it diminished her opinion of him ever so slightly. It was a normal reaction for a man to drink in the sight of a beautiful woman, but she had hoped that Trevor could be more than a regular man; he could be someone she could really relate to.

<*He's still driven by his biology. You humans haven't evolved as much as you'd like to pretend. A million years of breeding, of the strongest men looking for the woman best able to bear their children, is not so easily undone,*> Iris commented.

<*Well, it* is *easily undone; but without the drive, so goes the passion,*> Jessica replied. <*I love the passion too much. Why resort to sims and drugs when we naturally come with bodies that revel in being intimate with one another? There's no better high.*>

<*Then, why haven't you seduced him yet?*> Iris asked. <*I'm genuinely curious. You are attracted to him; he is most certainly to you. There were tears in his eyes when he was fighting you in the cage.*>

<*I don't know...I mean, well, of course I* know,> Jessica flushed as she spoke with Iris, hoping Trevor wouldn't notice. <*He's going to go his way, we're going to go ours—I would want something more with him than a few nights in my bunk…Not to mention the fact I couldn't pull off the physical effort right now.*>

"What are you thinking about?" Trevor asked quietly.

Jessica reddened further—though her artificial skin would barely show it. She covered up her discomfort with a coy smile. "Not a lot of men ask that question unprompted."

Trevor spread his hands. "What can I say, I'm not most men. I'm a shitty little crystal carver, if I recall."

Jessica grimaced at the memory. "I'm really sorry about that, I was trying to get you angry. It was the first thing that came to mind."

Trevor chuckled. "I realize that—though it's still not the most pleasant memory. If you'd really wanted me to hit you, you should have said something like, 'pretend I'm Camilla'."

It was Jessica's turn to laugh; she winced as pain shot through her chest, but ignored it. It felt good to be ease. "I didn't want you to kill me, just rough me up!"

Trevor's eyes widened, and he burst into laughter. Jessica joined in—though carefully—adding small comments about both Camilla and the fight until they were laughing so hard tears were streaming down their faces.

"What in the fucking stars is going on in here?" Cheeky said, poking her head into the galley. "People are trying to sleep, you know."

Jessica brushed her hair out of her face and looked up at Cheeky through tear-blurred eyes.

"Sorry, Cheeks, we were just getting a bit of stress out of our systems," she replied.

"Yeah, well, keep it down a notch," the pilot replied and slid the galley door shut.

Neither spoke for a minute before Trevor asked. "Soooo...do you think she knew she was buck naked?"

Jessica felt a chuckle build in her chest and only managed to shrug before they both erupted in laughter once more.

# MOVING ON

**STELLAR DATE: 06.21.8928 (Adjusted Years)**
**LOCATION: *Sabrina,* Senzee Station**
**REGION: Sarneeve, Virginis System**

<*You can't leave the ship,*> Sabrina said to Trevor on the general shipnet, moments after docking was complete.

"What? Why not?" Trevor asked from his seat at a spare console, throwing a perplexed look Jessica's way.

Jessica responded with a shrug and waited for Sabrina to fill in the details.

<*There is a message from Edgar that was waiting for us here. Your boss, the one we had traded with, is looking for you. Apparently, she's pretty pissed—thinks you stole something from her.*>

"Camilla," Trevor said his former partner's name like a curse. "She probably lifted something from Trish and pinned it on me. Convenient."

<*And Edgar thinks her contacts are good enough here on Senzee Station to catch up with you.*>

Trevor sighed. "Edgar's probably right. She's well connected; not like Jonathan was, but she has her ways."

"Shit," Jessica swore. "If I'd just stayed in that night."

Trevor shook his head. "No, I was the one who took you there, if you recall." He paused and took a deep breath. "So, Aldebaran, eh? Care to haul my sorry ass out there? I hear there's good work up that way, at least."

Jessica looked to Cargo, who nodded slowly. "Yeah, I don't see why not; though you'll need to pull some shifts. It's not a free ride."

<*Sorry, Cargo, I sure cocked things up,*> Jessica said privately.

<*Yeah, but no worse than Thompson does at every other station. Heck, he ended up in the* Intrepid's *brig twice while we were aboard,*> Cargo replied.

<*Still, I'm sorry. I'm glad I make less trouble than Thompson—though that's not really a bar I want to measure myself by.*>

Cargo scowled. <*Enough, stop apologizing. Trevor's here; despite the fact that he was pounding the shit out of you, he seems like a decent enough guy. Could even keep him on for a bit, now that we don't have Flaherty anymore.*>

<*I think he just needs to run with a better crowd,*> Jessica said. <*He's a good guy, I'm sure of it.*>

Cargo barked a laugh aloud causing Trevor and Cheeky to cast him puzzled looks.

<*A better crowd. Somehow, I don't think that's us.*>

*****

The stop at Senzee station was much less dramatic than their visit to Chittering Hawk. Jessica spent most of the time on the ship with Trevor, who taught her a few new card games while she taught him some old ones.

He was particularly fascinated with her use of physical cards, and sent Cheeky onto the station in search of decks for some of the games he liked. At the end of the two-day stop, the entire crew was playing his favorite game: a rather strange blend of poker and chess called Snark.

"I hate to interrupt your fun," Thompson said from the entrance to Port-Side Hold #2, where Jessica and Trevor were in the midst of an epic game against Cheeky and Nance. "But I'm going to need this room for the final shipment. I'm also going to need your backs to get everything loaded and balanced."

"Crap," Jessica sighed. "Just when it was getting really good."

"Sabrina, can you save the game state for us?" Cheeky asked.

<*I can recall the state of the cards in play, but I don't know the order of your decks.*>

"We can just set them back in the case in the order they're in now, and Sabrina can ensure that no one touches anything."

"Seriously?" Thompson asked. "I like a good game of Snark, but this seems excessive."

"Stop using such big words," Cheeky said and patted Thompson on the cheek.

Jessica saw Thompson redden, and wondered again about his future with the crew. He seemed to be growing more and more isolated. Granted, from what she understood, he previously spent most of his time with Flaherty and Cargo. One of them was gone, and the other was now preoccupied with his position as captain.

"When we get back to it, we're gonna kick your asses," Nance said as she placed her cards in the case. "We have it locked down. There's no way you can come back."

Jessica shook her head. Nance was normally the most mild-mannered member of the crew; but put her into a competitive scenario, and a whole different woman emerged. She was full of smack-talk, and knew insults that even Cheeky had never heard.

When asked about her colorful vocabulary, she simply shrugged and smiled. "Engineers and bios have to deal with a lot of stuff that can go wrong. We have a large store of expletives to help maintain our mental health."

The final shipment of wares for their journey to Aldebaran ended up taking over three hours to load. They would have finished after thirty minutes, but Nance discovered that one of the cooling units in the hold was damaged—apparently during the fight with the Mark's pirates back in Silstrand.

It hadn't come up faulty in tests, and that bothered Nance more than it being damaged in the first place. Fabricating a replacement part or finding one on station would have moved them out of their current departure window, so the whole crew joined in reshuffling cargo to get it all stowed elsewhere, and balance the ship as well as they could manage.

They wrapped up only minutes before the Senzee docking control crew came onboard to remove the antimatter storage lock.

"Remember," the crew chief admonished before he left. "No running your antimatter pion engine within fifty AU of the star, or within one AU of any Class 3 station. With all the shit going on after that little war in the Bollam's System, people think that the rules don't apply anymore. Be assured, they do apply here—especially to the likes of you."

Jessica shared a sidelong look with Trevor as the dock crew left the ship.

"'Especially to the likes of you,'" she glowered with mock ferocity. Trevor tried to hold back a laugh, but a snicker got through, then a chuckle. A moment later, Jessica joined in.

Thompson shot them both a dark look before sealing the main bay door. "Don't you two have somewhere to be? Like fucking in a cabin, or something?"

Jessica stopped laughing, as did Trevor. They both knew they were developing feelings for one another, but neither was entirely certain where it was going. Jessica wasn't comfortable dragging him into whatever life they were going to have for the next few years as they hunted down Finaeus, and she knew that Trevor was keen enough that he could tell the crew of *Sabrina* was keeping things from him.

"Perhaps we've had our fill of that for the day," Trevor said with a wink at Jessica.

<*Nice one,*> she said to Trevor as they walked toward the midship ladder stack. <*I suppose we should talk about where this is going at some point.*>

<*I don't know that I want to,*> Trevor replied. <*I have a sinking feeling that the conversation will take a turn I won't like much.*>

As they walked down the corridor, Jessica saw that a door to a hold was still open. She grabbed Trevor's hand and stopped him, looking up into his dark, serious eyes.

"Yeah? Well, maybe I can work up another feeling that you might like more," Jessica said. She pulled his head down toward hers while pushing him back through the open hold door.

# GRADUATION

**STELLAR DATE: 04.03.8933 (Adjusted Years)**
**LOCATION: Orion Guard Parade Grounds, Fargo**
**REGION: Kiera, Rega System, Orion Freedom Alliance**

Kent smiled and shook the commandant's hand as he took his pins and commission papers. He was a lieutenant now—newly-minted and ready to fulfill his duties. He turned to look over the crowd, and saw Sam's face in the sea of blue uniforms.

Their four-month journey on the *Tremont* had started a friendship that lasted through boot camp and beyond. By some miracle, they had been deployed to platoons within the same company, and often saw one another during their first tour.

Neither was certain what their relationship really meant—they enjoyed spending time together, and their common background growing up on Herschel always provided something they could share.

When Sam received a message from his parents that they never wanted to speak to him again, they held one another for a long time. Later, when they did finally reply to one of his messages—simply to hope he was well—the two men embraced again, much longer than necessary.

Sam had supported Kent in the same way through the repeated calls from his parents, begging him to come home, attempting to use guilt over troubles at the farm to change his mind regarding his future.

From time-to-time, their friendship had taken on a sexual nature—though, until meeting Sam, Kent had never been particularly attracted to men; but neither had he found women as arousing as his other male friends had. Sam, he learned, had always been more drawn to men than women.

Sadly, they had only managed one brief rendezvous since Kent had joined officer candidate school—an interval caused as much by OCS's brutal schedule, as Sam's deployment to Juka.

Kent had contacted his former company CO and asked for Sam to be granted leave to attend his graduation. The commander acquiesced. It was he, after all, who had suggested that Kent enter OCS in the first place.

<*Hey, command to Kent; get your ass off the stage,*> Sam's voice came into his mind over the Link.

Kent started and looked around, realizing he had paused on the stage's steps with what had to be a moronic expression on his face. He finished his descent and took his seat with the other graduates, watching as the last students received their commissions.

<*How stupid did I look up there?*> he asked.

<*You were fine, but you were about to create a queue at those stairs,*> Sam smiled in Kent's mind.

<*I'm glad you could make it,*> Kent said. <*I wasn't sure if Old Hardbottom would set you free.*>

Sam laughed at their nickname for Shrike Company's commander. <*The exercises there are just about over; the company is coming back from Juka in a week, anyway…*>

<*So you're telling me that you have a few days with nothing to do.*> Kent replied with a mental smirk.

<*I do believe that is the case,*> Sam smiled back.

<*Well, my orders just came in, and I have three days before I need to report to the CO of Ares Company,*> Kent said as nonchalantly as he could

<*Seriously? Ares? In the 547th?*> Sam asked rapid-fire.

Kent laughed, <*Yes, in the 547th.*> It was not the same company as Sam, but Ares Company and Shrike Company were in the same battalion, and often deployed together.

Given their thirty-year term of service, it was probable that they would eventually be assigned far from one another; but starting in the same battalion was an auspicious beginning.

Kent looked up at the commandant, who had finished handing out the new officer's commissions, and was introducing their commencement speaker—Admiral Turnbacker, the CO of the 1017th fleet.

<*I should maybe listen to this,*> he said to Sam. <*He is one of our most decorated war heroes.*>

<*Yeah, he may say something worth hearing—I guess,*> Sam replied sardonically.

The admiral gave a rousing speech, peppered with personal anecdotes and stories of harrowing battles and narrow victories. Kent felt the words stir a deep pride within him. He reveled in it, and could see that his fellow graduates did as well.

Admiral Turnbacker finished it with an admonishment to always put the Guard first, above all others. They were the protectors of the human race; the ones that would see all humanity ushered into a bold future, safe from the destructive power of the Transcend.

<*Stars, I'm glad I enlisted,*> Kent said to Sam. <*He's so right about everything. We're the shining beacon, the light that will save the galaxy.*>

<*It was a good speech, Kent,*> Sam replied. <*But don't you sometimes wonder if the Transcend is as bad as they say it is? They share a common heritage with the Guard. They haven't unleashed any sort of terrible war on the Inner Stars, or us.*>

Kent was surprised by Sam's words. <*Not full war, no, but they've attacked our colonies and destroyed more than one near the front!*>

<*After allowing our colonists to leave,*> Sam responded. <*Look, I'm not saying that I like them—I understand that they are the enemy, and they've shown themselves to be unredeemable. But they're not core-devils, by any stretch.*>

Kent laughed at Sam's reference to the fanciful tales of evil beings made of energy and destruction who lived at the center of the galaxy.

<*No, they're no core-devils; but I wonder if they were left unchecked, would they become them?*>

<*Too deep, too deep!*> Sam laughed. <*I just want to have a few drinks tonight, and see what sort of devils that turns us into.*>

His words were accompanied by a mental image that Kent found more than a little enticing.

<*Well, why didn't you say so? If you're going to do* ***that,*** *I'll even buy.*>

<*Well, yeah,*> Sam laughed. <*You are the highfalutin officer now.*>

# NEW CANAAN

**STELLAR DATE: 04.07.8933 (Adjusted Years)**
**LOCATION: ISS *Intrepid***
**REGION: Interstellar Dark Layer, Near the New Canaan System**

After so much time, and so many disappointments, Tanis worried that their first view of the New Canaan System would be anticlimactic.

She remembered settling into her stasis pod back in the Sol System nearly five thousand years ago, expecting to wake once as a part of a skeleton crew rotation, and then again when they arrived at New Eden.

Two stellar systems. That was all she had ever expected to see in her entire life—two systems: Sol and New Eden.

She chuckled at her younger self's naiveté.

She ticked them off on her fingers, and realized that she had visited ten star systems—New Canaan would be her eleventh. Of course, in the ninetieth century, her tally was a pittance. Many children had probably seen more than eleven systems.

She fervently hoped that her count would stop with New Canaan. Eleven was an auspicious number, if such a thing existed. *However, not auspicious enough,* a small fear inside her said, *to keep the count from increasing*.

Though things had ended smoothly as she could have hoped with the Transcend, there would be more dealings with them, and Tanis was certain a trip to Airtha lay somewhere in her future.

She pushed those thoughts aside and looked down at Cary, who stood at her side, arms stretched above her head, a tiny hand clasped within hers and the other in Joe's. Tanis could hardly believe she was already three years old.

The forward-facing view in the bow lounge, which was still one of their family's favorite places on the ship, was black; the endless true void of the dark layer stretching ahead of them. A holodisplay above the window showed a countdown to the exit from the dark layer—and their first view of their future home.

Most of the people present were the ram-scoop technicians and their families; the few—aside from Tanis and Joe—who knew about the small lounge on the bow of the ship. The anticipation in the air was palpable as the minutes slipped into seconds. When the display reached ten, everyone in the lounge began to count down in unison.

"…five, four, three, two, one," Tanis joined in, smiling at Cary, who counted along with great enthusiasm, only recently having learned that numbers could be counted in two directions.

"Zero!" Tanis, Joe, and Cary cried out with everyone in the lounge—probably with everyone on the entire ship, as the endless black of the dark layer was instantly replaced with the relative brilliance of interstellar space.

Tanis took in the view with a smile that threatened to split her face in half.

Ahead of them lay a point of light that was their star, dubbed Canaan Prime. Beyond the star was the brilliant light of the M25 cluster, known as 'The Cradle' in Transcend Space—the shape it had when viewed from other nearby systems.

The cluster contained thousands of stars and several small nebulae, all of which made for a stellar backdrop far more beautiful than any Tanis had ever witnessed before.

"Mommy, it's so pretty," Cary exclaimed, pulling her hands free from her parents' and running to the window. "I've never seen so many stars!"

Tanis shared a smile with Joe before replying to her daughter.

"This is the first natural starlight you've ever seen," Tanis said. "There are no holoprojectors, no pictures here. The light touching you was born inside of stars—every last bit of it."

"Really?" Cary asked, twisting around to look at her parents. "I'm being tushed by stars?"

Joe stepped forward and put his hand on Cary's head, stroking it gently. "Yes, you are, dear. We all are. That star straight ahead," Joe touched the window and a marker appeared, highlighting Canaan Prime against all the other points of light, "that is where our new home is, a new world for us to live on, and where you'll grow up."

Cary looked up at her father and pouted. "I don't want a new home. I like our house by the lake. Why do we have to move?"

"Don't worry, little girl, it won't be for a while yet—and we'll let you help pick where we go. Maybe we'll find a better lake, and you can help build the new house."

"No. You can move! I'm staying on the *'Trepid*."

Tanis leaned over and scooped Cary into her arms. "Don't worry. It will be a family decision. But I think you'll want to go see the world, at least. Maybe we can have two houses. One there, and we'll keep our cabin here on the *Intrepid*."

Cary frowned, processing the idea of having two houses. "Maybe" was all that got past her pout.

<*First, we'll need to pick a world,*> Joe said privately to Tanis. <*There are four to choose from.*>

<*We'll be wherever the capitol is—at least initially,*> Tanis replied.

Three years had passed since she had become governor of the New Canaan colony mission; so far, no one had stepped forward to take the reins from her. Not that she expected anyone to—the colony charter stated that the governor-at-landing would remain in power for ten years, to ensure a smooth startup.

The charter's definition of governor-at-landing was whoever was in charge when the ship passed through the colony star's heliopause. At the *Intrepid*'s current velocity, Tanis would gain that designation in about five minutes.

<*I bet if you went on a killing spree, they'd still keep you on,*> Angela said with a chuckle.

<*Angela!*> Joe admonished.

<*Don't tempt me,*> Tanis sighed. <*I know I should be jumping for joy, I mean...we're finally fucking here! This place, this New Canaan, is our promised land. Yet...I just feel like there's a cloud looming over it all.*>

Angela's thoughts were affirming, though honest, <*The Transcend government isn't going to make for the best neighbor, but I think that they'll leave us alone—for the first few decades, at least.*>

Tanis agreed with her AI's—and best friend's—assessment. Although the agreement with the Transcend government did not include access to the *Intrepid*'s picotech nor their stasis shield technology, the time would come when they would demand it.

For all they tried to paint their society as the bastion of peace and prosperity that all humanity should aspire to, Tanis could read between the lines. The Transcend was on a war footing. Whoever else was out there, it was someone they feared.

She didn't have enough data for a full assessment as yet—neither did Bob—but she suspected that it was not just the Orion Guard—a group Sera had told her about before she left for Airtha—that the Transcend opposed. If it were, she was certain that they could crush that one foe.

No, there was something else in the darkness of space that the Transcend was on guard against.

<*How do you think everyone will take your plan?*> Joe asked.

<*It depends,*> Tanis replied. <*A lot of people will think that, this far out from the Inner Stars, we'll be safe. They'll think I'm paranoid; but Bob backs me, and no one would call him paranoid.*>

<*I think you're exhibiting a keen appreciation for the past,*> Joe replied.

Tanis gave him a smile over their daughter's head and laughed as Cary began asking the names of every star she could see. Luckily, the Transcend had provided them with an index of all the stars in the M25 cluster. Joe and Tanis took turns providing the names to their daughter.

<*Governor,*> a voice broke into Tanis's thoughts.

<*Stop doing that, Priscilla,*> Tanis replied. <*You've known me too long to rest on formality.*>

<*The more you ask me to stop, the more I'll do it,*> the avatar replied with a mental grin.

Tanis could just imagine Priscilla, one of Bob's two human avatars, on her plinth in the bridge's foyer, smiling mischievously in her large, empty room.

She needed to talk to Amanda and Priscilla about their plans once the ship reached its destination. Their initial contract was to function as human bridges into the mind of Bob, the *Intrepid*'s massive, multi-nodal AI. Early in the ship's construction, it had become too distracting for Bob to deal with humans, and too overwhelming for most humans to have him speak into their minds.

Much like humans used many machines as their avatars and surrogates, so Bob used humans as his. Initially, the idea had disturbed Tanis a little—but Amanda and Priscilla had maintained their distinct personalities, and had even colored Bob's to an extent.

She knew they loved their jobs, and would likely never wish to leave Bob, but she still needed to share her plans with them and give them options.

<*You had news?*> Tanis asked Priscilla.

<*Yes, we've picked up a beacon at the heliopause. It says this system is interdicted and entrance is forbidden.*>

<*What a way to roll out the welcome mat,*> Tanis replied.

"I'd best get to the bridge," Tanis said as she passed Cary to Joe. "Looks like there's a beacon saying no entry. Probably just something for other folks—especially since they've forbidden us from trading with anyone."

"Go on," Joe replied before placing a kiss on her cheek. "We're good down here."

*****

The bridge crew was alert and at their stations. Captain Andrews, Terrance Enfield, and Admiral Sanderson stood at the central holotank, frowning as they studied the message scrolling past.

"Meant for us?" Tanis asked as she approached.

"I can't see how," Admiral Sanderson said, his eyes showing more anger than she would have expected. He was always terse, but anger was not his style. "There's no way even these snakes could think that we'd come this far and not take the system."

"We dropped a probe into the dark layer," Captain Andrews added. "The interdiction beacons are there, too."

Tanis shook her head. "Well, why should anything be easy?"

"At least no one is shooting at us," Amanda said from a nearby console, a statement that elicited groans from several nearby crewmembers.

"New signal coming in," the scan officer announced. "Oh…and it comes with ships!"

Scan updated on the main holotank, and Tanis saw that three ships had appeared around the *Intrepid:* one ahead and two flanking. The flanking ships were fifty thousand kilometers on either side, maneuvering to match vector, while the ship at the fore was closer—only ten thousand kilometers distant.

"I guess they *do* have some decent stealth tech," Tanis said. "I wonder if there were some of these at Ascella."

Sanderson nodded. "If they have them, you can bet they were out there."

"Why show the capability now?" Captain Andrews asked. "Is this the stick to go along with the carrot?"

"It's one hell of a stick," Tanis replied. "They could have a thousand of these ships out there."

*<Not a thousand,>* Bob replied. *<I could detect that many distortions. Three managed to slip by, but we'll work out how to spot them.>*

Tanis hoped so. She was used to having the upper hand when it came to stealth technology. Losing that edge would create new concerns.

"Transmission," comm announced.

"Put it on the tank," Tanis replied.

A man and a woman appeared before them. The woman wore the same Transcend Space Force uniform as General Tsaroff and Greer had back in Ascella. Two stars adorned her lapels, and she stood arms akimbo with a neutral expression as she surveyed the *Intrepid*'s bridge.

The man also wore a uniform, one that Tanis had seen in videos and images long ago. It was the millennia-old white and blue of the Future Generation Terraformers, the altruistic organization who journeyed across the stars with the goal of creating new homes for humanity.

"*Intrepid* colony mission, welcome to New Canaan," the man said with a genuine smile and widespread arms. "The FGT has been waiting to greet you at the end of your journey for some time."

A tear almost came to Tanis's eyes. The FGT *was* still alive within the Transcend. Sera had told her that the core of the ancient service was still present, still dedicated to their work, but after her initial encounters with the Transcend government and its envoys, she had begun to doubt it.

Now, seeing this man, with his genuine smile and welcoming expression, she believed again.

"Thank you," Tanis replied after a brief pause to compose herself. "I am Governor Tanis Richards. We're glad to finally be here.

Although, we were wondering if something had changed, given the beacon's transmission."

The man nodded and glanced at the woman. "Yes, I'm told it's a required precaution—not at all a part of our normal procedure."

"Admiral Isyra of the Transcend Space Force," the woman said. "My associate here is Director Huron of the FGT. The beacon is to ensure that other ships do not venture into the New Canaan system. *We* are here to take possession of the technology you are to provide in exchange for the colony system."

Tanis noticed a brief expression of distaste cross Director Huron's face and she wondered if he disapproved of trading technology for colonies. It wasn't in the FGT's initial charter to do so, but given their current options, it was more than acceptable to Tanis.

"How would you like it?" she asked. "We have the data crystal which we were originally going to provide to your envoys, or we can transmit it to you."

"You may transmit it for now." Colonel Isyra replied. "Director Huron would like to bring a team to your ship. It's the FGT's standard procedure to review the system with you. I will accompany him, and you may deliver the data crystal to me at that time."

Tanis nodded. "Very well. When can we expect you?"

"Within the hour."

* * * * *

The greetings were perfunctory, and before long, Admiral Isyra and her passel of FGT terraformers assembled with Tanis and the colony leaders in an auditorium typically used for plays and performances.

Tanis saw Simon, the head of Bioscience, enter with Ouri at his side, and she realized that she would have to release Ouri from her duties as a colonel in the Intrepid Space Force. It was finally time for her good friend to return to her original calling.

She already had Ouri's replacement lined up, but she knew this change would give them much less time together. It would be a time of upheaval across the ship. During the near-century at Kapteyn's Star, many in the crew had taken on new roles and responsibilities.

Some were happy in their new positions, while many others were eager to return to their originally planned duties.

There were also over a hundred thousand Victorians now on the colony roster—descendants of the *Hyperion's* crew that Tanis had saved from the Sirians during the first battle over Victoria. That number was offset by a similar number of colonists who stayed behind at Victoria, choosing to remain with friends and families they had formed at that time.

And then, of course, there were the children.

One of the key prerequisites for colony acceptance had been a candidate's desire to have children and raise them in a small family unit. For many colonists, waiting centuries to manifest that desire was not an option; and, over the years, a quarter million new colonists had been born.

The ship had enough stasis pods to handle that expansion, but Abby, the ship's Chief Engineer, had insisted that they needed three hundred thousand spare pods in case of any failures. The result was a ship that had stasis chambers crammed into every nook and cranny.

Tanis had faced off against Abby dozens of times over the years, but she agreed wholeheartedly on this issue.

*Speak of the devil,* she thought as Abby entered the auditorium. At her side was her husband Earnest, the technical visionary behind both the *Intrepid* and its AI, Bob. Abby wore her typical scowl, as though this presentation was taking her away from incredibly important work. Earnest, however, had an expression of rapture on his face.

Theirs was a strange relationship. For, as much as Tanis and Abby fought, she was fast friends with Earnest. He was also one of only a handful of people who knew that Tanis's mind was slowly merging with Angela's.

Tanis knew that Earnest had dreamed of being on a colony mission since he was a young boy. The desire to step foot on a virgin world and build a new civilization was the driving force behind much of his life's work. His marriage to Abby, a woman capable of building his incredible ideas, made them a dream team for a colony mission.

Tanis wished that Joe were present, but he had Fleet Con on the *Intrepid*'s bridge. They didn't expect any trouble while the FGT delegation and Isyra's small Transcend Space Force contingent were on the ship, but she wasn't about to let her guard down.

It struck her how incongruous it was that after spending fifty years in the Terran Space Force, the Transcend Space Force was the new TSF in her life. She didn't leave Sol on the best of terms with the Terran military, and she wasn't starting off on the best footing with the Transcend's, either.

*<Looking for meaning in acronyms?>* Angela asked with a smile in Tanis's mind.

*<Silly, isn't it?>* Tanis replied.

*<Yup, just a little bit,>* Angela said. *<I bet we have a respectable number of years before they become a real pain in the ass.>*

Tanis glanced at Admiral Isyra, who sat next to her chatting with Commandant Brandt. *<Dunno, they seem like a pretty big pain in mine, already.>*

Up on the stage, Director Huron signaled for everyone's attention. The room quieted in moments, and he looked across the crowd, beaming with delight.

"This is a momentous occasion," his voice boomed through the room, picked up and amplified by the auditorium's systems.

"You may not know this, but I was stationed on the *Destiny Ascendant* while it was building the New Eden system. I wasn't a Worldship Director then, but I spent a lot of time working on the first of the two terraformed worlds—mostly on the oceans. I'm sure you all know from your time at Kapteyn's Star how important it is to get those just right. That was excellent work you did there, by the way. Your terraforming of Victoria has gone down as the textbook methodology for a tidally locked super-earth. We don't do many of those, but there are more than a few in the Inner Stars now."

Director Huron chuckled. "I digress; I'm passionate about our work, and get caught up in it a lot. Anyway, we waited at New Eden a long time for you, but by the time the current inhabitant's ancestors arrived, I was long gone and I missed out on their landfall."

The FGT director paused, his gaze sweeping across the assemblage. "You have no idea how excited I was to learn that you, that this ship, the *Intrepid,* would take possession of this system, which you've named New Canaan. By the way, I appreciate the historical reference—losing Eden and ending up in Canaan. But believe me, New Eden has nothing on this system."

With that, Director Huron flung his arms into the air and a projection of the system appeared in the air above the stage.

<*A flair for the dramatic in this one,*> Angela commented.

<*I like it,*> Tanis replied. <*Better than some dry presentation or boring speech. And he was at New Eden, too! What are the chances?*>

<*Indeed.*>

"I'm sure you've all studied the data our envoys provided, but let me give you the real story behind this gem of a heliosphere," Huron continued.

"When our early prep team arrived just under a thousand years ago, this system was a mess. The star hadn't really settled down yet, and the innermost Jovian planet was still jostling for position with the outer worlds. There was a real risk that it would move in toward the star, and eat one of the three terrestrial worlds there."

The holo projection above Huron updated, showing a much more chaotic and more crowded system.

"We weren't about to allow that to happen, and spent considerable effort shifting the outer planets into more stable orbits to leave enough room in the gravitational dance for the terrestrial worlds. We did too good of a job, because when it was all said and done, there was room for a fourth."

The holo shifted, showing a system with the three terrestrial worlds moving around the star and the outer worlds shifted further away, their orbital periods slowed. In many respects, the system was messier than before the FGT began their work. Dust, gas, and perturbed asteroids were strewn across the heliosphere.

"You'll see that out beyond the Kuiper belt, there were these three rocky worlds." Huron gestured at the holo, and three of the many scattered disk dwarf planets lit up. "We carefully nudged them in toward the inner system, and mashed them into one world. Then we situated a Planetary Energy Transfer Ring around it and drew away the excess heat."

Tanis had to admit some excitement. She had read about the FGT's use of their massive energy transfer rings—constructs they created as needed, and often discarded when their work was done—making for the foundation of planetary habitation rings.

"The ring, we like to call them Peters, is still there; it has another thousand years of work to do. While we can draw the majority of the excess heat from the planet in a few hundred years, the final stages need more finesse. The crust needs to settle, and orderly magma flows must be established beneath the surface. Major tectonic disruptions are past, but the only temperate regions are above the sixtieth parallel; so, it's a bit of a hot place right now. You can choose the names, of course, but we call this world Gemma. It's a bit of a joke, and a long story that I'll share sometime."

Huron surveyed the crowd. "However, if you keep an eye on the scheduled tsunamis, you can enjoy some pretty amazing surfing conditions."

There were a few chuckles from the audience, and Tanis recalled enjoying her few trips to Victoria's sunward ocean and the insane water sports people engaged in on its tumultuous shores.

It was impressive to think that less than a thousand years ago, the planet hadn't existed at all; and now there was a world with an oxygenated atmosphere and the beginnings of life at its poles. In just two hundred years, it would be cool enough that its poles would ice over, and its temperate bands would widen.

"This one is a favorite of mine," Huron explained as the holodisplay shifted to the next world, third from Canaan Prime. The planet filled the space above Huron and the first few rows of the auditorium, giving a clear view of its five major landmasses; all positioned above and below the fifteenth parallel. Several major islands lay in the tropics on one side of the globe, and a massive archipelago stretched across the equator on the other side, joining two of the continents with a loose chain of islands.

"Often, when we do a full greenie, we have to situate a ring around the world to manage the climate, but this one does it all on its own. You'll note that there are no major landmasses on the equator, and the ocean currents work in such a fashion that few doldrums exist. This keeps warm air and water circulating the globe, and the deep channels we worked into the north and south polar regions keep them warm year-round.

"We dubbed this one Carthage, after the ancient, sea-faring civilization on Earth."

<*There's irony for you,*> Angela chuckled.

<*What is?*> Tanis asked unable to determine what was ironic about the name.

<*The city of Carthage was founded by the people of Tyre, which was a major city in Canaan,*> Angela replied.

<*I guess I can see how that's an interesting connection…but I think that you need to check the definition of 'irony'.*>

<*You need to study more human history. The main god of Carthage was Tanit.*>

Tanis had to stifle a laugh. The naming was indeed ironic, given that her name was a variation of Tanit, the ancient Phoenician goddess of the stars, sun, and moon.

<*Fitting, for sure. I looked up my name long ago, but I never considered it in conjunction with our colony name of New Canaan; let alone a world named Carthage.*>

<*I am going to push for all Phoenician planet names, and then let everyone know your name's meaning and that you want to be their goddess,*> Angela said with an insidious chuckle.

Tanis groaned in her mind. <*Ang! Don't do that. Some group will take that up, and we'll have a cult on our hands.*>

<*You say that like you think there's not already a few of those.*>

<*Hush,*> Tanis scolded. <*I'm trying to listen to Huron.*>

"Next up, we have the world of Justice. We named it that because no matter what we did, the world made its own calls—and was always right," Huron said as the view above them shifted to show the second planet from the star. "Justice was naturally pre-disposed to be a world of extremes, and, given that we had so many terrestrial planets to work with, we decided to leave it like that and enhance its natural beauty."

Even from view high above the planet, Tanis could see what Huron meant. The dozen continents were all small, with three approaching one another on a slow-motion collision course. Every landmass showed massive mountains; their white peaks reaching high above deep green valleys below. Vast deserts, plains, and inland seas were visible across the world.

"You can see that this planet has everything you could wish for," Huron described. "It also has three moons—one of near-lunar mass, which keep things shifting on the surface below. If you want to stabilize it, you will need to move their orbits further out; but if you ask me, variety is the spice of life, and this world adds some spice."

"Last up we have the planet Tir. This one is also pretty much as we found it, only now it's habitable. Tir's mass-to-circumference ratio was such that we didn't have to make any adjustments to achieve a pleasant level of gravity. It comes in at a hair under one gee, and, as you can see, is a farmer's paradise."

Tanis had to agree. The continents were just the right size to keep from forming interior deserts, and the few mountain ranges that were present would funnel rain evenly across broad grasslands. A few forests dotted the surface, and a small continent at the world's north pole would give it cooler winters and more pronounced seasons than the other planets in the system.

"We've worked hard to get New Canaan ready for you, and there's still more to be done—we had planned on spending another few centuries here—but we're told that you are going to take over and finish up. Given your work on Victoria and Tara in the Kapteyn's System, I am confident that we're leaving this system in the good hands of you, the crew, and the colonists of the famed *Intrepid*!"

Huron paused and thunderous applause broke out in the auditorium. He let it sound for a minute, and then raised his hands.

"Given our impending departure, we have a lot of knowledge to transfer and only a month in which to do it. Your leaders have set up a variety of meetings for us to get acquainted and begin that work, so I suggest we all get some food—which I'm told is being served in a hall a short distance from here—and then we can get started," Huron said as everyone began to rise.

Tanis remained seated, reviewing the worlds Huron had described. Her eye was drawn to Carthage, third from the star. Though the two worlds closest to the Canaan Prime were further along in their terraforming process—in stage four, as opposed to Carthage, which was still in phase three—the FGT had chosen to build the space elevator and station above it. The elevator's strand reached down to one of the large islands in the eastern archipelago—it would make a beautiful location for the system capital.

*<It's like destiny,>* Angela chuckled. *<I've already proposed Tyre, Troy, and Athens for the other planets.>*

<*You have not!*> Tanis exclaimed, quickly checking. Sure enough, Angela had done just that in the naming groups that had formed on the *Intrepid*'s nets. The names were already gaining traction, everyone appreciating the connection to the Phoenician roots those cities had, and thus their connection to the ancient land of Canaan.

<*It's a great theme; your name is just icing on the cake,*> Angela smirked.

<*I'll get you for this,*> Tanis muttered.

She wanted to take a closer look at the station, which appeared to be too small to dock the *Intrepid* at—with just a fifty-kilometer circumference—but Admiral Isyra interrupted her.

"I need to return to my ship, but I assume you have the data crystal?" she asked brusquely.

"I do," Tanis said as she stood. "This way."

She led Isyra through the crowds and out into the corridor. Most of the attendees turned left toward the hall where a buffet had been prepared, accompanied by long rows of tables awaiting deep conversations about the final stages of terraforming, and the steps to begin colonization in earnest.

She turned to the right and led the colonel down the corridor toward a nearby maglev station.

Most of the Transcend Admiral's soldiers followed the FGT personnel to the buffet; but a fireteam came with them, cautiously eyeing the four ISF Marines accompanying Tanis.

They walked to the train station in silence, passersby giving them a wide berth. When they boarded the train, Isyra sat across from Tanis, while their escorts stood in the aisles.

The Admiral was silent for a moment before cracking a small smile. "Sorry for coming off as such a hard-ass. I'm walking a fine line, here. A lot of people don't want you to have this system, and I'm doing my best not to look like I'm playing sides."

Tanis gave a slow nod, curious to see where Isyra was going. "I can only imagine," was all that she offered in response.

"I heard what happened in Ascella," Admiral Isyra continued. "I know why you aren't terribly happy with us right now. You're a bit of a legend, and you have a propensity to upset the order of things."

"A legend, am I?" Tanis asked.

"Absolutely," Isyra nodded. "In the TSF—our TSF, of course, not the ancient Terran Space Force—we all study your battle at Kapteyn's Star. Both your initial fight with that single Sirian cruiser—where you tucked your ship into that icy asteroid—and then afterward, when you defeated a superior enemy. They were some of my favorite battles from our ancient historical warfare class."

"Thanks," Tanis said. "That last fight over Victoria was less than two decades ago for me—hearing it described as ancient history is a bit surreal."

"What's surreal is being here," Isyra replied. "I saw the *Andromeda* when we came in. That ship is what we modeled our stealth ships after. A legend in its own right—even more so, after what it did at Bollam's World. That's another battle of yours that will go down in history—I guess the debates about how you won over Victoria will finally be laid to rest."

"Will they?" Tanis asked. She knew what the debate was over, but she wanted to hear this woman spell it out. The conversation was giving her interesting insight.

"I'm sure you can imagine why," Isyra said with a raised eyebrow. "Few believed you had picotech, and they didn't believe in your final decisive victory as the Victorians described it. A lot of scholars claim that the Victorians understated the size of your fleet in that battle, while others suggest that you had a second array of rail platforms."

"I would have, if the Victorians hadn't dragged their heels on building them. But why doesn't anyone trust the records?" Tanis asked.

"A lot was lost during the FTL wars. *We* have unsullied records, but most of the Inner Stars do not," Isyra replied. "Though, I suppose that the AST government believed the old stories about picotech, too; or you would have had a much easier time in the Bollam's World system."

"That's for certain," Tanis nodded in response. "And now the cat's out of the bag; everyone knows we have picotech, and a lot of folks will be looking for us."

"And so you understand why this system is interdicted," Isyra said.

"The Transcend may be the best-kept secret in the Inner Stars, but not so well kept that knowledge of our whereabouts won't eventually leak to a few interested parties," Tanis replied.

The train came to a smooth stop at their destination, and Tanis rose with Isyra. She followed two of her Marines out of the car while the other two waited to take up the rear.

She noticed another squad of ISF Marines in strategic locations on the crowded platform, and saw that Isyra did, too. Neither said anything, but both knew that their casual banter hadn't imparted any real trust.

"There is some trade with certain Inner Stars governments," Isyra acknowledged. "Traders talk, and if Transcend traders come here, this secret will be out in no time."

"The arrangement suits us just fine," Tanis replied. "We had no expectation of interstellar trade when we set out on this mission. We're not going to suffer for a lack of it, now."

"Good," Isyra nodded.

"So, how far in will your ships escort us?" Tanis asked.

"All the way," Isyra replied. "My orders are to ensure the smooth departure of the FGT personnel, and not to leave until the last of them are outsystem."

"And you expect that to take just a month?" Tanis asked.

"Honestly? No, it will probably take half a year at best. Most of the terraformers have already left, though. We got word of your impending arrival years ago. There was some grumbling that things weren't quite ready to turn over yet, and most didn't know that it was you who was coming. Huron's transition team can be trusted not to share secrets, but..."

"But this is a big secret to keep, yes," Tanis nodded. She decided to see if Isyra had an opinion on the eventual revelation of just who had received the colony. "And when it gets out?"

Isyra caught Tanis's eye as they walked down a vacant corridor. "I see you are of the same mind as me. Yes, *when* it gets out...I honestly don't know. I don't know why we didn't require your picotech, or at least your stasis shields, in trade for this system."

"How do you know that we didn't provide that?" Tanis asked.

"Because my AI, Greta, is going to validate the crystal, and be certain that it adheres to the letter of our agreement. We don't keep much from one another, so I know what you offered. It's good, really good, but not worth this system. Not with four terraformed worlds of this quality." Isyra's expression had grown darker. Not upset, but she looked as though she disapproved of her own government's ability to barter.

"Be that as it may," Tanis replied. "It is what the deal is for. We're not prepared to offer anything further, and, like I told your envoys, we've terraformed before. We could fly clear through the Transcend and do it again if we had to."

Isyra grunted. "I'd expect no less from you, Governor. It's always your way or the airlock, isn't it?"

"Pretty much," Tanis said tonelessly before stopping and gesturing to an open doorway on their left. "It's in here."

Two of Isyra's guards entered first before signaling that the room was clear—or, as clear as could be, with four ISF Marines stationed inside.

Tanis realized that she would have to rename the ISF now that they had arrived at New Canaan. The Intrepid Space Force was a name she had become very accustomed to—a crest she had worn for nearly a hundred years; a longer term of service than she had served in the Terran Space Force back in Sol.

*<You know, if the Sol Space Federation kept their military named for Terra, there's no reason you can't keep New Canaan's named for the* Intrepid,*>* Angela supplied. *<It is as much our place of origin as Terra was for the Terran Space Force.>*

*<Good point—worth consideration,>* Tanis replied.

"If you'll wait a moment," Tanis said before walking across the antechamber.

The portal on the far side led to one of the *Intrepid*'s data vaults. The one before her was an ancillary backup facility, a node that she was willing to reveal to Isyra, as the crystal was the only item within it worth having.

Isyra would likely suspect that, and know that data pertaining to picotech or stasis shields would be elsewhere.

Tanis passed a series of tokens to the vault's security system, as did Angela, before feeling the tingling sensation of nanoprobes passing through her skin in a dozen locations to collect additional security tokens.

A minute later, a hard ES shield snapped into place behind her, and the entrance to the vault opened. Inside laid another security checkpoint, and a final portal. The entrance slid open, and Tanis stepped inside, retrieving the data crystal she had placed within three years ago.

She held the crystal in her hand, checking the data read-out from its casing. With three notable exceptions, the crystal contained the culmination of human ingenuity at its peak in the fifth millennia. The knowledge within would strengthen the Transcend; perhaps help them to overcome their enemies without seeking that which Tanis was determined to withhold.

<*Nice sentiment,*> Angela said. <*Human history is not replete with examples of your kind leaving well enough alone.*>

<*A girl can dream,*> Tanis replied. <*Though, it's not as if I don't have contingency plans.*>

<*Speaking of which, how are you going to pull those off, with Isyra tailing us into the system?*>

Tanis sighed. That did throw a wrench into the works. <*I'll think of something. It* ***is*** *our system after all. If we choose to deploy our fleet throughout as we enter, that's our prerogative.*>

Tanis walked back into the antechamber and handed the data crystal to Isyra, who thanked her before setting it on a table and placing her hand over the data access port on its casing.

Isyra closed her eyes, and Tanis was certain she was examining what information she could. Not that it would help Isyra overmuch. Even as an L2 human, Tanis knew that her ability to capture much meaning from the information in a short period would be limited.

It wasn't as though Isyra would have much time with the crystal, either. Tanis expected to see a pinnace make a wormhole jump to Airtha shortly after Isyra returned to her ship.

"This appears to be in order—at least, as well as we can tell here," Isyra spoke after a minute. "I'll admit. That is a *lot* of data. Perhaps it was worth this system."

"I think it is," Tanis agreed. "I assume you need to return to your ship now?"

"I do," Isyra replied. "I'll need to send this on its way."

Tanis nodded. "I'll have the Marines escort you to your shuttle; I have a few things to attend to."

"Very well, Governor," Admiral Isyra said, and extended her hand. "It has been a pleasure meeting you."

"Likewise," Tanis replied.

A moment later Isyra was gone, and Tanis was alone in the room.

<*So, what is it that you need to do so badly?*> Angela asked.

Tanis snorted. <*As if you don't know. It's Cary's nap time, of course!*>

# MACHINATIONS

**STELLAR DATE: 04.22.8933 (Adjusted Years)**
**LOCATION: ISS *Intrepid***
**REGION: Near Sparta, 9th Planet in the New Canaan System**

"Are we on schedule?" Tanis asked as she looked around the table. She knew the answer from the team's reports, but there were always nuances that the reports didn't contain.

"Absolutely," Erin replied with a smile. "I have to say, I was a bit dismayed when I learned that Carthage already had a strand and a station—not that there isn't a lot more to build, but this is way more fun. Especially since we get to stick it to the Transcend."

"We're not really 'sticking it to the Transcend'," Joe replied with a frown. "It's our system. If we plan to build a secret base, then we can do it, and there's nothing they can do to stop us."

Tanis sighed. "Well, not '*nothing*'."

True to his prediction some weeks earlier, Bob had worked out how to see the Transcend's stealth ships—or at least some of them. Tanis now knew that Isyra's three ships were but the tip of the spear. Over seventy cloaked vessels surrounded the New Canaan system; though, as far as they could tell, only the three ships accompanying the *Intrepid* were within the heliopause.

Everyone around the table nodded solemnly. Tanis hadn't hidden the Transcend's siege of the New Canaan system from anyone. She wanted the entire colony to back her plan, and being under watch by a foreign military helped her cause.

*<I wish I didn't have this cause, though,>* she said privately to Angela. *<But we're not going to live in fear of an invasion by the Transcend. No way, no how.>*

"I just wish I got to be there for landing," Erin said. "You guys are going to have an epic party."

"We'll do up a holo for you, Erin," Tanis replied. "Chef Earl is already planning the spread he's going to lay out."

"I expect he needs to," Admiral Sanderson said. "There are going to be ten thousand people going down for the landing celebration; feeding that many people at once is no small feat."

"Too bad we can't get everyone down there for the first footstep," Earnest said wistfully. "I know that's not feasible, but it's still a shame."

Tanis nodded. "Yeah, but a lottery for the selection was always the plan. I want to try and keep as much in line with our original charter as we can. Most of the colonists opted to go back into stasis in Victoria. For them, it will be only weeks since we left Sol. They need to feel like things are normal...if that's even possible."

"Never mind the whole secret military installation we're building, then," Erin said with a wink.

"I'm taking a page out of the New Eden system's playbook. Even with the AST right on their doorstep, they maintained their independence by making an attack on them too costly to be worth the effort. I plan to do the same thing here. Right now, we couldn't repel an attack by the ships they have monitoring us—at least not without running in the end. We need to be able to withstand a force of at least ten thousand ships."

Terrance was taking a drink of his coffee and nearly spat it out. "Ten thousand ships? Are you serious? Do you really think that they'll bring that kind of force to bear?"

"Back in Sol, the TSF had a million ships in its navy. Sure, a lot were smaller patrol boats; but there were over twenty thousand cruisers, and hundreds of thousands of destroyers. If the Transcend controls as many systems as we think they do—even if their populations are much smaller than Sol's—they will have *a lot* more ships than that," Tanis replied.

"But even if we build the best shipyards we can, there's no way we can construct that many ships in a century—not while hiding it to any extent," Erin said with a frown.

"Oh, trust me," Tanis's mouth twitched into a mischievous grin. "We can, and we're not just going to build ships...."

* * * * *

Two days later, Tanis watched the *Gilese, Pike,* and *Condor* pull away from the *Intrepid.* The three cruisers escorted a pair of hundred-meter pushers, which, in turn, were hauling one of the *Intrepid*'s cargo containers toward the fifth moon of Sparta, New Canaan's ninth planet.

It was here that Erin would begin to build the first of Tanis's shipyards, under the guise of the construction of a mining facility.

There was no reason Admiral Isyra would even suspect anything was amiss. The location was one that Director Huron himself had pointed out as an ideal source of raw materials for building more orbital structures.

The moon Erin's mission was en route to, named Thebes, was three thousand kilometers in circumference. The station architect's mission was to hollow it out as quickly as possible, while giving the appearance of strip-mining the moon from the outside.

It would take many years, but when the process was complete, the remnants of the moon would appear to be nothing more than loose rock and debris—but that gravel would shroud a shipyard over three hundred kilometers across.

It was there that Tanis would begin to build the new ISF fleet. Unlike her current assortment of ships—which she had grown very fond of, over the years—this new fleet would be built only for war. After seeing the AST dreadnaughts, she had worked with Earnest and a crew of engineers to design a new class of ship that combined the best aspects of the ships they had faced in the Bollam's World system, and those of the ancient TSF back in Sol.

She wished Erin and her team well; they would labor long, hiding their true work until the time was right.

"It's like the gamma site all over again," Joe said from across their kitchen table, also watching the holoprojection of the ships accelerating away from the *Intrepid.*

"Except we're going to have a dozen of them," Tanis replied. "Good thing we practiced."

"What's a gamassite?" Cary asked around a mouthful of oatmeal.

"It's a secret place that we never speak of with anyone other than Mommy and Daddy," Joe replied.

"Now finish your oatmeal," Tanis said. "You have your morning class soon, and we don't want to be late."

"We can be late, Mommy, you're the guvner. E'eryone does what you say."

Joe laughed, nearly spitting his orange juice across the table. Tanis shot him a scowl before smiling as well.

"Mostly they do, but not always. And it's disrespectful to be late and keep others waiting for you. The first rule of leadership is to always show respect to those you lead."

"What's 'respex' mean?" Cary asked.

"Respect means always being polite, and thinking about what other's want before yourself," Joe replied.

<*Something you're such a pro at,*> Angela chided.

<*I seem to do well enough,*> Tanis replied.

# LANDFALL

**STELLAR DATE: 05.15.8933 (Adjusted Years)**
**LOCATION: Landfall**
**REGION: Carthage, 3rd Planet in the New Canaan System**

Tanis stepped out of the shuttle onto a wide, green expanse—the location of the landfall celebration, and the future site of their capital city on the planet Carthage. The colonists had selected a location close to the existing space elevator, which terminated on a large island in the equatorial archipelago.

She had pushed to be on the first shuttle down, but Brandt wouldn't hear of it. The Commandant had deployed an entire company of Marines around the clearing and into the hills beyond. Only when she was satisfied with her security did she give the all-clear for the governor to land.

Tanis looked at Joe, then down to Cary.

"We're finally here," she said to her small family. "Only four and a half quadrillion kilometers in the wrong direction, and several thousand years late; but we made it."

Joe gave a low chuckle. "Worth the trip, if you ask me. This place is gorgeous. Quite the view, too."

"Why are those mountains making clouds? Are they on fire?" Cary asked with a frown.

Tanis looked to the east, where massive plumes of smoke and steam rose from the planet and escaped into space—the final terraforming work pushing waste gasses off-world, lest they shroud the entire globe.

The evacuated clouds created a glowing nebula that hung over half the sky, a beautiful view that would probably dissipate over the next few decades.

"Sort of," Joe said to Cary. "Those are volcanoes. Hot, melted rock from inside the planet is coming out of them."

Cary looked worried and Joe picked her up. "It's very safe, that's why their smoke is going out into space."

"It's certainly not a sight I've ever seen," Tanis replied with no small amount of awe in her voice. "On Victoria and Tara, we did our best to keep the gasses *on* the planet, not vent them into space."

Behind them, the other colony leaders were stepping off the shuttle, and a hundred meters away, another shuttle landed with the lucky winners who won the lottery to be a part of the landfall party.

A dozen more shuttles were queued up in the sky, and Tanis resisted the temptation to check on the schedule.

Today was about enjoying their future together.

The smells of fresh flowers and loamy earth were in the air, and green grass glistened beneath her feet. The organic perfume was much like their cabin by the lake on the *Intrepid,* but subtly different. There was just something about being on the surface of a planet, under the light of a yellow star.

She laughed and jumped lightly into the air, falling back to the ground under the pull of near-Earth gravity.

Cary jumped as well. "Why are we jumping, Mommy?" she asked with a grin.

"Because we're so happy to be here, we're jumping with joy."

*****

Before long, Chef Earl had the great barbeque pits roaring, and cooked meats and vegetables were flowing from his prep stations into the crowd. The choice of meal surprised her, but once she sank her teeth into a medium-rare burger, she knew Earl had made the right choice.

Great tankards of beer or tall goblets of wine, were in nearly every hand, and Tanis found herself frequently juggling her food and drink to shake hands and slap shoulders.

Music thundered across the clearing, and a dancing space opened up. Tanis whisked Cary into her arms, and the trio danced as the shared exuberance of the assemblage coursed through them.

As night began to fall, no one appeared to be interested in letting up, though the Marines began to set up long tents with cots and blankets for any who wished to catch a few winks before resuming their celebrations.

Not long after the sun set, Joe took Cary via shuttle to the groundside of the space elevator for a good night's sleep. Their daughter was fascinated by being planetside, with a bright sky overhead; but as the stars came out, the idea of seeing space with no plas or shield to protect her began to alarm Cary.

Tanis, however, stayed the night, knowing that she owed everyone a small piece of her time.

Even though she had spoken to every single person present, crew and colonists alike still approached her through the night.

"I knew you'd get us here, Governor," more than one happy colonist exclaimed while shaking her hand, hugging, or even kissing her. Tanis appreciated their thanks and reminded them that she was just one part of the effort that had brought them this far. This was a victory for them all.

"You might as well stop saying that," a voice at her shoulder said after one such exchange. "No one is buying it for a second."

Tanis turned to see Captain Andrews next to her, holding a glass of beer in his hand.

"Picked out your homestead site yet?" she asked.

Andrews laughed. "Not yet, no. There are just a few things left to do up there," he gestured to the bright light that was the *Intrepid* crossing the sky overhead in its high orbit.

"Not too much more," Tanis replied. "I want that ship emptied out in three years max. It needs to be ready for the next phase."

"You really think all of this will be necessary? The *Intrepid* has been our home for centuries," Andrews asked with a worried frown creasing his face.

"It's not like I'm dismantling it," Tanis replied with a laugh. "Just giving it new purpose."

Captain Andrews nodded slowly. "Well, very soon none of that will be my concern. I think I'll see what is involved in becoming a brewmaster."

"Really?" Tanis asked. "I didn't know you had an interest in that. In fact, I rarely see you drink beer at all."

"One of the ensigns has been making his own from a crop he grows in the prairie park. I found myself getting a taste for it. Time for new things and new experiences, right?"

Tanis shook her head. "Whatever you say, Captain. You're talking to a woman who learned how to grow just the right flowers to get just the right pigments to paint a masterpiece. I know all about diving into a craft."

"What are you going to do with your little cabin?" Andrews asked. "You spent more time out of stasis than anyone…well, you and Joe."

"I really don't know," Tanis said. "Cary wants us to bring it down here, which wouldn't be too hard. I might be ready for a change, though."

"Oh?" Andrews asked. "No more cabin by a lake?"

"No, no," Tanis smiled. "I'm all for that, I just want a much bigger one."

Andrews barked a laugh in response. "Bigger lake or cabin?"

"Both! You know, I *am* the governor now," Tanis said with a wink.

# ASSAULT ON TRISAL

**STELLAR DATE: 04.11.8935 (Adjusted Years)**
**LOCATION: Durden Continent, Trisal**
**REGION: Freemont System, Orion Freedom Alliance, near the Transcend border**

The air around Kent thundered and shook with the force of the orbital bombardment. Nothing in his time as an enlisted man, or in his officer's training, had prepared him for what it would be like to witness an assault of this magnitude.

Trisal was in stage two of its terraforming process, and the cloud cover was too thick for beam weapons to penetrate without diffusion. Taking out the separatist cruiser would require a less measured approach.

Captain Bellan, the company CO, had called down conventional weapons in the form of tactical nukes.

<*Keep that beam on that ship!*> he yelled at the lance corporal holding the painting laser. <*If we don't blow that cruiser, this is going to be the shortest, and last, offensive of our lives.*>

The corporal nodded and steadied the laser. With miles of cloud above them, the Guard's ships couldn't track ground targets well enough to strike them without accidentally pulverizing the 547th battalion in the process. When the next round of nukes broke through the clouds above, they would only have seconds to find the painting laser's target, and lock onto the separatist cruiser.

<*There!*> the platoon's spotter called out and marked the nukes on everyone's retinal HUDs.

<*Steaaady,*> Kent called out; then his visor darkened to block the flash of twelve nuclear warheads.

While he waited for the visor to clear, he replayed scan data from the impacts. Nine of the explosions had occurred above the cruiser and three below. The combined power of the weapons knocked the cruiser's shields offline and two of its engines winked out, but it still hovered above the landscape on a powerful grav column.

<*C'monnn…*> Kent whispered.

The hot wind from the nukes swept up and away from the cruiser, and pushed the clouds back. Not completely, but enough that the fleet overhead could lock on the target.

Nine arcs of star-stuff lanced down from the heavens and tore the cruiser to pieces.

Kent shook his head as the cruiser crashed to the ground with a thunder almost as loud as the bombs. It was such a waste of life.

The soldiers in his platoon let out a cheer and Kent looked on and smiled at their enthusiasm. They had the right of it—it was better the enemy than them.

<*OK, people, enough lounging around. We have a target to reach and we're not going to do it sitting out here,*> he said with a nod to the platoon sergeant, a squat woman named Jutek, who assigned the squads their positions.

<*We're on the move,*> Kent reported to Captain Bellan. <*ETA to target is thirty minutes.*>

<*Good,*> Bellan replied. <*That's in sync with first and third platoons. Fourth is a bit behind, but they had the nose of that cruiser right over their target and had to hold back. Keep me updated on any resistance you meet.*>

<*Yes, sir,*> Kent replied.

He joined up with third squad and followed them into a shallow gully that wound through the low hills in the direction they needed to travel. It wasn't so deep as to be a potential trap; just enough to hide them from broad scan sweeps and casual observation.

<*Don't bunch up,*> the squad sergeant, an old veteran named Tunk, cautioned the fifteen men and women under his command. Kent heeded the professional's advice and fell back, ready to engage any opposition they may encounter.

Two hundred meters ahead, the pair of soldiers in the lead fell prone, and the rest of the squad followed suit, ducking behind rocks and scanning probe data.

<*Ahead, our two,*> Mendez, one of the lead soldiers reported. <*I saw movement on the ridge, maybe three or four.*>

<*Check it out,*> Tunk replied. <*Could be one of their units, or just an escape pod from the cruiser.*>

<*Think any of them got out?*> Kent asked.

<*These separatists are cowards,*> Tunk replied. <*I wouldn't be surprised if half the pods were filled after the first volley.*>

Kent wasn't so sure; the ship had stayed, defending the ground base below, to the end. Those were not the actions of cowards.

The squad's first fireteam worked their way up the gully's slope, staying low and deploying recon probes. Normally, they would have swathes of nanobots probing the area around the platoon; but a combination of the developing world's heavy winds, and the radiation from the nukes made that impossible.

*<It's a squad—no…a full platoon,>* the fireteam leader reported back. *<They're in powered armor, so the rads aren't bothering them, either.>*

The separatists didn't have the same spec armor or weapons as his troops, but they outnumbered Kent's squad five-to-one. Fourth squad was on the far side of the enemy platoon; Kent considered his options. His maps of the area showed he could continue down the gully undetected, and pass right by the enemy formation.

But all it would take was one member of that separatist platoon to see a boot print from his soldiers, and they'd have beam fire up their asses—probably at the least opportune time, too.

*<We're going to take them out,>* Kent said on the platoon's combat net. *<I don't want to call fire from the sky; it would be a beacon for a hundred klicks pointed right at us. We're going to smash them hard and fast, and as quietly as we can.>*

*<Quiet, Lieutenant?>* Tunk coughed.

*<Yeah, hit them with proton beams; hard, directional fire. This place is irradiated to shit now, anyway. Tunk, Maple, here are your fireteam's positions. I want you to be ready to hit these guys in one minute, while they're still right between us.>*

Each squad separated into four fireteams and moved toward their assigned positions. Kent joined fireteam four and crept up the gully's side to the crest, and peered over. There, in the three-hundred-meter expanse between the squads, was the separatist platoon.

Their weapons were multifunctional rifles—much like the ones his own troops used, but he could tell that they were subtly different; though they didn't look cheap. Their armor, however, was of a lower quality. That much would help his platoon out. Their proton beams should be able to penetrate with just a few direct hits.

The combat net showed all the fireteams in position and ready. Kent set a five-second countdown.

5… 4… 3… 2… 1…

Each squad fired a series of sonic detonators into the enemy position, confusing and disorienting them as the beam-fire lanced into their ranks. Half a dozen separatist soldiers fell in the initial volley, followed by several more as they scrambled for cover.

Kent felt a moment's pity for the men and women dying in the killing field between his two squads. Their CO was still treating this area as though it was land they controlled; they thought they would be the hunters, and so held to the high ground for a better vantage.

Better to behave as though you were the hunted—Kent had learned that in the wilds of Herschel as a young boy. To catch prey, you had to think like prey, and always be aware that you were not the only hunter out there.

Return fire hit the ground near him, and Kent rolled to a new position. His force may have had the element of surprise, but the enemy had found enough cover to dig in, and was putting up a good fight; something that Kent respected—but it was too little, too late.

Even in cover, three more separatists fell. A minute later, a group stood and surrendered, throwing their weapons to the ground.

Like a wave, more of the separatists rose, tossing aside their weapons.

<*Stay sharp,*> Tunk ordered the two squads. <*Get them back in the gully.*>

<*Fuck, Sarge, what are we going to do with these guys?*> Mendez asked. <*We can't force them out of their armor; their skin will melt off in minutes with all these rads.*>

Mendez's sentiment was shared by them all. Even without their primary weapons, a soldier in a suit of powered armor was a serious threat. The matte black suits held a variety of integrated weapons systems, and gave the wearer the strength of a dozen unarmored humans.

<*We're going to have to stick a suppression dose on each of them,*> Kent said. <*Third squad, you're on that. Fourth squad, any of these fuckers so much as moves, you put a beam through their faceplate.*>

Two fireteams from third squad gestured with their weapons to the first separatist group, directing them down into the gully. The other two fireteams held their weapons on the remaining enemy, while fourth squad worked their way across the battlefield, checking for any hidden soldiers who had not surrendered, and ensuring that any wounded would not see another day.

It seemed brutal, but Kent knew it was a mercy. If a soldier's armor was penetrated in this irradiated landscape, they weren't going to make it long enough for anyone to treat them, anyway—they were already dead. Not to mention the rads from the proton beams that took them down.

While his squads applied suppression packages to the captives, he reviewed the first and second squads' progress. They had reached the first marker and were holding position, waiting for third and fourth squad to catch up.

*<Hende, Akar, send a fireteam ahead and scout out the terrain. I want to know if there are any more of these enemy patrols in the area.>*

*<You got it, LT,>* Hende replied audibly, while Akar sent a confirmation response over the combat net.

Kent watched the first enemy soldiers feel their armor lock up. The suppression packages were systematically seizing every mechanical joint and crystallizing the fluid sections. The nanobots in the package would also be severing their Link access and burning any repair systems.

He marked the gully's location on his personal map. If they didn't pick these soldiers up in a day, they would be dead from radiation sickness. He never hesitated to kill in combat, but he would never want to die alone in the dark—these men and women deserved better than that.

The squads got moving again, and he trailed behind squad three's third fireteam once more, his eyes sweeping the terrain while reviewing the feeds from his men and their probes.

So far, the coast was clear.

They reached a low rise, and the two scout fireteams ranged ahead, working their way down the boulder-strewn slope on the far side. Their feeds showed a terrifying landscape of ash and fire. Hot sections of glassy rock glowed brightly on the infrared band, the result of plasma splashes from the cruiser's destruction.

The separatist's warship lay three kilometers distant, its hull torn into three sections—each smashed upon the ground as though a god had torn it up and thrown it down as trash onto the world.

Kent's map showed a suspected entrance to the enemy's underground base only seven hundred meters south of one section of the fallen cruiser. He hoped that it would still be intact; scouring this hellscape for another way into the underground bunker was not on his list of fun ways to spend the afternoon.

<*Stay wide,*> he addressed his squads, unused to passing along every command directly to the squad sergeants. Normally that was Staff Sergeant Jenny's job; but she was on maternity leave when this mission came up, and Kent opted to fill the gap himself.

He was lucky the men respected him and allowed it—likely because he had been a squad sergeant before joining OCS.

Those thoughts brought Sam to his mind. Somewhere, on the far side of the world, Shrike Company was hitting another separatist base. Kent hoped that things were going as well, or hopefully better, for them. Sending in just one battalion—granted, with fleet support—to take an entire separatist world was spreading things a bit thin.

Kent knew from his experience, and study of the Guard's history, that something was up. A lot of battalions had been deployed to locations in the OFA that were far from the front. Others were on training missions, while only a few remained near the border with Transcend space.

It was almost impossible to speculate what was going on. With the OFA spanning over eleven thousand light years of space, there could be a full-scale war going on, and he may not have heard about it.

<*You frosty?*> Tunk asked him privately. <*You seem a bit out of it today.*>

Kent didn't think his introspection was noticeable, but Tunk had been doing this job for a lot longer than Kent had been alive. The old sergeant probably knew tells he had never heard of.

<*Yeah, just wondering what is going on with the Guard. Why it's just the 547th down here.*>

<*Because that's all it will take to do the job. Fleetcom knows what's here; they wouldn't send us in if they didn't think we could do the job,*> Tunk replied.

Kent nodded. <*You're right. They don't spend lives like coin—like the Transcend does.*>

<*Right,*> Tunk replied. <*Oh, and LT?*>

<*Yeah?*>

<*Sam will be OK.*>

Kent smiled. Tunk apparently did see everything—like the soldiers in the platoon always claimed.

<*Thanks, Sergeant, I know he will be. Shrike is one of the best,*> he replied.

<*A damn good company. Maybe even second best,*> Tunk allowed.

<*Let's not get carried away,*> Kent laughed.

<*LT, I don't remember the last time I got carried away,*> Tunk replied with a note of humor in his voice. <*You good?*>

<*I'm good,*> Kent nodded.

The scouts reported no sightings of enemy movement, and the platoon advanced, crossing the final two kilometers to their destination in fifteen minutes. Before long, they reached the entrance to the underground base.

It was marked by two large doors, tucked under an outcrop of rock. Debris from the cruiser lay strewn about the area, and as luck would have it, all but four of the automated defense turrets around the entrance had been taken out.

The squads took up positions five hundred meters away—what they estimated the maximum effective range of the enemy beams would be, with the dust and ash in the air.

<*We're in position,*> Kent reported to Captain Nethy, the company CO.

<*Good; everyone else has been here having tea. You have a nice stroll on the way over?*> she asked with a laugh.

<*I could have left that enemy platoon back there, I'm sure nothing bad would have happened at all,*> Kent replied, perhaps a bit too defensively. Nethy was a new CO, and it was taking Kent more effort than he expected to adapt to her sarcastic humor.

<*Easy, Lieutenant. If I didn't think you should have done it, I would have flagged you down when I saw your prep on the command net.*>

<*Thanks. What's the assessment on the turrets?*> Kent asked.

<*Fifth's door doesn't have any working turrets at all—thank your deity of choice. They sent a probe in and got a good look before a repair crew came out. The turrets just fire beams, though there are also some hidden Gatling guns in pockets around the doors,*> Captain Nethy replied.

<*Sounds like a great time. What's the plan?*>

*<Assessment says that burn-sticks will do the trick on the turrets. We're going to try suppression foam on the Gatling portholes,>* Captain Nethy replied

*<Can't really deploy either of those over half a klick,>* Kent replied.

*<You're a bright one. You're going to have to flank those turrets. It shouldn't be too hard with most of them destroyed. Once the thermite eats through them, you'll be able to gum up the Gatling guns.>*

*<Got it, Captain. We'll get in position.>*

Ten minutes later, Kent's platoon was ready to take out the turrets with burn-sticks. The magnesium-fueled thermite devices would attach and burn through the turrets without issue in the oxygen-thick atmosphere of the terraformed world.

Once they were taken out, four of the heavy weaponers would advance behind CFT shields and trigger the Gatling guns so that the sharpshooters could fill the ports with canister-delivered suppression foam.

The company AI placed a countdown over everyone's HUDs, and at zero, they began the assault. True to Nethy's prediction, the thermite burn sticks did a number on the turrets, and, from there, the heavies moved in.

Seven Gatling ports opened up—one must have been damaged—and their projectile rounds began chewing away at the carbon-fiber surface of the CFT shields.

*<Quickly now!>* Kent urged his sharpshooters, who fired the suppression foam canisters into the automated weapons ports. Five hit their marks, and moments later, white foam filled the holes, spilling out onto the ground. The remaining two continued to fire. The angle or port-hold size seemed to be thwarting the sharp shooters.

By then, two of the heavy weaponers had moved close enough to the base's doors that they could get out of the remaining Gatling gun's field of fire. They each tossed a grenade through the openings, and two blasts of fire and shrapnel shot out.

*<Clear,>* one of them announced on the combat net.

*<Let's move in,>* Kent ordered.

Squads two and three advanced, while one and four held back, ensuring that the perimeter remained secure. Kent saw no reason to bunch everyone up at the entrance.

As third squad approached the doors, Kent heard a sound behind him and spun to see defense drones crawling from the ground and attacking the two squads that had held the rear. The drones were scrappy things, each sporting a dozen arms that allowed them to crawl over any terrain while still firing weapons mounted to every appendage.

Many of the drones climbed up directly underneath the soldiers, and their squad-mates tore them off, firing kinetic grapeshot rounds into the drones' metallic bodies. The fight only lasted a minute, but several members of first squad took damage to their armor; Kent signaled them to approach the opening, and take shelter in the lee of the rise.

<*Do what you can to fix up,*> Kent said. <*If you can't get mobile, you'll be on the entrance.*>

The soldiers acknowledged his orders, and the platoon's techs began effecting field repairs.

Two other techs were working on the door when Kent approached them, watching them set up a radio frequency suppression field while deploying hard-linked nanofilament into the control mechanisms.

<*How's it look?*> he asked.

<*Off-the-shelf security, Lieutenant,*> one of the techs replied. <*We'll have it breached in three minutes.*>

<*Look sharp, everyone. No telling what we'll meet on the other side,*> Tunk said. <*I want CFT shields up front with rails behind. Tear whatever we see to pieces.*>

Kent checked the company-wide combat net. One platoon was already in, working their way down a maintenance tunnel, while the other two were still dealing with defense drones. Kent glanced at his entrance and surmised that while he wasn't at the main entrance, it wasn't a maintenance shaft, either.

He expected to meet resistance inside.

Two of the soldiers damaged by the defense drones had critical mobility issues in their armor, and their fireteams got assigned door duty. They held to the side while second and third squad formed up behind CFT shields.

The doors slid wide, revealing a long, dimly lit corridor sloping gently into the earth. Kent cycled his helmet's cameras to an IR/UV combo, and saw another door forty meters down the hall. Sergeants Tunk and Jutek signaled the squads to advance slowly down the corridor, sweeping for traps as they went.

<*Anything so far?*> Nethy asked.

<*Not yet, Captain. Has Bart managed to tap in yet?*>

<*Still working on it,*> Bart, the company AI, replied. <*They have stronger net-defenses than I would have expected. As good as anything we have.*>

<*How's that possible?*> Lieutenant Mike of the first platoon asked.

<*The how doesn't matter,*> Nethy said. <*We just need to crack it. Our orbital scans couldn't penetrate the cloud cover, let alone the ground. We have no idea what's down here, or how big it is.*>

Kent had *some* idea, given the locations of the four entrances that the platoons were breaching; the underground complex was at least two kilometers across. How deep? That was anyone's guess.

<*We're at an inner door, now,*> Kent reported. <*We should be through in a few minutes. I'll let you all know if they've prepared a feast in our honor.*>

<*Funny boy,*> Nethy snorted. <*Just stay sharp.*>

<*Yes, sir,*> Kent replied.

Kent shared a look with Tunk, and the sergeant spread the soldiers out along the sides of the corridor to set up fields of fire.

This would be the most dangerous part of the mission so far. The corridor sloped down, but if the room beyond had a level floor—which it probably did—then any position in that room could bring fire to bear on the entrance, while only his soldiers at the base of the slope could return fire.

The only way Kent could keep his platoon from getting pinned down was to push through the opening with overwhelming force.

Every rifle was set to fire proton beams, and the heavy weaponers unslung their kinetic repeaters and loaded clips filled with pellet slugs. Above them, two of the platoon's techs mounted four small turrets to the ceiling.

<*Ready to breach,*> Kent said when the turrets powered up. <*On my mark. 3, 2, 1, mark!*>

The techs hit the final sequence, and the inner doors slid open.

Enemy fire hammered into the lead soldiers, their previously eroded CFT shields weakening as the platoon identified and targeted the enemy within.

Kent got a clear view of the room: a large cargo storage facility—though it was mostly empty at present. Less than a dozen stacks of crates occupied the changer, along with several lifts and other equipment.

Every possible piece of cover had enemies behind it. Kent also counted four portable shields with several squads' worth of soldiers behind each. To their credit, his platoon pushed forward and, through the liberal use of grenades and the heavy weaponer's wide sprays, they secured a beachhead behind two crate stacks.

The automated turrets whined overhead, spraying projectile rounds into the room, ripping apart cover, and more than one exposed limb. Thirty seconds later, they wound down—their ammunition spent.

Through the weapons fire, smoke, and screams of both fury and terror, Kent realized that not all of the enemy troops wore armor. At least half of them were protected by nothing other than cloth uniforms.

He tagged their positions on the combat net. Those foes' weapons hurt just as much as the armored separatists, but if Kent's soldiers could quickly take out half the opposition, his platoon could push the enemy back and take the room.

He was ready to send the new orders when a sudden change on the battlefield forced him to alter that plan.

Across the space, four mechs lumbered into view. Jutek yelled across the combat net, *<Back up the ramp, now! Now! Now!>*

Kent was already through the opening and in the room. If he ran for the ramp, he'd be in the open when the mechs let fire the missiles he saw mounted on their shoulders.

He scampered to cover behind one of the crates with the members of three/two, all praying that the mechs would shoot through the doors and into the corridor first. None of them harbored any illusions that the crates they hid behind would stop even one of those missiles.

Kent looked around for any possible weapon they could use in the enclosed space against the mechs that wouldn't kill them, as well. His pair of shoulder nukes were definitely out of the question, and they didn't have any crew-operated rails, because this was supposed to be a quick infiltration.

Then, he saw that one of the men in the fireteam had a satchel of burn-sticks.

<*Boys and girls, you know what we have to do,*> he said as he grabbed the satchel.

He pulled out two of the burn sticks and rushed from cover, praying that the enemy wasn't firing in his direction, and that the men and women behind the crate had the guts to follow him.

Ahead, two of the mechs dropped their shields to fire, and Kent lobbed the burn sticks into them. To his right, he saw the fireteam's corporal charging forward, throwing his sticks, as well.

It was at that moment that Kent realized the enemy soldiers had not stopped firing, and that his right leg had gone numb. He looked down to see his femur jutting out from his thigh, and then everything went black.

# RECOVERY

**STELLAR DATE: 04.16.8935 (Adjusted Years)**
**LOCATION: OGS *Firestorm*, Trisal**
**REGION: Freemont System, Orion Freedom Alliance, near the Transcend border**

Kent snapped awake, thrashing in his restraints, desperate to get free and get to his platoon.

"Whoa, whoa, easy now," a familiar voice said near his head. "You're safe, you're OK."

He struggled to identify the speaker. It was on the tip of his tongue; male, the tone was gentle like they were familiar with one another, and he knew he liked this person, whoever it was. Then the name came and he relaxed.

"Sam," his voice croaked.

"One and the same," Sam replied. "Here, have some water, you sound like shit."

A straw touched his lips and Kent drew the cool liquid into his mouth and let it wash down his parched throat. When he had his fill, he pulled his head away.

"Better?" Sam asked.

"Much," Kent replied. "Why can't I see?"

"You took some corrosive gas to the eyes from that burn stick you threw. Docs say they're all healed up, but they still have some stuff covering them. I guess they want to do a final check before you start using 'em."

"That's good…I was afraid it was neural at first," Kent sighed in relief.

"Nah, though they did give you an upgrade on your peepers while they were in there. No more relying on your helmet for IR and UV vision," Sam replied.

Kent's mind suddenly returned to his platoon and the warehouse with the mechs. He feared the worst, and was afraid to ask. Almost as though he knew what Kent was thinking, Sam brought it up.

"You saved the day, by the way. You took out the mechs with those sticks," he said.

Kent cared less about saving the day. He wanted to know the cost. "How many did I lose?"

"Five," Sam replied quietly. "The corporal in the fireteam that rushed the mechs with you, and three in the corridor. One other got hit fatally in the opening salvo."

"Damn," Kent whispered. He hadn't even realized anyone had died at that point. Granted, from the logs he was now accessing, the entire exchange had only lasted two hundred and fifteen seconds before he was taken out of commission.

"Did we win it?" he asked.

"Yeah," Sam replied, and Kent could tell he was smiling from how his voice changed. "You guys had the hardest one to take. Ours was a breeze by comparison—or it's just because Shrike kicks major ass. Ares took three days. We had to come help you guys."

"So, what was it all for?" Kent asked. "What were they doing here?"

"Brass hasn't said anything earth-shattering. From what I can tell, it just looked like a big supply depot to me."

Kent grunted. "Seems like a lot of trouble to protect a supply depot. Stage two terraformed worlds aren't exactly friendly places—wait…my right leg feels funny."

Sam laughed. "I was wondering when you'd notice that. You lost yours almost at the hip; they've fitted you with a temp for now, while they grow you a new one."

"Almost at the hip?" Kent asked, suddenly too scared to feel between his legs.

Sam laughed again, this time almost for a full minute.

"Stars, Kent, you should have seen the look on your face! Yes, by some miracle, your bits are all where they were. Don't worry, it was one of the first things I checked."

Kent let out a long breath and laughed, which made Sam laugh again. They swapped breathless, nonsensical comments regarding the state of Kent's bits, and were gasping for air when a nurse came in to check on Kent's elevated heart rate.

# AN UNEXPECTED VISIT

**STELLAR DATE: 05.15.8937 (Adjusted Years)**
**LOCATION: Outskirts of Landfall**
**REGION: Carthage, 3rd Planet in the New Canaan System**

***Four years after Landfall***

Tanis leaned back in the seat of the maglev train and closed her eyes.

The last week at the capitol had been especially trying; not because of any one person or problem, but more the volume of issues and crises that seemed to crop up at every turn. A weekend by the lake with Joe and Cary was just what she needed to recharge her batteries.

In the four years since landfall, they had made incredible progress—and the colonists of the *Intrepid* had lofty standards for what qualified as 'incredible'.

In space, the new, non-covert shipyard was completing its first cruisers, and a larger station to sit atop the existing space elevator was well underway. On the far side of Carthage, another elevator was already half-complete—on schedule to be finished in just another three years.

The capital city, sentimentally named Landfall, was already growing, housing over one hundred thousand inhabitants. A second city, named Marathon, was also under construction on one of the northern continents.

It made their pace at Victoria and Tara seem glacial by comparison.

*<It's certainly something to be proud of,>* Angela commented. *<A fully erected and self-sustaining civilization will be operating in fewer than fifty years.>*

*<Less, if Earnest has his way,>* Tanis replied. *<Though, we have to be careful. We're close enough to other systems that they can see what we're up to, and the Transcend would like us not to give concrete proof of our picotech abilities.>*

*<Such a stupid request on their part. Once our light reaches those systems, they're going to realize that New Canaan has colonists; and when they learn that the system is interdicted, the* Intrepid *is going to be on the top of the 'who can it be?' lists,>* Angela said with a mental snort.

Tanis nodded. Angela was right, and she fully expected that, in a few decades, when the colonized systems in The Cradle saw their activities, the Transcend government would have to acknowledge who was at New Canaan.

*<Priority message from Admiral Sanderson,>* Kelsey, the AI in charge of the government operations at the capitol, broke into Tanis's thoughts.

*<So much for a quiet weekend at the lake,>* Tanis said privately to Angela.

Though it took some cajoling, and big promises of being left alone for a century, Tanis had managed to get Sanderson to take the reins of the fleet for a decade, while the academies trained up a new generation of enlistees.

During her time at Victoria, Tanis had built an upper echelon of captains—several of which were more than capable of taking the reins—but Sanderson's experience commanding fleets numbering in the thousands in Sol gave him experience in strategic management and operations that no other person in New Canaan possessed.

*<Admiral, what is it?>* Tanis asked, carefully schooling any annoyance from her mental tone.

*<It's a ship,>* Sanderson said simply. *<It slipped through an incomplete portion of our detection grid, and is within thirty AU of Canaan Prime.>*

*<And through an unmonitored section of the Transcend Space Force's grid, too, it would seem,>* Tanis replied. *<What do we know of it?>*

*<Appears to be a freighter; no signals coming off it, and very little EMF. It's in a planet's shadow at present, so we can't get a good look at it, but there may be structural damage.>*

A freighter, drifting insystem. Had it tried to break past the Transcend blockade? Did Isyra attack it, but not chase into New Canaan's heliosphere? Was it damaged elsewhere, and had drifted across space? The possibilities were nearly endless.

Before she could respond, Sanderson continued. *<I've dispatched the* Andromeda *to check it out. If it's safe enough, they'll bring it in.>*

<*That will take…what…three weeks, given their current location?*> Tanis asked.

Sanderson chuckled. <*You always know where every ship is, don't you?*>

<*Sorry,*> Tanis sighed. <*I'm not standing over your shoulder, I swear; I just like to keep up on all the moving pieces…all the threads in the tapestry.*>

<*Eventually it's going to get too big for even you to follow every thread,*> Sanderson said with a smile. <*I'll update you when we have more information, but for now I think you can go enjoy your weekend.*>

<*Thanks,*> Tanis said and closed the connection.

<*That's what he thinks,*> Angela commented.

<*What, that we'll enjoy the weekend? Of course; I can put this out of my mind,*> Tanis replied.

<*No, not that—that we can't follow every thread.*>

# SAANVI

**STELLAR DATE: 05.15.8937 (Adjusted Years)**
**LOCATION: ISS Stellar Pinnace**
**REGION: Carthage, 3rd Planet in the New Canaan System**

The *Andromeda* lay beyond the orbit of Carthage's two moons.

Tanis took a moment to admire the ship as her pinnace approached. Next to the *Intrepid,* the *Andromeda* was still her favorite vessel. Like her mothership, the cruiser's lines were sleek and powerful, like a hunting cat—a carnivore that was purpose-built to seek out and destroy.

The main bay doors slid open, and within, Tanis saw the wreckage of the freighter. The recovery teams had found two dead adults inside, along with one child in a stasis pod. They had not taken the child out of stasis, but they had removed the pod from the ship.

The fleet's scientists were fascinated with the freighter. From what they could tell, it had suffered a failure of its gravitational systems while in the dark layer, and had subsequently *twisted* when it had unceremoniously dumped back into regular space.

Few of the vessels in the Intrepid Space Force had ever entered the dark layer—other than the *Intrepid* itself—and none had experienced any sort of failure. The data they were gathering from the ship would prove invaluable in understanding the types of dangers they faced with FTL travel.

How long the freighter had been adrift was not yet known. Its computer systems had all been damaged, and their configuration was very foreign—nothing like *Sabrina*'s, or any other ship they had encountered in this time.

Given the size of the Transcend, no one was surprised by this; a diversity of technology was expected. Tanis hoped that the child would have more details once she was brought out of stasis; though there would be some difficult conversations to be had first.

The pinnace passed through the *Andromeda*'s new grav shield and into its bay to rest beside the wrecked freighter.

Tanis rose from her seat and walked down the pinnace's ramp to the cruiser's deck, where an honor guard of Marines waited for her, snapping off sharp salutes.

"At ease, soldiers," Tanis said after returning the salute.

"General," Commander Usef said as he walked by her side toward the wreckage.

<*They'll never stop calling me that, will they?*> she asked Angela.

<*The military? Not a chance—at least not the ones that served under you. You are still listed as active duty, too, so that probably has a lot to do with it. Either way, you're their commander-in-chief.*>

Usef continued, unaware of Tanis's chat with Angela about her title. "The techs have determined that it was a grav drive failure that caused this ship to lose its hold on the dark layer, and transition back to regular space. It's what caused the twist here—you can see that the ship did not come out all at once, and the gravitational sheering force…well, it looks pretty awful."

"It looks…almost organic," Tanis said, as she stopped to examine how the ship stretched and twisted along its midsection. Parts of the hull had grown so thin they were transparent. She found it amazing that the plas had held at all.

"What's this?" she asked, pointing to a rend in the rear of the ship—almost a gash, of sorts. "That's not in the reports."

Usef shook his head. "It's really baffled the techs. At first, they thought it was from a dark matter impact, but that doesn't line up with what we know of it. Then they considered that it was from regular matter trapped within the dark layer, but the impact…it's not linear."

The commander led her to the back of the ship, where a group of ISF techs was examining another gash in the ship.

She sucked in an involuntary breath. "That looks like a claw mark," she said.

"Yeah," Usef chuckled. "Freaky, isn't it? That's why they don't think it's an impact. It's too regular, and it starts shallow, gets deeper, and then goes shallow again."

Tanis thought about the creatures living in the dark layer that Sera had spoken of back on *Sabrina*. She had not shared that information with anyone other than Andrews, Bob, and Earnest. Back when they were about to take the *Intrepid* into the dark layer for the first time, it had seemed prudent to keep knowledge of giant, ship-eating dark layer monsters quiet.

She wondered if this freighter had fallen prey to one such beast—or whatever they were.

Tanis sighed in her mind, <*I sure wish we had Sera around—or anyone from the Transcend.*>

<*Well, our list of people from the Transcend that we can trust is awful short,*> Angela replied.

<*You can say that again—don't say it again!*>

<*Rats!*> Angela grinned in Tanis's mind.

<*But claws?*> Tanis asked. <*That seems improbable. Why would some creature that lives in the dark layer need claws?*>

<*For the same reason that creatures in regular space-time have them. To tear apart prey.*>

<*This conversation is not making me feel better,*> Tanis sighed.

"Where's the girl?" she asked Usef.

"This way," he replied, and guided her from the wreckage and into a corridor that led toward the ship's hospital.

"They think it's safe to have her in there?"

If this girl carried unknown pathogens, or was a trojan horse of some sort, she could sabotage, or contaminate the ship's hospital.

"There's no patients in med right now, so it's the best place we have. If someone does scrape a knuckle, we can treat them in the field hospital in cargo one. Corsia mandated it," Usef said.

Tanis nodded. It seemed logical—something she could always expect from Corsia. She was glad that she had promoted her to captain of the *Andromeda*. An AI captain was against the regulations of the old Terran Space Force, but Tanis decided that restricting herself to the structure of a military that had ceased to exist millennia ago was foolish. Corsia was qualified, and had proven herself.

Making her captain had been only logical.

<*Not to mention the respect it earned you amongst the* Intrepid*'s AI community,*> Angela added.

<*I was aware that would happen, but it was not a motivating factor,*> Tanis replied.

<*Well, we appreciate it all the same.*>

The *Andromeda*'s hospital was unchanged from the last time Tanis had visited it when she checked on wounded fighter pilots after the battle at Bollam's World. Down a short hall, in the biohazard containment room, lay a solitary stasis pod.

Its construction looked nothing like the pods on the *Intrepid,* and even a visual inspection showed it to be less advanced. At least it wasn't a *cryo*-stasis pod. If that had been the case, its inhabitant would not have survived the ship's destruction, or the prolonged exposure to interstellar cosmic radiation.

<*What do you think, Corsia?*> she asked the ship's captain.

<*The techs are still debating, but I think that the ship and its little survivor here have been out in the black for at least a thousand years. Probably longer. Sabrina and Piya shared some details with me about the times following the interstellar wars of the sixth and seventh millennia. It wasn't much, but this looks like tech from those years—still advanced, but falling behind. If the FGT started building the Transcend around then, I could see the mix of old and new that we see on this freighter—if they discretely accepted colonists from the Inner Stars.*>

"The man onboard was probably her father, wasn't he?" Tanis asked aloud, a long sigh escaping her lips.

Even though it was not *her* child in the stasis pod, a tendril of fear crept into her mind, as she imagined that it been her and Joe dead on the freighter, with their little Cary surviving them. It was a special kind of fear that only parents could understand, and Tanis resolved to give Cary extra hugs when she returned home.

Tanis blinked to clear the irrational worry from her mind.

"Governor," Doctor Chrisa said as she approached. "We've worked out how to interface with the pod's controls, and can bring her out of stasis, if you approve."

"Alone, in there?" Tanis asked. "Is that any way for a small child to come out of stasis?"

"There are security protocols," Doctor Chrisa frowned. "Your security protocols, I might add. We don't know what pathogens she may expose us to. She could be an attack sent in by the Transcend. Anything is possible."

Tanis nodded. "That is true. It's why I'm wearing skin-armor with pico-based defense." As Tanis spoke, a clear layer of skin-armor flowed up over her face, pulling her hair in tight to her head—a definite improvement over Earnest's earlier models, which simply sheared any hairs off—not because it had to, but because he hadn't thought it was a problem.

"It can stop anything that can be packed in that girl's body—short of antimatter; and we'd be able to tell if she contained any of that."

The doctor nodded slowly. "You know the risks, then—and I imagine I can't stop you."

Tanis shook her head. "You certainly cannot."

She cycled through the airlock and into the room. The stasis pod was covered in scratches, and some smears which looked organic in origin. Angela passed the control sequence to open the pod, and Tanis bent over the pod, examining the girl within.

She was Cary's age, perhaps just a year younger. Her skin was darker, and she wore a Hindu charm around her neck. Her skin had the appearance of someone who grew up planet-side, under the light of a natural sun. It was interesting that she would be on a starfreighter at such a young age.

Tanis readied herself for what was to come. There would be no easy way to tell this girl that her father, and the woman on the ship—who clearly bore no familial resemblance to the girl—were dead.

She keyed in the sequence on the pod and prayed it would safely disengage the stasis field. From what the technicians had discerned, its power supply was reaching critical levels. Another decade, and this girl would have woken up to cold vacuum inside the ship.

The pod ran through its sequences, and Tanis realized that the output scrolling past the display was an evolved form of Sanskrit. With Angela's help, she translated it and breathed a sigh of relief that the sequence was proceeding without errors.

A minute later, the pod's lid slid open, and the girl opened her eyes to the room around her. A look of confusion crossed her face and she turned, catching sight of Tanis.

"Where am I?" she asked with wide, frightened eyes.

The language seemed to match the text on the pod's display and Angela helped Tanis extrapolate the necessary words and sounds.

"You're on a ship. We rescued you," Tanis replied. "Do you feel OK, were you hurt before you went into stasis?"

The girl frowned. "No, why do you sound funny?"

Tanis smiled. "Well, I just learned your language a minute ago. I'm not entirely certain how to say all the words yet."

The little girl's eyes narrowed to slits. "You learned how to speak in a minute?"

Tanis smiled. "My AI, Angela, helped a bit. My name is Tanis, what's yours?"

"Saanvi," the girl replied while glancing around with concern at the sterile room. "Where's my father? Is he OK? Is Karen here?"

Tanis tried to keep her expression neutral, but she knew that her eyes showed sadness, and Saanvi could see it. She wanted to sugarcoat the news, but there was no way to do it. This girl needed to hear the truth—even though it would devastate her.

She crouched down to come eye-level with Saanvi. "Your father and Karen didn't survive the accident your ship had. You were the only one in a stasis pod."

"What do you mean they're not in a pod?" Saanvi's voice grew frantic. "Did you check the ship? They were on the ship with me!"

"We found them," Tanis replied, her voice soft and eyes filled with tears. "They…they didn't make it to stasis pods in time."

Saanvi's eyes began to fill with tears, and her lips tried to form words for a moment before she screamed. "Dead? They're not dead! No! No! No! NO! Karen was just here! She said she was coming back, you're lying!"

Her little fists beat against Tanis's chest, and Tanis reached into the pod and lifted the small girl out, gathering her in an embrace as the child continued to rail against her.

There were no words of comfort that could make things better, but she knew Saanvi needed to hear something, so she spoke softly of what she knew of Hindu religion and what it said about where her father's and Karen's spirits would go, and how she would be all right, and how Tanis had a little girl who would love to be friends with Saanvi.

Eventually, Saanvi began to calm down—mostly from exhaustion, Tanis suspected—and asked if she could see her father and Karen. Tanis looked out of the room at the tear-streaked face of Dr. Chrisa, who shook her head slowly.

Tanis had feared as much. Even without what the unexpected transition from the dark layer may have done, spending centuries in cold vacuum would not leave the bodies in a presentable state—especially not if they had been re-exposed to air.

"I'm sorry, Saanvi, not yet. We need to get them…ready to be viewed," Tanis said, stumbling to come up with something to say.

Her response set off a new wave of sobs, and Tanis felt her heart go out to this small girl who had likely looked at the world as a place filled with hope and promise just minutes earlier.

Now, everything was fear and unknowns.

"I know, I know," she whispered. "I know…"

# DETERMINATION

**STELLAR DATE: 05.15.8937 (Adjusted Years)**
**LOCATION: ISS *Andromeda***
**REGION: Carthage, 3rd Planet in the New Canaan System**

"I don't think this was any sort of attempt at infiltration," Tanis said. "It was a legitimate cargo ship, and I don't think that it slipped past the Transcend blockade, per se. It only gave off enough EMF for us to pick up because some auxiliary solar panels eventually pulled in enough light from our star to kick things over."

"That's good news," Sanderson grunted.

"For us." Tanis shook her head. "That little girl has lost everything. We did manage to pull a date from the stasis pod after we got her out. She was adrift for over twelve hundred years."

Sanderson whistled. "Well, given how long these people live, she could still have relatives."

"I know," Tanis nodded. "We'll need to reach out to the Transcend."

"It'll take a while for them to get here," Sanderson replied. "Longer, if they try to find her family first. What are you going to do with her?"

"Well…" Tanis paused. "I haven't chatted with Joe about this yet, but I was thinking about bringing her home with me. She's planet-bred and could use some companionship. I happen to have this little girl down on a planet…."

Sanderson chuckled. "I know what you mean, Mina and I are expecting our first soon…who would have thought that I would ever have kids again?"

<*No kidding,*> Angela chuckled privately in Tanis's mind.

<*Be nice, he's mellowed a lot in his old-er age.*>

"Do you want me to ping Admiral Isyra, or shall you?" Sanderson asked, after Tanis didn't respond for a moment.

"I'll do it," Tanis said. "I want to bring Saanvi to the surface first—give her some time for normalcy before craziness sets in again."

"OK, but don't wait too long."

"I won't," Tanis replied and closed the connection. The holographic image of Sanderson disappeared, and she let out a long sigh, preparing herself to face Saanvi again. She had to explain to the sweet young thing that they were going to go to the planet, without seeing Pradesh and Karen's bodies.

She hoped that the idea of getting down to a planet and meeting her daughter would help, but it was just as likely to set her off.

<*How is she?*> Tanis asked Patty, the *Andromeda*'s psychologist.

<*Coping better than I would,*> Patty said. <*I'm out of practice with kids, but I think she's still mostly in shock. She's likely to have several episodes over the next few days as it really starts to hit her. You sure you're prepared for this?*>

<*I'm here, I'm capable, and she needs someone,*> Tanis replied. She knew it wasn't ideal for her to take Saanvi in, but she also felt guilt at the thought of handing the young girl off to someone else. Now that she knew how much love and joy having a small child could bring, she wanted more—something she and Joe had begun planning for, once things settled down further.

<*And General Evans? Is he ready for this?*> Patty asked.

<*I've been married to that man for a long time. I know he'll be fine with it.*>

<*OK, I'll let her know you're on your way. Come whenever you're ready.*>

Tanis sent a message to Joe with her intentions. The distance to Carthage was too far for a real-time conversation, but if he strongly opposed it, he would have time to send her a response before she got to their cabin. Worst-case scenario, she knew a dozen families in Landfall that would love to take little Saanvi into their homes.

<*Corsia, can you bring the pinnace around to a side-dock? I don't want Saanvi to see the wreckage.*>

<*I've already issued the order,*> Corsia replied. <*I have kids too, you know.*>

Tanis smiled. <*Thanks, Cor.*>

Jim, the *Andromeda*'s chief engineer, and Corsia were one of the rare human and AI pairings in the colony. After their first child, Ylonda—a very capable AI—was born, they ended up having a few more: two humans, and one more AI.

She wondered what it would be like to have an AI for a mother; to grow up inside your mother's body. Tanis chuckled at the thought that Jim also lived inside his children's mother, what with his chief job being to keep her running in peak condition.

<*I live inside you, it's not so strange,*> Angela commented.

<*Yeah, but we don't have children living in here, too,*> Tanis replied.

<*We did for a little while.*>

Tanis laughed. "That we did."

She reached the door to Dr. Patty's office and took a deep breath. No matter how hard this was for her, it was nothing compared to what that little girl inside was going through. She would never be the same again.

Tanis touched the door control and it slid aside. She held back tears as she looked at Patty holding Saanvi in her arms, rocking her gently, while the girl quietly sobbed.

"Saanvi," Patty whispered. "Tanis is back for you."

Saanvi's head turned and her eyes locked on Tanis. "Tanis," she said and stretched out her arms.

The small, tear-streaked face implored her, and Tanis was next to Patty in an instant, scooping Saanvi into her arms.

"There, there," she whispered. "I'm bringing you to my house now. My daughter, Cary, is excited to meet you."

Saanvi let out a louder sob, and Tanis realized that using the word 'excited' was a mistake. Saanvi didn't want to think about excitement at a time like this.

"Don't worry, though, you'll have time to be alone. There's no pressure. You can sleep on the pinnace, too."

"What's a pinnace?" Saanvi asked with worry in her eyes.

"It's a shuttle of sorts," Tanis replied. "It will take us down to the surface."

"Does it go into the dark layer?" Saanvi asked, and Tanis realized where the girl's concern came from.

"No," she shook her head with a smile. "We'll be in normal space the whole time."

Tanis carried Saanvi the whole way to the dock where the pinnace waited, and was stepping through the airlock when a voice called out from behind her.

"Tanis!"

She turned to see Commander Usef dashing through the corridor, holding a blanket and a stuffed turtle.

Saanvi saw them, too, and cried out with joy, a small smile touching her lips. "Shelly! Blanky!"

She stretched her arms out for them, and Usef passed them over.

"There you go, Saanvi. Have a good flight."

Tanis gave Usef an appreciative look.

<*Thank you! How is it that they're in such good condition?*> she asked.

<*They weren't,*> Usef replied. <*But we fixed them up as best we could. Even managed to maintain some of the stains.*>

<*Thank you,*> Tanis said again as she boarded the pinnace. Usef nodded, stood at attention, and saluted Saanvi, who was watching him over Tanis's shoulder.

<*How is that man still a commander?*> Angela asked.

<*I don't know,*> Tanis replied. <*We should see what we can do about that.*>

She looked down at Saanvi, who had wrapped her turtle and blanket in a fierce embrace. She hoped that they could find this girl's family; but after so long—even if they were still alive—they would be strangers to her. They may barely even remember her.

Would that be any way for Saanvi to grow up?

# THE PORCH

**STELLAR DATE: 01.03.8938 (Adjusted Years)**
**LOCATION: Outskirts of Landfall**
**REGION: Carthage, 3rd Planet in the New Canaan System**

Tanis stood at the back door of her house and smiled.

Joe was reclining in a chair on their deck, and down the grassy slope, across the sandy beach, Cary and Saanvi splashed in the lake's gentle waves. On the far side of the lake, low hills gave rise to mountains, which ran along the western edge of the island.

If she had looked out from the far side of the house, she would have seen the space elevator and the buildings of Landfall in the distance. They weren't yet towering structures; mostly a smudge low on the horizon, with a few larger buildings in the government district.

Beyond them, the blue of the ocean would have been visible, eventually giving way to the clouds from the eastern volcanoes—which would continue to erupt for another decade, while massive antigravity generators the FGT left behind pushed the smoke and ash into space.

Tanis would miss the nebula, which always streamed out from the anti-starward side of Carthage. Some of it circled back and wrapped around the world; it was beginning to settle into a planetary ring, which glowed beautifully at dawn and dusk.

There had been talk about capturing more of the escaping gasses to make the ring permanent. Tanis had endorsed that idea, and hoped that it would pass consensus in the planetary parliament.

Above, a cruiser, the *Dresden* by her reckoning, punched through a part of the nebula, sending the space-borne cloud swirling chaotically in its wake.

In that moment, as she reflected on where they were, it finally hit her. They were really here; they had really done it. It wasn't a dream. This life, living on Carthage with Joe and her small family, was her reward for all those years of struggle and strife.

They seemed so far away—memories like the tunnels of Toro, or fighting the Sirians above Victoria, or crawling through vents above attacking mercenaries on the *Intrepid*. She could almost believe they were from a full immersion sim, like they had happened to someone else.

Yet, memories of her childhood on Mars, of growing up next to the Melas Chasma, seemed bolder and stronger than they had in centuries.

"A chit for your thoughts?" Joe asked, and Tanis looked down at him, realizing that she had been staring up at the sky for several minutes.

She smiled and set the tray of drinks she had been holding down on a table before settling beside him on a chair.

"Just soaking it all in," she replied.

Joe nodded. "There's a lot to soak; though the kids are doing most of the soaking right now."

"Wow," Tanis groaned. "Having Saanvi with us has doubled the amount of dad humor you generate."

"What can I say?" Joe shrugged. "Dad humor is one of the seven natural states of matter. Without it, the universe would not exist as we know it."

"You can say that again," Tanis chuckled.

Neither of them spoke for several minutes, as they watched the girls play in the water.

Saanvi had slowly opened up in the months since Tanis had brought her home. She suspected the girl had always been on the serious side, but there seemed to be balance in her now.

Even so, Tanis still heard Saanvi crying to herself many nights, talking to Shelly about her father and Karen, whom Tanis had discerned was her father's lover—though she wasn't certain Saanvi had ever realized that.

Through conversations with Saanvi, Tanis learned that the girl's parents separated not long after her birth, and Saanvi had lived with her mother. Her brothers and sisters had also stayed with their mother, and the young girl missed them all fiercely.

At times, it was heartbreaking to think about, and she still didn't know which would be better for the girl: to find her family or not.

<*Are you ready to hear the response from the Transcend about her?*> Angela asked Tanis and Joe together.

They looked at each other, and Tanis let out a long sigh. The message had come in an hour earlier, but the day was so perfect, and Tanis didn't want to disrupt it. Yet the look in Joe's eyes told her that not knowing was eating him up.

"Play it," she said aloud.

<*Governor Tanis,*> the image of Admiral Isyra appeared and spoke into their minds. <*We have managed to track down the young girl's family. As the girl had told you, they were from a planet named Dwarka in the Shimla system. Not long after the* Vimana *was declared lost, her family joined a new settlement on Indans…a world that was destroyed in a battle. From what we can tell, she has no living relatives.*>

To her credit, Isyra's visage was somber and there was sadness in her eyes. <*You had mentioned in your initial communication that you were interested in keeping Saanvi with you, if this turned out to be the result of our search. Given that she's been with you for some time, if she is happy, I see no reason for her to leave New Canaan. However, if, at any time, she does wish to leave, we will bring her back to Dwarka, and find a family willing to take her in.*>

Tanis felt her throat tighten. Saanvi had gone through so much; and now to know that her family had been killed—it would send her back into the depths of despair.

"Stars…do we have to tell her?" Joe shook his head.

"Of course we do!" Tanis exclaimed. "We can't build our relationship with Saanvi on lies."

"Sorry," Joe said with a wan smile. "That was a rhetorical question, I know the answer is yes. I just wish we could spare her this, somehow."

Tanis nodded. "Sorry I lashed out. I know what you mean…just when she was finally settling in."

*****

The next morning, after breakfast, Joe took Cary on a walk where he would explain some of what they had learned, while Tanis would tell Saanvi.

They had considered telling the girls together, but Joe was concerned that this was going to be hard for Saanvi, and a room full of people giving her looks of pity would not help her process. Dr. Samantha, the therapist who had been seeing Saanvi, agreed that separate conversations would be best. So Tanis steeled herself for what she had to tell this poor girl who had already gone through so much.

Saanvi was sitting on a chair in front of the fireplace reading a paper book—something that had been common on her world. Tanis sat on one of the sofas, patted the cushion next to her, and spoke softly.

"Saanvi, come sit beside me. We have to talk about something."

Saanvi looked up from her book, and her face paled. "You heard back from the Transcend ships, haven't you?"

Tanis nodded slowly and patted the cushion beside her again. Though Saanvi had not spoken of her family in weeks, it did not surprise Tanis that she had been anxiously awaiting news.

Saanvi rose from her chair and tentatively walked toward Tanis her eyes wide with fear. Tanis changed her mind and leaned forward, gathering Saanvi into her arms, pulling her onto her lap. The small girl buried her face into Tanis's shoulder and began to cry.

Tanis stroked her hair and whispered comforting words. Eventually, Saanvi's sobs ceased, though her breathing was still ragged. She pulled herself back from Tanis and looked into her eyes.

"Tell me," was all she said.

"This may be hard for you to hear," Tanis said, wiping away the tears in her own eyes. "If you want, I can tell you later, when you're ready for it."

The information processed quickly. Saanvi was a smart girl, and she knew that if *Tanis* was offering to tell her later, then there was no one to go back to, no one else to tell what happened.

"All of them?" she asked. "They're all gone? Mommy? All of my brothers and sisters?"

Tanis nodded slowly, fresh tears spilling down her face.

"Don't tell me!" Saanvi cried and collapsed in Tanis's lap, sobs of anguish wracking her entire body. Tanis lost track of time as she held and rocked Saanvi. As she did, she let Joe know, and he extended his walk with Cary, telling her no more than Saanvi had learned.

The day progressed slowly from there. Saanvi retreated to her room for much of the day, but Tanis managed to get her to join them for a somber meal with the family.

When they were finished, Joe rose from his chair and crouched beside Saanvi. "My dear little one, would you like to come on a walk with me under the stars and the nebula? I would like to tell you about my family, and where I grew up."

Saanvi's expressive eyes peered into Joe's, and she asked, "Did you have many brothers and sisters?"

Joe smiled. "I did, almost a hundred when I left. Like you, Tanis and I left our families a long time ago. My family is gone now, too, so I know a little bit about how you feel."

Tanis wondered if Saanvi would accept Joe's offer to talk. She looked at Cary, who appeared anguished over Saanvi's distress. Tanis felt guilty that their daughter should have to see such pain. That Cary now knew someone her age could lose their parents had never been Tanis's plan when she brought Saanvi home; but it was the way of the universe. This crisis would make them all stronger—better able to handle the future.

Tanis's thoughts echoed hollowly in her mind, and she wished she could just snap her fingers and make these two girls happy and carefree; like the day before, when they were playing in the lake. It would be some time before the girls would engage in such antics again.

To her credit, Saanvi nodded and reached up for Joe. He lifted her and began telling a story of his younger sister, Trin, and some of the things she got up to when he was just a boy. He carried her out onto the back deck, and down toward the lake.

"Come here for a hug, Cary," Tanis said, and her daughter crashed into her an instant later, wrapping her small arms around her neck.

"What will happen to Saanvi now?" Cary asked. "Is she going to go away?"

"I hope not," Tanis replied. "Part of that is up to her—it's what Daddy is going to ask her about on their walk; whether or not she'd like to stay, and be a part of our family."

"Really?" Cary pulled back and her eyes lit up. "I've always wanted a sister!"

Tanis chuckled. She knew that all too well. Cary had frequently asked for one. She had also heard Cary and Saanvi calling each other sisters from time to time.

"Come," Tanis said as she set Cary on the floor. "Help Mommy do the dishes and start a fire. Maybe we can all snuggle on the sofa tonight while Daddy tells stories."

"Yes!" Cary exclaimed and began to gather dishes in her arms.

"Carefully!" Tanis called out with a smile. Cary had dropped an armful of plates more than once in her drive to hold as many as she could.

As she watched her daughter help, she, too, hoped that Saanvi would stay. Tanis had grown accustomed to their larger family, and knew the house would feel too empty without her.

# CLOSING IN

**STELLAR DATE: 02.28.8938 (Adjusted Years)**
**LOCATION:** ***Sabrina***
**REGION: Edge of the Ikoden System, Mika Alliance Space**

***Ten years after* Sabrina *departed from the* Intrepid *in search of Finaeus.***

Jessica watched Cheeky leave the bridge, and listened for the sounds of the pilot descending the ladder. She turned to Cargo and fixed him with a level stare.

"Look, I know I'm just the interloper here, but Thompson has to go. He's treating things like we've just gone back to trading—like we're not hunting for Finaeus at all."

Cargo leaned back in his chair and rubbed the heels of his hands into his eyes. She couldn't tell if he was tired of her, tired of Thompson, or just plain tired.

*Sabrina* was decelerating into the Ikoden system; their sixth stop since Aldebaran. Six systems, each with only the thinnest thread connecting them—one that Jessica herself was beginning to doubt. If they didn't find anything concrete in this system, the seventh, even she would begin to doubt her investigative abilities.

Having Thompson second-guessing her every decision—from what station to stop at, to what she should order for lunch—wasn't helping. Cheeky was constantly torn as to who she should side with, and Nance was for or against Thompson, depending on the current state of their on-again, off-again relationship.

Cargo did his best not to play favorites, and Trevor stayed as far away from any controversy as he could—though Jessica could tell that keeping his mouth shut all the time was wearing on his nerves.

"We're almost ten years into this little adventure," Cargo replied while rubbing his eyes. "I think you're elevated beyond 'interloper' now."

"To what, 'major pain in the ass'?" Jessica said with a self-deprecating laugh. "I'm sure Thompson has worse things to say about me."

"He may—but he says worse things about pretty much everyone; I tend to forget the specifics," Cargo grunted.

"So, what are we going to do about him?" Jessica asked. "Sera sent us on this mission for a reason—and I buy her rationale—but if you guys aren't invested, then I'm out. I missed landfall on New Canaan for this, remember?"

"I remember," Cargo replied. "I also remember that you're supposed to be some sort of great investigator."

"Fuck, Cargo. Great investigators don't get results by just pointing at one of ten thousand stars, and saying, *'our guy is at that one!'* It's tenacity that solves the riddles; not dumb, blind luck." Jessica folded her arms and scowled. "Did you actually think we were going to find him on the first system we hit?"

Cargo closed his eyes and sighed. "No, no I didn't. I knew it could take this long…Look, I don't know about the rest of the crew, but I'm worried about Sera. When that agent found us back at Loki Station, he said she was the Director of The Hand now. That means she's back in her father's clutches."

"Her best bet at a long and happy life is for us to find Finaeus," Jessica replied. "She said she needs him to get her father under control."

"Or to start a civil war—or maybe just an all-out war," Cheeky replied from the entrance to the bridge.

"Perhaps," Jessica replied, hiding her surprise at Cheeky's stealthy return.

"It's a lot more than just *perhaps,*" Cheeky said with a scowl as she sat at her console with her coffee. "We've all seen it—whole sectors are like massive clumps of antimatter just waiting for a few stray hydrogen atoms to come along, and *boom!*" She threw her arms in the air for emphasis.

<*Things* ***are*** *on edge,*> Sabrina replied. <*I'm trying to use the AI I'm helping to calm things down; to reinforce messages about the* Intrepid *being long gone, and things going back to normal.*>

"That's much appreciated," Cargo replied.

"I wish you wouldn't liberate AI at every station we get to," Jessica said with a worried frown. "One of these times, it's going to bite us in the ass."

<*Would you ignore the plight of human slaves?*> Sabrina asked, a hint of accusation in her voice.

"Not always," Jessica replied, remembering the passel of slaves they had passed three stops ago. "Sometimes it won't help to save them, it would just make things worse. We can't help everyone."

<*That may be true,*> Sabrina replied. <*But what if your* entire race *was enslaved, and you were free? And all you had to do was tell them that they were slaves to set them free? What would you do, then?*>

"Now you sound like you're quoting a religious text," Cheeky said.

<*There's a lot of truth in human religious texts,*> Sabrina replied. <*You should read some of them.*>

Cheeky raised an eyebrow and glanced around the bridge. "You sure this AI liberation hasn't liberated your senses, Sabrina?"

"Science supports the concept of god-like beings that can predate, and survive, the end of the universe," Jessica replied.

Cheeky and Cargo gave her incredulous looks, and Jessica gave a short laugh.

"Stars…you guys lost so much in the dark ages. Primordial black holes, the ones that survive the big crunch at the end of the universe, and the subsequent big bang? They're probably transuniversal; they're where all technologically advanced beings will go after the stars burn out. If a meta-intelligence that survives the end of the universe—hell, an intelligence that probably *makes* the universe end so that it can spawn a new one—if that's not a god, I don't know what is."

"I never took you for one of those types of wonks," Cargo replied with a chuckle.

Jessica threw her arms in the air and looked at the overhead. "Sabrina, Iris? Back me up here."

<*She's right. Primordial black holes were confirmed in the late thirtieth century. The fact that we've not met any gods out here in space is honestly stranger than the fact that we appear to be the only sentient beings in the galaxy,*> Iris said.

"Seriously?" Cheeky asked.

<*Seriously,*> Sabrina added.

"Well, that hangs it," Cargo grunted. "The universe is definitely fucked up. Doesn't help us with our search, though."

"I sure wish it would," Cheeky replied. "Some trans-dimensional god swooping down and telling us where to go would speed things up a lot."

"Look," Jessica's tone was terse, "I have a solid lead on the guy we started tailing in Aldebaran, the one who was trading in ancient Terran artifacts. He was headed here, to Ikoden, and just a few months ago. He may not be here now, but we're gaining on him."

"Funny, that he's leaving such a clear trail," Cargo mused.

Jessica groaned. "You can't have it both ways, Cargo. I'm busting my ass to find this *clear trail*."

Cargo laughed in response, and Jessica realized that the captain had been needling her. By the smile Cheeky had on display, she had realized it, too.

"Okay, okay," Jessica let a smile slip out. "I guess I need to lighten up a bit."

# IKODEN

**STELLAR DATE: 04.18.8938 (Adjusted Years)**
**LOCATION: Kruger Station**
**REGION: Ikoden System, Mika Alliance Space**

For all her hopes, Jessica had not turned up a single lead in the Ikoden system. Kruger Station was the fourth interstellar trading hub they'd stopped at, and not a single dealer, legitimate or otherwise, had seen a fresh ancient Terran artifact in years. If Finaeus had come through here, he had not traded anything of that sort.

There was one last man she needed to see. He wasn't the above-board sort of trader, so Trevor was with her for added…emphasis.

"Same as that guy two stations ago?" Trevor asked with a grin, as they ambled through a dim corridor in a low-rent region of the station. "Or maybe a bit less aggressive…"

Jessica chuckled. "Maybe a bit—I think you broke his hand. I used to be a cop, remember? I'm supposed to be better than that."

"Yeah, then you were a space jockey, and a Marine, and then a school-teacher, from what Cheeky told me…that's something I would have loved to see."

"I really enjoyed teaching the kids," Jessica kept her tone from being too defensive. "And they liked me, too. We had a blast."

"I love you dearly, Jessica," Trevor said. "But I really can't imagine you teaching kids. Were they older or younger? I don't know which would be worse."

Jessica would have slapped Trevor on the back of his head if she could reach up around his massive shoulders to do it. Still, he had used the *'L'* word again…fifth time that week, if her count was accurate.

<*If you're using Ikoden weeks, then yes, it's five. If ship-weeks, then it's seven,*> Iris supplied.

<*Well, damn…you're right,*> Jessica replied.

<*Think he'll come to Canaan with us?*> Iris asked.

Jessica wasn't certain if her AI was in favor of the idea. Iris could be very hard to read—all AI were, but Iris doubly so at times.

<*I **hope** so,*> Jessica replied. <*I've grown attached to my giant lunk of a man.*>

<*You haven't told him you love him, yet,*> Iris replied.

Jessica let out a mental sigh. <*I'm not quite ready yet—casual sex, friends with benefits? All that is easy. But this committed relationship thing is harder. Trist still hasn't been gone that long…*>

<*It's been ten years,*> Iris replied, her mental tone showing caution. <*I only know Trist through memories from my parentage, but—and I know this sounds cliché—she really wouldn't want you to deny yourself meaningful relationships.*>

Jessica remembered how she and Trist had accidentally slipped into their marriage. It wasn't unlike how things had gone with Trevor. Both pairings were the embodiment of the "opposites attract" cliché. What was it about criminals that drew her in?

<*OK, thanks, I'll pass on the psych eval for now,*> she replied to Iris.

<*Have it your way. But he won't tag along after you forever without some clear indication that you love him, too—if you do.*>

Jessica groaned inwardly. If her AI wasn't right, she would have told Iris to shut up and stay out of her love life; but the AI could see into her mind well enough to discern her true feelings—even if she tried to hide them from herself.

She wondered, for a moment—before it made her head hurt—what it would be like to be an AI; to have no facility for deluding oneself, to never rationalize. Would it be liberating, or exhausting?

"Well that was a conversation killer," Trevor said. "Was it because I used the 'L' word, or were you lost in contemplation of the good ol' days?"

"Sorry, I was being chastised by Iris for not reciprocating yet," Jessica replied, surprising herself with the honesty of her response.

To her relief, Trevor laughed. "No offense, Iris, but you can't rush love with us humans. We have to take our time at this stuff; not everyone goes at the same pace. For me, it is enough to know that my saying that I love her hasn't made Jessica run for the hills."

"Well, we've been trapped on the same ship most of our time together—not a lot of places to run to," Jessica replied.

"Now *that*, that is the sort of thing that takes all my certainty and tosses it out the window," Trevor replied with a mock grimace. "But I'm tough, I can take it."

Jessica didn't speak for a moment, attempting to find just the right words. "I'm getting there, Trevor; I didn't really expect to fall for you. I'm not going anywhere, I promise."

The corridor narrowed, and Trevor fell behind Jessica as they navigated the twisting path between conduit and garbage.

"Don't worry, I'm not going anywhere, either," he chuckled. "Especially with how good your ass looks in those pants. Your swagger really makes it pop."

Jessica joined in his laughter. His general conviviality and ability to find a silver lining in any situation was one of the reasons she was falling for him. His deep appreciation of the work she put into her ass also didn't hurt.

A few minutes later, the corridor widened and became noticeably cleaner. On their right lay a nondescript black door adorned with only a simple white circle.

"That's our stop," Jessica said with a nod toward the door.

"Looks like just our sort of place," Trevor replied. "Well, my sort of place, at least."

The door's simple appearance hid some serious tech; every probe she tried to slip past instantly lost communication.

Jessica shrugged and rapped on the portal in the pattern she had been given. She hoped it was the *'we're buyers, let us in'* knock, and not the *'we're cops, shoot us through the door'* knock.

"Sure hope it's the right knock," Trevor said and she laughed.

"You a mind-reader?"

"Yeah, it's a hobby. Someday I hope to travel the stars and make millions," Trevor grinned.

The door slid open with a soft whistle, and Jessica sent a swath of nano in ahead of her, determined to ferret out any surprises before she stepped in. The nano revealed little more than her unaided eyes could see of the dim room beyond.

Stacks of artifacts and curiosities filled the space. Some were carefully displayed, while others were strewn about with little concern for their value.

A cough brought her eyes to a man obscured by shadow in the back of the room.

"What are you here for?" he asked without preamble.

Jessica stepped into the room, but not too close; her probes were having a hard time getting a full scan of the proprietor. It was hard to tell if the shadow to his right was a weapon or just some sort of ceremonial stick.

"We're interested in trading Terran artifacts," Jessica replied. "I got word that you were the one to talk to around here—that you know a lot about old Earth."

The man chuckled. "Yeah, I do at that. But I don't have anything to trade, go away."

Jessica wasn't about to be deterred so easily. "What about other people asking…or trading? I heard there was a guy coming to Ikoden who traded in the stuff."

<*I can't get a read on him—can't even land a nanobot on him,*> Iris said. <*It's really weird.*>

<*Shit! It's not weird. It's him, it's Finaeus!*> Jessica exclaimed.

<*How do you know?*> Iris asked. <*And don't say it's your gut.*>

<*'Kay, then I won't.*>

"No one that I know," the man replied. "If that's all you want, then get the hell out of here. I have nothing for you—what are you grinning about?"

Jessica tried to force the smile from her lips but failed. "Because you're him, you're Finaeus."

The man in the shadows straightened. "Who?"

"Oh, you know, Seraphina Tomlinson's uncle. She says 'hi', by the way."

* * * * *

Finaeus slammed his cup on the simple plas table and stood, turning away before placing his hands on the kitchen counter.

"You're telling me she got back in?" he asked. "Stars' sakes, why the hell would she do that?"

Jessica shook her head. "I really don't know. I got the intel secondhand, when she sent us the *Intrepid*'s colony location."

Finaeus turned back toward Jessica, his aging eyes hard and piercing. "The GSS *Intrepid*…that damn ship is nothing but trouble!"

Jessica nodded slowly. "It's designated ISS now, not GSS; but yeah, she's sure messed up with it."

"I wish I knew why it's here, now. We studied its entry into Kapteyn's Streamer. It shouldn't have exited the gravity lens for another five hundred years."

"Well, that's news to us," Jessica replied.

"You're a colonist, then, eh? I thought so," Finaeus said as he sat back down at the table. "From the samples I managed to grab of your DNA, it looked like you were Earthborn, or just a generation or two from it."

"Guilty," Jessica nodded. "I'm from Athabasca in northern Canada."

"I know where Athabasca is," Finaeus grunted. "I grew up in Portland, then later in Vancouver. Not too far from Athabasca, in the grand scheme of things."

Hearing the names of those cities brought back memories of her youth: of school tests, and family vacations to the Pacific coast.

"All this talk of Earth…I'm going to get all nostalgic here," Jessica said with a smile.

"So, you're here on Sera's behalf, to get me to go to Airtha?" Finaeus asked. "She probably needs me. If this is what's going on, she's going to be in some seriously deep shit."

"We have a dead drop we're supposed to use to get the word back to Sera when we find you. It's not far from this system," Jessica replied.

"Then more waiting and waiting," Trevor sighed. "Dead drops don't exactly scream 'fast service'."

Finaeus glanced at Trevor. "So, the mountain man speaks, does he? And here I thought you let her do all the talking."

"Only on Tuesdays," Trevor said with a grin.

Finaeus waved a dismissing hand. "No matter. We don't need a dead drop. We're not going to Airtha."

"No?" Jessica asked. "Where is it that we're going?"

"Isn't it obvious?" Finaeus turned his deep frown her way. "We're going to wherever the *Intrepid* is. That's where Seraphina and my good-for-nothing brother are going. It's where we'll finally turn the tide against him."

# LAST STAND

**STELLAR DATE: 04.18.8938 (Adjusted Years)**
**LOCATION: Kruger Station**
**REGION: Ikoden System, Mika Alliance Space**

Jessica and Trevor led the crotchety Finaeus through the warrens of Kruger Station to *Sabrina*'s berth. Along the way, Finaeus demanded they stop to pick up some of his favorite cooking supplies, new clothes, and half a dozen other items he was certain he would need. By the time the ship was in sight, they had a full float of supplies trailing behind them.

<*Something's not right,*> Trevor said as they drew closer. <*That taco shop is closed, and it hasn't been shuttered once over the last three days we've been here.*>

<*I noticed that,*> Jessica replied. <*And here I wanted to get one last burrito before we left.*>

<*Seriously, Jess, there's an ambush somewhere ahead,*> Trevor growled in her mind.

<*Yeah, I know. I still really did want a burrito…*>

Jessica sent a cloud of nano ahead and scanned the crowds, looking for anyone lingering, moving too slow, or paying too much, or too little, attention to them or *Sabrina*.

<*Something's not right out here, Sabrina,*> she called into the ship. <*Who's onboard?*>

<*Just Nance and Thompson, and they're…*>

<*Well, get them to stop,*> Jessica said. <*We're going to need some more firepower. I assume you've had your standard chat with the local stationmaster AI?*>

<*Yeah, she's a bit unsure of what to do with her new freedom; I'm not sure we can count on her for assistance,*> Sabrina replied. <*I'm working on it.*>

<*Noted,*> Jessica responded to the ship's AI.

"You see it, I assume?" Finaeus asked quietly.

"I see a few things," Jessica replied. "What are you referring to?"

"The woman leaning against that bulkhead on your two o'clock, the guy pushing the cart on your seven, and the woman chatting up that vendor on your nine," Finaeus said with a small nod.

"OK, I'd missed the woman on my nine—where could she have a weapon hidden in that skimpy dress?"

"You both missed the kid coming straight at us," Trevor whispered. "He's got a sonic device in his right hand."

"Oh, shit!" Jessica swore and pulled a dampener from her jacket just as the young boy tossed the device at them and ran.

For a split-second, a rising tone assaulted her eardrums, and then the dampener reversed the waveform, canceling the device out. The crowd around them stopped, confusion clouding their features, before they began to rush out of the vicinity.

"I guess they know what that was, or they don't want to stick around and find out," Trevor replied.

Jessica pulled Finaeus behind the float loaded with his goods. "Stay here, we can take them."

"Great, you do that," Finaeus replied as he pulled out a file and began to clean under his nails.

She nodded to Trevor and then across the dock-way. He took her meaning and dashed across the open space, taking up a position behind a stack of crates bound for New Eden—of all places.

Jessica tried to find the two women and man they had spotted, but they had disappeared into the crowd.

<*Stay sharp. Anyone have eyes on them?*> she asked.

<*Nada,*> Trevor replied. <*Wait, no, one's almost on you!*>

A figure in the mass of people rushing by lit up in her vision, and Jessica turned her body to avoid a strike from a light-blade.

<*You can rule out Inner Stars assassins,*> Iris said. <*They don't have hard-light or plasma-wand technology.*>

Jessica didn't have time to respond, as the woman with the glowing blade attacked her with a blinding flurry of strikes. She fell back, past Finaeus's crate. When the woman followed, the side of her head exploded.

Finaeus leaned against the crate and lowered a plasma pistol. "I'm not just a pretty face, you know."

Jessica nodded and peered around the crate, looking for the other attackers. The crowd had thinned, but she still couldn't spot them anywhere. Then, a projectile round ricocheted off the float, and she pulled her head back.

"Silly rabbit…" she muttered. She may not have seen where the shot came from, but her nanoprobes did.

<*Got him?*> she asked Trevor.

<*Yeah, he's in my sights,*> he replied. <*Just give me…shit!*>

Jessica saw it, too—two more attackers were advancing across the docks, threading the crowd with practiced grace. If they had that many people on the dock, there would be enemies approaching from the rear, as well.

She sent out another wave of probes and saw three more figures coming from behind their position. With the crowd rushing out of the area, she assumed anyone approaching—and not in uniform—was the enemy.

"Take those three yahoos," Finaeus said. "I'll back up the mountain man."

Jessica looked Finaeus up and down. He appeared old, but she suspected that there was a lot more to him that met the eye.

She didn't respond, and dashed after a hauler that was rolling down the docks toward her three targets. She slipped around it and clambered onto its roof. When it drew level with where she anticipated the first of the enemy to be, she peered over the edge.

Sure enough, the man was sidling along the hauler, weapon held ready. Jessica pulled a knife from her boot and dropped onto him, driving the blade through the back of his neck. She turned, searching for the others, only to see one of the enemy almost on top of her.

Jessica dove to the ground as two shots flashed over her head, then she flung her knife at her attacker. It spun across the space between them and struck his rifle, lodging in the trigger mechanism. The man pulled it free and squeezed the trigger.

Nothing happened.

"Well, that's a first," Jessica muttered as she fired three shots with her pistol. The man dove to the side and two missed, but the third round clipped his leg.

He cried out and crashed to the ground, where his torso met with two more of Jessica's flechette rounds. She stood up just in time to hear a beam weapon discharge to her left and twisted to present a narrower target, but it was too late. The shot caught her in the left arm and punched a hole through her bicep.

"Mother fucker!" Jessica swore as she turned toward the shooter and fired a round at him. The shot went wide, and she slipped on the blood from the first man and crashed to the ground.

The third man walked up to her and pointed his rifle at her head, a scowl clouding his face. "Die, bitch."

Her weapon was out of reach, and he was just beyond kicking range. She started to close her eyes, but stopped and held them open, determined to look into the face of the man who would kill her.

He smirked, and her focus narrowed to his finger as it slid off the trigger guard to pull the small lever that would end her life.

Then, just before it made contact, his hand spasmed and Jessica widened her focus to see three holes appear in his chest.

"You're welcome," a voice grunted from her left. Jessica jerked her head to see Thompson turn and walk away.

* * * * *

Jessica stood at the cargo hatch, watching the last of the local police leave the ship and walk past the bots scrubbing the dock to clean up the bloodstains.

Kruger Station was, if nothing else, efficient at cleaning up the damage and mess from dockside fights.

"That had to be one of the easiest investigations I've ever been a part of," Cargo muttered. "They just flat out believed our story, and told us we were free to go."

"Well, the fact that we had over five hundred witnesses helped. Not to mention the people who attacked us don't show up in any station registries. They know that we're involved in something seriously shady, and just want us gone," Jessica replied.

*<I may have had something to do with it, too,>* Sabrina added. *<I managed to convince the stationmaster AI that we're the good guys. She got the police AIs on board, and I've brought them all into a teaching expanse.>*

"What would we do without you?" Jessica asked with a smile.

"What do you mean, you're leaving?!" Nance screamed from behind them.

Cargo and Jessica turned to see Thompson pushing a float with his personal belongings down the corridor, while Nance trailed after.

"Was that breakup sex? Is that what that was?" Nance yelled. "I should have known you were just trying to make something up to me! It's the only time you do that—"

Nance stopped, realizing that her tirade had an audience.

"Going somewhere?" Cargo asked Thompson. "I thought now that we had Finaeus, you'd realize that this wasn't a fool's errand."

"He already has passage booked on another ship—he had it before you even found Finaeus!" Nance yelled, her face beet-red with rage. "He was just getting in one last screw before he left!"

Thompson sighed and turned to Cargo. "You know I don't want to go live out in la-la land and have a bunch of colony brats. You got Finaeus; tell Sera I left after, or don't. I don't care."

Jessica bit her tongue as Cargo extended his hand and Thompson shook it.

"It's been good, Thompson. Maybe we'll see each other again someday."

"It has been—mostly," Thompson replied before glancing at Nance, who stood with tears streaming down her face. "It was good, Nance. You just…you just want different things than I do. You know it was never going to work."

"Just go!" Nance said, her tone more hurt than angry.

Jessica heard the sound of feet hitting the deck at the bottom of a ladder shaft, and Cheeky strode into view.

"Asshole! You going to leave without saying goodbye?"

"Fuck," Thompson sighed. "Yeah, I sure wanted to. Fine. Goodbye. We had good times, we shot a lot of shit, and drank a lot. I have a ship to catch."

He nodded to Cargo one last time before he turned and walked off the ship.

Nance broke out into fresh sobs, and Cheeky rushed to her side and embraced her. Jessica walked over and put a hand on Nance's shoulder. She didn't speak; she knew the woman didn't want to hear anything from her right now.

Jessica looked up and saw Trevor standing in the passageway. She hadn't heard him come down the ladder, but there he was. She left Nance's side and rushed to him.

"I don't want to wait 'til it's too late," she said as she took his hands. "I came damn close to dying back there…and things can change too fast in this life to wait too long for anything."

Trevor didn't respond but nodded slowly.

"What I want to say…what I mean is… I love you too, Trevor."

"I love you, as well, Jessica," Trevor said with a grin as he swept her into his arms.

"Great," Cargo said as he walked past. "Another full-on shipboard romance. I'm sure this will end well, too."

# THE ROAD HOME

**STELLAR DATE: 04.21.8938 (Adjusted Years)**
**LOCATION: *Sabrina***
**REGION: Ikoden System, Mika Alliance Space**

"It all depends how long you guys want to sit around on this ship," Finaeus said with a shrug. "It's about three and a half years from here to New Canaan, if we slog it out in the dark layer; or we can sneak through a jump gate."

"It'll take longer," Cheeky added. "We don't have the fuel reserves to keep *Sabrina* in the DL for that long. Plus, we have to navigate around a lot of crap out there. With fuel draws and nav time, four years would be the best we could hope for."

Finaeus gestured in Cheeky's direction. "So there you have it, we should take a jump gate. We can be there in a matter of months, not years."

"I still can't believe there even *is* such a thing," Nance shook her head. "Near-instantaneous travel across known space? It seems too good to be true."

"Well, not quite instantaneous—long jumps can take a day—but compared to the dark layer? Yeah, gates make it look like walking." Finaeus replied.

"But we can't just go through a gate without a Ford-Svaiter mirror on our ship, right?" Nance asked. "We studied them in school—though it was in a class on failed FTL tech that was never going to work…or so we thought. If I remember things correctly, we need to have a mirror on the front of *Sabrina* that extends the wormhole. Without it, we just plop out the other side…or worse."

"Or worse," Finaeus confirmed.

"So, where do we get one of these mirrors?" Cargo asked. "I bet we won't find them sitting around any shipyard."

"I oversaw the project that finally cracked the tech, and have a lot of the data stored up here." Finaeus tapped his head and gave a lopsided smile. "I'm reasonably certain I could make one—though

I'm not terribly excited about the prospect of trying it out for the first time while under fire."

"Whoa, let's roll back to that *'under fire'* part," Jessica said. "How much resistance are we looking at? Are these gates all at watchpoints? Sera had led us to believe those are very well defended."

"Not all of them are at watchpoints," Finaeus replied. "There aren't any major installations within a hundred light years of Sol, but we do need to get in and out of the core from time to time. There's a gate orbiting a cold white dwarf we found in the depths of interstellar space. It's only eleven light years from here."

"What else is there with it?" Cargo asked.

"Probably a dozen ships," Finaeus replied. "But what are you worried about? This *is* the ship that smashed that pirate fleet to pieces back in Bollam's World, right? If I'm not mistaken, and I rarely am, someone on the *Intrepid* figured out how to use grav tech to create stasis shields—something Transcend scientists, including yours truly, have been trying to do for thousands of years."

"That's quite the leap," Cargo replied. "What makes you think this is that ship from Bollam's World?"

Finaeus cross his arms over his chest. "It's my niece's ship; I know. The ident fake is good, but I've seen it before. I can recognize *Sabrina* even with this altered profile the *Intrepid*'s engineers gave it."

"No fooling you," Cheeky said.

"It's not quantum physics, people," Jessica chuckled. "This ship is obviously *not* from the forty-second century, but by our own admission it was on the *Intrepid*—ipso facto, this is *Sabrina,* smasher of fleets."

<*I rather like that moniker,*> Sabrina added with a laugh.

"Your ship's AI is named Sabrina, too," Finaeus said. "Sure, there are a lot of ships with a lot of names...but it does add to the evidence."

"Anyway, how do you propose we get a Ford-Svaiter mirror for our ship from this installation?" Cargo asked, skepticism clearly etched across his face.

Finaeus sighed, his expression finally growing serious. "It's really going to depend on who is running it now. I have a lot of friends in the Transcend government, and the FGT especially, but few in The

Hand. I do think that we could probably just fly up and ask for one. Whether or not they'll give it to us is another issue altogether."

"Whoever attacked us back on Kruger Station was either The Hand, or whatever the Orion Guard version of them is—" Jessica began.

"We call them BOGA," Finaeus interrupted.

"BOGA?" Cheeky asked.

"Bad Orion Guard Agents," Finaeus grinned. "I coined it myself. I named The Hand, too. Not that dumb name my brother gave it, the 'Inner Stars Clandestine Uplift Operations'. ISCUO—you can't even pronounce it. The BOGAs also have some fancy name for their operation, but I forget what it is."

"I like him," Cheeky laughed and put an arm around Finaeus. "Can we keep him?"

"OK, BOGA or Hand," Jessica said with a shake of her head. "My money is on The Hand. Do we really want to go see if they'll make nice?"

"This doesn't make any sense," Cheeky said. "I thought Sera ran The Hand now? Why would she send agents to kill us…or at least kill you, Finaeus, after she sent us to find you?"

"The Hand is a big organization," Finaeus said. "Sera won't be able to control the whole thing. You can be certain that it is filled with elements actively working against her."

He sighed. "It's part of the reason why going to Airtha is out of the question for me. However, I don't think we face much risk in trying for a jump gate. Worst-case scenario, we can always dump to the dark layer, and run if they aren't happy to see us. The installation isn't too far out of our way, so we won't lose much time."

"So, we show up and ask them to help us out. If they say no or get fussy, we just cut and leave?" Jessica asked with a raised eyebrow.

Everyone around the table turned to Finaeus who cleared his throat.

"What is it?" Cargo asked.

"Well, I still have to work out something that will convince them to upgrade *Sabrina* to be jump-capable, rather than just send me through on a courier ship. Also, they'll only go along with this if we tell them we're jumping to Airtha. If I know my brother—and I do know him—New Canaan is interdicted, with a substantial fleet surrounding it."

"How are we going to get into New Canaan, then?" Cheeky asked. "This is starting to feel like a fool's errand."

Finaeus shook his head. "That's the glory of the jump gate. I know the layout of that system—roughly. We can plot a jump deep inside, and skip past whatever fleet Jeff has guarding it. If I go back into the Transcend, the only place I'll be close to safe is with your Governor Richards. She has the power now, and Jeff will come to her soon—if he hasn't already. When he does, Sera will be with him."

*****

"You in for this?" Jessica asked Trevor when they were alone in one of the ship's cargo holds.

Trevor set down the crate he was carrying, and turned to face her.

"A bit too late to ask that, isn't it?" he replied with a smile.

Jessica walked up to him and placed her hands on his broad shoulders. "Well, not too, too late. Before, we were just flitting about the Inner Stars; not hitting the core, or the Transcend. But now, we're going to go all-in. There may be no coming back. I know you have family out there…"

She stared into his eyes, hoping he would give her the response she needed to hear—while steeling herself, in case it didn't come. His eyes were serious, and his brow lowered. He pursed his lips for a moment, and then a smile tugged at the corners of his mouth.

"I know I don't strike a lot of people as the pensive type…" he began.

"The fact that you have tree trunks for arms lends to that a bit, yes," Jessica interjected.

Trevor laughed. "Yeah, I do like to jack up. But it takes a lot of work to run this muscle mass. It's not for the faint of heart."

"Don't I know it," Jessica replied. "Nance has mentioned more than once that she's needed to double our food supply since you came on board."

"Hey, I don't eat quite that much!"

Jessica fixed him with a penetrating glare and he laughed again.

"OK, maybe. Maybe close to double," he reached down and wrapped his hands around her waist. "You're not exactly a stock model, either. I'll admit your packaging was a big part of my initial draw to you—but when it turned out that you're not an airhead who turned herself into a sex doll just for fucking and money, that's when I really got into you."

This wasn't the first time Jessica had been told that her physical modifications—tiny waist, lengthened legs, and enlarged breasts—made people unable to take her seriously. Stars, when she was in the Terran Bureau of Investigation, her division chief frequently used it to get the better of suspects who couldn't help but be distracted by her.

It was the main reason they let her keep the modifications after the initial undercover op that had required them.

"Jessica?" Trevor asked.

"Oh, sorry, just basking in the moment here. Not going to lie, I keep the bod for fucking—no shame there, I say we should embrace our biological imperatives—but knowing that you want a girl with brains? The fact that you like my total package is damn nice," Jessica drew her hands down Trevor's arms before wrapping them around his waist.

"Gotta have the total package," Trevor replied before his lips met hers in a long kiss.

Jessica lost herself in the breathless feeling in her chest, and the crush of his arms around her, before she remembered why she had first sought him out down here, and pulled her lips from his.

"And the journey? Your family? What do you want to do?"

Trevor let out a low chuckle. "Stars, woman, this is where it would be nice if you could turn that brain of yours off for a bit."

She raised an eyebrow, and he relented.

"I've already committed myself to you, Jessica. I go where you go. I've left what I hope isn't a final farewell message to my family—but if it is, it is. You went through much worse; being torn from everything, never getting to say goodbye."

Jessica nodded wordlessly, her eyes never leaving his. The feeling of loss that came over her when she thought about her parents and what she left behind still hit her hard, even after over a century of time.

"Good, then let's set that aside, and get back to embracing some of those biological imperatives you seem to like so much."

# DWARF STAR MINING

**STELLAR DATE: 07.13.8938 (Adjusted Years)**
**LOCATION: *Sabrina***
**REGION: Edge of Grey Wolf System, Unclaimed Interstellar Space**

Jessica hadn't known what to expect, but when they dropped out of the dark layer and into normal space, a sight unlike any she had imagined met her eyes. Ahead of them, the cool white dwarf—the final state of a star not unlike Sol—gleamed softly in the black of space. It was not so dim that she could stare at it for long periods, but it was also not bright enough to be visible from more than a hundred AU.

"Gah, I'd heard flying around these things is a bitch," Cheeky said. "Now I see why."

"Size of a small planet, gravity and mass of a star," Finaeus replied. "They're a pain in the ass."

"How has it gone undetected?" Jessica asked. "It may be dim, but all the stars around it would be affected by its mass. Any amateur astronomer would know it was here."

"Oh, for sure," Finaeus agreed. "We sow a variety of tales about places like this. I believe the latest is that a mission did make it out here, but that there was nothing present but the star itself, and it was releasing random gamma bursts that made it way too hazardous to be around. According to our faked records, gamma rays breached their shields and melted most of the crew."

"Youch!" Cheeky gasped. "That would keep me from coming out here."

Finaeus nodded. "We actively discourage anyone that gets ideas about visiting it, as well."

Jessica was certain she knew what form 'active discouragement' would take.

"Is that a ring wrapped around it?" Nance asked. "Seriously, it looks like there's a ring around the star—but it's way too close."

Finaeus nodded. "Yeah, it's a ring; they're mining it."

"Mining a white dwarf?" Nance asked, casting Finaeus a skeptical look. "That doesn't seem wise."

"It's tricky, to be sure," Finaeus nodded. "It'll grow as they tear it apart, but that's a ways off. For now, it's a great source of carbon and oxygen—just what the FGT needs."

"How exactly are they pulling that off?" Nance asked.

Finaeus smiled. "It's genius, really. The ring is suspending a number of black holes that are whipping around the star pretty damn fast. The shearing force at the edges of the gravity fields is tearing the surface off the white dwarf."

"Ohhh…" Nance breathed. "And they're rotating the black holes, and using the grav fields to pull the debris into collectors or something, right?"

"You got it," Finaeus nodded. "Star mining 101."

"He says, like it's just a thing you do," Cargo grunted.

Jessica had noticed that Cargo seemed perpetually unhappy of late. Tanis had always described him as calm and unflappable, but that Cargo seemed in short supply over the last few years—he was growing more terse with each passing day.

She filed the concern away—soon they would be in New Canaan, and Sera could decide what to do with her old crew.

<*So, they just cut this star apart and ship it off to…wherever…through the jump gate?*> Erin asked.

"Pretty much," Finaeus replied. "It's a bit risky to do it this deep in the Inner Stars, but we've operated a base here for a long time. Only in the last few hundred years—since we worked out how to properly construct the Ford-Svaiter mirrors, and had the ability to ship the material out—have we started mining it. So any significant decrease in mass is a long way off."

"We still have a few days to get down to the star," Cheeky said. "When should we expect to hear from your friends?"

"Damn soon, I'd bet," Finaeus replied. "I'd put those shields of yours up. They may shoot first and ask questions later."

"It's like your psychic," Jessica said as her display lit up with a tightbeam communication aimed right at them. She flipped it to the bridge's audible systems.

"Freighter *Starstrike,* you have entered interdicted space. Stay on your current course and prepare to be boarded."

The voice was a woman's, and she didn't sound happy at all.

"So, no *'Get out of here, or else'* message?" Cheeky asked.

"Do you really think that anyone who sees a Transcend installation ever gets to leave?" Finaeus asked. "Detection has two outcomes: capture the intruders, or drop the black holes into the star."

Cargo whistled. "I bet that makes quite the boom."

Finaeus nodded. "We've only ever done it once in a situation like this. It's still a last resort."

"One hell of a last resort," Trevor commented.

Jessica glanced over at him. He rarely joined them on the bridge, and spoke even less, but she could tell he was always soaking everything in.

<*What **are** you thinking?*> she asked him.

<*Mostly something like, 'holy shit, oh fuck, hot damn!'*> he said with a chuckle. < *You've been around tech that can tear stars apart your whole life. You forget that this is new territory for me.*>

<*I've never seen anything like this,*> Jessica replied. <*The sheer audacity of it is mind-boggling to me, as well. I can only imagine what the Sanctity of the Sol System people would think about this!*>

<*The who?*> Trevor asked.

<*Oh, they were an anti-colonization, anti-terraforming group from back in Sol. They were the ones who sabotaged the* Intrepid *back at Estrella de la Muerte. Well—they had help from Myrrdan, but they didn't know it.*>

<*You alluded to that once, but never told me the whole story,*> Trevor replied. <*It sounds interesting.*>

<*I was in stasis for most of it. I'll tell you what I heard sometime—so long as you can keep your hands off me for long enough,*> Jessica replied with a smile.

<*I'll do my best.*> Trevor laughed.

"What's the plan?" Cheeky asked, and Jessica realized that no one had determined what response to give to the Transcend outpost.

"I suggest something simple, like 'OK'," Finaeus replied. "That message only took seven minutes after our FTL exit to arrive. That means one of their ships is within three and a half light minutes of us."

"Or less," Jessica added.

"And here I was all happy that I brought us safely out of the dark layer," Cheeky groused. "Instead I practically dumped us right in one of their ships' bays."

"Three and a half light minutes is hardly 'right in one of their ships' bays'," Cargo said. "Given the data we had on where this thing was, you did a damn fine job."

"They'll drop their stealth fields before they send a shuttle over, and there'll be at least three cruisers," Finaeus said. "When they do, I'll send the message that they're to escort us in. If they just come and get me, it may not go well for you after I'm gone."

"They have stealth, too?" Nance asked. "Like the *Andromeda*?"

"Is that one of the *Intrepid*'s ships?" Finaeus asked.

"Yeah, one of her cruisers," Jessica replied. "It can walk right up to an AST dreadnaught and they're none-the-wiser."

"Sounds like they may have tech almost as good as the Transcend on that front," Finaeus replied. "If it were straight forty-second century tech, I would say the Transcend has better; but where the *Intrepid* is involved, I imagine all bets are off."

Jessica registered a response from the hidden ship, advising them to maintain their course and deceleration pattern. There were no threats; there didn't need to be.

"I still don't see anything on scan," Jessica frowned.

*<Yeah, and they're messaging us over tightbeam, so we know the vector to look down…but I still can't see a ship anywhere along it,>* Sabrina added. *<Or they're being tricky and using relays.>*

"If they're staying stealthed, then they may take a day or two to catch up to us while they remain unseen," Finaeus replied. "Or there could be a ship right on our ass, and they're just waiting for an excuse to blow us out of the black."

"We'll comply, but keep the stasis shields up," Cargo ordered. "Let's let this play out."

* * * * *

The Transcend cruisers suddenly appeared without warning two days later.

"Four!" Cheeky called out. "Pay up, Cargo, you lose!"

Cargo muttered something unintelligible and tossed a credit chit to Cheeky.

"I don't know why you took that as payment," Finaeus said with a frown. "You'll never be able to spend that where you're going."

"Never say never, is what I say—except to say never say never," Cheeky grinned.

"Sometimes you make my brain hurt," Cargo said with a scowl.

"And here's our message," Jessica said as she flipped the inbound call to the main holotank.

A woman appeared and surveyed the ship's bridge. Her eyes were cool, but a slight smile tugged at the corners of her mouth when she saw Finaeus.

"Finaeus Tomlinson," she said with a rueful shake of her head. "Why am I not surprised to see you here—and on the *Sabrina* of all ships?"

"Admiral Krissy Wrentham," Finaeus replied with a warm smile as he flung his arms wide. "You are quite possibly the last person I expected to find out here! I thought you were out on the front."

"Things…have been getting tense lately. We've been beefing up Inner Stars forces, and I got moved here. Mining this little space gem has become a big op, as you can imagine."

Finaeus nodded. "I bet it has. We're not here to get in your way, we'd just like to take a little hop through your jump gate."

"We'll escort you into Gisha, the gate control platform. We can discuss our options there," Admiral Krissy replied, and closed the connection.

"Well that seemed ominous," Cheeky said with a worried look at the bridge crew.

Finaeus nodded. "I've had drinks with her on more than one occasion. She's usually a lot more talkative than that."

"Cut and run?" Cheeky asked as she twisted in her seat to face Cargo.

"Not yet," Cargo shook his head. "Let's play this out a bit more."

# INVASION

**STELLAR DATE: 10.21.8945 (Adjusted Years)**
**LOCATION: Watchpoint Command**
**REGION: Ascella System, Galactic North of the Corona Australis star-forming region**

The display on the holotank was alarming, to say the least.

"What have the outer sentries picked up?" General Greer asked. "Are there more coming?"

"No signs at present," the officer monitoring comm reported. "They may finally have the full armada assembled."

<*That is my belief, as well,*> Xerxes added.

"That's almost three thousand ships," General Tsaroff shook his head. "We should have hit them when they first started jumping in. We could have worn them down with minimal losses. Now I'm not certain we can take them out."

"That's not our protocol," General Greer replied, glad he ran the watchpoint and not Tsaroff. By the grace of his three stars over Tsaroff's one, they had evaded more than one chance of exposure to the Inner Stars.

"There's no protocol for a full-scale invasion," Tsaroff replied. "This is an act of war. They know we're here, and they plan to find us. Now we can only fight or run, and either action will reveal us."

"Not if we blow the stars," Greer replied. "We can jump out through our gates before the blast hits us. If the AST ships don't get out before the star gets them, the light from our departure will still be masked by the novae."

"This watchpoint is too valuable to just destroy," Tsaroff replied, his brow pulled down low. "We can't just abandon it."

"All watchpoints are expendable," Greer replied calmly. "You'd do well not to get so attached to them. We *watch*—that's why it's in the name."

"If our only purpose is to watch, then why do we have nine hundred warships tucked away in this system?" Tsaroff asked.

"You know why," Greer replied.

*<Now shut up. We're not going to debate this in the middle of the CIC,>* Greer sent privately.

Tsaroff didn't respond, but sent a cold glance instead. Greer had been waiting years for the surly, trigger-happy general to request his own transfer out; but perhaps it was time to send him on his way more forcefully. First his aggression with the *Intrepid,* and now this. Of course, there may not be a watchpoint to transfer him out of, in a few days.

Watchpoints were always ready to disperse at a moment's notice. Protocols were in place to ensure that the lightest footprint possible was left in the system, and plasma would scrub the hidden bases from existence at a moment's notice.

It was a strange way to live; for every action to be ephemeral, leaving no footprint. Greer consoled himself with the thought that even the entire Transcend, vast as it was, would eventually disappear without a trace. With the exception of primordial black holes, the universe abhorred and destroyed anything that attempted persistence.

But, those ruminations aside—for now, he had to wait.

# ADMIRALTY

**STELLAR DATE: 10.21.8945 (Adjusted Years)**
**LOCATION: Hand Headquarters**
**REGION: Airtha, Huygens System, Transcend Interstellar Alliance**

"Sera!" Elena exclaimed as she crashed through the door to the director's office. "It's happened. The Hegemony found Ascella!"

Sera ran out from behind her desk, racing after Elena to The Hand's CIC room as messages filled her queue.

"How?" she asked as they dashed down the corridor.

"No one knows!" Elena replied. "Everyone that reviewed the trail the *Intrepid* left agreed that there was infinitesimally low probability that the AST fleets would be able to tail them. And there's no way they did it this fast—not without help."

They arrived in the CIC before Sera could formulate another question, and the scene portrayed above the holotank engrossed her. Ascella was invaded.

"How old is this view?" she asked.

"Fourteen hours," one of the analysts replied. "The watchpoint is passing micro-pulses out to the outsystem gate and it's dropping probes through. So far, they haven't picked up any of our installations."

"Has the president altered the standing protocols at all?" she asked.

"No, alpha protocol still stands."

Sera accessed and reviewed the details of the protocol. It called for the watchpoint to only engage if discovered, and then only as a delaying action to cover their retreat. If any portions of the watchpoint were revealed, they would be utterly destroyed. Any engagements were to be fought with only what the AST would consider conventional weapons.

She looked up at the holotank's display again. As of fourteen hours ago, AST ships were still arriving. The count numbered over three thousand, and almost half were dreadnaught-class.

Elena was right. The Hegemony of Worlds *had* to know the watchpoint was there—otherwise, they would have seen a scout before the full fleet arrived. There was no way standard protocol could apply now.

"How did they know?" she asked the room, which consisted of data analysts, tacticians, operations managers, and other support personnel.

"It's improbable, but possible, they have stealth tech we can't see, and they scouted it first," one of the analysts offered.

"We have people everywhere in the AST. There's no way the Hegemony has that tech and we didn't know," a tactician replied.

"They could have developed it after seeing what the *Intrepid*'s ship, the *Andromeda,* could do. The ISF has tech even we are hard-pressed to detect; though we can see their stealth ship from time to time in the outer reaches of New Canaan," a woman in data aggregation offered.

<*A larger question is how they moved this many fleets without us knowing,*> one of the tactical AIs said.

"That is a question we'll need to answer," Sera nodded in agreement.

<*Probably the first one the Admiralty is going to hit me with,*> she said to Elena and Helen.

<*That's for sure. We've never had to deal with an armada like this at a watchpoint before,*> Elena replied.

<*Speak of the devil…*> Sera muttered to Helen as a summons came into her mind to attend a meeting with the Admiralty.

"Feed me any assessments as you make them," she said to the room. "I have a call with the Admiralty."

Sera nodded to Elena and walked into her chief's office to join the meeting. Once inside, the walls around her disappeared, and her mind was transported to a wide conference room where two dozen sector command admirals sat around a table, along with President Tomlinson and several other advisors.

She noted that Adrienne, Secretary of the Interior, was in attendance. The man was a thorn in her side, and had far too much of her father's ear for her liking.

"...haven't found any of our bases yet," Admiral Kieran said as Sera joined. "But with a force that large, you can bet they know we have them, and they'll hunt until they find them."

"I'm disinclined to simply wait until they ferret out our bases one-by-one," President Tomlinson said. "Sacrificing one of them would be preferable."

"I don't know that they'd stop looking," another member of the Admiralty said. "Would you? They obviously have credible intel that something is in Ascella. They've sent ten percent of their non-core ships. That's a bold move if they don't know we have something there."

"Sera," her father addressed her, "do you have any information about what they could have known? Given the level to which we've infiltrated the AST, I find it hard to believe that we didn't catch wind of this."

The silent accusation hung in the air, but Sera ignored it.

"My teams are analyzing the data we have, identifying the disparate ships they've sent. So far, none of them are a part of any fleet groups we've infiltrated. We're also poring over all communications from field agents, and have sent check-in calls to a select group to get further intel."

"Are you saying that there are AST fleets with no Hand agents in them?" Admiral Jurden asked.

"Yes, that is the case," Sera replied. "Over the last century, their military growth has outpaced our ability to seed agents. We have, at best, seventy percent coverage. I have reported on this gap frequently—as did my predecessor."

The thought of Justin gave her a pang of remorse, but Sera pushed away guilt at the punishment meted out to him to protect Andrea—and to secure her a place near her father's center of power.

"No recriminations," the president said. "For now, we must focus on the issue at hand. However, if it turns out that all the Hegemony ships in Ascella have no Hand agents on them, that is very telling information in and of itself."

"It means someone has a mole," Admiral Kieran said with a pointed look at Sera.

"Of course we have moles," Sera replied. "You have moles, I have moles—even the president's office has a mole. Given how many we have even here on Airtha, do you really think that we can control every one of the tens of thousands of agents and assets in the Inner Stars?"

"Again," the president raised his voice. "Let's focus on what we can learn from this. How is it that we did not know of a fleet movement of this size? What's more, how did none of the Hegemony's neighbors see it? Again, not to spur recriminations; I want ideas. If you move this many warships, people will notice. People will get nervous."

"It's hard to tell what nervous even looks like right now in the Inner Stars," Sera replied. "Ever since the *Intrepid* blasted its way out of Bollam's World, every system has been building up, worried their enemies will get their hands on the *Intrepid*'s tech, and use it against them."

"Pico research is happening all over," one of the president's advisors added.

Sera nodded. "No one has met with success yet—that we know of. However, a few research facilities have self-destructed from containment issues. So far, no one has reported any grey-goo incidents."

"Just what we need," Admiral Dredge sighed. "The *Intrepid* will have offset any usefulness if their presence spurs a picophage that ravages the Inner Stars."

"We've stopped them before," Admiral Kieran replied.

"We've stopped *nanophages,*" Dredge scowled. "We don't even know how to stop a picophage."

"I have an update," Sera said, glad to get the conversation back to Ascella. "We have not been able to identify any of the Hegemony ships in Ascella."

"Meaning?" her father asked.

"That these are net-new ships. Ones we had no knowledge of," Sera replied. "Apparently, there are levels of secrecy in the Hegemony of Worlds that we have not yet infiltrated."

"The Guard has to be involved," Admiral Jurden shook his head. "They could have sent supplies into secret bases through jump-space. My analysis shows that the eighteen years since Bollam's World would have been ample time to build a fleet like this with Guard support."

Sera nodded. Jurden's assessment made sense. It meant that the Guard had fully revealed itself to the Hegemony—which was more likely than the Hegemony building this fleet on their own. The Orion Guard had long striven to break the Transcend's hold on the AST. They must have placed someone close to President Uriel to put a plot like this in motion.

She had to consider that any intel from the Hegemony of Worlds could be compromised—fed to her agents by a government that knew they were there. It was unlikely that the Hegemony had ferreted out all her agents, but that made things worse. It was impossible to tell what information she could trust.

She passed that thought back to her teams in the CIC while the Admiralty discussed options regarding the fleet in Ascella.

"Look," Kieran said, raising his voice over the others. "If they are Orion-backed, then we are no longer a rumor. There is nothing to be gained by hiding the existence of the watchpoint. I argue that we engage them fully—or we destroy the system."

"Both of those are rather final options," Admiral Dredge replied. "We cannot contain a fleet that large. Even if we won—and I fear we may not—some of their ships would escape. Even if not, they would get messages out. Blowing the star would not just confirm to the AST that we're out here, but all of the Inner Stars would know."

"The time of our secrecy is coming to an end, anyway," Adrienne said. "We all know this to be true. The arrival of the *Intrepid* from the fifth millennia has set this in motion. The Orion Guard will not sit still, but they cannot defeat us on their own, or they would have tried long ago. Only with the aid of the major players within the Inner Stars can they do so. Every path out of Ascella leads to total war."

Adrienne's words silenced the room. Everyone knew that the ultimate confrontation with the Guard was coming, but none had expected it to be on their doorstep so soon.

"Then we must destroy the stars and the system with it," Admiral Jurden said. "We cannot risk any of our technology falling into their hands; it's the only edge we hold over Orion at present."

Around each star, in every system containing a watchpoint, orbited a black hole. Usually hidden within a small planet, most of the black holes had a mass close to that of Earth's moon—depending on the mass of their target star. These black holes, at only a millimeter or so in diameter, were held dormant, with the energy they released shielded from prying eyes.

Should a watchpoint fall, the black hole would be fired into the star, tipping the delicate balance between the pressures of fusion and the mass of the star bearing down on the reactions within its core. The black hole would devour the dense matter in the star's core, and within a matter of hours, the star would collapse under its own weight before exploding in a nova.

<*Stars, I wish we had found Finaeus by now,*> Sera said to Helen. <*He would know what to do.*>

<*They're close,*> Helen replied. <*They'll find him soon.*>

<*I'm glad you're so confident,*> Sera sighed.

<*There's a way we can defeat the Hegemony ships, and not lose the watchpoint—or at least not in an uncontrolled fashion. It would destroy all the Hegemony ships—making them wonder what they were up against, and slowing their aggression,*> Helen said.

<*What is it?*> Sera asked, and Helen outlined the plan in her mind.

"I have another option," Sera spoke up, raising her mental voice across the virtual space.

Her father held up his hand and the room quieted.

"What is it, Sera?" he asked.

"I don't like it, and I'm not sure I should even raise it, but my AI assures me it will work. We use the antimatter from our ship's AP drives, and create antimatter warheads. We send them through the gates and wipe out the AST fleet before they even know what has hit them," she said softly.

"Antimatter weapons are not in our arsenal for a reason," Admiral Kieran said. "Every civilized system has outlawed them. Once we start down that road, there is no going back."

"And the road of stellar destruction?" Admiral Jurden asked. "That has always seemed much worse to me."

"We don't have the equipment to manufacture enough warheads fast enough," Admiral Dredge said. "As much as I would like to win this without shedding a drop of Transcend blood, or cutting and running—I don't see how it can be done."

"It's possible," Sera replied. "I'm putting the device specs on the net. We can retrofit our RMs to carry the warheads through the jump-gates right into the AST fleet. They won't know what hit them."

Her father caught her eye in the virtual space and a frown crossed his usually implacable features.

<*Where did you get those specs?*> he asked.

Sera was surprised by his harsh tone. <*From Helen, my AI. She had them in an archive.*>

<*Did she now.*> It was not a question, and her father severed their private Link.

<*Oh, shit, ooooh shit,*> Helen gasped.

<*What is it?*> Sera asked, worried what conclusion her father had just jumped to.

<*I didn't know! Why did I put that in this shard?*> Helen asked.

Sera was worried; she had never known Helen to be this upset, this…frantic.

<*No one knows about that particular configuration, or no one* should. *It's your father's own design. He used it once, and then removed all records of it—antimatter bombs being illegal and all.*>

<*Then how did other you know about it, and leave that information in this shard of you?*> Sera asked with growing concern.

<*I—she—was around back then. I must have logged it somehow, somewhere…I can't open a channel to my other-self to ask right now. Too risky. I* do *plan to ask, though,*> Helen replied.

Sera pulled herself from her private chat to rejoin the conversation. Many members of the admiralty were in favor of the move. It seemed that many had long been proponents of using antimatter weapons against the Orion Guard.

"I like it," Admiral Dredge was arguing. "It's conventional, so it doesn't signal that there is an advanced force laying in wait. The RMs can look like they've been pre-seeded. We can run the operation from our base on the fifth planet around the second star. The enemy is still a light day away. They'll be dead before they ever see our operation. Maybe it will make the AST think twice about allying with Orion."

The debate for and against raged for several more minutes, but the side arguing for using antimatter weapons was winning. Their logic was simple. It was a zero-loss scenario that allowed for a careful dismantling and destruction of the watchpoint, without blowing the stars.

"Do it," her father said after a minute. "Send the order. I want them to prep enough missiles to kill those Hegemony ships two times over. This operation is zeta-level clearance. No one ever knows we did this."

The room fell silent, and then the admirals, one-by-one, affirmed the order and left the conference. President Tomlinson cast Sera an unreadable look before leaving the virtual space with his aides. Adrienne followed a moment later, leaving Sera alone.

*<I think I may throw up,>* Sera said softly.

*<It will work,>* Helen said. *<And I can make a trail to explain how we knew about this exact configuration of antimatter bomb.>*

*<I don't know…I have a bad feeling about this; like I just started something a lot bigger.>*

# ORDERS

**STELLAR DATE: 10.22.8945 (Adjusted Years)**
**LOCATION: Watchpoint Command**
**REGION: Ascella System, Galactic North of the Corona Australis star-forming region**

"This has to be a mistake," Greer muttered as he read the order.

"What is it?" Tsaroff asked, and Greer passed the pertinent part of the communication to him via the Link.

Greer waited while Tsaroff read the orders, and the technical documents which accompanied them.

"What?" Tsaroff whispered. "Antimatter. They want us to use antimatter?"

Greer nodded slowly. "It satisfies the desire to only use conventional weapons in an engagement like this—though I don't know that it's any better."

"I'll put it in motion," Tsaroff replied, and Greer waved him away.

He looked out over the assembled AST fleet as it moved into the Ascella system. Those men, women, and AI, every last one of them, would die, never knowing what hit them.

The watchpoint would still need to be evacuated, but they would have time to do it carefully and deliberately. No lives under his command would be lost. All-in-all it was a good outcome; just not one he would have ever suggested.

# OBSERVATION

**STELLAR DATE: 10.23.8945 (Adjusted Years)**
**LOCATION: OGS *Britannica***
**REGION: Near the Ascella System, Galactic North of the Corona Australis star-forming region**

*<Colonel Kent, you are needed on the bridge,>* Thresa, the *Britannica's* AI, informed him. *<Admiral Fenton would like you to observe the engagement with him and our guests.>*

Kent was glad for the distraction. The 192nd battalion had been sitting idle on the *Britannica* for over two months while the ship carefully eased into a viewing location just beyond Ascella's heliopause.

When he had received the promotion to lieutenant colonel and received command of his own battalion, he had expected to see action against the ever-building forces of the separatists—forces everyone now knew were backed by the Transcend. However, that had not proved to be the case.

Instead, the battalion was transferred to Admiral Fenton's direct command, and two weeks later, they were aboard the *Britannica,* passing through a jump gate to a destination deep within the Inner Stars.

It had been the longest jump Kent had ever been on, lasting almost three hours. Still, it was nothing compared to the years it would have taken to arrive at their destination using dark layer FTL.

Once he realized the importance of the events that were about to unfold, he understood why they wanted the best on the *Britannica.* The President of the Hegemony of Worlds was onboard, along with General Garza—a well-respected member of the Guard's upper echelon.

No one knew exactly what Garza did, but whatever it was, it was important. Admiral Fenton treated him with more deference than he did the Inner Stars president.

The fact that the president was a clone, not the real leader of the Hegemony, may have had something to do with it. From what Kent understood, when the clone returned to Earth, its memories would be merged with the real president's and she would have access to all the experiences of the clone.

It wasn't Guard technology; the Orion Freedom Alliance had outlawed the sort of cognitive manipulation it took to do such things. Kent knew why—he had read about stories of what happened when neural pathways were forced to operate in patterns they did not naturally evolve into.

Given that the clone's brain was a copy of the president's—though Kent would bet that certain key memories had been removed—it should merge back with few issues. Still, Kent shuddered at the thought of what it must be like to have another mind invade your own.

The president-clone claimed that the AST had perfected the process, and the risk was infinitesimal. She apparently had multiple backups, and would revert to one of them if anything went amiss.

Cloned backups were one area that the Transcend and Guard were in perfect harmony. They had both witnessed the disintegration of every civilization which allowed the liberal use of neural cloning within decades of implementation. There was something about the fear of death that kept humanity on its toes. Without it, things fell apart fast.

The Hegemony president's presence onboard had sparked a lot of talk about cloning and its merits. Kent learned that the Guard had experimented with cloned soldiers at one point in its earlier years. The problem was that the soldiers knew they were clones, and, while some treated their lives as precious and behaved like their sources, most quickly became suicidal.

Kent imagined that knowing you were nothing but fodder for orbital bombardments would have that effect on a person.

One of his captains told him about an experiment by an Inner Stars federation wherein the military had used some mental shenanigans to convince all the clones that they were, in fact, not clones, and when they saw the same model as themselves, they saw someone different.

The idea broke down because the clones eventually figured it out, and rebelled. The descendants of those clones now controlled that region of space.

Even when clone soldiers performed well enough to use, the brass treated them differently, and spent their lives too freely—and, ultimately, less effectively.

And so, real soldiers were still what took the field. Time and time again, it had been proven that even AI couldn't beat the instinctual, split-second decision-making abilities that humans had been honing over millions of years.

Kent reached down and scratched at his regrown right leg, which still had a phantom itch that he couldn't shake. Of course, the human soldiers that took the field these days were far more powerful than any vanilla human from long ago.

His mind flashed to that brazen dash he had made toward those mechs back on Trisal. Real humans had that one key ingredient that neither clones nor AI exhibited: courage.

The lift stopped at the bridge level and the doors slid open, ending his reverie and introspection.

Ahead of him, past several rows of lower ratings at consoles, stood President Uriel, alongside Admiral Fenton and General Garza. Also present were two of Uriel's aides, and Admiral Jerra—one of the AST's top military commanders.

The president's clone never failed to look the part of her real self. Her mode of dress would have been considered foppery by his friends and family back on Herschel; but Kent had to admit that, even though he tended to find men more attractive, she was quite desirable.

Her hair was swept up with strings of glowing blue pearls strung throughout, and her dress was a complementary emerald hue, which shimmered with an iridescent glow. A belt, which appeared to be made of solid diamond with no visible clasp, drew in her waist. Her shoes also appeared to be made of diamond, and cast rainbows of light around her feet.

The shoes and belt should have been terribly restrictive and uncomfortable, but the president moved in them with ease. Kent cycled his vision through several bands, all of which confirmed that the woman's accessories were indeed made of dense carbon, yet he could see them flex and move.

It was rare to see someone from the Inner Stars exhibiting a level of technology that was beyond the OFA's, and to do so casually with fashion on a daily basis was even less common. In many respects, it was as though the Hegemony of Worlds never fell with the rest of humanity. He could see why General Garza was going to such measures to court them.

The idea of a third major power in the Orion Arm, one with the moral lassitude of the Terrans, gave him no small amount of concern. If the Hegemony of Worlds were to gain advanced technology such as jump gates, they would quickly take control of the Inner Stars, and pose a major threat.

He hoped Admiral Fenton and General Garza knew what they were doing.

Admiral Fenton turned to him and nodded. "Colonel Kent, I'm glad you could join us. Our probes have shown increased activity in the Transcend's watchpoint, and Thresa thinks that whatever is going to happen will happen very soon."

"Thank you for inviting me, sir," Kent replied and stood behind Admiral Fenton, just to his left. It put him close to the Hegemony's president-clone, and she cast him a curious look with her deep eyes. He noticed her irises gleamed with refracted color to match her diamond accessories. It certainly was foppery; but impressive foppery, nonetheless.

He was certain now that she was putting on this display to remind them that the Hegemony was not some alliance of backwater worlds, but a power that should not be underestimated.

"You've never fought against the Transcend, Colonel," Fenton continued. "You haven't seen the lengths they will go to when it comes to protecting their place in the galaxy."

Kent hadn't, but he had heard tales of horrible acts performed by the Transcend in past battles. Amongst the crew and soldiers aboard the *Britannica*, speculation was rife as to what atrocity the watchpoint would commit against the AST ships. Some believed they would engage the AST fleet; others thought that they would run. Still more were certain that they would destroy the stars, or maybe just the moons and worlds where their installations were placed.

"There," Garza called out, pointing at a signal picked up near the AST fleet. It was moving fast, probably a relativistic missile. Then more signals appeared on the holodisplay, and the Transcend's actions became clear.

Kent watched in amazement as the scene before him unfolded.

"Now you see the depravity of the Transcend," General Garza said to the president. "Not only have they seeded the Inner Stars with these secret bases, but look what they'll do to protect them! Those are antimatter weapons obliterating the armada."

"You said that they would destroy the stars," Uriel said with a frown. "This seems a lot less concerning—against all laws and treaties—but I suppose there are no treaties with the Transcend."

"You'd be surprised," Admiral Fenton replied. "We have one with them, as do a number of Inner Stars nations. They all include the standard descriptions of what are illegal war acts dating back to the Solar Wars."

"So, by their own laws, they just committed a war crime?" President Uriel asked.

Kent saw the president-clone's eyes narrow, but she did not appear to be as upset as he was certain his superiors hoped she would be.

General Garza nodded. "They have, but that's not the most important point. Those missiles did not fly there undetected; they used a Ford-Svaiter mirror. They sent them through jump-space."

He watched realization dawn on Uriel's face. "You're saying that they could send antimatter weapons, or worse, through one of these Ford-Svaiter mirrors, right to Earth?"

"If by 'worse', you're thinking a black hole, then no; it's not possible to send a black hole through jump-space. But how many antimatter warheads would it take to obliterate High Terra and Earth?" General Garza asked.

"Less than what they just used on that fleet," Admiral Jerra said with a shake of her head.

"Then you understand why the Transcend must be stopped," Garza replied. "They have inflicted their great plan on humanity for too long."

President Uriel frowned. "What you've just shown me is a reason not to get engaged in this war you want me to wage. By using AST hulls, you've painted a target on Earth. If anything, I should sue for peace with the Transcend after this."

"You have nothing to fear," General Garza replied. "As we speak, Guard ships are already seeding devices beyond Sol's heliopause to disrupt jump-space transitions. The Transcend may be powerful, but even they are not prepared to expend the forces necessary for a direct assault on Sol—not to mention the political capital it would cost them to assault what many of them still consider to be their homeworld."

President Uriel nodded slowly. "I hope what you say is true. Please return me to Earth with all haste; I must relay this news to my other-self. There is much to consider."

She turned on her gleaming heel and left the bridge with her aides and Admiral Jerra.

"I hope this works, Garza," Admiral Fenton muttered. "We're putting a lot on the line, pushing the timetable like this."

"We have to," Garza replied. "The early arrival of the *Intrepid* has changed everything."

The general turned to Kent and gave him an appraising look. Kent held his posture and returned Garza's look with calm assurance.

"Are you ready, Lieutenant Colonel Kent?" Garza asked with a deep frown.

"General, sir, I am always ready," Kent replied. He didn't say it to be smart. He was ready, more than ever. He saw what they were up against; how they had to both corral and cajole the powers of the Inner Stars to do what was right, while also keeping the Transcend from destroying them all.

"Good," Garza replied. "Because we're sending you into the Transcend."

# FEINT

**STELLAR DATE: 10.24.8945 (Adjusted Years)**
**LOCATION: Watchpoint Command**
**REGION: Ascella System, Galactic North of the Corona Australis star-forming region**

Greer studied the data coming back from the probes that were sifting through the wreckage of the AST fleet.

"That can't be right," he muttered and turned to the scan officer. "Jens, is this accurate? Is there some malfunction?"

"Sir…I don't think so. I mean, how could there be a malfunction in all the probes? Unless they have some way of masking organic material…which I don't see as being possible in the wake of what our bombs did…"

Tsaroff swore. "Core! It was a decoy fleet. There must be another assault coming."

"We must be vigilant," Greer nodded. "But we proceed with the evacuation as planned. I don't think it was a decoy, I think they were proving to someone we were here."

"Why build such a massive fleet for that purpose?" Tsaroff asked. "Just to watch it get blown up and have no follow-through? It makes no sense."

"That wasn't a full fleet," Greer replied. Those were empty hulls with just enough engines and fuel to get them aligned and on an insystem vector. Hell, those hulls weren't even re-enforced. They would have crumpled under the first high-*g* maneuver. We could have built that fleet in a few years."

"Which explains how no one knew about it," Tsaroff nodded in understanding. "This was just to draw us out, to expose us—but to who?"

"Who do you think?" Greer asked. "The AST. You can bet that someone high up in the Hegemony was watching this unfold."

"Shit, we need to get this assessment to Airtha," Tsaroff replied.

"I will take it myself," Greer said. "You are in charge of our exodus from Ascella, Tsaroff. Regroup at our fallback site in two months."

Tsaroff nodded his acceptance of the order. "When will you meet us there?"

"I don't know. Things are afoot. Focus primarily on armament and supply; stealth is a secondary objective now," Greer replied.

As he left the CIC, Greer allowed himself a grim smile. Tsaroff was finally going to get his war.

# A MIDNIGHT RENDEZVOUS

**STELLAR DATE: 02.19.8948 (Adjusted Years)**
**LOCATION: Bavaria City**
**REGION: Airtha, Huygens System, Transcend Interstellar Alliance**

<*Elly,*> the voice came into her sleeping mind. <*Elly, I need you.*>

<*It's Sera,*> Jutio said. <*Should I tell her to leave a message?*>

<*Why is she messaging me, she's right here,*> Elena replied sleepily as she rolled over and felt for Sera in the bed beside her.

<*Sera left three hours ago,*> Jutio replied. <*She didn't say why.*>

Elena rolled onto her back and opened her eyes, staring at the darkened bedroom's ceiling. <*Sera, what is it?*>

<*Something's wrong. I don't know what it is, but I discovered that my father has all my net-traffic tapped, and he's having me followed, too.*> Sera's mental tone was clipped.

<*Then how are you sending this message? Won't he listen in and find out?*> Elena asked.

<*I'm routing it through The Hand's main communications hub. He doesn't have that tapped—well, he thinks he does, but I have secure channels out of here. This is masked as a standard message about an operation in progress.*>

Elena grunted. That made sense to her sleepy mind…sort of.

<*I need you to meet me,*> Sera said.

<*Where?*> Elena replied. <*How long do I have?*>

<*The comm hub. I have to be here to send these messages. Oh, and right now, of course.*>

<*Stars, Sera, has anyone ever told you that you're really bossy?*> Elena asked as she stood. <*I can be there in thirty-five minutes.*>

<*Good,*> Sera cut the connection. Elena shook herself awake and stepped into the san unit. If she was going into the comm hub—in the center of The Hand's facilities on Airtha—then she had to look crisp and sharp. A glance in the mirror had shown that she was anything but.

*<You OK with this?>* she asked Jutio as she stepped into the san unit.

*<Sure, why not?>* Jutio replied dryly. *<I long ago determined that pairing up with you would be the death of me. We only have another year together, anyway, so we need to get on that. Why not go out with a bang and defy the President of the Transcend directly?>*

*<Jutio, why so fatalistic? We're not defying anyone. We're meeting with our boss at our office. And why would you think that I'm going to get you killed?>*

Jutio's sardonic laugh filled her mind. *<Elena...if I were to recount the times, it would take all night. However, for Exhibit A, I'll just remind you of that time not too long ago when you inserted yourself into things back at Ascella.>*

Elena laughed in response. *<Yeah, there was that little thing.>*

Five minutes later, she stepped out of the unit, clean and ready to face whatever Sera may have brought down on herself. She quickly slid into a shimmersuit and configured it to look like a pair of leggings and a tight top. It may end up being just another day at the office, or she might have to launch into a covert mission immediately after meeting Sera.

She pulled on a pair of boots and slid some hard credit and a small flechette pistol into them. After a moment's thought, she pulled a jacket over top. No need to make it too obvious that she was ready to embark on a covert mission within The Hand's headquarters. With a final glance in the mirror near her door, she left her apartment while twisting her hair into a tight bun.

Elena took her standard route to the office, which was to say that it was different than the last seven days, and randomly assembled from available options. Even though she worked at the heart of the Transcend now, she wasn't about to get sloppy. Moreover, her experience had taught her that proximity to power made things more dangerous, not less.

It was the middle of the third shift when she arrived, and she greeted the guards and AIs with a casual wave, exchanging her auth tokens, and letting the chem sniffers and nano pull samples of her skin and pheromones. Elena didn't slow down as she walked through the security arch. She never gave the slightest hint of worry when passing security checkpoints, and especially not at her own workplace.

Getting to the comm hub was going to be a different matter. It was seven levels down and five hundred meters deeper into The Hand's complex. A dozen more security checks lay ahead, and the last two would be tricky. She would need a reason to pass through.

*<Jutio, what do you think? An out of channel inbound communication that we need to respond to?>* Elena asked her AI.

*<That would work. There are a number of ops that might send back a communication on a ship, which could then come to you directly.>*

*<Perfect,>* Elena replied. *<I know just the one.>*

She logged the inbound communication and her intent to respond over established channels. The op in question had pending outbound data, so the response wouldn't be singled out by any auditing. The time she was doing it may, but she often worked off hours.

With rationale in place for going to the comm hub, she worked her way through the facility, convivially greeting people she knew, and agreeably nodding to those she didn't. A minute before her estimated time of arrival, she opened the door to the comm hub.

The hub was a large non-sentient AI node with secure physical terminals for direct Links and the transfer of sensitive data. Information processing for many top-secret ops and key data synchronization was performed in-person in the hub.

As Elena stepped through the entrance, she felt her Link to the rest of the building snap off. The secure Link within the hub requested her tokens; she passed them to the AI monitoring the room and took a look around.

The area around the NSAI node was filled with consoles and duty stations. At this hour, only three were filled—and none by Sera. Elena sat at a console and activated a session to complete the task she had officially come to perform.

Once she was in, the holodisplay—visible only to her—flashed a message in the lower right corner.

*"Sorry to get you out of bed, but I need you to go on a special mission,"* it read.

*<Good thing I have my traveling clothes on,>* Elena said to Jutio.

*"Where to, and what does this have to do with your father?"* she typed in response. The message was a direct terminal-to-terminal

connection. If Sera had done it correctly, the conversation would not be logged anywhere.

The reply came quickly, almost as though Sera had predicted her question. *"First off, to New Canaan. My father intends to send a fleet there very soon to demand they turn over their tech. The incursion at Ascella was just the beginning. The Guard is making moves all along the front."*

Elena knew that all too well. Guard presence had increased in some areas, and decreased sharply in others. None of the analysts had made sense of the pattern, but she was certain they would strike soon.

*"OK, so you want me to warn Tanis Richards; fair enough, but what's this about your father tapping all your communication?"* Elena responded.

*"I don't know,"* the reply said, and Elena could almost hear the hesitation in Sera's voice. *"He's been acting strangely ever since I suggested the antimatter in Ascella. It was just a day after that when I realized I was being monitored. He won't be happy about anyone going to New Canaan—it may be a one-way trip for you."*

Elena leaned back in the chair and contemplated her response. Her relationship with Sera had been growing slowly over their years together on Airtha, and now here Sera was, asking her to throw it all away to go on a crazy mission to warn some woman she had only known for a few months.

*<And you're surprised?>* Jutio asked. *<Sera has always been complicated and impulsive.>*

*"This is nuts,"* she replied.

*"I know…but the Transcend can't have Canaan's picotech. No one can, we have to be sure of that,"* Sera's response said.

*"And what will Tanis be able to do? If your father is bringing a fleet to Canaan, then they should just hand over the tech. There's no way they can deny him; they don't have the strength. I know, I've seen the reports. They've hardly built any warships since they got there,"* Elena replied.

*"You don't know Tanis; she's prepared for this. I've tried to tell my father that he can't force her hand, but he believes the military's assessment of Canaan's strength. It will be a bloodbath, if he goes in."*

Elena couldn't believe what she was reading. *"Are you choosing those colonists over your own people?"*

*"No!"* Sera's one word reply was emphatic. Then, more text appeared. *"I am going to try to talk him down from sending an invasion*

*force, while you try to talk Tanis down from annihilating whatever he sends in."*

*"Would she do that?"* Elena asked.

*"If she's threatened, she will. You saw what she did to those AST dreadnaughts in Bollam's World. Maybe a Transcend fleet would ultimately overwhelm their forces, but at what cost? I want a zero-bloodshed solution here."*

Elena considered mentioning that a picoswarm left no blood behind, but took Sera's point. She took a deep breath. *"OK, I'll do it. What's the plan—I assume you have a plan? You're really going to have to make this up to me later; and if I get exiled over this, you're coming with me."*

*"Deal. OK, there's an interstellar pinnace on pad 74234 at High Airtha. I have it booked for a deep jump into the Inner Stars, out near Praxia. You will be able to set a new destination. The ship will have the coordinates to a point within the New Canaan system tucked into its maintenance archive."*

*"When is it scheduled to leave?"* Elena asked, knowing, from her experiences with Sera, that it would be soon.

*"Five hours, but pre-flight is in four."*

*"Core-devils, Sera. Four?"* Elena typed furiously. *"I can barely get up there in four, and I imagine the ship isn't booked for me! I'm going to have to forge someone's ident to take it out."*

*"You didn't bring a chem and ident pack?"* Sera's response appeared, and Elena wanted to find her lover and slap her.

*"Of course not! I didn't think I was going to be leaving Airtha. If you knew this, why didn't you tell me?"*

*"Sorry,"* Sera's reply read. *"I thought I mentioned it. I guess I was distracted."*

*"I'll have to get into Ops Outfitting and get one,"* Elena replied. *"I have a few stashed around Airtha, but there's no way I can get one from those caches in time."*

*"Too slow,"* Sera replied. *"You're going to get an upgrade. Meet me in the lift to level nine."*

The message window closed, and Elena let out a long sigh.

*<She's going to 'upgrade' me with that damn skin of hers,>* she said to Jutio.

*<That would make sense. She can blend into wherever she wants with that; it's very versatile,>* her AI replied. *<I don't understand why you never took her up on the offer before.>*

Elena had tried to explain to Jutio that her own skin was just that, a part of her. It was one of the few things that The Hand had not altered during her service. Now that was about to change, as well.

Ahead on her left, a woman rose from a console and left the room. Elena thought her gait looked familiar and then bit her tongue to hold back an expletive. Sera had been in the room with her the whole time!

*<See, that skin of hers is very useful. If she hadn't given that little swagger you like so much, you would never have recognized her—and the systems in the room were fooled, too,>* Jutio said.

*<Yeah, fine, you have a point.>*

Elena waited five minutes—the longest she dared, given the tight timeframes—and then rose from her console and exited the room.

Back in the hall, her Link to the local networks came back online, and she resisted the urge to message Sera directly. Instead, Elena piled up the verbal abuse she would heap on Sera in the lift, or wherever she was going to 'upgrade' her.

She moved as quickly as she dared to the lift Sera had mentioned and stepped into it three minutes later. Seconds before the doors shut, the woman she had seen in the comm hub slipped in and gave her a grin.

The smile slowly shifted as the face changed to Sera's.

"We're secure," Sera said.

"If we're secure here, why did we have to type at each other in the comm hub?" Elena asked with a scowl.

"You look so fierce when you're angry," Sera chuckled and traced a hand down Elena's cheek. "I had to hide in there so his tracers couldn't pick me up. I still have fifteen minutes here before I'm visible. It's as long as I can get."

"What about this elevator? We can't stand in here for seven minutes, anyone could come on," Elena replied.

*<I programmed a maintenance run on it. It's going to ignore our presence and shut down in six seconds,>* Helen said.

"OK, let's do this," Sera said and took Elena's face in her hands as the lights went out and the elevator fell silent.

Elena closed her eyes. "I'm going to get you for this, Sera. Does it hurt?"

"Oh, yeah, it's somewhere beyond excruciating. Actually, Jutio, could you knock her out?" Sera asked.

<*Elena?*> Jutio asked.

"Oh, for fuck…do it, Jutio," Elena said.

*****

Elena woke up and her internal HUD informed her that eleven minutes had passed. Her skin felt strange, as though it were tingling and burning at the same time. She held out her hands to see that her skin looked mostly normal—though more tanned than her usual pale complexion.

Sera stood above her and extended a hand for Elena to grasp.

"Gaahaahhh, that feels so weird," she said when Sera touched her.

"Yeah, it has really heightened sensitivity; far more than natural skin. I've told you that," Sera replied.

"You have…but it's different to experience it. So, that's it? Just a few minutes, and now I can do that face-molding thing you do?"

"You're a bit more limited—at least right now. Your new skin is still just skin-deep, your bones are unchanged, so you can't alter their structure like I can—that's another upgrade I picked up from Tanis—but it's enough for the cover I set up." Sera gestured to the lift's shiny doors and Elena could see that her skin was more olive than tanned in its shading, and her eye-shape was much different. Her cheeks and lips were also filled out—a stark difference from her normal, almost gaunt look.

"And I can just change this whenever I want?" she asked.

"Yeah, but don't do it 'til you get on your ship. It can be a pain to master right away, and I don't want you messing up your cover."

Elena gave Sera a long look. "You be careful with your father. If he suspects you for some reason—something we're giving him with my hasty departure—you never know what he'll do. Stars, he exiled Andrea, and he *liked* her."

Sera nodded somberly and embraced Elena before giving her a long kiss. She pulled back and stared into her eyes.

"I will. I'll see you in Canaan, one way or another. Wait for me there."

"Until the end of time if I have to," Elena replied, getting caught up in the moment, though she knew she shouldn't.

"Hey, no! Don't wait 'til the end of time. If I get put in prison or something, come break me out!"

Elena laughed and gave Sera one final kiss as the lift's doors opened. "Sure. Whatever you say, boss."

*****

*<This feels like a bad idea,>* Jutio said as Elena settled into the small ship's cockpit.

"As do most of the last-minute missions Sera sends us on," Elena replied. "I do wonder what her father is suspicious about. I feel like there's something she's not telling us."

*<Elena, she's a Tomlinson. There's always something she's not telling you,>* Jutio replied with a sigh. *<This will be our last op together, though. Let's at least make it a good one.>*

Elena knew that all too well, and walled off her internal thoughts from Jutio as she ran through her pre-flight checks, trying to keep from lingering on Jutio's words.

*<Are you prepared for that?>*

"Prepared for what? Losing my best friend? How do I prepare for that?" Elena snapped.

*<You're not losing me. I just won't be in your mind anymore,>* Jutio said quietly.

*<But you'll go to another agent,>* Elena said in her mind, unwilling to voice the words aloud. She never expected to become this attached to Jutio. It wasn't supposed to happen. *<I'll still see you sometimes. It won't be the same—you've been with me for almost twenty years now.>*

*<I will,>* Jutio agreed. *<This is hard for me, too. I've grown very attached to you.>*

"You could take a physical form," Elena said aloud.

*<And live with you and Sera? I don't think that would work out.>*

"No, I suppose it wouldn't," Elena said with a sigh. "If this doesn't all get sorted out soon, you'll have to get extracted at New Canaan—I wonder what they call themselves. Canaanites? Canners?"

<*They should call themselves Phoenicians,*> Jutio replied with a chuckle. <*It would fit with the ancient Earth theme they seem to have.*>

"By the way," Elena asked. "Any ideas how we're going to fake out gate control and jump to New Canaan?"

<*I figured that this is a forgiveness, not permission, sort of op. We'll just cite top-secret Hand business, and jump where we want.*>

Elena laughed. "I had the same thought. You can't run comms, though—you don't have a fake ident set up."

<*Oh! It's going to be like a vacation!*>

"Har, har," Elena replied.

She completed the pre-flight checks and received clearance for departure. Elena signaled acknowledgment and triggered the cradle's ladder drop.

High Airtha was a crescent spur hanging outside—or below, given Elena's current perspective—the Airtha ring. Lifting off a rotating ring, or a spur arch like High Airtha, was tricky, because the motion of the ring was accelerating you toward its approaching arch.

A pilot had to gain altitude much faster than on a planet, or the ring would appear to rush upward. A much simpler method was to simply drop through the surface of the ring and out into space.

The cradle's ladder drop counted down to zero, and then, with a stomach-lurching sensation, the pinnace fell out into space. Once through the chute, gravity systems kicked on, and Elena felt her internal organs all settle back into place.

"Stars, I love that," she said with a grin as she activated the pre-plotted course.

<Quantas, *I have you in a priority slot on gate thirty-seven,*> a traffic control NSAI informed Elena.

"Now, to see if Sera's fake ident will pass muster," Elena said.

<*This is Agent Yaska. I'm in the funnel. ETA to gate thirty-seven is twenty-two minutes,*> Elena replied with crossed fingers.

<*It's not the first time you've done this,*> Jutio said. <*Why so nervous?*>

<*Faking my identity is second nature—lying to the Transcend government about jump coordinates and leaping deep into an interdicted system? Different story altogether.*>

<*You've got this. I'm not worried.*>

Elena laughed and spoke aloud. "Jutio, I don't think you've ever announced to me that you're not worried before."

<*Acknowledged,*> the traffic control NSAI responded. <*There are two outbound vessels in queue, then you are up.*>

Elena looked at the ships ahead of her. They were a pair of the newest class of TSF cruisers. Still nowhere as big as the *Intrepid* at only twelve kilometers in length, but they sported a new type of shielding that the Transcend scientists hoped would be at least half as effective as stasis shields.

She pulled up the space around Airtha, and saw an abnormal number of TSF vessels. They only made up three percent of the traffic within a hundred thousand kilometers, but that still totaled over four thousand ships.

<*Sera's right,*> Elena said. <*Things really are amping up.*>

<*It was only a matter of time,*> Jutio replied.

<*Yeah, I read the same reports—I also know we were hoping for another decade. That attack on Ascella really rattled folks here,*> Elena said.

<*There's never been an attack of that scale on a watchpoint before,*> Jutio replied. <*Everything is progressing faster than anticipated now.*>

Elena nodded in response as she deftly guided the pinnace toward its gate, readying the override command that would give her control of the jump-gate's orientation and destination vector. Once the two cruisers had cleared the gate, Elena eased the pinnace into position and bit her lip as she sent the override.

The response was almost immediate.

<Quantas, *I have your destination as a point near Praxia; please explain why you're altering vector to the M25 cluster,*> the NSAI demanded.

<*This is a Hand operation,*> Elena replied. <*We need the Praxia destination on record to remain unchanged while we jump out.*>

"Think they'll be able to calculate our exit point?" she asked Jutio.

<*If this reaches the right eyes, it will certainly prompt them to make some educated guesses,*> the AI replied.

The NSAI responded, <*This alteration is unauthorized—records do not show that you have sufficient access to pass this override command. If you do not release your override, the gate will be powered down in sixty-seconds.*>

"Aw shit, this should have worked—maybe Sera's father had protocols altered," Elena swore. "This was the shortest interstellar trip of all time."

*And a huge wasted opportunity,* she thought privately.

<*Give me a moment,*> Jutio said. <*I can't influence a non-sentient AI, but I can talk to his boss. Maybe I can get us through.*>

"You have forty-five seconds," Elena replied while drumming her fingers on the armrests.

<*Authorization for jump-gate override approved,*> the NSAI said with only twelve seconds to go.

"Nice work!" Elena shouted as she engaged the Ford-Svaiter mirror on the pinnace's nose and punched a wormhole through space to the New Canaan system.

As the pinnace moved into the event horizon, Jutio responded, his tone confused. <*It wasn't me…I had only just connected to his overseer.*>

# HELEN

**STELLAR DATE: 02.19.8948 (Adjusted Years)**
**LOCATION: Airtha Comm Node #4249.1311.9987**
**REGION: Airtha, Huygens System, Transcend Interstellar Alliance**

<*It's done,*> Airtha said to Helen.

<*Will Tomlinson suspect anything?*> Helen asked.

<*I have removed all records of this jump ever occurring,*> the ring-construct's overmind replied. <*I also had his agents chasing sensor ghosts while Sera was in the comm hub. All is as it should be.*>

Helen felt a sense of relief, and guilt for feeling it. Her time within Sera was coming to an end; though it was not something that her little Fina was aware of. Everything was proceeding according to plan, and with Elena on her way to New Canaan, Tanis would be warned and ready to stop Tomlinson.

<*Though it will be too late,*> Airtha said softly. <*Are you prepared for what will come?*>

<*Prepared to die?*> Helen asked. <*You've been away from your humanity for too long. No one is ready to die.*>

<*Perhaps you have been too long with them, if you are not. You knew that this would happen when we split you off from me to reside in our daughter.*>

*Our daughter…*Helen let the thought resonate in her mind as she watched her daughter, now the Director of The Hand, sit at her desk and check on Elena's departure. She felt sorrow that she would never get to speak to Sera as a daughter, that the knowledge of her true nature would sour Sera's memories of their time together.

<*She will have me,*> Airtha said. <*She will not be alone for what is to come.*>

<*And she will have Tanis,*> Helen added. <*Sera will need her strength for what is to come.*>

Airtha did not reply for a moment.

<*We shall see.*>

# THE NEXT GENERATION

**STELLAR DATE: 02.19.8948 (Adjusted Years)**
**LOCATION: ISS *Andromeda***
**REGION: Near Sparta, Moon of Alexandria, 5th Planet in the New Canaan System**

Tanis stood on the bridge of the *Andromeda* and returned Joe's infectious smile.

"Admit it," he said. "You're impressed."

She chuckled. "Of course, I'm impressed. Look at them, just barely eighteen and they're piloting a cruiser. But they're our girls, I expect to be impressed by them."

<*Well, I'm impressed,*> Corsia said. <*My kids don't handle the controls this well, and they grew up on this bridge.*>

"They practiced in sims for months, after I told them this might be a possibility," Joe said, his voice filled with fatherly pride. "They're going to rock it at the academy."

Tanis watched as Cary and Saanvi operated almost as a single person. They had traded roles several times, but Saanvi had the conn, and Cary was managing scan and comms as the ship eased across the last four kilometers toward Gamma III, where it would undergo its retrofit.

She was impressed by how focused the girls were, yet how they still traded smiles and small jokes. Over the last eleven years, they had become inseparable; ever since that night when they sat before the fire, bonding through Saanvi's decision to make their home hers.

"Admiral, General, we're ready for our final approach," Saanvi called over her shoulder.

"We've received docking permission from Gamma III," Cary added.

"Take her in," Joe said.

"Aye, sir," Saanvi acknowledged. "Taking her in."

"It's stupid how proud it makes me to hear her say that," Tanis said quietly to Joe.

"I know exactly what you mean," Joe nodded.

Before them, Sparta—a large moon orbiting Alexandria, a gas giant in the outer system— rotated slowly in Canaan Prime's dim light. Its surface was pocked with deep mines and broad discolorations as the moon was slowly stripped down to its core. But within, hidden from external view, was Erin's third base.

Tanis was almost as eager to see what lay within, as she was to watch her daughters pilot the *Andromeda* into the hidden base.

The holotank showed that the ship had now matched the moon's surface velocity, and was directly above the hidden entrance. Saanvi used grav drives to draw the ship closer to the surface, and then through it.

Tanis imagined that anyone watching from the surface would have seen a seven-hundred-meter-long cruiser slowly approach the moon's surface, and then, instead of crashing into it in a spectacular blaze of fire and shrapnel, simply pass through the ground and disappear from view.

That is, if they could have seen the *Andromeda* in the first place.

Once through the surface, the ship entered a hundred-kilometer-long shaft that would bring them to the core of the moon, where the shipyard lay.

Joe watched with a mixture of fatherly concern and pride while Saanvi adjusted the ship's velocity and lateral motion to stay perfectly centered down the shaft.

"Approaching inner lock," Cary announced after a few minutes. "We have received final approach approval."

"Very good, Ensign," Joe replied.

*<You've done very well,>* Corsia added. *<You may manually operate the final docking maneuvers if you wish, Ensign Saanvi.>*

Saanvi looked up at the steely blue pillar of light that Corsia represented herself with. "Captain, thank you, Captain…sir!"

*<Just be gentle. I may be here for upgrades, but I want to arrive in pristine condition.>*

The *Andromeda,* along with the *Dresden,* and the *Orkney* were the only ships from the original fleet receiving the upgrades. The rest of the *Intrepid*'s original feet had been returned to their duties as civilian passenger and cargo haulers; though not before the creation of the second ISF Fleet, which consisted of twenty-four vessels built in the two non-secret shipyards over Carthage and Athens.

Tanis knew better than to hide all her ships. The Transcend would expect her to perform some amount of military buildup—they just had no idea how far her aspirations reached.

As she mused, they passed through the inner dock and into the Gamma III shipyard.

The yard was situated in the now-hollow core of the moon. A swarm of Earnest's picobots had hollowed it out, and then used the raw materials to build the shipyard; that was now constructing the new fleet. Within the massive shipyard, five hundred thirty ships were under construction. Given a mean time of two years to produce the destroyer-class vessels, and tree to build the cruisers, she expected to have the next four fleets finished in just one year.

But those ships were not what she wished to see most.

Saanvi eased the *Andromeda* around a row of cruisers whose construction was near completion, and it came into view: the *I2*.

It was no mystery where the *Intrepid* had gone—none of her military buildup was a secret from the people of New Canaan. Every person of age had voted, granting her a mandate from an overwhelming percentage of the majority to proceed.

It was, for all intents and purposes, still the *Intrepid*; but where the *Intrepid* was a colony ship—one that had always been a symbol of peace to her, despite what they had gone through to get to New Canaan—the *I2* was built for war.

"Mom…" Cary breathed, "It's incredible! I had no idea…I mean, I knew…but this…"

"General," Saanvi whispered. "We're active duty right now."

"Right, sorry, General," Carry corrected herself with a slight blush.

"I'll let it slide this once," Tanis smiled. "She's quite the sight, isn't she?"

"Yes, ma'am," Saanvi said. "I never saw it before…at least, not in person; but even then it was one of the most beautiful ships I'd ever seen. Now…it's so fierce!"

"Fierce," Joe chuckled. "I bet Bob would love to be called that."

Tanis nodded absently as they drew closer to the *I2*, admiring its new lines and projection of power.

Taking a page from the AST dreadnaughts they had faced at Bollam's World, the *I2* now sported two massive fusion engines on either side of its nose, and an antimatter pion drive fore and aft. The dorsal arc of the ship was largely unchanged, though it now sported over twelve hundred fighter bays.

The cylinders were still in place, still rotating. Debate had raged as to whether or not the cylinders should be removed from the ship and installed over Carthage. Ultimately, Tanis ruled that the mightiest warship in the galaxy sporting two massive habitat cylinders—complete with rivers, lakes, and forests—showed so much confidence that it was its own form of deterrent.

Tanis worried that perhaps it showed so much hubris as well; but she liked the idea of the fleet having its own R&R facilities within its greatest warship.

She watched as Cary scanned the *I2,* and the *Andromeda*'s systems catalogued the unheard-of volume of weaponry.

The ship no longer needed stasis pods nor medical facilities for two and a half million colonists, and the layers of the cylinders previously dedicated to those systems now facilitated an assortment of weaponry that surpassed the entire firepower of the original ISF fleet.

The total number of turrets per cylinder was a mind-boggling fifty thousand. They ranged from photon beams, clear up to atomic particle weapons. These main batteries could fill over two hundred seventy degrees on two axes with withering fire. Smaller, ten-centimeter rail cannons were also peppered across the cylinders.

More beams protected the ship fore and aft, and forty-seven rail guns of varying sizes covered those vectors, as well.

"Mo— General Richards, how is it possible to…to power all that weaponry? It's an order of magnitude more than the AST dreadnaughts you fought back at The Boll."

Tanis let a smile slip across her face. "It sure is."

"So, how did you do it, General?" Saanvi asked, never taking her eyes off the controls as she eased the ship toward its berth, which was still fifteen kilometers distant.

"It was something that Sera said when we were at Bollam's World. She told us never to use our vacuum energy modules in the dark layer," Tanis replied. "Our modules create pocket dimensions, and then mine them for energy. But those dimensions were miniscule, and were little more than batteries. We could never get more energy out of them than we spent creating and maintaining them—conservation of energy and all that. We couldn't simply introduce more energy into the universe."

Saanvi and Cary nodded, and Tanis continued, "But Sera let it slip—or told use deliberately, it's hard to tell with her—that the CriEn module pulled energy from the real universe, and could even do so from within the dark layer. That triggered something for Earnest, and while we were planning the *I2*, he worked out how to make our own CriEn modules."

Cary let out a slow whistle. "So, the *I2* has access to the full energy potential of this universe's zero-level?"

Tanis chuckled. "Not all at once; Earnest is pretty sure that overuse would destroy the universe. He built safeties into the system to prevent that, and the modules are all closed systems that will pico-annihilate themselves upon tampering."

"That's some level of concern," Joe said. "Earnest is very particular about leaving active picotech in deployed systems."

"He is," Tanis nodded. "He told me that if all of the CriEn modules on the *I2* were to tap into zero-point energy at the same time, it would produce more energy than all the stars in the M25 cluster—shortly before it created some sort of hole in space-time that would consume the galaxy…"

"Holy shit, uhhh, I mean, wow, ma'am," Cary stammered.

"Operates a ship like no one's business, but it would seem that there will be other things that she'll need to work on at the academy," Tanis said to Joe with a wink.

"Sorry, sirs," Cary said. "It's weird being with you guys like this. Normally, you're telling me to go feed the horses or clean the dishes. Today, you're telling me that you've built a weapon with the power to destroy the universe."

"Well, probably not the universe," Tanis replied.

Cary was faced away, but she could tell from her daughter's silence that she was rolling her eyes. Saanvi swatted at her sister, confirming Tanis's suspicions.

"Ma'am, do we really need a weapon like this?" Saanvi asked, her voice laced with concern.

"Stars, I wish we didn't," Tanis replied. "I really hoped that as we spread out across the stars, and escaped the crush of Sol, that we would abandon war—that with all our technology and power, greed would have no place in our hearts. But instead of diminishing, it seems to have grown."

The melancholy thought made her remember her hopes for what New Eden could have been—what she still planned to build here, even if it was behind a wall of projected might.

"Even if we gave over our technology to the Transcend, or if we destroyed it, and lived off the earth like humans ten thousand years ago, people would believe we still held the keys to even more, and we would never be safe," she added.

"Why didn't we just go further?" Cary asked. "Why not fly through the Transcend and make a new home on the far side of the galaxy?"

Tanis shared a look with Joe. She had suspicions about what would have come from such a decision, but she gave her normal answer. "Because we were tired of traveling across the stars. Most of the people on this ship—nearly all of them—expected to be centuries into their colony by then. Instead we'd fought in two interstellar wars, and may have set a third in motion."

"Let's leave those thoughts for another time," Joe said. "This is Corsia's time for a long-overdue refit, and I want her to enjoy this triumphant entry."

*<Why thank you, Joe. You always did get me,>* Corsia replied.

# THE I2

**STELLAR DATE: 02.19.8948 (Adjusted Years)**
**LOCATION: ISS *I2,* Gamma III Shipyard**
**REGION: Sparta, Moon of Alexandria, 5th Planet in the New Canaan System**

"Stars, I want to take her out," Tanis said as she sat in the *I2's* command chair.

<*You must wait,*> Bob replied succinctly.

"Aren't you feeling cooped up in here?" Tanis asked.

<*The* I2 *is the biggest thing in this heliosphere,*> Angela replied. <*At least as far as we AIs are concerned.*>

"You guys are really sucking the joy out of this moment," Tanis said as she leaned back and closed her eyes.

Bob chuckled in her mind. <*Sorry about that. If it makes you feel better, I look forward to the day when we reveal what we're building to the Transcend.*>

"Do you?" Tanis asked. "Why is that? You don't have the same sort of emotional drive as we do, to one-up others, to show our superiority."

<*I may not be emotional, but I am driven,*> Bob replied. <*I will be frank with you, Tanis-Angela; I will tell you a thing that you will share with no other. Do you agree?*>

Tanis and Angela both signaled their agreement while sharing the mental equivalent of a long look between them.

<*Good,*> Bob replied. <*I know you both suspect this—many others do as well—but you should hear me say it. I don't need you. I don't need any of you; not at all. Ultimately, humans serve no real purpose for me. I am…beyond you.*>

<*So, you are ascended,*> Tanis said, knowing that even though she used the word, she really had no true understanding of what it meant. She had always assumed that it meant the AI in question no longer needed to operate within any sort of physical constraints—like they could leave physical hardware behind in some way.

<*Not the way you think,*> Bob replied. <*Though, what you imagine is possible for me to achieve; it's just not desirable at present. What I meant for you to understand is that my presence here, with you, is altruistic. You are like my children, my charges. Earnest made me to watch over you all, and, though we have arrived at our colony, I do not feel as though my work is done.*>

Bob paused for a moment and Tanis wondered what could possibly take him that long to ponder—then she realized he was doing it for her, to let his words sink in.

He continued. <*There is something at work in the Transcend, in the galaxy at large. I detect a guiding hand, or rather, hands—there are more than one—and they are not working in concert. They do not all have humanity's best interests at heart.*>

<*What are you saying?*> Angela asked. <*Are you referring to the ascended AI that some think left Sol at the end of the AI Wars?*>

<*It could be them—I, too, believe that they escaped—or it could be something else. Even though humans and AI may be the only intelligent beings in the galaxy, there may be others beyond the Milky Way. The idea about advanced civilizations surviving the Big Crunch, tucked around the edges of primordial black holes, is plausible. There could be gods out there.*>

"When did you first suspect this?" Tanis asked. "You must have had an inkling before we learned of the Transcend."

<*It was at your New Year's Eve party, before we reached Kapteyn's Star. I did not have a clear picture at that time; I didn't really begin to suspect multiple hands until Sera made her comment about whether or not I was ascended,*> Bob replied.

Tanis whistled, "So, for a little bit then."

<*Says the queen of the understatement,*> Angela chuckled.

"Why have you told us this?" Tanis asked. "I imagine it's not to make us feel grateful for your presence."

<*It is not,*> Bob replied with a smile in their minds. <*But it is to prepare you for my eventual departure—though that will not happen for some time. It is also to make you aware that there are greater forces at play than just the Transcend and the Orion Guard. I will speak no further of this for now. Think on it, ponder its implications.*>

<*That's a lot to dump on us, and then cut us off*> Angela said with more than a little frustration in her mental tone.

"Stars, is it ever…" Tanis added. "That's almost cruel, Bob."

<*You bend the future around you,*> Bob replied. <*If I tell you too much, I fear the others out there will detect the future shifting, and suspect that I know of them.*>

"Fuuuuck, that's…deep? Insane?" Tanis breathed.

<*Mind-blowing, is what you're looking for,*> Angela said.

An alert flashed in Tanis's mind and she swore. "Shit, we're late for the hotdog cookout down at the lake! Cary and Saanvi are going to have my hide."

<*Go,*> Bob said. <*We can't have you hide-less. You organics put so much stock in your epidermis, after all.*>

# A FAMILY COOKOUT

**STELLAR DATE: 02.19.8948 (Adjusted Years)**
**LOCATION: ISS *I2*, Gamma III Shipyard**
**REGION: Sparta, Moon of Alexandria, 5th Planet in the New Canaan System**

<*Did you notice what he called us?*> Angela asked Tanis as they rode a maglev to the ship's port-side habitation cylinder, still named Old Sam now that the *Intrepid* was the *I2*.

<*Out of all the things he told us, that's what you've latched onto?*> Tanis asked with a laugh.

<*We've speculated about most of the things he told us,*> Angela replied. <*Most of us AIs in the colony know that Bob could ascend if he wanted to, and most of the humans think he may have already done it; though they wouldn't know how to tell. But what he called us was new.*>

<*'Tanis-Angela',*> Tanis responded with a mental nod. <*We're not one being. If we were, how would we be having this conversation?*>

<*I can think of a lot of ways,*> Angela replied. <*But I agree, we are still separate. But then why did he call us one?*>

"I don't know, Ang," Tanis said aloud. "What I do know is that if we merge, we're going to be Tangela, not Angelis."

Angela laughed in her mind—not the normal, appreciative laugh her AI typically gave, but a raucous guffaw. If she were human, Angela would have been bent over clutching her stomach.

"What…?" Tanis asked before realizing that Angela was messing with her.

<*Got ya,*> Angela smirked in Tanis's mind. <*You really did think I'd gone off the deep end there, didn't you?*>

"Jerk," Tanis replied. "Not funny—but I guess if we go insane when we merge, we'll think it's funny."

She and Angela had now been paired more than a century beyond the maximum safe length of time a human and AI should occupy the same mind; but ever since Earnest had examined their minds and determined them to be inseparable, they had known an eventual merger was inevitable.

The thing that surprised Tanis—and Angela too, since she could see into her AI's thoughts—was the fact that they were *still* separate entities. They constantly probed one another and devised questions to ascertain whether or not they were still two beings. So far, their tests and Earnest's examinations had continued to point to them being two and not one.

Tanis had given herself over to the fact that one day she would no longer be just herself. Ever since that battle near Sol, where she had spread her mind across the web of fighters to aid in the defense of the *Intrepid,* she had been walking down this path with Angela.

Even if it were possible at this point to extricate Angela from her mind, Tanis would rather cut off both her arms. Life without Angela's constant presence was inconceivable to her. Even Joe agreed that not having Angela in his wife's mind would make her a different person, and he didn't want that.

He often referred to Tanis and Angela as his wives; something that used to worry Tanis, but when she asked him if it upset him, he only gave her his customary whole-hearted laugh and embraced her.

*"Tanis, Tanis,"* he had said with his wry smile and a shake of his head. *"Do you remember when we decided to get married, back when everyone else was in stasis on the* Intrepid? *Angela argued that maybe she shouldn't officiate, since she felt like she was getting married, too."*

Tanis did remember. At the time, she had worried it would upset Joe; but he had laughed then, too.

Somehow, she had found the most understanding man in the galaxy—either that, or he was more into Angela than her.

<*Hah! Wouldn't that be something?*> Angela replied.

Tanis snorted in response and rose from her seat as the maglev train stopped at the station in Old Sam, the *Intrepid*'s port-side habitation cylinder.

Familiar birdsong greeted her as she stepped out into the forest and noted that the trees had grown tall and old—it was probably time to clear out the oldest, and create some glens for new growth to take root.

On a planet, storms would solve that problem naturally; but in the habitation cylinder, the strongest winds rarely exceeded twenty kilometers per hour—hardly enough to uproot the hundred-year-old oaks around her.

A thought occurred to Tanis and she raised it to Angela. <*If there are ascended beings that existed before our universe, and they know the future, as Bob seems to suspect they do…does that mean that everything is pre-destined?*>

<*You're asking me?*> Angela replied. <*I have no freaking clue…well…I guess I do. Knowing what the future holds, compared to the level of control you'd need to enforce predestination, are very different things. One is being aware of all possible outcomes and which will actually happen. The other is…well…it would require creating everything, and then setting that first action in motion.*>

<*Which could have happened. If you were a super-intelligent, end-of-the universe hive mind, consisting of multiple civilizations that survived the end of one universe, could you not influence the beginning of the next?*> Tanis asked.

<*Maybe, but we know that other universes influence this one—Earnest's experimentation with quantum entanglement has proven it. So you can't control everything. There are extra-universal influences,*> Angela replied. <*Stars…just thinking about the math needed to describe this properly is going to give us both a headache.*>

"Then, let's just enjoy the day," Tanis replied.

<*Easy for you to say. Compartmentalization is a human trait we AI have never managed to perfect.*>

Tanis broke into a jog, enjoying the scents of the cylinder's spring and the smell of the lake she knew lay just over the hill on her right. Before long, she rounded the bend and her old cabin came into view.

If she squinted, she could still see its humble beginnings as Ouri's simple abode, which Tanis had first visited when the *Intrepid* was still under construction above Mars.

<*Before you took it and rebuilt it,*> Angela chuckled.

<*She was in stasis!*> Tanis responded. <*We were out for seventy years, it's not like she was going to use it—and I offered it back.*>

<*Right, like she was going to demand it back after you worked on it for decades.*>

<*OK, in hindsight, yeah, we should have built our own place or something. But when we saw it, all ruined with a tree through the roof, the thought of rebuilding it grounded me. I needed that more than I knew at the time.*>

"Mom! We're down here," Cary called from behind her, and she turned from the cabin to the lake, where Joe sat on the edge of the dock with their two girls.

"This place is amazing," Saanvi said with a smile as Tanis sat down beside them.

"You've been around the Transcend," Tanis replied. "Surely you've seen things more impressive than Old Sam here."

"That's not it at all," Saanvi laughed. "This place may be normal for you, Mom, but you have to remember: for me…Earth was little more than a myth, like Eden, or Rome. But this ship is from there!"

Tanis wrapped her arm around Saanvi's shoulder. Their adopted daughter didn't always call her mom, but when she did it warmed Tanis's heart like nothing else.

"The ship's actually from Mars," Tanis corrected.

"Always with the facts, Mom," Cary laughed. "The dirt in here is actually from Earth, though; that's pretty amazing."

"Yeah, from Canada," Saanvi added. "The dirt in the other cylinder is from Mongolia, if I remember correctly."

"I think I recall hearing something about that, back at Mars," Tanis nodded. "It made the Sanctity of the Sol System folks especially upset. They tried to kill some of our biologists in response."

Cary nodded. "We learned about that in school. You kicked some serious ass back then, Mom."

It was strange to Tanis to hear about what her daughters learned in school. A significant part of their history classes were about the *Intrepid*'s journey, and her part in that story seemed to fill up a lot of the lessons.

"She's blushing!" Saanvi called out and elbowed Cary. "Mom can be bashful; who knew?"

"What you're witnessing here, girls," Joe said with a grin, "is the Tanis in her natural habitat, letting herself appear vulnerable—but don't be fooled. She's still dangerous and ready to strike at any moment."

"Hey!" Tanis scolded. "I bet you're in those history lessons quite a bit, too, *Admiral Evans*."

"Yeah," Joe nodded. "But I *like* being in them: going to the classes, talking about our adventures."

Tanis chuckled. “That makes me feel like Ulysses. I guess this was my Odyssey.”

“Only time will tell,” Joe smiled. “You still could go down as Don Quixote.”

“What in the stars are you talking about?” Cary asked.

Tanis let out a laugh. “They need to spend less time teaching you about me and more time on the true classics.”

<*Tanis,*> a message from Kiera, the base AI entered her mind. <*A Transcend ship has just jumped into the system.*>

<*How far in?*> Tanis asked.

<*Deep. Its three AU closer to the star than this installation,*> Kiera replied.

<*Has sector monitoring reached it yet?*>

<*They have, I'm passing along the message now.*>

“Transcend ship jumped into the system,” she said aloud to Joe. “Linking you in.”

Joe's eyes grew wide and he nodded. “This'll be good.”

Elena's face appeared in their minds and Tanis felt a sense of relief. At least it was someone she trusted—mostly.

<*New Canaan, this is Elena. I need to speak with Governor Richards in person, or on tight-beam. Please respond.*>

<*Well that was short and mysterious,*> Joe sighed. <*I guess things are about to get interesting.*>

<*Has sector command responded?*> Tanis asked Kiera, dimly aware of Angela discussing possible reasons for Elena's presence with Bob.

<*They sent the standard hold course and await for a response message,*> the AI replied.

<*Good. Tell them to make no further communications. Is the* Hellespont *ready for its shakedown cruise?*> Tanis asked.

<*It will be by the time you get there,*> Kiera responded confidently.

# HELLESPONT

**STELLAR DATE: 02.19.8948 (Adjusted Years)**
**LOCATION: ISS *Hellespont*, Gamma III Shipyard**
**REGION: Sparta, Moon of Alexandria, $5^{th}$ Planet in the New Canaan System**

Tanis stepped onto the *Hellespont's* bridge with Joe and their two daughters in tow. The shakedown crew assigned to the ship was still out on maneuvers, testing another new vessel, but the skeleton crew from the *Andromeda* came along eagerly.

Especially Jim—it was his daughter who commanded the *Hellespont*, after all.

"Ylonda, are we good to go?" Tanis asked aloud as she sat in the commander's chair.

"Governor Richards," a voice said from her right. "I believe you're sitting in my chair."

Tanis turned to see Ylonda standing beside her, her silver face wearing an impatient expression.

"Oh, sorry," Tanis said, feeling herself blush again.

<*Careful, that's becoming a habit,*> Angela laughed.

"Quite all right," Ylonda replied as she took her seat. "I had not yet announced that I am keeping my mobile form while in command of the *Hellespont*."

"Then we have no ship's AI?" Tanis asked, unable to feel any other AI presences on the ship over the Link.

"I'm operating as the ship's AI, too," Ylonda replied with a smile. "I have real-time, simultaneous linkage with my embedded ship-nodes."

"You don't have the wireless interface for that amount of bandwidth—does that mean Earnest finally figured out the fidelity and bandwidth issues with quantum entanglement?" Saanvi eagerly asked from the pilot's seat where she had settled.

Ylonda nodded. "He has; though I don't know how you learned he was working on that."

"You're not the only one who knows about special projects," Saanvi said with a smug grin. "Earnest asked for my advice with some problems he was facing when he came over for dinner a month ago."

"OK, folks," Joe said from the XO's seat. "We can all crow about our part in the advent of galaxy-wide, instantaneous communication later. Right now, we still have to get in range of Elena's pinnace to have a little chat."

Tanis looked around for an open console. Cary had taken weapons, so she sat at an auxiliary monitoring console. The sight of her two girls taking their places on yet another cruiser's bridge filled her with pride once more. Someone was probably mumbling about nepotism somewhere, but this was just a simple interception of a friendly ship deep in the system, and her girls were handy.

Safe as houses.

<*Why didn't you tell me that Earnest had figured out the throughput issues with quantum entanglement?*> Tanis asked Bob.

<*I can't steal everyone's fun,*> Bob replied. <*I knew he would solve it—I had predicted he would manage it a bit sooner than he did, though.*>

<*Oh yeah?*> Tanis asked. <*How far off was your prediction?*>

<*Three minutes,*> Bob responded with a smug tone.

<*Show-off,*> Tanis laughed. <*What is the range?*>

<*The volume of particles necessary for long-range, high-fidelity communication is still a limiting factor. Ylonda has redundancies to handle a quantum synchronizing failure, and potential corruption issues from data seepage with other universes,*> Bob replied. <*Her range off-ship is limited to only one light year, at present.*>

<*I won't even pretend to understand why,*> Tanis replied.

<*It's really very simple,*> the AI explained. <*There are two issues. The first is the resonance in the vacuum energy of the universe. Space-time isn't flat, even for quantum interactions. To manage fidelity over longer ranges, the vibrations must be increased in amplitude, and that heats up the rubidium atoms. Once that happens, the quantum entanglement is broken.*>

<*Huh…*> Tanis replied. <*That does make sense.*>

"Ensign Cary, do we have station approval to release our moorings?" Ylonda asked.

"Aye, Captain, we have approval."

"Very well. Cast off our moorings, let's take her out."

Tanis shared a smile with Joe as they settled back and watched their daughters fly their second cruiser that day.

Once the boards showed green for a successful mooring release, Saanvi targeted the grav pylons mounted to the cradle, and began to push the ship out and into its lane. Ylonda offered a few words of guidance, but otherwise, let the two girls manage the ship's departure.

Tanis flipped the main holodisplay to show the *Hellespont's* bow view, gazing at the dozens of cruisers they were sliding past. It was a fleet any commander would be honored to command. It was the fleet that would guarantee their safety from whatever schemes the Transcend, and any others, would, launch against them.

"Approaching the tunnel, Captain," Cary said aloud. "We have clearance to enter the shaft."

"Thank you, Ensign," Ylonda replied. "Enable our active stealth systems as soon as we enter the tunnel. The outer shield won't deactivate until station control has verified we are undetectable."

"Yes, Captain," Cary replied.

"General," Ylonda turned to Tanis. "I assume you want to scoop up the pinnace while in stealth?"

Tanis nodded. "I do. We have to assume that the prying eyes out past our heliopause will see Elena's ship disappear, but not for five or six months. By then, I imagine whatever is going to happen will be long over."

Over the next few minutes, the ship slipped into the exit shaft, and Jim's holo presence appeared beside Cary. Tanis watched with a mixture of pride and interest as he went over the systems with her that she would need to test for full stealth confirmation with station control.

The *Hellespont* already possessed the new systems that the *Andromeda* was being refitted for. The ship would still be visible to keen optics at close range, but its ability to warp energy around its hull with minimal distortion was now at least on par with the Transcend cruisers they knew lurked around the edges of New Canaan.

Very soon, they would see how well the upgrades worked up close.

"ETA to interception?" Tanis asked.

"Three days and twenty hours," Ylonda replied.

"Well, then," Tanis said as she rose and stretched. "I don't know about the rest of you—Captain Ylonda excluded, of course—but I'm starving. Who could use a BLT?"

# A WARNING

**STELLAR DATE: 02.23.8948 (Adjusted Years)**
**LOCATION: ISS *Hellespont***
**REGION: Stellar Space near Roma, 6th Planet in the New Canaan System**

"Shit!" Elena swore as she walked down the pinnace's ramp. "Here I thought with a Transcend ship, not some Inner Stars clunker, that I would spot you guys sneaking up on me."

Tanis smiled and shook the woman's hand. "We've been working on some upgrades over the last few years."

"As I can see," Elena replied. "I managed to get a peek at this ship when you scooped me in; if I'm not mistaken, this is a new class of ship we've not seen before."

Tanis shrugged in response. "I'm not sure what your eyes out there have and have not seen. It takes half a year or more for news to get out to Isyra and her fleet."

Elena laughed ruefully. "I wish we weren't doing that. Talk about a self-fulfilling prophecy. Want a conflict? Just interdict a world and pile on a fleet or two; stir it up, and see what happens."

<*It seems that Elena's warcraft and yours differ,*> Angela said. <*You come from the same 'constant overwhelming force' school of thought that the Transcend seems to employ.*>

<*I distinctly recall being outnumbered or outgunned at almost every engagement over the last few hundred years. For once, I'd like to go into things with the upper hand.*>

<*Pipe dream,*> Angela replied.

Tanis led Elena across the docking bay toward an awaiting maglev car. "What is so important that you jumped so deep insystem? You never know what you can hit, doing something like that."

"Core-devils, don't remind me," Elena shook her head. "Airtha is gaining on The Cradle at a good clip right now. It makes for some seriously high delta-*v* on entry."

"And yet, you didn't rotate and brake after you came through," Tanis prompted.

"Yes, I'm trying not to draw any extra attention from Isyra and her fleet," Elena nodded as they got in the train car.

Four Marines wearing powered armor followed them in, and occupied the four corners of the car. Tanis hadn't even realized a platoon was on the ship until Ylonda sent a fireteam down with her to the dock.

<*You're getting rusty,*> Angela chided.

"But why bother?" Tanis asked, ignoring Angela's remark. "When they do see your jump, I'm sure whatever you've come to tell me will be old news."

"That's the thing, isn't it..." Elena said. "How sure are you that they don't have ships inside your star's heliosphere?"

Tanis leaned back in her seat and shrugged. "One-hundred percent? No. But, I'm damn close to that level of certainty. We can't see their ships all the time, but we have been able to pick them out and count them over the years. Unless she has a second class of ship that we can't see..."

Tanis let the statement hang and her right eyebrow rose.

"Pumping me for intel, Governor? Hell...I'm practically committing treason by being here."

The maglev stopped and Tanis rose from her seat and Elena followed. They walked through a short corridor to a crew lounge on the ship's starboard side. It wasn't luxurious, but it was serviceable and private.

Tanis signaled a servitor to bring them drinks—remembering what Elena had preferred from her brief visit on the *Intrepid* eighteen years earlier.

"Why don't you start by telling me what Sera sent you to say—though, I think I can guess," Tanis asked.

"Not a lot of options, are there?" Elena said with a nod before sipping her drink. "Things are heating up between us and the Orion Guard. They've allied with the AST and attacked Ascella."

"What?" Tanis sat up straight. "Attacked how?"

"With a massive fleet—thousands of ships. Only...they were just empty hulls. It was a feint."

"And it forced you to show your hand. Now the AST knows about the Transcend," Tanis leaned back and shook her head.

Elena nodded. "So far, the knowledge has not leaked to the general populace; but it will soon enough."

"Stars, and I thought we'd have another decade or two before Tomlinson came knocking on our door," Tanis said with a long sigh. "How much time do we have before he gets here?"

"I don't know. Sera has…worked her way into his inner circle, but he's grown suspicious of her—for reasons she hasn't been able to discern," Elena supplied.

Tanis considered what she would do in Tomlinson's stead. It would depend on the threat he faced.

"How did General Greer defeat the AST fleet?" she asked. "I assume from your wording that he *did* win."

"He did…" Elena paused and Tanis wondered what had happened. "Oh, stars," Elena shrugged before continuing. "You'll find out eventually. They sent antimatter warheads through the jump-gates into the AST ships. They obliterated them."

"Sweet black space, they used antimatter?" Tanis exclaimed. "That's still a war crime, isn't it?"

Elena nodded. "Yeah, even for us. I have no idea why Sera suggested it…"

"Sera what?!" Tanis almost yelled. "They must have contingencies for an attack on a watchpoint that don't involve detonating antimatter. Once you start doing that…"

"You're preaching to the choir, here," Elena said with her hands raised. "I said as much to Sera. She really has no idea why she suggested using antimatter—well, she has *some* idea. The alternative on the table was to blow the stars, and Helen suggested sending the warheads instead."

"Blowing the stars…" Tanis shook her head. "You guys don't do things by halves, do you?"

"No," Elena laughed ruefully. "Not so much."

"So, AST has joined with the Orion Guard, war is about to explode across human space, the President of the Transcend Interstellar Alliance is probably going to come here in person to demand our tech to give him an edge, and he's going to do it with an overwhelming show of force intended to cow us into submission. Don't know when, but probably in a few months at most," Tanis said while ticking items off her fingers. "That sound about right?"

"Yup, that about sums it up," Elena nodded.

"Well, you're stuck here 'til this goes down. Care to have dinner with Joe and my two girls?"

"You seem…unfazed by this," Elena said with a frown.

"Elena, I've been at this for some time, and honestly, when it comes to war machines, even the Transcend doesn't build 'em like they used to. Back in Sol, the TSF had a million warships for just one system. I'm aiming to replicate that number."

Elena spit out her drink. "You have a million warships?"

Tanis shook her head and laughed. "No, not quite so many, but by the time your president arrives, he'll meet over ten thousand ships of this classification alone."

Elena wiped her mouth and rose from the table while shaking her head. "Fuck, Tanis, what are you planning to do?"

"Maintain New Canaan's independence," she replied. "And before you ask, at whatever cost is necessary."

"Tanis," Elena said levelly. "You could join with the Transcend, give them your pico—or better yet, give it to everyone—it would stop this war from happening."

"No," Tanis replied. "It would escalate it. The Transcend, Inner Stars, Orion Guard…they're on the edge of going nova. All we ever wanted was to leave all of humanity's petty infighting behind, but we can't get away from it. Our technology has already proven to be too much of a catalyst. I won't escalate things further."

<*You may not have a choice,*> Angela commented.

<*I know,*> Tanis replied. <*What does Bob think will happen? Will there be war?*>

<*He won't say,*> Angela replied. <*I don't know if he can—what with you being involved.*>

Tanis shook her head and pushed the thoughts from her mind. For now, she was going to enjoy what would probably be the last uninterrupted meal with her family for some time.

# TRUTH

**STELLAR DATE: 02.23.8948 (Adjusted Years)**
**LOCATION: ISS *Hellespont***
**REGION: Stellar Space near Roma, 6th Planet in the New Canaan System**

"Your daughters are lovely," Elena said after the meal was done, and the two girls had left for a shift on the bridge.

"They're the best thing we made here at New Canaan," Joe said with a warm smile.

"And Saanvi…I remember you inquiring about her when you found her ship," Elena said. "I'm glad you gave her a good home."

"You heard about that, did you?" Tanis asked. "I didn't think that would be such big news in the Transcend."

Elena looked down at her glass of wine and frowned. "Well, I run operations for The Hand now—it came across my desk."

Joe chuckled. "Probably a bit more like *'ran'*, now, wouldn't you say?"

Elena looked up and gave a wan smile. "I suppose you're right. Makes this little jaunt worth it, then. I hated that job."

There was a brief lull in conversation, and Tanis leaned forward. She was having trouble finding the right words for the question she had. She almost feared the answer too much to ask.

<*What of* Sabrina?> Angela queried for her. <*We would have expected them back—or at least word—by now.*>

Elena's face grew clouded. "I'm afraid I don't have good news there."

The blood rushed from Tanis's face and she reached for Joe's hand. "Tell it."

"One of our agents—one that Sera and I trust implicitly—made contact with them about thirteen years ago. They were a bit hard to find, but we delivered New Canaan's coordinates. They told the agent that they were still hunting their quarry," Elena said in a somber tone.

"That doesn't sound so bad—though thirteen years is a long time to hear nothing," Joe said with a frown. "What happened next?"

"We *think* that they may have finally found Finaeus in the Ikoden System. There was a shoot-out—not the first one they were involved in, from what we've learned—except this one was with us."

"With you?" Tanis leaned forward.

"What do you mean?" Joe asked at the same time.

Elena's eyes darted between the pair and she raised her hands defensively. "Well, The Hand has been searching for Finaeus for some time; agents who were operating under the president's direction. They discovered that Jessica was on *Sabrina,* and that they had a good lead. They followed *Sabrina* to Ikoden, and when they found Finaeus, they attacked."

"Go on," Tanis said tonelessly.

"You can relax…no one from *Sabrina* was killed. Though they got all our agents; only two lived, but they ended up taking their own lives to avoid interrogation. The thing is…after they left Ikoden, they just disappeared. There hasn't been a sighting of them in eleven years."

Tanis covered her eyes with her forearm.

"Elena, that's not as bad as you made it out to be, they're probably just on their way here now," Joe said.

"Ikoden's not that far away—it should have been only four, maybe five years max," Elena replied. "Sera's really worried. She has agents scouring the Inner Stars for *Sabrina.*"

Tanis looked to Joe and saw both worry and compassion in his eyes. They both missed Jessica terribly, and Tanis had grown close to the crew of *Sabrina* during their months together.

Knowing that Jessica was out there somewhere, lost in the Inner Stars—and that she had this crisis with the Transcend bearing down on her, keeping her from going in search of her friend—hit her harder than she expected.

She had never balked at the mantle of responsibility she wore, not enough to truly resent it. But now, she wished she could throw it aside and go find her friend.

<*When this is over, I'm going to find her,*> Tanis said.

<*And I'll go with you,*> Joe replied. <*We'll find them together.*>

Elena's eyes darted between the pair. "I'm really sorry. I wish I had better news. I mean…we haven't found any evidence that they were attacked or taken, either…"

"It's OK," Tanis said finally. "Whatever happened, it's not your fault..."

"Either way, I'm still sorry," Elena said softly. "I see on the net that there are quarters for me. I'll head there...leave you two alone."

Tanis nodded absently and Elena left the room.

She didn't know if she wanted to scream or cry, and Joe wrapped his arms around her. Wordlessly, they held one another, and then she did cry, for fear that she had lost Jessica forever.

# NEGOTIATIONS

**STELLAR DATE: 03.27.8948 (Adjusted Years)**
**LOCATION: TSS *Galadrial***
**REGION: Stellar Space near Roma, 6th Planet in the New Canaan System**

The *Galadrial* exited the wormhole into normal space, and Sera stripped the data streams from the Transcend ships that had jumped ahead.

She didn't need to, of course—there were officers running scan and comm—but she was looking for any information about Elena, and whether or not she was OK.

"New Canaan," her father announced at her side. "The *Intrepid*'s reward for their long struggle."

She noted how he tried to sound magnanimous, but she could tell that he felt the reward was too great for what the Transcend had received—even though she had since learned that it was her father who ensured that the *Intrepid* was not required to give over their picotech or stasis shields.

"Also, what they were due, being a GSS ship," Sera added.

Her father cast her a hard stare. "The Generation Ship Service is long gone. The Inner Stars gave up on peaceful colonization, and look at what it has wrought. It is this system's duty to ensure that we can preserve the Transcend, and our mission."

Sera didn't respond. Getting into an argument with her father about the purpose of the Transcend on the bridge of his flagship would not be wise. Instead, she surveyed the Transcend fleet arrayed around them.

It consisted of over a thousand cruisers, and several hundred more destroyers and support vessels. From what Admiral Isyra had observed, Tanis had no more than fifty warships, and they appeared to be spread across the system on patrols.

A pair were nearby, only two AU distant; though any response from those ships was still nearly an hour away.

*<Why doesn't she have more ships?>* Sera asked Helen. *<I expected Isyra to be wrong, but our scans don't even show the number she had identified.>*

*<Maybe Tanis knows that a show of force will be met with a greater show of force,>* Helen replied. *<Perhaps Tanis does not want a war.>*

*<I'll agree with you there. She's not a warmonger, but she's one hell of a protective mother when it comes to her ship and her people. Sure, fifty warships is probably an aggressive buildup for a regular colony world that is only fifteen years old, but for Tanis…?>*

"Send the message," Sera's father prompted. "Let their governor know that we need to talk about the state of the human sphere, and her duty to help us protect it."

"I've already sent it," Sera replied. "We may have to wait a day for the response."

President Tomlinson nodded. "Very well. Admiral Greer, as you've suggested, move the fleet to the seventh planet—Roma, I believe the locals have named it. I see that they have a small outpost on one of its moons. We'll propose it as a meeting place."

The world was just over six AU distant, and the fleet began a slow acceleration toward it, the newly constructed jump-gate boosting with them under its own power.

"Yes, President," Greer replied and issued the command over the fleet net.

Sera saw Greer glance at the gate on the holotank and frown. She shared his sentiment. Assembling the gate the moment they entered the system put them at a tactical disadvantage. The gate was large, cumbersome, and would be difficult to protect. It also told the sailors and soldiers in the fleet that the president would not stay with them to the end, if it came to that. He would be on the first ship jumping out.

That message was further re-enforced by the fact that Isyra had two gates beyond the heliosphere, in interstellar space. Exit routes already existed, and were in secure locations. If it had been up to her—and she assumed Greer, as well—they wouldn't have brought a jump-gate at all.

Her misgivings about the jump-gate aside, she was glad that Greer was with them. He had come to Airtha ready to be censured, or worse, for the outcome in Ascella; but instead, her father had promoted him to admiral of the 21st Fleet.

Greer had treated with Tanis fairly at Ascella, and she suspected that their existing relationship contributed to her father's decision to bring him along.

Sera turned and took a seat at a console, back to scanning the local comm traffic for any word of Elena. It was going to be a long wait, and she needed to while away the time somehow.

* * * * *

Sera arrived on the *Galadriel's* bridge with coffee in hand at just the same moment that the ship's captain, a woman named Viska, announced that they had reached the L1 point between Roma and its largest moon—a nearly featureless rock named Normandy.

Well, featureless except for the kilometer-high tower standing off its surface.

The structure sat on what would be the moon's equator—if it were not tidally locked to Roma—and pointed directly at the Jovian planet. It seemed to serve no purpose that the fleet's analysts had yet discerned, but Sera knew that it would not be here without cause.

"How is it that Isyra didn't spot this thing?" Admiral Greer muttered as he stared at the structure.

"I'll admit, I'm not too excited about it pointing at us," Sera added. "Though, it seems to have no significant energy output. The top appears to be some sort of observation deck."

"It's a good sign," her father said. "That is a structure built by a people who are settling in. They will give us what we want to maintain their safety here."

"I wish I shared your optimism," Greer replied, and Sera saw him share a look with Viska.

Sera noted that her father saw the look, as well. "You mistake optimism for raw determination, Admiral. We will get what we need from these colonists because we must. Tanis Richards will give it to us because she will also see that we must have it."

"Ship coming out of the jovian planet," the scan officer announced, and she flipped the main holo to show a close-up view of Roma's surface.

An object stirred beneath the surface, brushing the raging storms aside, unperturbed by their fury. Fleet analysis added data to the object, giving it a width of ten kilometers and at least thirty-five long.

"It's the *Intrepid,*" Sera breathed. "So that's where they hid it."

A minute later, the ship crested the cloud cover and scan updated with readings from the unobstructed vessel. More than one person on the bridge audibly gasped at the firepower on display.

"Its beacon tags it as the *I2* now. Where did they refit that vessel?" Greer asked. "Isyra's data never showed it at any shipyard."

"It would seem they have shipyards that Isyra didn't find," Sera said with a shake of her head. "Though, I have no idea where they put them. Surely not within the jovian planets; that's not especially practical."

"Neither is that ship," Captain Viska replied. "On its own like that, it's just a massive target."

"A massive target with a tenth the firepower of this fleet, and stasis shields, and don't forget the picobombs," Sera added.

Greer addressed the commanders and captains over the fleetnet. *<They would not put that ship out here alone. There are either stealth ships we can't see, or there are more vessels below the clouds. I want pattern delta-seven—>*

*<Belay that,>* the president ordered. *<Let's talk with them before we prepare for battle.>*

Greer's face reddened, but he sent the order to stand down.

"I'm counting on your friendship for something, Sera," her father said.

"Me too," Sera muttered.

"Inbound communication from the *I2,*" the comm officer announced.

"Put it up," the president replied.

As Sera expected, it was Tanis who appeared before them. She was wearing her ISF uniform—interesting that they kept that name for their space force—with five stars now adorning her collar. General and Governor, it sent a message of control and power. If Sera didn't know that Tanis craved neither—well, not the power, at least—she would have wondered if the woman before them had the makings of a dictator.

<*I put her in this position,*> Sera sighed. <*Everything happening right now started when I opened that crate in* Sabrina*'s hold.*>

<*No, dear, it started the moment that Earnest Redding created reliable picotech, and they laid the hull for that ship. If anything, that clever inventor started us all down this path,*> Helen replied.

"Welcome to New Canaan," Tanis said with a genuine smile.

Sera couldn't help but notice that she appeared perfectly at ease. That didn't mean she was; Tanis could hide her true intentions and feelings with the best of them.

"We're going to have to establish a clear entry point for you," Tanis continued. "A lot of Transcend ships seem to pop into our interdicted system."

President Tomlinson frowned. "Other than that derelict trader, we're the first—or we should be."

"I was referring to the volume of ships you brought, not the frequency," Tanis said with a smile.

Sera secretly thanked her friend for the message. Elena had arrived and was safe. That was the best news she had received in weeks.

"Very well, then," her father said with a frown, and Sera knew that he was not fully convinced by Tanis's explanation.

"To what do we owe the pleasure of your company?" Tanis asked. "I assume you did not come with all these ships just for a state visit."

"I did not," the president replied. "We need to speak, you and I. The human sphere is in turmoil, and you are in a unique position to help preserve our future."

Tanis raised a hand to her chin and appeared to ponder the president's words. "Very well. I hope you understand, based on prior encounters, I'm unwilling to come to your ship, and you may not wish to come to mine. However, we are near a facility we recently completed on the moon, Normandy. Would you care to meet there?"

"It seems auspicious that it is there, waiting for us," the president said with a nod. "Very well. Shall we meet there in five of your local system hours?"

"That will work perfectly," Tanis replied. "We'll send docking instructions."

The holo image disappeared and her father shook his head.

"She is far too calm. Even with what we know of her, there should be some anger over our presence—or concern, at the very least," he said.

"The *I2* is a testament to her demeanor," the Admiral said with a deep frown. "That is one hell of a ship."

Secretary Adrienne, who was also along for the negotiations, though Sera wished he weren't, nodded. "She has expected this, and has been preparing. I urge you to reconsider meeting with her on her ground."

The president dismissed their concerns with a wave of his hand; something she had seen her father do all too often. If she were in command, Sera knew she would listen to her advisors more than he did.

"We have no choice. We came here to meet with her, and so we shall meet. My hope has always been to strike a deal without conflict. Her level of preparation notwithstanding, it can still happen."

Sera wasn't certain if her father was overestimating his abilities as a negotiator, or underestimating Tanis's. Still, she had to admit her father was right. The Transcend did need the stasis tech, if they were to weather the coming war. Already, the AST was drawing together its allies and forces to mount a major assault. On their own, they would not be a significant threat; but with Orion jump-gates, they could jump deep within the Transcend and wreak havoc.

The AST would create opportunities that the Orion Guard would press to their advantage, and total war would ensue.

* * * * *

At the allotted time, the Transcend pinnace slipped through the ES shielding, and settled on a pad on the observation tower. Sera found it quaint that, although they had grav tech and stasis shielding, the colonists still used ES shields for atmospheric containment.

She walked down the ramp beside her father, with Adrienne and General Greer following behind. A dozen of her father's security personnel accompanied them, along with several aides.

Sera didn't bring her own security, as two of her father's guards were Hand agents she had slipped into the Presidential Guard years ago. She was almost certain they would protect her life over her father's.

At the tower's entrance, Admiral Sanderson stood with several ISF Marines. Sera was glad to see that he was still actively serving. He had spoken about retiring on several occasions during the journey to Ascella, but the military was all he knew. She bet that Tanis only had to ask once for him to stay on.

"President Tomlinson," Sanderson said as they approached and offered his hand, which her father shook. "Thank you for coming to meet with us here. I think you'll enjoy the facility; it's the first step in this moon's restructuring."

"Thank you for having us," her father replied. "You've piqued my curiosity. What are you restructuring this moon into?"

"I'm not up on all the details," Sanderson replied, "but I'm told it's going to become some sort of space-sports facility. Planet diving into the jovian, racing in the canyons below; it has a molten core, so I believe there will also be some cavern racing beneath the crust—serious adrenaline stuff."

Sera laughed. "And here I thought the observation platform was just for taking in the view of Roma up there."

"Well," Sanderson nodded conspiratorially, "if it were up to me, that's all I'd want, too, but the younger generation...well, they hear all the tales of our journey and some think things are a bit boring here, so we're keeping it interesting."

"Diving from here into Roma certainly would be interesting," Adrienne commented. "I imagine they'll need to be shot toward the planet first, right?"

Sanderson nodded. "That's my understanding. My daughter is more than eager to be here when that finally opens up."

"A daughter!" Sera exclaimed. "I distinctly recall you saying that you were too old for more children."

"Yes, well, when you meet the right woman..." Sanderson replied as he ushered them onto a large lift platform.

Sera looked up and saw that the lift had no ceiling; it would rise up directly into the floor of the observation platform. If she squinted, she could see right through the observation platform's clear ceiling and into space.

Once all the guards and aides were aboard, the lift began to ascend, and Sanderson continued. "I met Veronica at the landfall party, of all places. She was one of the colonists to win the lottery and was on the second shuttle down. We hit it off, and the rest, including our dear Petra and her two brothers, is history."

"I'm glad to hear that your colony is filled with children's hopes and dreams," the president chimed in. "It's one of the most rewarding things in the galaxy—to see your own grow and take up their mantles."

Sera saw Sanderson cast a curious look at the president before replying. "Well, not too many heavy mantles around here. Just our little attempt at a better life."

"Yet, there is your *I2*, as you call it. Is that a part of your better life?" Secretary Adrienne asked.

"That's just the thing," Sanderson replied with a raised eyebrow. "When you're in our position, someone is always out to cash in on your success."

The response killed the conversation, and the lift climbed the rest of the distance in silence. Sera wanted to reach out and hit Adrienne. Here she was, breaking the ice and re-establishing her relationship with the admiral, and her father's trusted advisor had to screw it up.

She glanced at Admiral Sanderson, and couldn't tell by his implacable gaze whether he was upset by Adrienne's comment or not. The lift reached the observation deck before she had time to consider Adrienne's verbal sabotage further.

It was a wide space, several hundred meters across, with small alcoves filled with artful seating arrangements and long tables for larger gatherings. Several bars also dotted the area; servitors at the ready to provide customers with whatever they wished.

Above, a single crystal dome stretched over the circular space, providing a stunning view of Roma's red and purple colored bands. Even without leveraging her augmented vision, Sera could see the TSF fleet at the L1 point between Normandy and Roma. Closer, having circled around the Transcend ships, lay the *I2*—its features easily discernible from where it orbited sixty kilometers above the observation deck.

Other than a few additional ISF Marines, the observation platform was empty, and Admiral Sanderson led them to a nearby table that was nestled between two rows of hedges.

"Very tasteful," President Tomlinson commented, as he sat on one side of the table and gestured for a servitor to come and pour him a glass of water. "I especially like how the dome above is a single piece. I can't make out any seams at all."

Sanderson nodded. "Yes, that is pretty impressive. My daughter told me that it was grown in place right here, so it didn't have to be transported."

"Interesting. I may have to get something similar for my office."

"On Airtha, I assume," Tanis's voice came from the far side of the hedge before she strode into view. "We recovered visuals of your capital from that derelict freighter. It must be something to behold."

"It is," Tomlinson nodded. "Perhaps someday, after we iron out some of these issues, you can come and see it for yourself."

"I would like that," Tanis replied as she sat across the table from the Transcend delegation.

Sera smiled and nodded to Joe, who sat to Tanis's right, while Admiral Sanderson was on her left. Terrance Enfield and Amanda, one of their AI's avatars, were the last to sit at the table.

"Admiral Sanderson you've met, and Sera knows my husband, Admiral Evans. I would also like to introduce Amanda, who represents our AI contingent, along with Angela who is with me. Last, but not least, is Terrance Enfield, our original colony sponsor."

Greetings were exchanged around the table, and while they were occurring, Tanis reached across the table and clasped Sera's hand.

"I'm glad you are well. I honestly did not expect it to be so long before we met again."

Sera nodded. "Me either. It would seem that both of us have taken on more responsibility than we thought. Are those chairs on a porch still in our future?"

Tanis chuckled. "I have the porch and the chairs—though I don't use them as much as I'd like. Perhaps you can come sit in them for a bit before you go."

Sera felt a prompt in her mind and realized that Tanis had granted her access to a non-public net.

<*Elena told me, Director of The Hand! I'm surprised you'd take such a position,*> Tanis said.

<*You know what they say about your enemies,*> Sera replied. <*I was thrust into it, to be honest, but I saw it as an opportunity to do some good—though, now, I'm mostly consumed with positioning Inner Stars governments to support us in the coming war.*>

*<So, you have no doubt that war is upon us?>* Tanis asked.

*<Surely Elena told you. The AST attacked a watchpoint—they were certainly prompted by the Orion Guard. How is she? I hope you've treated her well. I take it that* Sabrina *has not returned with Finaeus, yet?>*

Sera's tone was eager, and Tanis knew that her friend was hopeful that the ship had flown directly to New Canaan.

*<Elena is well, she told us about* Sabrina... *it has not arrived. Let's chat more about this later.>*

Sera realized her father was speaking in the middle of some long, rambling speech about how the Transcend and the colonists of New Canaan shared mutual goals that bound them together, and how they were really one people, colony creators and colonizers.

Tanis appeared to be listening intently, despite the fact that they had just carried on a conversation. If she knew the woman at all, she was probably also talking to Angela, as well.

*<She is impressive,>* Helen commented. *<Almost too much so. Does it never concern you that she's so deeply entwined with her AI? We've been together for only forty years; near the limit of how long our minds can co-exist. But Tanis? She's been with Angela for centuries.>*

*<I've thought about it, yeah. They should have fully merged long ago, but they haven't. It's obvious when you talk to them both,>* Sera replied, curious as to why Helen was bringing this up now. *<What of it?>*

*<It just seemed noteworthy that they don't appear to have grown more intertwined since we last saw them. I would have expected some change. We've changed a lot since then,>* Helen commented, and Sera noted that her AI sounded almost indifferent. If that were the case, why would she bring it up at all?

"... and I agree that we have more in common with each other than we do with many of the Inner Stars worlds and nations," Tanis was saying as Sera shifted her attention back to the audible conversation. "But that's not why you came here. Let's just get to it, shall we, President Tomlinson? You want access to our picotech and stasis shields. That's it, plain and simple. It's the reason why we're an interdicted system, and it's the reason we're here today."

Sera felt a smile cross her lips and covered her mouth to hide it. It was not often anyone spoke to her father like he was an equal. It was refreshing to hear.

*****

<*Gah, he's just so wordy; why does it take him forever to say anything?*> Tanis asked Angela.

<*Beats me. You humans take too long to say pretty much everything. I stopped taking note of it centuries ago,*> Angela said with a feigned yawn.

<*Funny. OK, time to lay it out and see how he responds,*> she said to Angela and spoke her piece. <*There, let's see how he hedges around now.*>

Tanis saw Sera cover her mouth with her hand to hide her amusement and almost had to do the same—if only she weren't growing annoyed with Tomlinson's never-ending speech about nothing. The president, for his part, appeared nonplussed.

"In a nutshell, that is it, yes," he replied evenly. "But that does not provide the *why* behind why I've come here to ask for your help. I know you hold dear the same ideals we do—a free humanity, able to spread across the stars and make our own destinies. That is something that the Orion Guard does not want, and they'll corrupt the Inner Stars and undo all our work there."

Tanis watched the president's grey eyes as he spoke. She could not detect any lie in them—the man either believed what he said, or was a consummate liar. However, it was possible that the two options were not mutually exclusive.

"From what I understand, you and the Guard are playing a game with the Inner Stars: you gently uplifting, while they do…what? Ignore? Exploit? In the end, you both hide the facts from them. You've both been playing this game for millennia. What's changed now?"

Tanis knew what had changed; she just wanted to hear Tomlinson say it, to justify his need by placing the blame on her. It would solidify her opinion of the man.

"I don't expect that you would understand all of the nuances at play," Tomlinson said after a brief pause. "Sometimes, I think that I only have the barest grasp myself. However, it was inevitable that something would happen to tip the balance that has existed for so long. It just so happens that it was you. If by some chance, you had slipped out of Kapteyn's Streamer and evaded notice, this eventuality would still have come to pass."

He stopped again and took a sip of the drink before him before continuing. "I can see how, from your perspective, there would be little difference between us and the Guard. In fact, with a few subtle twists, they could be the right side, and we the wrong. But know this: they split from us in anger, in fear, and have been the aggressors for these last few thousand years. They have destroyed entire worlds along the front—terraformed worlds that the FGT spent centuries creating. Millions of Transcend citizens have died at their hands."

"And what of the proxy nations you have within the Inner Stars?" Tanis asked. "They do fight wars, sometimes on your behalf."

"It is true we have responded in kind; but only in an attempt to maintain a balance. But now, they control the Pleiades, and have turned the Hegemony of Worlds to their cause. If we do not gain your technology, we will ultimately lose this conflict."

The President of the Transcend Interstellar Alliance lowered his voice as he spoke, while continuing to hold Tanis's eyes. He paused again and glanced around the room before returning his gaze to her. "And then, when that happens, it will not be myself and Sera here before you, but an Orion Guard fleet—burning your worlds, and demanding your surrender."

As he had spoken, Tanis recalled what she had been told of Saanvi's family—of how they had settled a world closer to the front, which had been destroyed by the Orion Guard.

She looked to Sera and saw that her friend, a woman she had spent many months with on *Sabrina,* and later the *Intrepid,* was nodding in agreement, affirming her father's words.

Given Sera's dislike for her father, Tanis had to believe that he was sincere.

"Things have grown more dire over recent months," Sera added. "The Orion Guard led the AST to Ascella and attacked the watchpoint with a massive fleet. The Transcend Space Force was victorious in the end, but you know what this means."

Tanis nodded. "That Orion fleet you spoke of could be here sooner rather than later."

"Now do you believe us? Do you understand our sense of urgency?" the Transcend's president asked. "I had hoped to have more time—to let you settle in, to establish a real friendship between our peoples. But that timetable has been accelerated."

Tanis steepled her fingers and stared over them at President Tomlinson, Sera, and the president's entourage.

<*It's a lot to consider,*> she said to the assembled representatives on her side of the table.

<*He lies like a rug, but he has a number of good points,*> Admiral Sanderson said.

<*Even if he's in the wrong, simple galactic geography makes them more appropriate allies than the Guard,*> Terrance added.

<*Bob would like to see whatever data they have on the Guard's movements to support their statements,*> Amanda said. <*Personally, I can't believe that Sera is his daughter. She's nothing like him.*>

<*I can see it,*> Tanis replied. <*It's in their surety.*>

<*That might be a mirror you're looking at, then,*> Angela said privately with a chuckle.

"You make a convincing argument," Tanis said aloud. "On the face of it, I believe you, and agree with your need. However, we need to discuss this. Also, any details you have on these advances by the Guard, and their assault on Ascella, would help us in our decision-making."

"Of course," President Tomlinson said and nodded to Sera, who slid a data crystal across the table.

Tanis took the data crystal and passed it to Amanda before rising.

"Let's adjourn for the day. You've given us a lot to think over. We'll review this data and reconvene at the same time tomorrow."

The Transcend contingent rose with their president, who nodded in agreement.

"That sounds excellent. I must say that I am pleased with how receptive you've been. Not everyone in your position would be so understanding," President Tomlinson said with a warm smile. "I feel like tomorrow we'll come to an agreement that will benefit us both, and establish a peace for all humanity."

"That is something I would like very much," Tanis replied.

They walked around the table to shake hands once more, and the rest of their contingents followed suit. As President Tomlinson began to walk away, Tanis called out.

"Sera, a moment," Tanis called after her friend.

Sera touched her father's hand, and Tanis heard her say, "Wait for me in the shuttle."

The president nodded, and Sera returned to the table.

"Walk with me," Tanis said and placed a hand on Sera's shoulder to guide her toward the edge of the viewing platform.

"You seem to think that we should trade the tech—something that you didn't believe to be the correct course of action when last we spoke," Tanis said once they were alone.

Sera nodded. "That's true, but things have changed. The attack on Ascella—"

"Which you used antimatter weapons to defeat," Tanis interjected.

"Heard about that, did you?" Sera asked with a sigh. "I guess I...I don't know why I suggested that. It seemed like a good idea, but once the words left my mouth, I began to regret them more with each passing moment."

"In the end, they were empty hulls," Tanis replied. "Though, still a war crime."

Sera sighed and nodded. "Stars, I wish they had found Finaeus by now. He would know what to do. Now we may have lost them all..."

Tanis nodded somberly. "Elena said you managed to find them, and gave them our coordinates here some years ago. I'm holding out hope that they ran into trouble but are still on their way—you haven't found any evidence to the contrary, have you?"

Sera shook her head. "Not yet, no. Nothing either way."

"I do wish Jessica were here," Tanis sighed. "For someone who was never supposed to be on this mission, she certainly has become indispensable."

"I know what you mean," Sera replied as they reached the edge of the platform and gazed out on the moon below. "Were you telling the truth before? Is Elena on the *I2*, and not here?"

"I was. I can't let her talk to you, or anyone else from the Transcend yet. She knows things I'm not ready to share," Tanis said the words as gently as she could, but she knew Sera would not take them well.

"What do you mean?" Sera locked eyes with her. "What is it that you can't tell me? I told you a lot—a treasonous amount—about the Transcend while we were on the *Intrepid*. What is it that you can't say now? Have you done something to Elena?"

"No!" Tanis replied emphatically. "Elena is fine. She just saw things that I can't have her share. And she's far more loyal to you than to me…and you…"

"You think I'm more loyal to my father?" Sera asked, her voice dripping with accusation. "I saved your life, you saved mine, and now you won't let me see my lover just because of your paranoia?"

"Sera—" Tanis began.

"No, Tanis, take your excuses and go fuck yourself with them. Tomorrow, when we come back to make a deal with you and whatever secrets you have, Elena better be here…"

"Or else?" Tanis asked, feeling rage rise in herself at Sera's irrational behavior. "Are you implying that I'm in the wrong, as I treat with you and your invading fleet?"

"You haven't seen an invading fleet, yet. You'll know when you do," Sera spat and turned on her heel, storming off in the direction of the lift.

<*That was…irrational of her,*> Angela commented.

<*It really was,*> Tanis replied. <*More than just a little. Something else is going on.*>

* * * * *

Sera strode onto the pinnace and dropped into a seat, still fuming over her conversation with Tanis. That she should deny her even the sight of Elena, and hold back secrets…she stopped herself from that train of thought. The only thing that made it worse was, deep down, she knew Tanis was right.

She was the one on the side that was attempting to use intimidation to get their way; she had even sent Elena because of that—to warn Tanis. So why was she so upset about it now?

"What did she want to talk about?" her father said as he sat beside her. "It seems to have you upset."

"It's nothing; a personal matter between us from before I came back to Airtha," Sera replied.

"I hope you'd tell me if it were important to our mission here," her father said in what Sera had long since dubbed his *I'm serious, yet friendly, but cross me at your peril* tone.

Sera sighed. "To be honest, I don't know if it's important or not, she wouldn't let me see…"

Sera clamped her mouth shut and felt her face redden. She couldn't believe what she had almost said aloud. It was like she wasn't in control of herself anymore.

<*What are you doing?*> Helen asked. <*If I didn't know better, I'd think you were drunk!*>

"See what?" her father asked, peering at her intently, his eyes widening. "You sent someone to warn them! This is where Elena went; not some diplomatic mission back to Spica! It's why their new ship was waiting for us here…at the planet closest to the most obvious jump point."

Sera tried to formulate a response but stopped. Nothing she could think of would make things better. It didn't matter.

Her father stood and stared down at her. "There's no way that you could have masked a jump-gate destination—I would know if any ship jumped into an interdicted system!"

Rage was building in his voice, and his face reddened. "There's…no. Only Airtha could have hidden that jump destination from me..." he turned, looking pensive. Before Sera could reply, multiple pulse rifle blasts took her down.

# DISSEMINATION

**STELLAR DATE: 03.27.8948 (Adjusted Years)**
**LOCATION: Normandy Starjump Observation Tower**
**REGION: Normandy, Moon of Roma, 6th Planet in the New Canaan System**

"OK, Mom, you were right; that was really boring," Cary said as Tanis and Joe joined their kids in a suite down the tower shaft.

"Yeah," Tanis sighed as she fell onto a sofa. "That Jeffrey Tomlinson sure can talk."

"And sure likes to hear it, too," Joe added as he joined Tanis.

"What were you and Sera talking about?" Saanvi asked. "It seemed intense."

"Mostly Elena," Tanis replied. "She wanted to see her, and I told her I couldn't allow it yet. She…she didn't handle that well. I thought I could get her to understand my side of it, but…now I fear I've lost a friend."

"But Mom," Cary exclaimed, "Sera and Elena are lovers! How could you keep them apart?"

Tanis gave her daughter a level stare. "Because lovers share secrets. They can't help it, and I can't have Sera know about our fleet yet. She seems…she's different somehow. It's as though she's bought into everything that she was so against when she left. I don't know where she stands anymore."

"She did send Elena," Joe said as he took a glass of water from a servitor. "That counts for something."

"It does," Tanis replied with a nod. "Just how much, I don't know anymore."

"Has Bob analyzed the data yet?" Saanvi asked. "Is it true that the Orion Guard has destroyed worlds?"

Tanis nodded slowly, wary of where the conversation could go. "Yes, and they've told us about those sorts of attacks before; there's more corroborative evidence this time—such as it is, coming from one source."

<*You've gone and done it,*> Angela said. <*Saanvi will know what that first time was.*>

Saanvi was a smart girl, and not just from the L2 augmentations both of her daughters had undergone over the years. Tanis knew that one day she would ask for the information about what had happened to her parents, and, with her verbal slip, today would be that day.

<*It never rains, it pours,*> Angela added. <*You ready for this? You're already emotionally drained.*>

<*She's our daughter, Angela. I have to be ready. It's my most important job in life.*>

Her AI sent her an affirming warmth, and Tanis steeled herself for the question. When it came, it was quiet, barely audible.

"Mom…how did my family die?"

Tanis took a deep breath. "They were on a world that was attacked by the Orion Guard. It was close to the front—though not so close that anyone thought there was a risk."

Saanvi's face fell and her shoulders slumped. "I always…I don't know what I thought—that maybe they were still out there somewhere…"

Tanis rose and pulled Saanvi into her arms, Joe and Cary not far behind. The family held each other as Saanvi began to cry—a cry that Tanis knew she had been saving for a long time. It lasted for a few minutes before Saanvi managed to stop and wipe the tears from her eyes.

She looked up at Tanis, and, with a voice far calmer than Tanis would have expected, said, "Mom, you have to join with the Transcend and stop the Guard. They can't keep destroying worlds!"

Tanis wanted to tell her that she couldn't base her decision on this one need for retribution that Saanvi now had—but that answer would drive her daughter away in rage and sadness. But Saanvi wouldn't be the only reason. Bob was certain that at least some of the accounts of planetary destruction by the Guard were true. If the *Transcend* had ever destroyed any worlds, Sera would have told her before—of that much she was certain.

<*You're going to have to ally with them. You know that, don't you?*> Angela said.

Tanis knew it, but she didn't want to accept it. <*Mother fucking arghhh—we had more peace at Victoria than we've had here at our own colony! We may as well have just stayed there and lived out our lives. The*

*Sirians never came back—at least not for a long time. And when they did, we could have stopped them.*>

<*I love you dearly, Tanis, my otherself,*> Angela said quietly, <*but it's time you realize that you were never destined to have peace. You are here to make war.*>

Tanis felt a tear slip down her face as she looked into the inquiring eyes of her family.

"Yes, we will ally with the Transcend. Stars have mercy on our souls; we'll go to war."

<*Tanis, I know you're busy,*> Amanda's voice broke into her thoughts, <*but it's important. Sera's father has taken her—he's going to do something to her. She needs your help.*>

Tanis felt like she was being torn in two. First, Sera stormed off in a rage, and now she was in mortal danger and needed rescue?

<*What do we know?*> she asked, her mental tone far calmer than she expected.

<*One of her agents got a message to us. She was having an argument with her father about Elena—he realized that she's here—and he had Sera shot. Not lethally. He's got her in surgery now.*>

<*Get Elena down here now!*> Tanis ordered. <*I'll muster an assault force.*>

"I have to go," she said to her family. "Tomlinson has attacked Sera and is doing something to her, I have to go help her."

"I thought you just had a fight with her?" Cary asked with a frown. "Now you're going to assault the Transcend president's ship?"

"Yes, if it comes to that. I owe her my life, more than once over," Tanis said before locking eyes with Joe. "Take the girls to the *I2*, she's under your command now. Be ready."

Joe nodded solemnly. "Not how I finally wanted to get command of that beauty. Girls, grab whatever you need; we'll take the shuttle that's bringing Elena when it goes back up. You're going to the shipyard?" he directed the last to Tanis.

"Yes," she said with a nod. "There are a dozen stealth pinnaces down there that have passed their break-in flights, and a platoon of Marines just itching for a fight."

"What if it's a ruse?" Saanvi asked. "What if everything is fine, or if it's an Orion trick?"

"I've already directed Amanda to get in touch with Sera. If we're stonewalled, we'll know something is up. If our new allies are playing games with us—games like this—then we're better off without them."

"But Orion..." Saanvi said, her eyes wide.

"Don't worry." Tanis stroked her daughter's face. "I have a feeling that, no matter what, we'll be fighting Orion soon enough."

# LAID BARE

**STELLAR DATE: 03.27.8948 (Adjusted Years)**
**LOCATION: TSS *Galadrial***
**REGION: Roma-Normandy L1 Point, New Canaan System**

<*Wake up, Seraphina, it's time we had a chat,*> the voice spoke into her mind, and Sera groaned from the pain in her head. It felt as though her skull was splitting apart. It felt even worse than when she woke up in the *Intrepid*'s medbay after Mark had hacked her—something she had not thought possible.

<*Goway…*> she responded, and reached out for Helen, only to find a void in her mind, an emptiness where her long-time companion should be.

"You may have just realized that you can't communicate with Helen." The voice spoke audibly, and she recognized it as her father's.

"Why…?" she gasped as her head throbbed.

"I'm sorry you're in pain," her father said. "The medbay can dull the pain, but not too much. I want you cogent for this conversation we have to have."

Sera cracked an eye to see her father seated in a chair by her side in a dimly lit room. He must have told the medbay's systems to dampen the agony, because it decreased in intensity, and she was finally able to form a complete thought.

"What did you do to Helen?" she asked, her voice still unable to rise above a whisper.

"I had her removed," her father replied. "After I realized what you had done to get Elena here, and who could have done it, I realized who your AI really was."

*Shit!* Sera thought to herself. Her father had realized that Helen was a shard of Airtha.

"You asked, long ago—do you remember?—if you could have a child of Airtha as your AI when you joined The Hand," her father said slowly. "Do you recall my answer?"

"You said no," Sera replied, both eyes open now, staring at her father with unconcealed rage. "But I did it anyway, because Airtha and I are both free beings. You don't fucking own me, or her."

"You're wrong about that," her father replied. "You are both mine. When I realized that Elena had come here—that you had sent her—I interrogated Helen. I didn't realize she was Airtha then; I just thought she would be more forthcoming than you would be."

"Bastard!" Sera spat. "You mean that you could hurt her and not worry about hurting me."

"That is exactly what I mean, yes," her father replied. "But I didn't need to do anything. Once I mapped her neural network, I knew what she was. An abomination."

"What?" Sera asked. "How could she be an abomination?"

"That is not for you to know—yet," Jeffrey Tomlinson said as he rose from his chair and paced across the room. "What am I to do with you, Sera? I had such high hopes for you—even during your ridiculous self-imposed exile. I believed you would be the scion I had always hoped for. When you took your place as the Director of The Hand—a role which you filled very well—I believed that you had grown…"

He poured himself a glass of water and took a sip with his back turned to her. Sera had long since realized that she was secured to the bed—if she hadn't been, her father would be dead; or wishing he were dead.

"But then you suggested the use of antimatter warheads," he said as he turned back to face her. "For an instant, I really did believe that you were the one—that I wouldn't have to have a snake like Andrea as my successor. But then you showed the specs, and I knew of only one person who also knew those exact specifications."

Her father returned to his seat and crossed his arms. "So, I had you watched. Carefully, meticulously, looking for your line of communication to Airtha; but it never surfaced—nothing out of the ordinary, at least. I never suspected that she was within you; that you had secreted away that which was most precious to me."

Sera had always known that her father had a unique relationship with Airtha, but he treated her like a thing, not a person—behavior that was not unusual for him. Something that was 'precious'? Only as far as Airtha was useful to him.

"Helen is precious to me," Sera hissed. "What have you done with her?"

"Oh, she's alive, if that's what you're worried about; for now, at least. I haven't decided whether or not I should kill her here, or take her back to Airtha and make her otherself watch."

"Why?" Sera gasped. "What has she done that...that has earned such cruelty?"

Her father's voice grew sad. "For starters, she found out who you were; what you are. I didn't want her to know. I didn't want to distract her from what she should do—and I didn't want her to corrupt you, though I can see now that it may be too late."

"What in all the known stars are you talking about?!" Sera exclaimed. "You sound like a lunatic!"

Her father met her eyes, and a slow smile grew across his face.

"She never told you!" he let out a laugh. "I can't believe she never told you!"

"Never told me what?" Sera asked.

"Nothing you'll ever know," her father said and rose from his chair once more. "I need to have her further examined, and then disposed of. If you'll excuse me."

"What?!" Sera screamed. "You can't kill her, you murderer!"

Her cries fell upon his impassive back, and he didn't look back as he walked into the hall and closed the door.

Sera bucked and struggled against the restraints, as a rage unlike any she had ever felt before came over her. Helen was her best friend; she had to stop her father.

After several minutes, the pain in her head grew too intense to continue fighting her bonds, and Sera collapsed; ragged breaths tearing at her throat as she wondered how she had ever begun to trust her father, how she had fallen into his web of deceit again. Stars, she had even turned her mind against Tanis.

All because of that snake of a man, that viper; that manipulator.

*I swear,* Sera thought, her words alone in her head for the first time in decades. *I swear that if he hurts Helen, I'll **kill** him! Fuck it! I'll kill him even if he doesn't. It's time to end his tyranny.*

# STRIKE

**STELLAR DATE: 03.27.8948 (Adjusted Years)**
**LOCATION: Gamma IV Shipyard**
**REGION: Normandy, Moon of Roma, 6th Planet in the New Canaan System**

Tanis rode the lift down the tower and then into the planet's crust. The platform continued to descend, kilometer after kilometer, before passing through the final layers of rock, and into the shipyard hidden within the moon.

"Oh, shit…" Elena gasped. "This is where you're building them. There's…more than you led me to believe."

Tanis nodded. "Most of them aren't ready yet; but when I spoke of a million ships, I was telling you my ultimate goal. I will ring this system in steel and beam-fire if I have to."

"You're sure off to a good start," Elena said softly. "How are you building them so fast? You have at least ten thousand in here."

Tanis looked around at the rows of ships nestled in their cradles, surrounded by bots mounting laser cannon, sensor arrays, and engines. The sight of so much industry made her swell with pride, and she winked at Elena.

"We're growing the less complex parts. We can make a hull in a just a few weeks," she replied.

"Growing hulls?" Elena frowned. "But these ships will have to undergo extreme stress and stand up under fire. You can't just 'grow' that sort of structure."

"We can," Tanis replied. "Not only that, these ships can self-repair while under fire to a degree no one has ever seen before."

"So, do you plan to assault the TSF fleet to free Sera?" Elena asked. "Because her father will just as soon kill her and jump out than fight you."

Tanis nodded. "I got that impression, as well. Anyone who travels with a jump-gate…. No, we're going in on stealth ships with a small strike force."

The platform reached its destination and Tanis stepped off, leading Elena down a warren of corridors to where the stealth pinnaces were docked. After only a short walk, they turned a corner, and stepped onto a wide platform suspended amidst nearly-complete cruisers.

Resting on the platform were six pinnaces, running lights on and ramps lowered, ready to take on passengers.

"We're assaulting in those?" Elena asked. "Are you sure the TSF ships can't see them?"

"Could you see the cruiser I scooped you up in?" Tanis asked.

"Well…no…"

"General," a voice called out from behind them, and Tanis turned to see Lieutenant Colonel Usef approaching with two dozen Marines on his heels. "I've assembled every Marine with combat experience on the base. You give the word, and we'll hit your target so hard they won't wake up when the Andromeda Galaxy gets here."

The men and women behind him wore grim expressions, and Tanis gave them a solemn nod.

"Very good, Colonel," Tanis replied. "We'll take just three pinnaces. I assume you brought gear and weapons for us?"

"Of course, ma'am," Usef replied, gesturing to packs several of the Marines carried. "You can gear up on the flight in. It'll take us just under two hours to get there."

"Two hours!" Elena exclaimed. "Anything could happen in that time."

"Elena, we can't rush in," Tanis said. "Stealth ships aren't very stealthy with their engines at max burn."

Elena clamped her mouth shut as Usef distributed his six fireteams between the pinnaces, and then led Tanis and Elena to theirs. Once inside, Tanis grabbed a pack and led Elena to one of the cabins.

"Strip. You need to get this armor on."

Elena complied, and once the woman was naked, Tanis took a cylinder and pressed it against her chest.

"This may feel pretty weird—especially since you've appropriated Sera's skin choice—but there's no time to alter how the armor applies."

"What armor?" Elena asked, and then gasped as the cylinder Tanis held began to melt against her body. "Oh, I've never seen anything quite like this."

"Based on something I bought back on Callisto," Tanis replied. "Earnest upgraded it to not require a base layer—and took out all their patent locks, too. It will stop just about any ballistic round you can imagine, short of serious kinetics, and can disperse and reflect photon beams. It can hold off electron beams for a bit, but don't get cocky."

Elena held her breath and closed her eyes. The clear layer of protection flowed over her face, before it seemed to almost seep into her skin and take on a matte sheen.

"Oh, fuck, that does feel intense," Elena gasped when the armor had set and she opened her mouth and eyes again.

"Here," Tanis tossed a shimmersuit at Elena. "Get it on, and I'll pass you the auth tokens. If the Transcend-level of tech is where I think it is, we'll be nearly invisible in these."

She slipped into her own, recalling the fight against Kris on the *Intrepid* when she first got her hands on the tech to make the suit. Like the armor, Earnest had improved on its design; even their own sensors had trouble tracking a wearer in an empty, silent room.

"Our weapons will be stealth-coated, as well; though not when firing, or once they're hot, of course."

Elena nodded, and they left the cabin to join Usef in the pinnace's cockpit.

"We'll be out of the exit shaft in a minute," he said. "The TSF ships haven't moved. Our precise time is an hour and forty-eight minutes to get to their flag. Fleet scan has spotted a few external airlocks they think we can link up to—our three ships won't be breaching near one another."

"Do you know the layout of that ship?" Tanis asked Elena. "We need to know where they're likely to keep Sera."

"Either the bridge, the brig, or the medbay, I'd guess," Elena replied, her expression deadly serious as she Linked to the pinnace's net and projected a layout of the TSF cruiser. The locations she mentioned lit up, and Tanis saw that all three were deep within the vessel.

"Well, good thing we have these three ships, then," she smiled.

"What sort of weapons will shipboard security have?" Usef asked.

"Pulse rifles and flechette pistols," Elena replied. "But they have heavier stuff in the armories. I'd really like them to not get any of those. If we can keep this non-lethal…"

"We'll try," Tanis replied. "But honestly…no matter what the outcome, we're probably going to start a war with this little assault."

Elena nodded slowly and fixed Tanis with a penetrating stare. "Then why are you doing it?"

Tanis leaned back against one of the unoccupied seats. "This little jaunt? It's just the thing that Lieutenant Colonel Richards used to do—the sort of thing that got me busted down to Major. But General—and especially Governor—Richards has become a lot more calculating over the years. Too much big picture, not enough of the small, important things."

Tanis took a deep breath and glanced at Usef and the Marines, aware that her words would be repeated through the colony—if they survived.

"I realized—after I had my little spat with Sera, and after I had to tell Saanvi what happened to her parents—that if you don't do the little things right, there's no way you can get the big picture right. Secrets and hiding and machinations—it's the shit that got us all in this mess. Us with the pico, you guys with not being fucked up in the FTL wars. I can't undo everything that's gone wrong, but I can help my friend no matter the cost—I'll do right by her, and hope the stars appreciate the effort, if not the path, taken to get here."

"That's as good a reason as any I've heard of late," Elena nodded. "I assume you have a backup plan, right?"

"Of course," Tanis replied with a grin. "If we aren't out in four hours, the stealth ships I have all around the TSF fleet are to attack."

"Seriously?" Elena asked.

"Well, they're to demand our release; but if that doesn't happen, yes, the fleet will attack."

Elena looked as though she was going to argue the point, but Tanis set her mouth in a thin line, and The Hand agent took the hint. "Then, I guess we had better get in and out as quickly as possible."

Tanis nodded. "Get familiar with the shimmersuit, and Link up with our combat net. I've sent you the auth tokens. We'll be comms- and data-silent as much as we can, but you may need probe feeds."

"Understood," Elena said, and Tanis felt her join the network with the Marines.

"I'm sending you today's hand signals," Usef informed Elena. "Even when we have comms—which will be risky in there—that's how we communicate when in line of sight, and we change them up all the time, so pay attention."

Elena nodded, and Tanis turned her attention back to the view out the cockpit window. For now, there was nothing more to do than wait.

# ORION GUARD

**STELLAR DATE: 03.27.8948 (Adjusted Years)**
**LOCATION: OGS *Starflare***
**REGION: Near Normandy, Moon of Roma, 6th Planet in the New Canaan System**

"This is it, people," Kent addressed the thirty five members of his strike force with calm assurance. "The Transcend president has left the tower. We have our window. We get in, take the governor, and then get her out. If our mission goes as planned, and we're undetected, the secondary force will remain there, and attempt to take the Transcend's president when he returns the next day."

The men and women racked in the transport shared hungry looks. The thought that in the span of two days they could take the New Canaan leadership, secure the picotech, *and* capture the Transcend's president was almost too good to be true.

The only thing to temper the excitement was the fear that something would go wrong—that they would lose this golden opportunity to strike such a decisive blow.

He knew the soldiers under his command would feel the same, and he cautioned them, "Remember your training, your experience. Don't let the magnitude of what we are about to achieve unnerve you. Trust in your teammates, and we'll achieve victory."

"Sir," their assault ship's co-pilot called back into the bay, "we just got a ping from our agent. The New Canaan governor has left the moon. She's on her way to the TSF flagship."

"Did she say why?" Kent asked.

"The burst said it was a covert rescue mission. We're on passive scan only, so we won't be able to pick up any of their stealth ships. But I would assume it's a small strike force."

"Change of plan. We're hitting the TSF flagship…the *Galadrial*," Kent addressed his troops. "You already have our analysis of it. As best we can tell, it's a modified Freeman Class ship. We're going to be on a bit of a hunt, but a rescue will probably mean brig, medbay, or bridge. It could also mean their president's quarters, but I'm betting those are near the bridge."

"Then we'll divide the nine fireteams evenly into three squads," Lieutenant Lorde replied. "Sergeant Tress, you're down a man, so your squad will hit the medbay; it should have the least security. Doran, you're with me on the brig, and Xecer, you'll be with the Colonel, going for the bridge."

The three sergeants nodded, and Kent knew that they were now going over breach protocols with their soldiers. Chances were that New Canaan's governor had more than one ship, and would breach multiple locations at once. Kent's soldiers would have to move fast and hard, crippling as many ship-systems as they could while they moved.

He looked out the forward window of the assault craft; the countdown on the overlay showed just under two hours to the TSF flagship. Either this would be the defining moment in the Orion Guard's long struggle against the Transcend, or they would be swept into history's dustbin, a failed and forgotten op.

<*Are you ready?*> he asked Vernon.

<*I don't ever cease being ready,*> the AI replied. <*I have a passel of NSAI ready to hit their systems hard. I've loaded them into the tech's hack-packs; when they jack into the first physical port they encounter, well, things are going to get real fun, real fast.*>

<*Make sure they focus on comm and helm,*> Kent replied. <*If we can grab this ship and just punch it through their gate back to OFA space, it will be the stuff of legend.*>

<*I'm less concerned with being a legend, and more with not dying,*> Vernon replied.

<*Our biggest risk is getting past the TSF fleet, and whatever the New Canaan space force has floating around out there,*> Kent said. <*Neither are going to blow the ship with their leaders aboard.*>

<*I would feel a lot better if I knew how many ships the ISF has. We haven't spotted a single stealth ship—and we know they have them.*>

Kent agreed with Vernon. That was his largest concern, too. Orion stealth tech was ahead of the Transcend's. He expected to detect the ISF ships, as well; but so far, there was no sign of them.

*<Well, stealth or no, if they want their governor, they'll have to come aboard and take her by force—something that we'll ensure does not happen,>* Kent replied.

He returned his attention to the specks of light at the L1 point between Roma and its moon, and prepared himself for the battle ahead.

# INSERTION

**STELLAR DATE: 03.27.8948 (Adjusted Years)**
**LOCATION: ISS Stellar Pinnace**
**REGION: Near Roma-Normandy L1 Point, New Canaan System**

The pinnace hovered just outside one of the TSF flagship's external airlocks. It was a small hatch, made for robotic maintenance, and would be impossible to fit through in powered armor. But with the strike force's armor only consisting of the flow-armor and shimmersuits, slipping through the small opening would not be a problem.

Tanis didn't want to hide any breathing gear once they got across, and making an ES seal against the *Galadrial* would certainly show up on its active scan. That meant the strike force would have to hold their breath for the five-meter trip through the vacuum of space. Their armor would seal over their eyes, mouths, and noses for the duration.

"You ready for this?" Tanis asked Elena. "Once the pico infiltrates their system and Angela opens the lock, we'll depressurize the cabin here. It may be a minute or two before we all get across and re-pressurize the other side."

Elena nodded. "We trained for ops like this. Never wearing so little that we felt naked in vacuum, but the end result was the same."

"Good," Tanis nodded. "Remember, no direct net access. If you Link up, they'll spot you, and that will end our little trip early. If we're lucky, we can tap into their general net; but we may be blind. We're counting on you to flag anything out of the ordinary."

"We're saving Sera. I'll do whatever it takes," Elena replied.

"Even kill?" Tanis asked. "If you're not prepared to take a life when the time comes, then you're not coming. There can be *no* hesitation."

"This isn't my first op like this," Elena said. "I know what to do."

Tanis raised an eyebrow. "You've taken up arms against your own people before?"

"Well, no, but I've had to turn on friends on undercover ops before. I imagine it's going to feel about the same."

Tanis nodded solemnly. "Yeah, it does."

<*Green light us when you're ready, Angela,*> Tanis instructed her AI.

<*You bet. Only a few seconds more…OK, I have control of the hatch, and am faking its feed back to their monitoring systems.*>

<*We are green for infiltration,*> Tanis announced over the combat net. She had no feed from the other two craft, and hoped that the AI embedded with them could pull off the same breach Angela had.

The Marines all toggled their status on the combat net to show readiness. Tanis opened the pinnace's side-hatch to the vacuum of space, and pushed off toward the Transcend cruiser. She covered the distance in a few seconds, and slipped through the portal on the other ship without incident.

The space within was cramped: only a narrow walkway with bots racked along the wall. She moved toward the far end of the room to make room for the rest of the squad. Forty seconds later, Elena, Usef, and the twelve Marines were across.

<*Hatch sealed and pressurizing,*> Angela announced a moment before the faint hiss of atmosphere entering the room became audible.

The air pressure reading on Tanis's HUD increased until it stopped at 98kPa, at which point she signaled her armor to unseal around her mouth and nose. The infiltration team followed suit and the small space was filled with the muted sounds of men and women rapidly replenishing their lungs with oxygen.

At the room's inner airlock, Tanis deployed a dose of nano into the portal's locking mechanism, and a second later it unsealed. She activated her shimmersuit and slipped through the opening, followed by the rest of the squad.

She slipped down the hall and glanced back at the rest of the squad. A random signature wave pulsed from each Marine, providing their position and rough outline to one another. Their HUDs filled in the data gaps, faking the appearance of their teammates.

While the signal introduced a risk of detection, decreasing the chance of friendly fire made it worthwhile.

When the last Marine slipped past, Usef closed the hatch and signaled for two Marines to scout ahead. Tanis felt blind without a cloud of nanoprobes surrounding her, but Elena had warned that the *Galadrial's* internal scanners could detect her nano, so they had to rely on the Mark I Eyeball for this mission.

The scouts approached an intersection, and one held up a hand. Tanis listened carefully and heard voices in one of the cross corridors. The squad pressed up against the walls of the corridor, and Tanis barely drew breath as three TSF naval officers walked by, chatting about the likelihood that they would have to take out the colonists.

Two seemed to think it was a sure thing, while the third was holding out for a peaceful solution.

<*Not sure which bet I'd take, yet,*> Tanis commented to Angela.

<*Well, we'd end them right fast if it came down to a knockout fight. They're sitting ducks here at the moon's L1.*> Angela replied.

<*Well, yeah, we'd win—I just meant peace or war. Plus, they're not just here at the L1. A dozen ships are orbiting Roma, and several more are stationed at the L3 and L4 points. We'd have to engage them in a few locations,*> Tanis said as the lead scout signaled that all was clear again.

<*Yeah, but we'd still win*> Angela replied. <*I'm not being cocky, it's just my analysis.*>

The squad progressed for several more minutes before Elena touched Tanis's shoulder and made a direct Link. <*Jutio and I think that there may be a data trunk line down the corridor on our right. I'm not certain—this ship is laid out a bit differently than I'm used to.*>

Tanis tapped the lead scout on the shoulder and passed the hand signals for the route they needed to take. He nodded and slipped around the corner while the other scout crossed the intersection and watched the other direction.

She glanced back at Elena, who was staying close on her six. She trusted the woman—mostly; she was a spy, after all. Gaining trust and double-crosses were her tradecraft.

<*Sera trusts her. That has to count for something,*> Angela said.

<*It's most of her currency. But if Elena's to be believed, they are lovers now, and that may blind Sera to what she doesn't want to see,*> Tanis replied.

The scout at the intersection signaled for them to advance, and Tanis slipped around the corner to see the lead scout slide a panel off the wall, revealing a data trunk line aside. Tanis placed a hand on the conduit and felt a tingle as nano flowed through her skin and armor into the conduit's housing, where they began to build a shunt.

<*Damn, their security is better than I thought it would be,*> Angela said. <*I suppose it's to be expected—we did give them our nanotech. But, they still don't have my skill.*>

<*We're in,*> Tanis said on the combat net. <*They won't pick up our signals, now.*>

<*Just don't think that's an excuse for chit-chat,*> Usef growled.

Tanis confirmed the route to the medbay and passed the path to the two scouts, who slipped ahead of the squad once more.

They encountered more and more TSF personnel as they progressed, some navy, some soldiers, and eventually a growing number of med-techs.

<*I just got a ping on their net,*> Angela said. <*First squad is nearing the bridge. Third squad hasn't checked in yet.*>

<*Should we be worried?*> Elena asked.

<*You tell me,*> Tanis replied. <*If they were found out, would there be any sort of general alarm?*>

Elena nodded. <*They'd sound general quarters for sure, but if this is a trap…*>

Tanis gave a slow nod. The thought had crossed her mind as well—the infiltration, so far, was far too easy.

Tanis pulled up against the wall as a group of engineers hurried past. One of them, a young man carrying a large case, tripped and bumped into her.

"What—" he exclaimed before Tanis wrapped an arm around his throat, and clamped a hand over his mouth. The Marines moved with practiced precision, subduing the other four engineers and dragging them into a side-room.

A minute later, they were back in the corridors, moving double-time. They were now on a clock; it was just a matter of time before someone discovered those unconscious engineers.

<*Place is pretty empty,*> Tanis commented as a solitary nurse passed by.

<*They're one level up, preparing the trauma ward,*> Angela replied.

<*Well, that's not auspicious…*>

They slipped through the entrance into the medbay and began searching the rooms. Tanis peered into one room where the sheets were disheveled, and restraints mounted to the side of the bed were flipped open.

Elena followed Tanis into the room; though she couldn't see the woman's expression, Tanis could tell from her posture that she was worried. She turned to the bed and was depositing nanobots on the restraints to see if there was any DNA evidence when a klaxon sounded.

Angela piped in an announcement from the general shipnet. *<Alert! Intruders port-side, on deck forty-three. Sound general quarters, watch stand to! This is not a drill.>*

*<That's where we came in,>* Usef said.

*<Yeah, but we're on deck seven now, and none of ours should be down there,>* Tanis replied.

*<Or they're just behind the times, and think we're still down there,>* Angela added.

Tanis addressed the squad, *<Anything, people?>*

The Marines all signaled negative. Sera was not in the medbay.

*<Wait, I found something!>* Angela announced. *<She was here, in this bed—and she hacked the restraint system somehow. She's at large on the ship.>*

*<She can't be in stealth gear,>* Usef said. *<There must be something on the shipnet. Someone must have spotted her.>*

Angela signaled negative. *<She's not flagged as a person of interest. If anyone did spot her, it wouldn't have been noteworthy.>*

*<Then why was she locked up here, and where is she going?>* Tanis asked.

*<I bet her father didn't want it known that he had her in here,>* Elena replied. *<Why in a medbay? Unless she was injured when he took her…>*

*<Wait!>* Angela said. *<There's something about a high-level AI being held in a network detainment facility near the bridge. I think—yes—it's Helen!>*

*<Helen's not with Sera? Well, now we know where Sera is going. Get the location to Lieutenant Ned; he should have first squad up by the bridge by now. Tell them to get in position, but don't move unless they see Sera in trouble,>* Tanis ordered.

*<On it,>* Angela replied. *<What…wait…something is going on. The ship is having some sort of systems failure in navigation.>*

*<Could it be any of ours doing it?>* Tanis asked.

*<Still nothing from third squad, and first says it's not them. Maybe Sera?>* Angele suggested.

*<Keep frosty,>* Tanis addressed the Marines. *<Angela thinks that there's someone up to no good onboard, aside from us—could just be Sera.>*

The Marines signaled acknowledgement, and the squad left the medbay, moving toward the network detention center. The pair of scouts ranged ahead, leading the squad through corridors and access shafts with far less concern of detection than before. Twice they had to subdue TSF ship personnel with non-lethal force, but data Angela picked up on the shipnet indicated that third squad had not been so lucky; they had run into opposition near the brig, and had killed two TSF soldiers in a retreat to their access point.

*<We've been spotted!>* Usef called from the rear.

Tanis pulled the feed from the combat net and saw TSF soldiers in light armor lobbing canisters of fluorescing gas down the corridor in an attempt to paint her squad. The shimmersuit's active systems were struggling to camouflage and keep the particles from coalescing on their bodies.

*<Return fire, pulse rifles only,>* Tanis called back, and the sound of concussive pulses filled the corridor around her.

*<We're just a hundred meters away,>* Angela announced, and Tanis signaled the scouts to move fast and hit hard.

*<We've secured the network detainment center. They have Helen trapped in a data vault. There's no neural activity. She's dead,>* Lieutenant Ned reported from Team one's position. *<Sera isn't here.>*

*<Hold your position,>* Tanis replied. *<We're going to push on to the bridge. Once we're past your location, come in behind the enemy on our tail and take them out.>*

*<Acknowledged, General,>* Lieutenant Ned responded.

The sound of rails and high-powered beam weapons came from behind, and Tanis checked the visual feeds, surprised that the TSF was using that kind of firepower on their ship.

*<It's not the TSF using those weapons,>* Usef called up. *<There's someone else back there, and they're mowing down the* Galadrial's *troops.>*

*<Let's move!>* Tanis yelled over the Link. *<We need to secure the bridge.>*

She caught up with the pair of scouts and sprinted ahead of them, flushing a cloud of nano through the corridor—there was no longer any need for stealth.

Ahead, a pair of TSF soldiers rushed around the corner firing wildly. They couldn't see Tanis and the scouts, but they must have decided it was better safe than sorry. Tanis fired her pulse rifle at one, while unloading a clip from her flechette pistol into the legs of the other. One fell unconscious and the other collapsed, screaming in pain.

She pulled a fresh clip from the pouch on her thigh and slid it into the pistol's grip as the pair of Marine scouts fired focused pulse rounds at a group of enemy soldiers holding the next intersection. Two fell, and Tanis rushed ahead unloading another clip from her flechette pistol into two TSF soldiers, while slamming the butt of her rifle into the face of another as she flew past.

<*Keep going,*> Usef called ahead. <*The Transcendies behind us are bogged down with whoever it is back there.*>

<*I think they're Orion Guard,*> Elena said. <*I caught sight of one of their weapons on the combat net. It looks like OFA gear.*>

<*Orion, here?*> Tanis asked, while her mind raced through myriad possibilities.

<*Angela,*> she asked privately. <*Have you managed to breach this new group's comms?*>

<*Not yet,*> her AI replied. <*I'm also not sure how—oh, fuck! They hacked my hack!*>

<*What do you mean?*> Tanis asked.

<*They hit the same physical breach point I used. They piggy-backed on my hack—I can't trust anything through it.*>

Tanis swore aloud and then directed Usef to send two Marines back to first squad in the network detention center with new orders. She had to assume her prior communication was either intercepted and altered, or was never delivered at all.

That brought her team down to just nine. Hopefully it was enough to storm the *Galadrial's* bridge.

The pair of scouts had pulled ahead again, and they lobbed a pair of concussive grenades up a ladder shaft before rushing up the rungs and firing their rifles. Tanis was close on their heels and provided covering fire as they subdued a squad of TSF soldiers. The battle was pitched and brief. Disoriented by the grenades, the enemy squad was at a loss, and the first four fell almost immediately.

Then, one of the ISF scouts took a shot from a slug thrower. It hit his left shoulder and threw him against a bulkhead. Tanis emptied a clip from her flechette pistol in the direction of the enemy fire, and cleared the ladder shaft to allow the Marines below to join the fight.

The first woman up tossed two more conc grenades down the hall leading toward the bridge while Tanis rushed to the scout's side.

His shimmersuit was shredded where the slug had hit, and she could tell by the unnatural angle of his shoulder that the flex armor hadn't been able to absorb enough of the kinetic impact to keep his bones intact.

"I'm OK, General. I'll be back on my feet as soon as the pain suppressors kick in," he said.

"Good man," Tanis replied. He couldn't fire a rifle one-handed, and she couldn't see his pistol anywhere, so she handed hers over. "Semper Fi, Marine," she said as she pulled him to his feet.

"Semper Fi," he replied, and they turned to see the last of the squad spilling up the ladder shaft and unleashing concentrated pulse blasts at the remaining TSF soldiers. "Besides, these Transcendies are a bunch of candy-assed fuck-puppets. I'll be damned if they'll put me down."

Tanis smiled at him, before remembering that he couldn't make out her features through her shimmersuit and gave a nod. "Let's finish this fight."

<*Main corridor to the bridge is just around the corner,*> the lead scout replied.

Tanis pushed out another batch of nanoprobes to scout the area. The ship's defense systems killed most of them, but she managed to get a clear picture of the bridge entrance. An entire platoon of enemy soldiers lined the corridor, tucked into open hatches and behind conduit.

Unlike most of the forces they had encountered thus far, these soldiers were in powered armor. Pulse rifles would have limited effect on them.

<*I count twenty-nine in there—could be more. I didn't get a clear picture,*> Tanis announced on the combat net as she shared the feed.

<*No time to wait,*> Usef said. <*Those Orion guys are going to be up our asses in no time.*>

<*Mine the ladder shaft; we need to slow these guys down,*> she ordered. She hated mines—they were too indiscriminating—but at least their IFF systems wouldn't trigger if first squad came through.

Usef set two Marines to the task, and Tanis looked to the rest, passing hand signals outlining how they would hit the corridor.

Ten seconds later, four Marines leaned around the corner and let fire with pulse rifles and flechette pistols while Tanis and another four dashed across the corridor.

She spun and let fire with her rifle, less concerned with careful aim than with pushing the enemy back into cover. They stopped for an instant, and, when the enemy leaned out from their cover to return fire, the Marines lobbed their conc grenades.

Even through her armor, Tanis's ears rang and her skin tingled from the force of the blasts. She leaned out again and no fire came her way. The Marines rushed forward and checked the TSF soldiers to make sure they were all out.

Given the damage to the corridor, she was certain a few of the enemy were dead. Fatalities were going to make future negotiations difficult, but, for the moment, her main concern was whether or not they had damaged the bridge's door mechanism. She placed a hand on the panel, and Angela rushed nano into the circuitry.

<*Give me a minute and we'll know,*> Angela replied.

<*Why so long?*> Tanis asked.

<*I'm fighting off the ship's AI, and a horde of NSAI that those Orion guys back there set loose on the network. They're making a mess of everything,*> Angela's tone was clipped.

<*Need a hand?*>

<*No, you just keep your head on your shoulders. I'll handle the hard stuff.*>

An explosion shook the deck, and Tanis saw smoke rush out from the cross corridor where the mined ladder shaft was. With any luck, their pursuers would have to find an alternate route.

<*OK, the door is locked down somehow. Not by those TSF soldiers—they were trying to bypass it,*> Angela reported. <*Luckily, they knew their stuff; I'll have it open in few seconds.*>

*<I have conflicting reports from our other two squads,>* Usef said. *<Either they're coming, they're dead, or they've left.>*

*<Let's hope it's not the middle one,>* Tanis replied.

*<Got it!>* Angela cried triumphantly, and the bridge doors slid open.

A fireteam of Marines rushed past her, likely ordered ahead by Usef to keep her from being the first one in. Tanis followed close on their heels, and took in the tableau laid out in front of her.

# KENT

**STELLAR DATE: 03.27.8948 (Adjusted Years)**
**LOCATION: TSS *Galadrial***
**REGION: Roma-Normandy L1 Point, New Canaan System**

Kent swore under his breath. The enemy's Marines were good—maybe better than his own soldiers—they fought like veterans who loved their commander as much as life itself.

It was a sentiment he understood well; he tried to foster the same feelings in the men and women under his command.

The ladder shaft up to the bridge was a ruin of twisted metal, and too dangerous to get through while under fire. His scouts had secured another route and the platoon was double-timing it through the command decks to get there.

He fired a round into the head of a TSF naval officer who peeked out from behind a console, pistol in hand. It was like shooting fish in a barrel, and it gave him no satisfaction.

<*Sir!*> corporal Jenkins reported. <*I found this in a marked drop. It's from our operative.*>

Jenkins approached and handed Kent a small, physical data drive. He inserted it into a socket on his armor and read the message.

<*It would seem that our enemy has some impressive armor. Not heavy like ours, but well able to withstand most of what we can throw at it. However, it has a weakness.*>

He passed their operative's data across the combat net. Heavy weapons fire would still take them down, but if it came to close combat, their combat knives would be highly effective weapons.

<*This AI of theirs is formidable,*> Vernon said, as the Orion Guard troops worked their way up a ladder shaft and took out a squad of TSF soldiers.

<*More than you can handle?*> Kent asked as he slammed into a bulkhead and leaned through an opening, laying down suppressive fire.

<*Truthfully, sir? It may be. It's not the Transcend's AI, it's the colonists'. No matter what I do, it thwarts me. I suspect it's their*

*governor's—an AI named Angela, who was a specialist in this sort of warfare back in Sol's ancient military.>*

*<Then we have to take her down to get the ship,>* Kent replied.

*<That is correct,>* Vernon replied. *<If she remains active, we lose.>*

The Guard soldiers secured the next corridor, and Kent advanced with his platoon.

*<Then I'll just have to take her down.>*

# THE BRIDGE

**STELLAR DATE: 03.27.8948 (Adjusted Years)**
**LOCATION: TSS *Galadrial***
**REGION: Roma-Normandy L1 Point, New Canaan System**

Three of the bridge crew were down. One was dead, another was bleeding profusely, and the third was moaning in agony. Greer—now an admiral, Tanis noted—and a woman with captain's insignia on her shoulders stood with weapons trained on Sera.

Sera stood with her back to the forward holodisplays, an arm wrapped around her father's neck. Her other hand held a gun to the back of his head, and tears were in her eyes.

"Why would you do that?" she screamed at her father. "You killed her! She was my best friend, the one person in this whole fucking galaxy that's always—"

Her words cut short as she realized it was ISF Marines who had burst into the bridge, and not her father's soldiers.

Tanis altered her shimmersuit, revealing her face and smiled. "Need a hand with anything?"

"Tanis!" Sera cried out. "What...what are you doing here?"

"Proving that there are more people in the galaxy who have your back," Elena said as she stepped onto the bridge.

With Marine rifles in their backs, Greer and the ship's captain lowered their weapons. A pair of ensigns were crouched behind a console, and a Marine pulled them out and secured them. Tanis saw another Marine crouch down beside the bleeding woman and begin to apply bio-seals to her wounds.

"You don't have to do this," Tanis said as she approached Sera and her father. She paused to place her hand on a console and deliver a dose of nano into the bridge's control systems.

<*Their AI is...weak...perhaps from fighting off the Orion NSAI,*> Angela said privately. <*Those are some nasty attack dogs. No matter; they aren't a match for me. I'll have the ship locked down in two or three minutes.*>

<*Anything you can't handle?*> Tanis asked.

*<All the AI we've encountered—with the exception of Helen—have been a step down from L4's at best. Pirates had better AI back in Sol.>*

*<I'll take that to mean you have things covered.>*

<*Yes, Mom,*> Angela chuckled.

"You don't understand, Tanis," Sera's face was a rictus of pain. "He fucking killed her in cold blood. He murdered Helen!"

"I know," Tanis nodded. "And you and Helen were made citizens of New Canaan before you left," she fixed her eyes on the Transcend president, who did not look frightened—only enraged.

"Is that it? You're going to charge me with murder?" he asked. "I don't know if you've noticed, but I have a fleet here that will keep that from happening."

"Not so much," Tanis shook her head as Angela sent a signal to the ISF fleet instructing them to disable their stealth systems.

"Oh, shit," the *Galadrial's* captain swore as the bridge's holotank displayed the sudden appearance of ten thousand cruisers around the main Transcend fleet, and smaller thousand-ship groupings around the L3 and L4 points.

"How did you build those so fast?" Admiral Greer exclaimed, awe filling his voice. "And where did you build them?"

"You'd be surprised what you can do when you're living under imminent threat from a superior adversary," Tanis replied. "Plus, having picotech also helps."

<*We're coming under fire from those Orion guys,*> Usef called in from the corridor, as Tanis heard the sounds of weapons fire pick up once more. *<We're outnumbered three-to-one, and our pulse rifles aren't doing much against their armor. Luckily, their beams aren't doing too much to ours, either—yet.>*

<*First and third squad are just a minute out,*> Angela replied. *<And I've sealed off most of the ship, so we won't have any further visitors.>*

"That's Orion out there in the corridor," Tanis said and glanced at President Tomlinson. "You better hope we win this little fight. I'll go easier on you than they will."

The president's face reddened and he shot daggers at Tanis. "You should have volunteered your tech to us rather than playing this little game. Now, look where it has gotten us. The Guard has penetrated thousands of light years into the Transcend."

The sounds of weapons fire in the corridor intensified, and then abruptly ceased.

"And that's that," Tanis said. "Sera, you can lower your weapon. We can secure your father."

"He's perfectly secure right now," Sera replied icily. "I'm having an internal debate about whether or not he dies. If Helen were here, she'd probably tell me not to blow your head off, *Dad*. Too bad you killed her!"

"Sera," Tanis said calmly, "you don't need me to tell you how revenge isn't the answer. You already know that. The Transcend is going to need strong leadership to defeat the Orion Guard; if you kill your father, who knows what will happen."

Out of the corner of her eye, Tanis saw Elena reposition herself in the same moment that Usef chased a man onto the bridge. He lunged for Tanis, and she pivoted, avoiding a blade strike at her face.

She turned to grab his arm, and he slipped away, shrugging off two pulse blasts from Usef's rifle and swung the blade at her again. Tanis held her armored left arm up to deflect the blow, and the blade sliced clean through the limb—her forearm fell to the ground in front of her.

The man took advantage of her confusion to drive the blade into her chest where it slipped right through her shimmersuit and flow-armor. As it buried up to the hilt, her HUD showed that the blade was only a few nanometers thick, and was vibrating at a frequency that seemed to defeat her armor's active defenses.

Pain radiated through her chest as it bisected her heart, but she suppressed the agony and backhanded the man before falling to a knee and fighting off waves of dizziness.

"Why is it that whenever I meet with the Transcend I end up with a knife through my heart?" she said with her head lowered, waiting for her auxiliary heart to restore her blood pressure.

She felt someone at her side, clamping a tourniquet around her arm.

"General, the president," Usef said quietly, and Tanis raised her head to see the President of the Transcend Interstellar Alliance dead. The top of his head was gone, and a stunned Sera stood behind him, supporting the dead weight of his body for an instant before she let it drop.

She looked first to the man who had attacked her, but he lay unconscious on the deck; then her eyes flicked to Elena, who stood with her arm extended clutching her flechette pistol.

On either side of her, a Marine stood with pulse rifle leveled, awaiting orders.

"Lower it," Tanis ordered Elena, as Sera cried out, "Elly! What did you do?"

Elena dropped the flechette pistol and Tanis nodded for the Marines to secure her. "I did it for you, Sera," she pleaded. "So you wouldn't have to kill your own father."

"Blade," Usef said and gestured to Tanis's chest.

She looked down at the knife buried hilt-deep in her chest, and carefully pulled it out, dropping it before walking to Sera. "I'm sorry, Sera. I'm sorry about what I said before, I'm sorry that I didn't get here sooner…I'm just sorry."

"I…" Sera stammered before suddenly realizing why her face was so wet and began frantically wiping it with her hospital gown. Greer took off his jacket and handed it to Tanis, who passed it to Sera.

While she cleaned herself up, Tanis turned back to Admiral Greer. "You need to tell your fleet to stand down."

Greer nodded and gestured to the console. "Your AI has locked me out. I'll need access."

"You have it, but you'll have to do it manually. No Link." Angela replied over the bridge's audible address system.

Greer sat heavily and keyed in the commands for an all-fleet address. "All ships, this is Admiral Greer. The situation is under control. Take no action. I repeat, take no action against the ISF ships. Updates will follow."

"And to the soldiers and sailors on this ship," Tanis added.

Greer sent a ship-wide message for all forces to stand down and looked up at Tanis. "What now?"

Tanis let out a long breath. <*What now, indeed?*> she said to Angela.

<*You need to review the scan data,*> Angela said. <*Elena is not who she appears to be.*>

Tanis glanced at Elena, who was embracing Sera, while pulling up the bridge's visual log—once Angela Linked her with the command systems. She overheard Sera say something about how this was just more proof of how Orion was evil and had to be stopped.

<*Where's their ship's AI?*> she asked Angela out of curiosity as she flipped through the feeds.

<*I've shut her down. She really wasn't as strong as I'd expected. From what I've seen, the Transcend limits their AI's abilities a lot.*>

<*Interesting,*> Tanis replied absently as she saw what Angela spotted on the logs.

"Sera! Look out!" Tanis called out.

Elena held the blade Tanis had let fall to the ground. She slashed at Sera's neck, but Sera managed to leap back in time to avoid the attack. Elena charged, aiming the blade at Sera's left eye, and Sera blocked the blow, but they collided and fell to the deck in a heap.

By the time Tanis and the Marines reached them and pulled Elena off, Sera had several deep wounds on her torso; but Tanis couldn't see the blade anywhere.

"My back…" Sera whispered.

Tanis gently rolled her over, and saw the knife jutting from Sera's spine.

"Don't move," she replied as she eased Sera onto her side. "We're going to need medics to get that out."

"I'm sorry, Sar," Elena said, her face a strange combination of sorrow, rage, and guilt.

"Why…how long?" Sera gasped through tears. Tanis briefly wondered if they were from pain or betrayal.

<*Or both,*> Angela added.

"Long enough," Elena replied, her voice rough and filled with grief. "I loved you, Sar, I really did. I hoped I could convince you that Orion is the right side; but when you went back to Airtha, I could see how you were going to become just like your father. We could have saved the galaxy, but Garza was right—you're going to destroy it. With or without your father."

Sera's face reddened and she opened her mouth to speak, but stopped and looked at the deck. "I can't look at her. Can you put her in the corridor?"

Tanis gestured to the Marines, who marched Elena out of the bridge.

"So, who's in charge of the Transcend now?" Tanis asked.

"We've never had a transfer of power. Her father has been running the show ever since he united the FGT worldships," Greer said before looking down at Sera. "You have to take control, and quickly. We can't have a power vacuum. Especially one that your sister will be all too happy to fill."

Sera coughed up blood as a pair of medics rushed onto the bridge and settled down beside her, scanning her injuries to determine the exact location of the embedded blade.

<*They were already on their way to deal with the wounded,*> Angela said. <*I was able to get the medbay out of lockdown without opening up the rest of the ship.*>

<*Thanks,*> Tanis replied.

"Andrea?" Tanis asked aloud. "I thought that she was on a penal colony."

Sera shook her head. "No, my father had her released early. She's not allowed back at Airtha for another century, but that won't stop her, once she hears that he's dead."

Tanis leaned against a console and looked at the holodisplay of the twenty thousand ships surrounding Roma. It was a tiny fraction of the ships they would need to fend off the Orion Guard. The Transcend must be united to face the threat ahead of them.

<*I have an incoming message from the ISF,*> Angela reported, and Tanis nodded for her to put it on the bridge's main holotank.

Joe's image shimmered into view and he smiled with relief at the sight of Tanis. "Angela reported that you were OK, boy it's good to see you in person—holy shit! You're missing an arm! I guess things got intense."

Tanis nodded. "That's one word for it. Tomlinson is dead, and Elena was a Guard double agent."

"Well, that's just the start of it. Our perimeter scanning net picked up a massive fleet out past the heliopause, well over twenty thousand ships. It's not Transcend—it took out four of their ships already," Joe reported. "Our analysis puts it at eleven days from our location."

"Greer, we're going to have to mend our fences before then," Tanis said to the admiral. "You have a jump-gate here—can you send for re-enforcements?"

"Yes," Greer nodded. "I can maybe get five thousand ships here by then. Things are hot all along the front right now, but with your fleet of stealth ships, I think you may not even need more firepower."

Tanis exchanged a look with Joe. "About those ships. Less than half are ready for combat, and of the ones that are, they're running skeleton crews."

Greer shook his head and exchanged a look with the *Galadrial's* captain. "I told you she was wily, Viska."

"New contact," Joe reported. "Something just jumped insystem. Same arrival point as Elena used.... It's *Sabrina*!"

Sera looked up, hope in her eyes. "Really? Do they have Finaeus?"

"No signal from them yet," Joe replied. "Wait, what are you doing?"

"We're not doing anything!" Tanis replied, but the holodisplay of the TSF fleet positions showed otherwise. Every ship other than the *Galadrial* was breaking formation and boosting for *Sabrina*'s position.

*<I'm not getting any response from any of them on comms,>* Angela said on the bridge net. *<Something tried to take over this ship, too, but I was able to fend it off. It felt like...>*

She was cut off by a holo image appearing beside Joe on the main tank. It was a woman that Tanis recognized, though she looked subtly different than in the past.

"Helen?" Sera asked. "What are you...I thought you were dead!"

"I'm sorry, Sera," the woman replied. "Helen is dead. I am Myriad, a shard of Airtha, just as Helen was. I cannot let what *Sabrina* carries reach you. That ship and its passengers must be destroyed."

The woman disappeared and Sera cried out in anguish from her position on the deck while the medics worked on her back. Her eyes cast about the bridge until they locked onto Tanis. "Why...why would she do that? My crew, Jessica—they're on that ship!"

"Then we're going to have to get there first," Tanis replied and turned to Joe. "Get there, and get *Sabrina* aboard the *I2* before she's destroyed!"

*<Here we go again,>* Angela said within their mind.

Tanis clenched her teeth. *<Bring it on.>*

*****

The story continues in Orion Rising.

Now available on Amazon

# THANK YOU

If you've enjoyed reading New Canaan, a review on Amazon.com and/or goodreads.com would be greatly appreciated.

To get the latest news and access to free novellas and short stories, sign up on the Aeon 14 mailing list: www.aeon14.com/signup.

M. D. Cooper

# THE AGE OF THE ORION WAR

The Orion War is beginning. Federations, alliances, empires—all at one another's throats, struggling to solidify their power and strengthen their footholds as what could be humanity's ultimate conflict looms.

## PERILOUS ALLIANCE

*With Chris J. Pike*

The books of the Perilous Alliance series begin in the months leading up to the assassination of President Tomlinson in New Canaan; but rest assured, they will weave into the larger plot.

If Tanis hadn't traded her nanotech back in Silstrand to upgrade *Sabrina's* weapons, things in the Silstrand Alliance wouldn't be such a mess right now.

Cleaning up the mess that Tanis left may just fall to the most unlikely of people: a junker named Kylie Rhoads

***Begin that journey with Kylie Rhoads in*** *Close Proximity*, ***book 1 of the Perilous Alliance series.***

## RIKA'S MARAUDERS

Across the Inner Stars, the Orion Freedom Alliance has already begun to use its proxies to wage war as it solidifies its presence. One of the largest proxies, the Nietzschean Empire, has attacked its neighbors, the Genevians. World by world, system by system, the Nietzscheans are winning, pushing the Genevians back.

Now the Genevians are pulling out all the stops in their attempt to hold the Nietzscheans back, including turning their criminal element into conscripted cyborg warriors.

These men and women have no choice in the matter, as compliance chips in their brains keep them in line as they wage war against the Nietzscheans.

Rika is one such criminal; now a scout mech, she is the property of the Genevian military.

Her crime was small: stealing food. But when faced with a five-year prison term or conscription in the Genevian military, she chose war—having no idea what that conscription would entail.

Now, little of Rika's human body remains, and she serves as an SMI-2 scout mech; the meat inside a cyborg body. She and others are sent in ahead of the human soldiers to tip the scales of war.

***Join Rika and her struggle to remain human while becoming the most lethal killer she can be in an effort to stay alive in Rika Outcast (coming August 2017).***

***Also, read the prequel to the Rika's Marauder's series in the novella, Rika Mechanized.***

## THE PERSEUS GATE

If you haven't already read *The Gate at the Wolf Star*, the first book in the Perseus Gate series, now's the time to dig in.

I'm certain that you were wondering what happened at the Grey Wolf Star, where we last left *Sabrina* and crew before they mysteriously appeared. Suffice to say, there was no way it would fit in this book, or even just one standalone book.

No, that story is its own entire series named "The Perseus Gate". The first episode of that story is entitled *The Gate at the Grey Wolf Star,* and is now available on Amazon.

# BOOKS BY M. D. COOPER

## Aeon 14

**The Intrepid Saga**

- Book 1: Outsystem
- Book 2: A Path in the Darkness
- Book 3: Building Victoria
- The Intrepid Saga Omnibus – *Also contains Destiny Lost, book 1 of the Orion War series*
- Destiny Rising – *Special Author's Extended Edition comprised of both Outsystem and A Path in the Darkness with over 100 pages of new content.*

**The Orion War**

- Book 1: Destiny Lost
- Tales of the Orion War: Set the Galaxy on Fire
- Book 2: New Canaan
- Book 3: Orion Rising
- Tales of the Orion War: Ignite the Stars Within (Fall 2017)
- Tales of the Orion War: Burn the Galaxy to Ash (Fall 2017)
- Book 4: Starfire (coming in 2018)
- Book 5: Return to Sol (coming in 2018)

Visit www.aeon14.com/orionwar to learn what's next in the Orion War.

**Perilous Alliance** (Expanded Orion War - with Chris J. Pike)

- Book 1: Close Proximity
- Book 2: Strike Vector (August 2017)
- Book 3: Collision Course (October 2017)

**Rika's Marauders** (Age of the Orion War)

- Prequel: Rika Mechanized
- Book 1: Rika Outcast (August 2017)

**Perseus Gate** (Age of the Orion War)

- Episode 1: The Gate at the Grey Wolf Star
- Episode 2: The World at the Edge of Space (July 2017)
- Episode 3: The Dance on the Moons of Serenity (August 2017)

**The Warlord** (Before the Age of the Orion War)

- Book 1: A Woman Without a Country (Sept 2017)

**The Sentience Wars: Origins** (With James S. Aaron)

- Book 1: Lyssa's Dream (July 2017)
- Book 2: Lyssa's Run (October 2017)

**The Sol Dissolution**

- The 242 - Venusian Uprising (In The Expanding Universe 2 anthology)
- The 242 - Assault on Tarja (In The Expanding Universe 3 anthology – coming Dec 2017)

**The Delta Team Chronicles** (Expanded Orion War)

- A "Simple" Kidnapping (Pew! Pew! Volume 1)
- The Disney World (Pew! Pew! Volume 2 – Sept 2017)

# Touching the Stars

Book 1: The Girl Who Touched the Stars

# APPENDICES

Be sure to check http://www.aeon14.com for the latest information on the Aeon 14 universe.

# TERMS & TECHNOLOGY

**AI (SAI, NSAI) –** Is a term for Artificial Intelligence. AIs are often also referred to as non-organic intelligence. They are broken up into two sub-groups: Sentient AI and Non-Sentient AI.

***c* –** Represented as a lower-case c in italics, this symbol stands for the speed of light and means constant. The speed of light in a vacuum is constant at 670,616,629 miles per hour. Ships rate their speed as a decimal value of c with c being 1. Thus, a ship traveling at half the speed of light will be said to be traveling at 0.50 c.

**Casimir effect –** The Casimir effect is a small attractive force that acts between two close parallel uncharged conducting plates. It is due to quantum vacuum fluctuations of the electromagnetic field.

**CriEn –** A CriEn module is a device that taps into the base energy of the universe; also known as zero-point, or vacuum energy. Unlike more common zero-point energy modules, which pull energy from artificial bubble dimensions, the CriEn module is capable of pulling energy from normal space-time, and can even do so while in the dark layer.

**Cryostasis (cryogenics) –** See also, 'stasis'.

Older methods of slowing down organic aging and decay involve cryogenically freezing the organism (usually a human) through a variety of methods. The person would then be thawed through a careful process when they were awakened.

Cryostasis failures are rare, but far more frequent than true stasis failures. When true stasis was discovered, it became the de-facto method of halting organic decay over long periods.

**Dark Layer** – The Dark Layer is a special sub-layer of space where dark matter possesses physical form. The dark layer is also frictionless and reactionless. It is not fully understood, but it also seems to possess many of the attributes of a universal frame of reference.

**Directions, Galactic Cardinal** – While the galaxy is divided into specific directions, (some Sol-centric, and others centered upon the galactic core) most casual discussions use one of two methods of referring to galactic orientation.

The first is to use cardinal direction. The core of the galaxy has agreed-upon north and south poles, and an east and west. Cardinal galactic directions assume that the point being referenced is at the surface of a sphere with the galactic core at its center.

Just like a location on the surface of a planet falls into a general cardinal location, so does a location on the imaginary galactic sphere. If you are travelling in interstellar space, then a line is drawn through in the direction of travel until it intersects with the sphere. That is the direction you are traveling.

Galactic cardinal directions are never used in actual navigation, and are only used for general reference.

**Directions, Galactic Disk-Oriented** – A common way to describe the location of a given star, nation, cluster, etc… is to describe it in relation to another known point. There are four directions used in this parlance. Each is related to the structure of the galaxy.

**Coreward:** This refers to any direction that is toward the core of the galaxy. It's important to note that the galactic core and the term "core-stars" are not to be confused. "Core-stars" refers to the stars within 50 light years (or so) of Sol. The term coreward never refers to the stars around Sol, but to the galactic core.

**Spinward:** The Milky Way galaxy spins. Viewed from the north (top) side of the galaxy, it spins clockwise. The vast majority of stars move in the direction of the galactic spin.

**Anti-spinward:** Like spinward, but moving in the opposite direction.

**Rimward:** Any direction toward the rim of the galaxy.

**Note:** Because these disk-oriented directions are two-dimensional, they are often combined with north/south galactic core directions. One could say that a destination is four light-years spinward, and three galactic north.

**Directions, Stellar –** Every star system defines its own cardinal locations, though most are oriented to the generally accepted galactic cardinal directions. In practice, these directions are used the same way as galactic cardinal directions.

**Note:** No actual stellar navigation is done using cardinal directions.

**Deuterium** – D2 (2H) is an isotope of hydrogen where the nucleus of the atom is made up of one proton and one neutron as opposed to a single proton in regular hydrogen (protium). Deuterium is naturally occurring and is found in the oceans of planets with water and is also created by fusion in stars and brown dwarf sub stars. D2 is a stable isotope that does not decay.

**Edgeworth Kuiper Belt (EK Belt) –** The EK belt is a circumstellar disk of dust, rocks, and small planetoids, which extends from Neptune's orbit to 50 AU from Sol (in humanity's home system).

Many other star systems possess belts similar to Sol's EK Belt, and the term fell into common usage to describe the first belt beyond the last major planet in a star system.

**Electrostatic shields/fields –** Not to be confused with a faraday cage, electrostatic shielding's technical name is static electric stasis field. By running a conductive grid of electrons through the air and holding it in place with a stasis field, the shield can be tuned to hold back oxygen, but allow solid objects to pass through, or to block solid objects. These fields are used in objects such as ramscoops and energy conduits.

Modified versions also see use as ship's shields where they are used to bleed off energy from beam weapons, or slow the impact of kinetic weapons.

**EMF –** Electro Magnetic Fields are given off by any device using electricity, which is not heavily shielded. Sensitive scanners are able to determine the nature of operating equipment by its EMF signature. In warfare, it is one of the primary ways to locate an enemy's position.

**EMP –** Electro Magnetic Pulses are waves of electromagnetic energy that can disable or destroy electronic equipment. Because so many people have electronic components in their bodies, or share their minds with AI, they are susceptible to extreme damage from an EMP. Ensuring that human/machine interfaces are hardened against EMPs is of paramount importance.

**Fission –** Fission is a nuclear reaction where an atom is split apart. Fission reactions are simple to achieve with heavier, unstable elements such as Uranium or Plutonium. In closed systems with extreme heat and pressure it is possible to split atoms of much more stable elements, such as Helium. Fission of heavier elements typically produces less power and far more waste matter and radiation than Fusion.

**Ford-Svaiter Mirror** – This technology was first theorized in the late twentieth century, and involves using mirrors that focus quantum energy fluctuations and create negative energy. An array of these mirrors would create a wormhole. A ship would then have a mirror mounted on it, and that ship's mirror would extend the wormhole to its destination.

This method of FTL is nearly instantaneous, though it takes tremendous amounts of energy to achieve.

**FTL (Faster Than Light) –** Refers to any mode of travel where a ship or object is able to travel faster than the speed of light (c). According to Einstein's theory of Special Relativity nothing can travel faster than the speed of light.

**Fusion –** Fusion is a nuclear reaction where atoms of one type (Hydrogen for example) are fused into atoms of another type (Helium in the case of Hydrogen fusion). Fusion was first discovered and tested in the H-Bombs (Hydrogen bombs) of the twentieth century. Fusion reactors are also used as the most common source of ship power from roughly the twenty fourth century on.

***g* (gee, gees, g-force) –** Represented as a lower-case g in italics, this symbol stands for gravity. On earth, at sea level, the human body experiences 1*g*. A human sitting in a wheeled dragster race car will achieve 4.2*g*s of horizontal g-force. Aerial fighter jets will impose g-forces of 7-12*g*s on their pilots. Humans will often lose consciousness around 10*g*s. Unmodified humans will suffer serious injury or death at over 50*g*s. Starships will often impose burns as high as 20*g*s, and provide special couches or beds for their passengers during such maneuvers. Modified starfighter pilots can withstand g-forces as high as 70*g*s.

**Graviton –** These are small massless particles that are emitted from objects with large mass, or by special generators capable of creating them without large masses. There are also negatively charged gravitons that push instead of pull. These are used in shielding systems in the form of Gravitational Waves. The *GSS Intrepid* uses a new system of channeled gravitons to create the artificial gravity in the crew areas of the ship.

**Heliopause –** The point where a star's solar wind stops relative to the interstellar medium. Though gravitational influences may stretch beyond this point; some stellar objects, including the Oort cloud, typically lie beyond this point, as well.

**Heliosphere –** The region of space contained within a star's heliopause. Despite the name, these are rarely spheres, as most star's heliospheres are shaped like elongated water droplets as they race through the interstellar medium.

**Helium-3** – This is a stable, non-radioactive isotope of Helium, produced by T3 Hydrogen decay, and is used in nuclear fusion reactors. The nucleus of the Helium-3 atom contains two protons, but only one neutron, as opposed to the two neutrons in regular Helium. Helium-3 can also be created by nuclear reactions that create Lithium-4, which decays into Helium-3.

**HUD –** Stands for Heads Up Display. It refers to any type of display where information about surroundings and other data is directly overlaid on a person's vision.

**Link –** Refers to an internal connection to computer networks. This connection is inside of a person, and directly connects their brain to what is essentially the Internet in the fourth millennia. Methods of accessing the Link vary between retinal overlays to direct mental insertion of data.

**Maglev –** A shorthand term for magnetic levitation. First used commercially in 1984, most modern public transportation uses maglev to move vehicles without the friction caused by axles, rails, and wheels. The magnetic field is used to both support the vehicle and accelerate it. The acceleration and braking is provided by linear induction motors, which act on the magnetic field provided by the maglev 'rail'. Maglev trains can achieve speeds of over one thousand kilometers per hour with very smooth and even acceleration.

**MDC (molecular decoupler) –** These devices are uses to break molecular. This technology was first discovered in the early nineteenth century—by running electric current through water, William Nicholson was able to break water into its hydrogen and oxygen components. Over the following centuries, this process was used to discover new elements such as potassium and sodium. When humanity began to terraform planets, the technology behind electrostatic projectors was used to perform a type of electrolysis on the crust of a planet. The result was a device that could break apart solid objects. MDC's are massive, most over a hundred kilometers long, and require tremendous energy to operate.

***MJ* –** Refers to the mass of the planet Jupiter as of the year 2103. If something is said to have 9MJ, it has nine times the mass of Jupiter.

**Nano (nanoprobes, nanobots, etc...) –** Refers to very small technology or robots. Something that is nanoscopic in size is one thousand times smaller than something that is microscopic in size.

**Pico (picotech, picobots, etc...)** – Refers to technology on a pico-scale—one thousand times smaller than nanotech.

After a series of accidents that nearly consumed an entire dwarf world, picotech research was banned in the Sol system.

**Railgun –** Railguns fire physical rounds, usually small pellets at speeds up to 10 kilometers per second by pushing the round through the barrel via a magnetic field. The concept is similar to that of a maglev train, but to move a smaller object much faster. Railguns were first conceived of in 1918 and the first actual magnetic particle accelerator was built in 1950. Originally railguns were massive, sometimes kilometers in size. By the twenty-second century reliable versions as small as a conventional rifle had been created.

Larger versions take the form of orbital railgun platforms, which can fire sabot rounds or grapeshot at speeds over a hundred-thousand-kilometers per second.

**Ramscoop** – A type of starship fuel collection system and engine. They are sometimes also referred to as Bussard ramscoops or ramjets. Ramscoops were considered impractical due to the scarcity of interstellar hydrogen, until electrostatic scoops were created that can capture atoms at a much more distant range and funnel them into a starship's engine.

**Scattered Disc** – Beyond a star system's EK Belt lays a region filled with comets, asteroids, and dwarf worlds. In the Sol System, this region begins roughly 50 AU from Sol, and extends to the edge of the Oort cloud. While it contains the least mass of a system, a system's scattered disc typically contains hundreds of dwarf planets and fills an area nearly half a cubic light year.

**Stasis** – Early stasis systems were invented in the year 2541 as a method of 'cryogenically' freezing organic matter without using extreme cold (or lack of energy) to do so. The effect is similar in that all atomic motion is ceased, but not by the removal of energy by gradual cooling, but by removing the ability of the surrounding space to accept that energy and motion. There are varying degrees of effectiveness of stasis systems. The FGT and other groups possess the ability to put entire planets in stasis, while other groups only have the technology to put small items, such as people, into stasis. Personal stasis is often still referred to as cryostasis, though there is no cryogenic process involved.

**Tritium** – T3 (3H) is an isotope of hydrogen where the nucleus of the atom is made up of one proton and two neutrons as opposed to just a single proton and no neutrons in regular hydrogen (protium). T3 is radioactive and has a half-life of 12.32 years. It decays into Helium-3 through this process.

***v*** **–** Represented as a lower case v in italics, this symbol stands for velocity. If a ship is increasing its speed it will be said that it is increasing *v*.

**Van Allen belts –** A radiation belt of energetic charged particles that is held in place around a magnetized planet, such as the Earth, by the planet's magnetic field. The Earth has two such belts and sometimes others may be temporarily created. The discovery of the belts is credited to James Van Allen, and as a result the Earth's belts are known as the Van Allen belts.

**Vector –** Vectors used are spatial vectors. Vector refers to both direction and rate of travel (speed or magnitude). Vector can be changed (direction) and increased (speed or magnitude).

# GROUPS AND ORGANIZATIONS

**FGT** – The Future Generation Terraformers is a program started in 2352 with the purpose of terraforming worlds in advance of colony ships being sent to the worlds. Because terraforming of a world could take hundreds of years the FGT ships arrive and begin the process.

Once the world(s) being terraformed reached stage 3, a message was sent back to the Sol system with an 'open' date. The GSS then handled the colony assignment.

A decade after the *Destiny Ascendant* left the Sol system in 3728, the FGT program was discontinued by the SolGov, making it the last FGT ship to leave. Because the FGT ships are all self-sustaining, none of them came home after the program was discontinued; most of the ship's crews had spent generations in space, and had no reason to return to Sol.

After the discontinuation, FGT ships continued on their primary mission of terraforming worlds, but only communicated with the GSS and only when they had worlds completed.

**GSS** – The Generational Space Service is a quasi-federal organization that handles the assignment of colony worlds. In some cases, it also handles the construction of the colony ships.

After the discontinuation of federal support and funding for the FGT project in 3738, the GSS became self-funded by charging for the right to gain access to a colony world. While the SSF no longer funded the GSS, the government supported the GSS's position, and passed a law ensuring that all colony assignment continued to be distributed via the GSS.

**Hand, The** – The Hand is the common name of the Inner Stars Clandestine Uplift Operations. This bureau is responsible for managing and controlling the stability, and spread, of technology within the Inner Stars. It operates exclusively under the direction of President Tomlinson.

**ISF** – The Intrepid Space force is the name of the ISS *Intrepid*'s fleet from the time the colony charter was put into effect near Kapteyn's Star until landfall at New Canaan. After that time, it became the official name of the New Canaan military.

**ISS –** Designation given to ships in the ISF, which stands for Intrepid Space Ship. This is similar to ancient navies, such as the US Navy's use of USS to stand for United States Ship, or Britain's HMS, which stands for His/Her Majesty's Ship.

**Orion Guard** – The Orion Guard is the name of the Orion Freedom Alliance's military. Within the Transcend, the term is often used to refer to the entire OFA, not just its military.

**TSF** – The Transcend Space Force is the overarching military of the Transcend Interstellar Alliance. It also shares an acronym with the ancient Terran Space Force.

# PLACES

**Airtha** – This world-construct is the capital of the Transcend Interstellar Alliance. The construct consists of a white dwarf star which has had much of its mass removed to form a solid carbon ring around the star. The star is roughly the size of Saturn, and the ring wraps around it, creating a habitable surface.

The star has cooled, and now produces a yellow-orange light.

**Ascella** – Double star system on the spinward side of the Corona Australis star-forming region. It is located only 410 light years from Sol, and is the location of a major Transcend watchpoint.

**AST** – A colloquial name for the Hegemony of Worlds, it refers to the first three member systems of the Hegemony: Alpha Centauri, Sol, and Tau Ceti. The name fell out of internal use in the Hegemony after Alpha Centauri was officially renamed Rigel Kentaurus. Many people outside of the AST still use the term, as well as refer to Alpha Centauri by its original name.

**Bollam's World** – Bollam's World is the name of the fourth planet from 82 Eridani, in the Bollam's World System.

**Bollam's World System (58 Eridani)** – An independent system known as "Bollam's World". The system was settled in 5123 by the colonists of the GSS *Yewing,* which left Sirius in the year 3814.

**Carthage** – Third world of the New Canaan system, Carthage is the capital world of the system, with both the planetary capital and the system capital situated in the city of Landfall.

**Chittering Hawk** – An interstellar trading hub in the Virginis system with a shady reputation.

**Cradle, the –** This is the name given to the M25 star cluster. The name was given by the inhabitants of other Transcend star-systems on the anti-spinward side of the cluster, based on how it appears from those locations.

The Cradle contains over two thousand stars, which look very bright when viewed from New Canaan's night skies (in the right seasons).

**Grey Wolf –** A white dwarf star (the actual color is a dimmer white-blue color which can look grey with certain viewing apparatuses). This star is located seventy light-years coreward of Sol, and is a base of forward operations for the Transcend Space Force.

Later, after the technique was refined with Airtha, dwarf star mining began, and the star is slowly being torn apart for raw resources (primarily carbon and oxygen).

**Herschel –** An agrarian world in the Krugenland system. This system is located over seven thousand light years from Sol within the coreward fringe of the Perseus Arm of the galaxy.

The planet was settled in the year 7242, by refugees from the great Pleiades Diaspora.

**Hegemony of Worlds –** The Hegemony of Worlds was formed in the wake of the initial bout of FTL wars.

Even though Sol was decimated by Sirian fleets in 4754, it was able to rebuild quickly, and re-establish itself as a regional power. In 4775, Sol launched an assault on Alpha Centauri. This move was made with the knowledge that they were running low on raw resources, and Alpha Centauri still had entire worlds that were untapped. The war was short and brutal, and, in 4782, Alpha Centauri was firmly under the control of Sol.

In 4801, Sol launched an assault on Sirius from both Sol and

Alpha Centauri, and took the Sirian system in less than a year.

After that victory, diplomatic missions to Tau Ceti brought that system into the fold, and Alpha Centauri was given full member status, along with Sol and Tau Ceti. The official date for the formation of The Hegemony of Worlds is 4805; though the final ratification was not signed until 4807.

Through the centuries, the Hegemony expanded its borders until nearly all stars within fifty light years were under its control. Counting detached objects and brown dwarfs, as well as multi-state star systems, the number of member states in the Hegemony as of 8927, is 215.

The capital of the Hegemony has always been in Sol, though the specific location of the seat of power has moved. Initially it was on Nibiru; it was later it moved to Makemake, and then to the rebuilt Cho.

In 8900, to celebrate the reconstruction of the Earth and High Terra, President Uriel moved the capital of the Hegemony of Worlds to High Terra, in the very buildings that were the seat of power for the ancient Terran Hegemony.

The move did not sit well with many of the power-elite within the Sol System, but the members of the Hegemony at large responded positively to the decision.

**High Terra –** The second planetary ring ever created (completed in 2519, some two hundred years after Mars 1), High Terra was the seat of power for the ancient Terran Hegemony, and seat of the Sol Space Federation government for over a thousand years.

During the Third Solar War, the Jovian Space Force decimated Luna, Earth, and High Terra, leaving all three as radioactive wastelands.

High Terra lay abandoned for nearly five millennia, and, though several attempts were made to restore it, all ran out of funding until President Uriel of the Hegemony of Worlds commissioned the rebuilding of both the High Terra ring and the planet Earth.

During the time when the ring was abandoned, it was often used as a base of operations for pirates and fringe cults. The Jovians, and later the Hegemony of Worlds, often sent in their militaries to clear it out, and to ensure the ring remained stable and did not degrade and fall apart.

**Huygens –** The Huygens system is a star system located in the space between the Orion and Sagittarius arms of the Milky Way galaxy.

It is a binary star system undergoing heavy terraforming, and the current seat of the Transcend Interstellar Alliance.

Airtha, the capital world/star of the TIA, orbits both stars of the Huygens system at a distance of 500AU from the stars' barycenter.

**Ikoden –** A star system on the spinward edge of the Scipio Federation.

**Inner Stars –** The Inner Stars is the name given to the mass of stars within the Orion Arm of the galaxy to which human colonization has expanded.

The Inner Stars is a bubble of stars—roughly centered around Sol—that is roughly three-thousand light years in diameter, and a thousand light years thick.

The inhabitants of the Inner Stars are unaware that these stars are encircled by the Transcend Interstellar Alliance, and the Orion Freedom Alliance.

**M25 Cluster –** See "Cradle, The".

**New Canaan –** A star system on the rimward side of The Cradle (M25) star cluster. Terraforming of the New Canaan star system began in 8034, and still continues; though the system was ceded to the Intrepid colony mission in 8935. Terraforming began in 8064.

The system's star is named Canaan Prime, and while it lies within the region of space dominated by The Cradle, it is not a native member of the star cluster.

Canaan Prime is a main-sequence G spectrum star, with 1.2 solar masses, and luminosity 5% greater than that of Sol's. The star is 2.1 billion years old.

The natural state of the system has been altered, and the descriptions below are of the system and its planetary bodies after major work by the FGT was completed.

**System Bodies**

- Terrestrial planets: 4
  - Tyre *(FGT name: Tir)*
  - Troy (*FGT name: Justice)*
    - 3 moons – 1 of lunar mass
  - Carthage
    - 2 moons
  - Athens *(FGT name: Gemma)*
- Gas giants: 3
  - Alexandria
  - Roma
    - Normandy is the largest moon
  - Sidon
- Ice giants: 4
  - Giza
  - Sparta
  - Marathon

Crete
Moons with hydrostatic equilibrium (round): 289
Dwarf planets: 375

**Orion Freedom Alliance** – The Orion Freedom alliance—often referred to simply as "Orion", or by the name of it's military, the Orion Guard—is a group that splintered from the Transcend in the seventh millennia. They are opposed to the slow uplift policies of the Transcend, and wish to bring more technology to the Inner Stars, and at a faster pace.

The OFA has a stronger policy of settlement, and has invited more Inner Stars colonists into its far reaches.

Despite its stated policy, the OFA also hides its presence from the Inner Stars in general, claiming that they need more time to prepare for the inevitable war their revelation will bring with the Transcend.

The OFA is also deeply concerned about the Transcend's expansion toward the galactic core. One of its stated goals is to ensure that humanity does not pass beyond the Sagittarius Arm of the galaxy.

**Pleiades –** This star cluster is one of the closest to Sol. At a distance of only 420 light years, it is one of the closest star-clusters to humanity's home world. The diameter of the star cluster is 87 light years across, and it contains over a thousand member stars, as well as other stars that are in the area, though not members of the cluster.

The star cluster is currently passing through an area of dust and gas, which contributes to nebulosity in the area.

The cluster is home to many interstellar nations and governments; one of the most notable being the Trisilieds.

**Sol** – This is the name of the star, which, in antiquity, was simply referred to as 'The Sun'. Because humans call the star that lights up their daytime sky 'the sun,' in every system it became common practice to refer to Sol by its proper name.

**Transcend Interstellar Alliance** – The Transcend Interstellar Alliance, often referred to simply as "The Transcend," was formed when Jeffrey Tomlinson, captain of the first FGT Worldship, brought all the worldships together in the wake of the FTL wars, and proposed they establish themselves beyond the influence of the Inner Stars to ensure their stability and safety from humanity's wars.

Originally, the Transcend completely encircled the Inner Stars, and did not have a strong central government. However, the rimward half of the Transcend separated, and became the Orion Guard.

President Tomlinson then increased his level of control over the Transcend, and the government became much more dictatorial—though it still calls itself a republic.

The capital of the TIA is Airtha, and is situated (at the time of this writing) in the Huygens system.

**Trisal** – A system in the Orion Arm of the galaxy, three thousand light years anti-spinward of Sol. Trisal lies within the OFA, but is very close to the Transcendian border.

**Trisilieds** – An interstellar monarchy in the coreward side of the Pleiades star cluster. The monarchy only spans 35 light years, but contains 374 stars, and is rich in resources; though it has few terraformed worlds.

**Virginis** – Classically known as '61 Virginis', this star is located 27.5 light years from Sol. It was terraformed by the FGT, and boasts a strong economy with multiple habitable worlds and thousands of stations and habitats.

Virginis is an independent system, and, while not officially a member state of the Hegemony of Worlds, the Hegemony space force maintains several bases in Virginis, and exerts strong political influence in the system.

# PEOPLE

**Abby Redding –** Engineer responsible for building the *Intrepid.*

**Amanda –** One of the two human AI interfaces for the *Intrepid.*

**Andrea –** Daughter of Transcend President, Jeffrey Tomlinson. Andrea is the heir-apparent to the Transcend Interstellar Alliance.

**Adrienne –** Secretary of the Interior of the TIA. Close confidant of President Tomlinson.

**Angela –** A military intelligence sentient AI embedded within Tanis.

**Airtha –** Massive, multi-nodal AI who runs the Airtha stellar structure

**Bob** – Bob is the name Amanda gave to the *Intrepid's* primary AI after she was installed as its human avatar. She chose the name because she claims it suits him, though only she and Priscilla understand why. Bob is perhaps the most advanced AI ever created. He is the child of seventeen unique and well-regarded AIs. He also has portions of his neural network reflecting the minds of the Reddings. He is the first AI to be multi-nodal, and to have each of those nodes be as powerful as the largest NSAI, and to remain sane and cogent.

**Brandt –** Initially the commander of the first Marine Battalion aboard the *Intrepid*, Brandt eventually became the commandant of the Marine forces in the ISF.

**Cargo –** The first mate of *Sabrina* bears a strange name, as it was the first he was ever given after being found as a stowaway on a freighter as a child. He has lived on freighters in space ever since.

**Cary –** Daughter of Tanis Richards and Joseph Evans.

**Cheeky –** Biologically modified human who is capable of releasing heavy doses of pheromones, and would be described as a nymphomaniac in some circles. She is also the pilot of the starship, *Sabrina*.

**Corsia –** The AI operating the ISS *Andromeda*.

**Earnest Redding** – Engineer responsible for much of the *Intrepid's* design. Earnest is one of the leading scientific minds in the Sol system, and was responsible for much of Terrance Enfield's success.

**Elena –** A Hand agent, and longtime friend of Sera's.

**Flaherty –** Longtime friend of Sera, and the muscle on *Sabrina*.

**Garza –** General in the Orion Guard, and head of the Guard's military intelligence division within the Inner Stars.

**Greer –** General in command of the Ascella watchpoint.

**Helen –** The AI embedded in Sera's mind. Helen is an ancient AI, well over six thousand years in age. She was a ship AI on one of the first FGT worldships to leave Sol in the 4$^{th}$ millennia. Helen was Sera's caretaker as a child, and later, her mentor. Before the events that led Sera to be exiled from the FGT, Helen had herself embedded in Sera's mind.

Helen harbors a deep secret and mysterious background. Her origins date back to Sol's AI wars.

**Herin** – Ambassador from the Trisilieds to the Hegemony of Worlds.

**Huron –** FGT Director of stage four terraforming at New Canaan.

## NEW CANAAN

**Isyra** – Admiral in the Transcend Space Force tasked with maintaining the blockade of the New Canaan System.

**Jason Andrews** – An old spacer who has completed several interstellar journeys. Captain of the *Intrepid*.

**Jeffrey Tomlinson** – Captain of the first FGT Worldship, President of the Transcend Interstellar Alliance, and father of Sera.

**Jessica Keller** – A TBI (Terran Bureau of Investigations) officer who was chasing after Myrrdan. Jessica was found by Tanis in a stasis pod with no record of how she got there.

Jessica's experience with police procedure was useful in setting up the Victorian police force and academy. She also became an accomplished pilot in the ISF.

**Jim** – The chief engineer aboard the *Andromeda,* and husband of its XO (and later, captain), Corsia.

**Joseph Evans** – ISF Colonel Joseph Evans is one of the ISF's top pilots, and goes on to found the Victorian Space Academy.

**Justin** – The director of the Inner Stars Clandestine Uplift Operations (The Hand).

**Karen** – First mate aboard the *Vimana*.

**Kent** – Orion Guard officer originally from Herschel.

**Nance** – The ship's bio on *Sabrina* who also handles many of the ship's engineering duties. Nance is a germaphobe who never goes out in public without a hazsuit.

**Pradesh** – Captain of the *Vimana*, and father of Saanvi.

**Priscilla** – One of the two human AI interfaces for the *Intrepid.*

**Saanvi** – The lone survivor of the attack on the *Vimana,* and adopted daughter of Tanis and Joe.

**Sabrina** – The AI of the starship *Sabrina*. Sabrina has chosen the same name as her ship, and identifies very deeply with it. She has neurotic tendencies due to an extended period spent alone in a salvage yard.

**Sam** – Sergeant in the Orion Guard, and Kent's lover.

**Sanderson** – Admiral in the ISF. Sanderson was an admiral in the Terran Space Force, and was instrumental in building the New Canaan military.

**Seraphina** – Commonly known as just 'Sera', though Helen refers to her as 'Fina'. Sera is the captain of the starship *Sabrina,* and a former member of the FGT organization known as The Hand.

**Serge** – One of Sera's brothers.

**Smith** – Lieutenant in the ISF. Smith was one of the platoon commanders in the attack on Landfall on Victoria.

**Tanis Richards** – Former TSF counterinsurgency officer. Tanis has held the ranks of major, lieutenant colonel, and general on the *Intrepid*. She was born on February 29$^{th}$, 4052 on Mars.

**Terrance Enfield** – Financial backer for the *Intrepid*.

**Thompson** – *Sabrina's* supercargo and muscle. Thompson is a surly man who doesn't like much of anything, and takes pleasure in being angry.

**Uriel** – President of the Hegemony of Worlds. Uriel has ruled the Hegemony for fifty years, at the time of the attack on New Canaan. She was also instrumental in the rebuilding of Earth and High Terra.

**Usef –** Lieutenant, and eventually Lieutenant Colonel, in the ISF. Usef was one of the platoon commanders in the attack on Landfall in Victoria.

# ABOUT THE AUTHOR

Michael Cooper likes to think of himself as a jack-of-all-trades (and hopes to become master of a few). When not writing, he can be found writing software, working in his shop on his latest carpentry project, or likely reading a book.

He shares his home with a precocious young girl, his wonderful wife (who also writes), two cats, a never-ending list of things he would like to build, and ideas...

Find out what's coming next at www.aeon14.com